Obsession: The Awakening

Carole McEntee-Taylor

Copyright © Carole McEntee-Taylor, 2016.

The right of Carole McEntee-Taylor as the Author of the Work has been asserted by her in accordance with the Copyright, Designs and Patents Act, 1988.

First Published in 2016
by GWL Publishing
an imprint of Great War Literature Publishing LLP

Produced in United Kingdom

Apart from any use permitted under UK copyright law, this publication may only be reproduced, stored or transmitted, in any form, or by any means, with prior permission in writing of the publishers or, in the case of reprographic production, in accordance with the terms of licences issued by the Copyright Licensing Agency.

All characters in this publication, with the exception of any obvious historical characters, are fictitious and any resemblance to real persons, either living or dead, is purely coincidental.

ISBN 978-1-910603-25-3 Paperback Edition

GWL Publishing
Forum House
Stirling Road
Chichester PO19 7DN
www.gwlpublishing.co.uk

Carole loves writing and loves history, so it's no surprise that she writes historical books! She enjoys writing both military history and historical fiction and the idea is to give the author royalties of any military history titles to military charities, whilst proceeds from the fiction go to Carole, to help fund the research into both – at least that's the theory! She currently has six military history books published with Pen & Sword, with more in the pipeline.

Carole is retired and lives in Lincolnshire with her husband, David.

Also by Carole McEntee-Taylor

Fiction:

Lives Apart: A World War Two Chronicle –
Book One - Separation
Book Two - Change
Book Three - Love
Book Four - Deception
Book Five - Retribution

Betrayed

Non-Fiction:

Herbert Columbine VC

A Battle too Far: The True Story of Rifleman Henry Taylor

From Colonial Warrior to Western Front Flyer: The Five Wars of Sydney Herbert Bywater Harris

The Battle of Bellewaarde, June 1915

Surviving the Nazi Onslaught: The Defence of Calais to the Death March for Freedom

Military Detention Colchester from 1947. Voices from the Glasshouse

Dedication

To the many thousands of allied Prisoners Of War who never returned home from Eastern Europe at the end of The Second World War.

Acknowledgements

I would like to thank my husband David for his continued help and encouragement and my publisher for her patience!

Cast of Characters

Germany
Hans Kohl	
Karin Kohl	Hans' sister
Agata Kohl	Hans' mother
Christophe Kohl	Hans' father
Andreas Sturm	Hans' friend and Karin's husband
Claudia Fremont	Andreas' mistress
Heidi	Claudia's daughter
Franz Emmett	
Hannah Emmett	Franz' wife
Gerhard Emmett	Franz and Hannah's son
John Carstairs	British spy

England
Rob Davies	
Bill Davies	Rob's father
Mike Jacobs	Rob's best friend
Annie Parker	Rob's girlfriend
Harold Parker	Annie's father
Ivy Parker	Annie's mother
Daisy Harris	Annie's best friend
Albert Harris	Daisy's brother

Poland
Wiktor Sosnkowski	
Magda Sosnkowski	Wiktor's wife
Stanislav (Stani)	Oldest son
Aleksander (Alek)	Second son
Felcia	Oldest daughter
Raisa	Middle daughter

Ala	Youngest daughter
Iwan	Felcia's husband
Mariusz	Felcia and Iwan's son

Prologue
Munich, Germany
February 1915

It was freezing in his room. Through the open curtains, ten year old Hans could see the snow settling on the window sill outside, and ice forming on the inside of the glass. He realised he was holding his breath and exhaled slowly. Clouds of white steam filled the air, but Hans hardly noticed. His heart was pounding against his chest and he was shaking violently. But it wasn't the cold making him shiver. It was fear.

He had woken suddenly and, in the first instance of consciousness, he'd thought he heard someone crying, but before he was really awake, the noise had stopped and now he wasn't sure whether he'd been dreaming. He held his breath and strained his ears but all was quiet. The silence felt suffocating, as if some unseen terror lurked just out of sight. Hans wriggled down under the blankets, closed his eyes again and tried to think of something nice to take his mind off the feeling of dread that wouldn't leave him.

He was just beginning to doze off again when he heard something else. He tried to ignore it, but the noise was persistent and seemed vaguely familiar, rather like the sounds he sometimes heard from his parents' room in the middle of the night. But his father wasn't here and it didn't sound like his mother.

He cowered under the covers wishing he was brave enough to investigate. Then he thought about his father. While he was away fighting for his country, Hans was the man of the house. Scared as he was, he would have to make sure his mother and sister were alright.

He forced himself to climb out of bed; the thick rug felt warm under his bare feet, providing him with a brief moment of comfort. Hans edged slowly towards the door until his feet met the harsh cold wooden floorboards. The sudden contrast made him shiver but he couldn't turn back now. He reached the door and gently eased it open. The noise was louder now and he could hear something else. His heart pounding uncomfortably against his chest, he crept forward onto the landing and listened again. The noise was definitely coming from his parents' bedroom. Hans breathed deeply, turned left, took a few halting steps along the landing, flung open his parents' bedroom door and stared in horror.

Chapter One
1923

Munich, Germany

Nineteen year-old Hans Kohl rushed home to their large, slightly dilapidated detached house following the latest meeting of the National Socialist Party. He was full of excitement after listening enthralled to its leader, a young man called Adolf Hitler, railing against the Treaty of Versailles and the reparations which were crippling Germany.

The street was in a quiet part of the city and was full of houses that had seen better days. As usual, the road was deserted and Hans had no inkling of the horror he was about to find. He flung open the solid wooden front door and pulled up abruptly, unable to believe what he was seeing. It took him several seconds to realise that the object swinging from the rope attached to the bannister rail was his father, Christophe. He could hear sobbing coming from the drawing room to his left, but he couldn't take his eyes away from the lifeless protruding eyes of his father.

He was vaguely aware of footsteps crossing the drawing room and entering the hall, but he couldn't move. This couldn't be happening. Perhaps he was asleep and this was some terrible dream? He closed his eyes and then opened them again, but nothing had changed.

"Hans!" His mother's plea finally broke through his horrified disbelief and he spun round.

"What happened? Why...?" He stopped and turned back to his father. "We should get him down. It's not right to leave him there."

Agata didn't answer, her eyes were glazed over in shock and she was repeatedly muttering something under her breath.

"What?" Hans asked automatically, his gaze still focused on his father's body.

Agata looked up at him and shook her head. Hans frowned; his mother looked terrified. "What do you mean, 'he found out'?" He took a guess at what he thought she'd said and her face paled even more.

Hans stared at her, wondering if he should insist that she explain herself, but as a memory threatened to fight its way to the surface, he suddenly changed his mind. Perhaps it was best not to know.

"Go and get help." He turned his attention back to his father's body and, ignoring her sobs, he climbed up the narrow carpeted stairs until he reached the sturdy bannister rail to which the rope was tied. Agata watched him for a few seconds then, once she was sure he was no longer paying attention, turned away and disappeared in the direction of the kitchen.

Hans didn't notice. He was trying to work out the best way to get his father down. Christophe was too heavy for him to lift on his own. His only option was to cut through the rope and allow the body to crash to the floor. He hesitated, unable to heap the final indignity on his father, even if he did feel Christophe had taken the easy way out.

He glanced at the clock. Karin, his seventeen year old sister, would be home soon. He was very protective of Karin and he didn't want her seeing this. She had been very close to their father, unlike Hans, who had soon lost patience with the man he'd previously idolised.

Born in August 1904 in Munich, Hans had just celebrated his tenth birthday when he'd stood waving his flag excitedly while his father marched off to fight in the Great War. As he stood there cheering the men off to war, their heads held high, full of pride in their country and the Kaiser, Hans couldn't wait for his turn to come. Throughout the following years, Agata constantly regaled him with heroic tales of his father and the other men who had gone to fight for the Fatherland and his biggest fear was that the war would be over before he too could be a German hero. When the Armistice was declared in 1918 and his father returned home, a shattered wreck of his former self, Hans was bewildered. This wasn't the upright, proud man he remembered.

But before long his confusion was replaced by an all-consuming rage as the rumours quickly began to circulate that Germany had not actually lost the war as they had been told, but instead had been betrayed by troublemakers at home, predominantly Jews and Communists.

Unemployed and disillusioned, Hans only really felt at home with people who believed the same as he did and he threw himself into the thick of the fighting against the communists with enthusiasm. After a failed coup in Weimar, Munich had become the headquarters of the right wing opposition to the Republic and, throughout the next few years, Hans became involved with various extreme right wing groups.

Then things deteriorated even more. Hans could only watch helplessly while his parents gradually lost everything, leaving them almost penniless. When Germany had been unable to meet its reparation payments, French and Belgian troops had occupied the Ruhr, the Germans' major industrial area. The leading industrialists in the area organised passive resistance, but the French brought in their own workers and arrested the leaders of the resistance. The German economy collapsed, leading to massive unemployment and inflation and the German Mark became almost worthless. While Agata turned to cheap alcohol to help her cope, Christophe sank further into depression, eventually refusing to leave the house at all.

Hans shook his head to clear the memories and, returning his attention to his father's lifeless body, he tried to control his rage. He didn't blame his father for feeling defeated but he did blame him for giving up. Christophe's death might have ended *his* suffering, but it had just added to that of his wife and children. Hans was now head of the family, responsible for his sister and mother. He took a deep breath. Somehow that made this decision easier. His father was beyond pain now, unlike his family who would have to live with the shame of Christophe's suicide.

There was no time to waste if he was to protect Karin. Hans pulled out his knife and began sawing through the thick rope.

****

Hackney, East London

Ten year-old Mike Jacobs stared at the small circle of boys surrounding him in the playground, a defiant expression on his face.

"We don't want Jews in our school." The speaker, Steven Kelly, was tall for his age and a natural bully. The other boys muttered their agreement, even though Mike doubted they really understood what they were saying.

He clenched his fists and prepared to defend himself. His father had always told him not to fight but he wasn't going to back down, not when he hadn't done anything wrong.

"Let's get him," Steven yelled and Mike tensed. The taunting grew louder and the boys began to close in on him.

"Leave him alone, or you'll have me to deal with." The voice was clear and strong.

The row of taunting boys fell silent and turned as one towards the speaker. Although the same age, Rob Davies was taller than Steven Kelly, broader across the shoulders, with blond hair and blue eyes that were blazing with anger.

"Well?" Rob repeated, his eyes still boring into those of Steven Kelly.

Steven took a step forward and Rob squared up to him. "Are you sure you want to risk taking me on?" Rob indicated the other boys who were muttering amongst themselves and then smiled as they gradually dispersed. "Looks like you might be on your own."

Steven glanced round and paled. The odds had changed now. He backed away but couldn't resist one last threat: "He won't always be here to protect you, scum." He spat in Mike's direction before running off towards the other end of the playground.

Mike stared at his rescuer in gratitude. "Thank you. I'm Mike, Mike Jacobs."

Rob grinned. "Rob Davies. Don't take any notice of Kelly; he's an idiot." He reached into the pocket of his short trousers. "Here, have a liquorice bar."

Mike took the offered sweet just as an older boy walked past ringing the bell to signify the end of the morning break. The two boys headed towards the classroom, chatting away, their friendship sealed.

****

Munich, Germany

Twenty-one year-old Andreas Sturm climbed reluctantly off the bed and began getting dressed. He gazed down at the girls' naked bodies and smiled.

"I have to go, ladies, but thank you for a wonderful time. I'll see you both next week, same time?"

Bertha smiled up at him and Helga nodded. He was one of their better clients. He treated them with respect, almost as if they were his girlfriends, and he paid well.

Andreas finished dressing, put some money on the bedside table, left the room and wandered back down into the street. He glanced at his watch. Time for a quick beer and then he would go home.

He was heading towards the local bierkeller when he heard a piercing scream. Andreas hesitated and then, as another scream rent the air, he hurried towards the sound, caution forgotten.

****

Romford, Essex

Eight year-old Annie Parker was cuddling her favourite doll and sitting on her mother's lap in the small front room of their terraced house. Her mother was reading her fairy tales and Annie loved listening to the stories, especially the ones where the handsome prince carried the beautiful princess to his castle and they got married. She didn't really understand what that meant, but her mother had explained that every girl was waiting to meet a handsome prince who would rush her off her feet and sweep her to happiness. Annie's mummy had told her she would meet her own prince one day and Annie was already excited.

"You're filling her head with nonsense." Annie's father's voice was gruff, but she knew he didn't really mind. A supervisor at the local Ind Coope brewery, Harold Parker idolised his daughter and loved to see her enjoying herself.

"Plenty of time for the real world when she grows up." Ivy, his wife, echoed his thoughts as she turned the page of Annie's story book. "Life will get in the way soon enough, Harold. Let her enjoy her childhood."

He sighed, shook his head and went back to reading the paper.

****

Munich, Germany

Karin stared at the lifeless body of her beloved father and screamed again. She had arrived home just as Hans finally managed to cut through the rope, and witnessed Christophe crashing to the floor.

"I'm so sorry, Karin. I was hoping to…" Hans tailed off, not knowing what to say.

Karin was still staring at her father, the door wide open behind her and he could see she was in shock. She was just about to scream for the third time when a man appeared in the doorway.

"Is everything alright?" The voice was solicitous and Hans spun round.

"Of course it fucking isn't!" He indicated his father. To his surprise, the man, who was about his own age, didn't take offence.

"I'm sorry. That was a really stupid question. Is there anything I can do to help? I'm sorry for intruding but I heard someone screaming."

Karin turned to look at him for the first time. He was tall and well-built with short blond hair and blue eyes. She could see a small scar on his left cheek and he had a slightly crooked nose. But there was something calming and reassuring about his presence.

"My father... I came home..." She stopped. Hans put his arm around her protectively.

"He was hanging from the bannister, I was trying to get him down before Karin came home. I'm Hans, by the way."

"Andreas. And this is your sister?"

Hans nodded.

Andreas took control. "Your mother?"

"I sent her to get help." Hans frowned. "She's been gone ages. Perhaps I should have gone myself but I could hardly leave her with the body. She's had plenty of time to get to the police station, though. She should be back by now."

"Well, don't worry about that at the moment. While we're waiting, I think you could both do with a drink. Then if you tell me where I can find something to cover the body?"

Hans nodded and indicated a door at the end of the hall. "There's a bottle of cognac in the cupboard under the sink in the kitchen and some blankets upstairs." His face darkened. "I think I'd better go and look for my mother."

Andreas leaned forward and patted his shoulder. "She's probably in shock, Hans. It might be taking her a while to explain to the police if she's very upset. Why don't we go into the kitchen and I'll get you both a drink. Then I'll cover the body before going to the police station myself. I'll see if there's any sign of your mother and bring her back... If that's alright with you of course?"

Hans nodded, relieved to have someone else make the decisions. He took Karin's hand and guided her towards the kitchen.

"Thank you." To Hans' surprise, Karin's voice was calmer now. He breathed a small sigh of relief. At least he wouldn't have to deal with an hysterical teenager. Andreas followed them down the hallway, but they stopped abruptly when Hans opened the kitchen door. Andreas saw Hans' shoulders slump and heard him give a loud sigh. Andreas peered past him. He could see a middle-aged woman, who he presumed to be Hans' and Karin's mother, sitting at the small wooden table. She was staring into space, a half empty bottle of cognac in front of her.

Chapter Two

Berlin

Nine year-old Gerhard Emmet held tightly onto his mother's hand as they hurried through the wide, tree-lined streets of Berlin. He could hear the sound of scuffles and the odd gunshot in the distance and he could feel his mother's nervousness. He couldn't remember a time when he hadn't heard fighting in the streets, sometimes close to where they lived, at other times further away.

"Hurry up, Gerhard. Let's get home before dark." He quickened his step to keep up with hers, his shoes echoing on the cobbles. His heart was thudding loudly against his chest and he could feel the sweat trickling down his back, despite the chill in the air. Just when he thought his heart would burst, he realised they had reached the edge of town. He could see the vast emptiness of the park ahead and he began to relax. They were home. Just around the corner was the large comfortable detached house he'd always lived in. He was safe.

"I was starting to worry." Gerhard's father, Colonel Franz Emmet, a tall, well-built man with a military stance that befitted an ex-soldier, was standing by the ornate door waiting for them. "You should let me go in future." He waited until they were inside the house, then closed the door firmly behind them.

Hannah shook her head. "It's much safer for us to be out there than you. No one will suspect a woman and child out 'looking for food'." She took off Gerhard's coat while she was speaking.

"I wouldn't count on it." Franz waited until she'd finished and Gerhard had gone running into the drawing room before pulling her into his arms. He closed his eyes, grateful they were both safe, before whispering, "Did you get the pamphlets?"

Hannah nodded and pulled them out carefully from under her warm winter coat. Franz took them and indicated the drawing room. "Come and have a drink while I read through them."

Hannah hung her coat on the hall stand and joined her husband and son in the ornately furnished drawing room. She walked over to the small drinks cabinet and poured herself a large glass of wine. Franz could see the strain in her face. It wasn't just the extreme right wing groups they had to be careful of; the Communists were just as dangerous. "It won't be long now. Weimar will soon put an end to the violence from both sides and democracy will flourish." *It has to*, he added to himself. *Anything else is inconceivable.*

Hannah didn't look convinced. "And if it doesn't?"

Franz frowned. "Stresemann has sorted out the currency, things are already beginning to stabilise. The extremes only flourish when there is chaos. You'll see; it's only a matter of time before we have proper peace and prosperity."

Gerhard hadn't understood most of the conversation but he knew his father was always right so he took his mother's hand. "Everything will be alright, Mutti. You'll see."

Hannah laughed and squeezed his hand. She turned her attention back to Franz. "Is that the last of them?" She indicated the small pile of pamphlets that were now in the corner of the room, hidden under some books.

He shrugged. "Let's hope so. Once I've delivered these, we should be able to relax."

Hannah drained the rest of her drink. "Come on, Gerhard, let's see what cook has for dinner. You must be starving; I know I am."

Gerhard nodded. Now he was home, he no longer felt afraid and his appetite had returned with a vengeance. He wondered briefly why the papers were so important, then his stomach took over and he followed his mother down the hallway into the kitchen where the smells of bierwurst and sauerkraut wafted appetisingly.

****

Munich, Germany

"Would you like another coffee?" Karin smiled up at Andreas. She was still in shock over her father's death but Andreas had been a tower of strength and she looked forward to his visits.

Hans also liked Andreas, who was two years older than him and considerably more worldly-wise. Andreas had helped him organise Christophe's funeral and all the paperwork, his mother having sunk into depression, fuelled by alcohol. To his delight, Hans had discovered Andreas was also a member of the Nazi Party and the two men had become good friends. But more importantly, Hans trusted Andreas with Karin, so he watched their growing friendship with little concern.

"Thank you, but I have to go." Andreas glanced reluctantly at his watch. "Hans and I have a meeting to go to in a few moments, but perhaps I could take you out to dinner tomorrow?"

Karin tried to ignore the sudden pounding of her heart and nodded without speaking. In the short time since her father's death, Andreas had taken the place of her father as her protector. And now he'd asked her out on a proper date. She was so excited she felt sick.

Andreas watched the differing emotions crossing Karin's face and hid a smile. "Goodbye. I'll pick you up at about eight?"

"Yes, that would be lovely." Karin knew she was gushing but she didn't care. She was so busy trying to decide what she could wear, she barely even noticed him leaving.

****

Outside Lublin, Eastern Poland

"She's beautiful." Wiktor Sosnkowski stared down at his newborn daughter. He already had two sons and two daughters, and he'd not expected any more children, so Ala was like a miracle.

"You're not disappointed?" Magda looked up at him from the bed, relieved to see him smile.

"Of course not. I'm delighted to have another daughter." He bent down, picked up the tiny bundle and walked towards the window. "You've been born into a free Poland, my darling. Your life is your own and I pray it will be a happy one."

Magda smiled. He'd said the same to the all the children. The girls, Felcia who was four and Raisa three, came into the room followed by their older brothers, Stanislav, known as Stani, aged seven and Aleksander, known as Alek, who was six. The children looked interested in the new arrival, except Raisa who gazed contemptuously at her younger sister and refused to give her a welcome kiss.

Magda was about to tell her off when Wiktor intervened. He ushered the children from the room, telling them their mother needed to rest and he would be along in a moment to read them a story. Once they had gone, he smiled down at Magda. "It's only natural, my love. She's no longer the baby. Give her time and she'll soon love Ala just as much as we do."

Magda nodded but she felt uneasy. In her thirties and after two miscarriages, they had thought her child bearing days were over, so Raisa had been spoilt. Still, Wiktor was probably right. She was very young, she'd soon get used to not being the baby any more. She put her misgivings to one side, smiled up at Wiktor and thought how lucky she was.

****

Hackney, East London

"My dad says you can come home to tea tonight, if you want." Rob grinned at Mike. They were in the playground playing football with the other boys. Since Rob's intervention, Mike had not had any more trouble with the other boys.

"Really?" Although he considered Rob to be his best friend, Mike was still astonished by the invitation. His dad had warned him that some of the parents didn't like Jews, so even though he and Rob were friends, it didn't mean Rob's father would accept him. Mike had found this very confusing and had spent a lot of time in the cramped bathroom of their terraced house staring at himself in the mirror to see if he looked any different from the other boys. But he hadn't been able to see anything that made him stand out, so eventually he'd given up.

Rob had already been to tea with Mike's parents after school a couple of times, but this was the first time Mike had been invited back.

"Yeah, we can call in at yours on the way, to tell them you're coming to mine. Dad says we can have fish and chips."

"Still playing with the yid then?" Steven Kelly's harsh accent drifted across the playground.

Rob stopped smiling, gave a loud theatrical sigh and turned to face him. "What's it to you, Kelly?" He clenched his fists.

Kelly gave an unpleasant smile. "Nothing, Davies. Nothing at all, except we don't want dirty yids in the playground and if you're with him, you're against us."

Rob had heard the boy's father make similar pronouncements outside the gate but both he and Mike had ignored him.

"I don't want you to get into trouble because of me…" Mike began, but he was too late. Rob launched himself at the other boy, taking him by surprise and knocking him to the floor. Before Mike could do anything, Rob flung himself on top of Kelly and began punching him. The two boys rolled around for several moments while a crowd of children grew around them.

To Mike's surprise, most of the children seemed to be backing Rob and he joined in enthusiastically before a teacher strode into the middle of the melee and pulled the boys apart.

Mike stared carefully at Rob and breathed a sigh of relief. His friend appeared to have come out of the fight better than his opponent who had two burgeoning black eyes and a cut lip.

"Who started it?" The teacher's voice rang loudly around the playground. There was silence. No one wanted to be a snitch.

"Right. To the Headmaster's office. Now! He'll soon beat the fight out of you. You'll get at least ten of the best. You'll also both stay after school and write a hundred lines. 'I must not fight in the school playground'."

Mike watched in despair while the two boys were marched up to the head's office to be caned. As they disappeared through the door, Rob turned around and winked at him.

Mike smiled uncertainly and then the bell rang and he followed the others into class and took his seat. He felt terrible. This was all his fault. Perhaps he should go and tell the Headmaster. But then he'd be a grass and be hated even more. Unable to decide what he should do, Mike did nothing. He turned his attention to the blackboard and tried to block out the feelings of guilt that he had let his friend be punished when he might have been able to stop it, if only he wasn't such a coward.

****

Romford, Essex

"What's the matter, Annie?" Ivy stared at her daughter with concern.

"Nothing, Mummy." Annie gave a heavy sigh and then began to cry.

Even more concerned, Ivy sat down next to her on the floral-patterned settee. "Whatever's wrong?"

There was a brief silence. "I'm scared that I won't find the right one for me. What if I walk past him in the street and don't recognise him, or I do find him and he doesn't like me? I'll be all on my own." The words came out in between sobs.

Ivy resisted the temptation to laugh. But she was so relieved there was nothing really wrong, she smiled. "This business of there only being one man, it's not really true, Annie. Real life isn't like a fairy tale." Seeing her daughter's horrified expression, she hurried on. "But you will find the right man, Annie, I promise, and then you will live happily ever after, just like in the books. You don't need to worry." Even as she said the words, Ivy wondered what Harold would say. He was always telling her not to fill their daughter's head with nonsense.

Annie didn't look very convinced. "Maybe I should ask Daddy?"

Ivy panicked. "There's no need to bother your dad, Annie. Come on, let's do your hair in a nice pony tail and we can go shopping. You'd like a new dress, wouldn't you?"

Annie immediately forgot about telling her father. "A real princess dress?"

"Yes, why not?" Ivy breathed a sigh of relief. "You can help me pick the material and then I'll make it for you."

"Can we buy some shoes to go with it?"

"Of course." Ivy had no idea if she had enough money, but anything was better than having Harold go on at her again.

Annie smiled happily and sat quietly while her mother combed her hair. She couldn't wait to grow up and meet her handsome prince.

****

Hackney, East London

"Are you sure you're alright?" Mike stared at Rob, his face anxious. He'd waited for Rob to come out after writing his lines, but he'd been worried about what sort of reaction he would get.

"Of course." Rob replied, ignoring the stinging pain in his buttocks that was making walking difficult.

"It was all my fault…" Mike began.

Rob stopped and stared at him. "How was it your fault? Kelly started it because he's an idiot."

"But if you hadn't been playing with me…"

"He would have found something else to fight with me about. Anyway, let's forget all about him now. He won't bother either of us again and, if he does, I'll soon sort him out."

Mike began to relax. He was relieved Rob didn't seemed to blame him, but he couldn't quite get rid of the feeling that it was his fault. He tried to push away the feelings of guilt and concentrate on what Rob was saying.

"Sorry?"

"I said I'm starving. I'm going to eat tons of chips, you see if I don't." He seemed to realise Mike was still worrying because he suddenly grinned. "Come on, I'll race you to your house. Last one's a sissy."

Chapter Three

Munich, Germany

Hans looked at the empty bottles strewn all over the house and cursed. His mother was getting worse. Unable to cope without Christophe, Agata had turned even more to alcohol to help her forget. He began picking up the bottles then, in a fit of rage, threw one of them across the room where it smashed loudly against the wall. Hans sighed loudly and stared at the broken glass for several moments before running his fingers through his hair and gritting his teeth.

He was about to clear up the mess when he heard what sounded like a groan from upstairs. Forgetting he still held one of the empty bottles and wondering if his mother was hurt, he headed up towards where he'd heard the sounds. As he grew closer, he realised Agata wasn't alone and his heart sank. He paused outside her bedroom and listened. He could identify at least two male voices and he clenched his fists. His mother was drunk. How dare they take advantage of her?

Without thinking, he shoved open the door. His mother was spread-eagled on the bed naked, her arms and legs tied to the pillars of the dilapidated four poster. A dark haired, swarthy man with an unshaven face had his penis in her mouth, while a fat man with short blond hair was thrusting hard against her, his back to the door.

A red mist swam before Hans' eyes, a roar escaped his mouth and, before either of the men knew what was happening, Hans had rushed into the room brandishing the bottle. He smashed it down hard on the head of the blond haired man who still had his back to him and, without stopping, rushed at the swarthy man. One glance at the bloodshot eyes in the unshaven face told Hans what he needed to know. The man was drunk and would be unable to react quickly. Hans lunged forward, the full force of the bottle smashing into the man's face. Blood spurted from the numerous cuts and rained down on Hans' mother together with shards of broken glass. She screamed.

Hans was beyond reason, he grabbed the pillow from under her head and pressed it over her face, anything to stop the dreadful shrieking. Feeling his mother struggling, Hans pressed harder until she finally went limp and there were a few seconds of silence. Hans let go and straightened up. He was panting with exertion and he closed his eyes while he tried to regain his breath.

Then he heard groaning by his feet. Hans glanced down at the fat man who was beginning to regain consciousness and, as the red mist descended once more, he kicked out again and again until the man's head lolled to the side and he too fell silent. Hans watched him for several seconds to make sure he was dead before stepping back towards the swarthy man who was still motionless on the blood-stained carpet where he'd fallen. Hans glanced around and saw the broken neck of the bottle lying a few feet away. He picked it up and, without hesitation, slashed the dark haired man across the throat. There was a strange gurgling noise, the bloodshot eyes opening wide in terror.

Hans watched calmly while the man gasped for breath and his blood ran freely onto the carpet.

****

Munich, Germany

Karin had finished work early at the dressmaker's shop and was rushing home to get ready for Andreas. He was taking her out for a meal that evening and she couldn't decide whether she was excited or nervous. Her mind was filled with images of him, his smile, his laughter, his eyes boring into hers. Her body began tingling in anticipation and she felt herself blushing. Perhaps she'd better think about what she should wear instead. Smiling to herself, Karin hurried up the path towards the front door and then stopped dead. The house was quiet, the door wide open.

She hesitated, a feeling of dread overcame her, reminding her of the day earlier in the year when she'd arrived home in time to see her father's body crashing to the floor in front of her.

Holding her breath, she stepped gingerly through the open space. The silence was deafening, the lack of any noise was unnatural and emphasised by the darkness in the empty hallway. She entered slowly, making her way towards the sitting room. The first things she saw were the empty bottles, then the broken glass. The room reeked of cheap cognac but there was no one there. Karin let out a slow breath and stepped back into the hallway.

"Mutti? Mutti, are you upstairs?"

There was no answer. Again she hesitated, then chided herself for being so stupid. Her mother had probably had too much to drink and gone out, forgetting to close the door behind her. It wouldn't be the first time. Karin relaxed. She had the house to herself.

Feeling more confident, she climbed the stairs, her mind back on what she could wear that evening. Although it was the end of September, the weather was unseasonably warm so she didn't want to wear anything too heavy. In any case, for some reason she always felt hot when Andreas was near her so it wouldn't do to wear anything that was likely to make her perspire. The thought made her shudder. No, light clothes would be best, but Andreas had seen most of her decent summer clothes now. Perhaps her mother had something she could borrow? A nice sleeveless dress and matching cardigan would be just right. She would take a quick look. Given her mother's alcohol consumption lately, Agata probably wouldn't notice if there were any clothes missing from her wardrobe. Karin pushed open her mother's bedroom door and stopped dead. Her hand flew to her mouth and she began screaming.

****

Munich, Germany

"I need your help." Hans rushed into the small local office used by the National Socialist Party. He was relieved to see Andreas was still there.

"What on earth…? You're covered in blood."

Hans drew in a breath. "I found two dirty Jews raping my mother. They'd smothered her with a pillow… I lost my temper and killed them. There's blood everywhere…" He tailed off.

Andreas didn't hesitate. He grabbed the phone. "Don't worry. We'll sort this out, Hans." He spoke rapidly into the receiver.

Hans listened while Andreas barked instructions at whoever was on the other end of the phone, before replacing the receiver and turning his attention back to the younger man.

"I'll come home with you and we'll wait for my men there. When the police arrive, you tell them you've been here with us all afternoon. You went home, found your mother and the two men dead and rushed back here because you didn't know what else to do. Alright?"

Hans nodded.

"We'll back you up. They'll assume someone just broke in and killed them all; a robbery gone wrong or something like that."

Hans nodded.

"Where's Karin?"

Hans glanced up at the clock. "She's at work. She won't be home for a couple of hours yet."

"Good. We don't want to upset her unnecessarily." An image of Hans' attractive younger sister came into his mind and he smiled to himself. Their relationship was developing nicely, although he was still seeing Helga and Bertha for sex because he knew Karin wasn't that sort of girl and he was hoping, at some later point, to ask her to marry him. Andreas turned his attention back to Hans "Don't worry, those filthy Jew scum won't get away with this. We'll take some reprisals just to make sure they get the message. Alright?"

"I want to come with you when you do." Having blamed the Jews for his mother's death and, unable to accept his own guilt, Hans was already half way to believing his own lies. "She was my mother, I should be the one to take revenge."

Andreas gave a cruel smile. "Of course you can. Now let's get round to your house and deal with the police."

****

Berlin

Franz was having an afternoon pastry and reading his newspaper in the large Wannsee Park when he was vaguely aware of a man sitting down on the bench next to him. Franz ignored him. He was deep in thought about the deteriorating political situation in Germany and wishing there was something he could do about it. He stared at the newspaper and resisted the impulse to screw it up in frustration.

"Difficult times." The man was about his age, his accent suggesting he wasn't German. Franz nodded and wondered if the man was English. The man's next words confirmed his suspicion. "John, John Carstairs. I work at the British Embassy."

Franz frowned and wondered if he would compromise himself if he allowed the man to engage him in conversation.

"I'm not going to beat about the bush," Carstairs continued. "I know you're a patriotic German and, as such, you must be horrified by the talk of separation."

Franz nodded but didn't answer.

Carstairs glanced around. There was no one close to them, but he wanted to concentrate on the man he'd come to meet. "Perhaps we could walk while we talk?"

Franz was about to refuse when his curiosity got the better of him. He stood up suddenly, taking Carstairs by surprise.

"What do you want?"

Carstairs smiled. "Your files suggested you always get straight to the point."

Franz stared ahead. "And what else do they say?"

"That you're an honest man who has Germany's best interests at heart; a brave man, decorated in the war and willing to do whatever it takes to preserve the Fatherland and democracy."

Franz didn't answer while he considered the other man's words. They were almost at the lake now; he could see the waves lapping gently on the shore. There were even fewer people here than nearer the streets, despite the good weather. Fear of the growing political storm and a repeat of the violence of the previous year were keeping Berlin's citizens indoors. "You obviously know a lot about me," he said finally. "Why?"

Carstairs debated briefly whether he should avoid answering until they'd talked longer, then changed his mind. Colonel Emmet must already know why and he'd still agreed to walk with him. Nothing would be gained by prevaricating; in fact the Colonel might be insulted if he tried to hide the reason. "We, the British that is, want to avoid another war at any cost and we think the majority of the German people feel the same. However, this business of the Rhineland is dangerous and we think the best chance of peace is for us to work with those who share our own goals." Carstairs didn't look at the Colonel and he resisted the temptation to hold his breath while he awaited his companion's response.

There was a long silence. Franz had realised long before they'd reached the deserted shores of the lake that Carstairs was trying to recruit him as a spy and he would have stormed off in protest, but he had a weakness. He had always admired the British: even when he'd been fighting them, he'd felt they were Germany's natural allies. Given the problems they were having with the French, and the support the British had tried to give them in the League of Nations, he was prepared to hear the man out.

They talked for over an hour and, by the end of the conversation, although nothing had been formally agreed, Franz knew he would meet Carstairs again. Franz did not feel like a traitor. Instead he felt he was doing his bit to help Germany. To keep the French in check, Germany needed to be united and grow strong again. Above all, they needed to avoid a repeat of the Great War and that aim could best be served by talking to the British, whose goals were the same as his.

****

Munich, Germany

"Karin?" Hans heard the screaming before he reached the house. Andreas was close behind him and, as the piercing shrieks rent the air, the two men increased their pace. They rushed through the open front door and up the stairs. Karin was still standing by the door staring into the bedroom.

Hans grabbed her arm and pulled her away. She made no attempt to resist him, nor did she give any sign that she recognised him. But at least she'd stopped screaming. Then she saw Andreas, her face crumpled and she ran to him. Andreas put his arms around her and, catching Hans' eye over her shoulder, indicated he would take her downstairs.

Hans nodded and followed them. In the distance they could hear the sound of sirens and, in his mind, Hans repeated the story he'd agreed with Andreas.

To his relief, the police showed no sign of not believing him. They listened patiently, offered their condolences to the two young people and spoke briefly to Andreas before arranging for the bodies to be removed. It was only when they left that Hans glimpsed the older of the two men giving Andreas the Nazi salute. For the first time since he'd come home that afternoon, Hans smiled. His friend obviously did have friends in high places. He would have to make sure Karin was suitably appreciative to her boyfriend. He would wait until they were on their own before having a little chat with her. Given her expression when Andreas was around, he didn't think he would have much trouble persuading her to sleep with him, but it didn't hurt to make sure.

****

Munich, Germany

Andreas turned down the gas light and returned to the sofa next to Karin. By the time the police had gone it had been too late to go out for a meal, so he'd suggested she come back to his house where she could spend the night if she wanted. He'd explained that she could have his bedroom while he slept on the sofa. Hans was clearing up the mess in their own house and Karin jumped at the chance. Andreas had expected some protest from Hans and concern about his sister's honour but surprisingly Hans had been even more enthusiastic. It crossed Andreas' mind that Hans was offering his sister as a thank you, but rather than annoying him, he found the thought exciting, so he'd said nothing.

Karin had insisted she wasn't hungry so instead he'd poured them both some wine and sat cuddling her on the settee while she drank two large glasses on an empty stomach. He knew he should probably feel guilty but her body was warm and inviting and he'd been seeing her for several weeks, so he felt he'd waited more than long enough.

Karin snuggled up against him, her face upturned and Andreas leant towards her. His lips brushed hers, gently at first and then with more passion. He felt her hesitation and then she began to kiss him back. He wondered briefly again if he was taking advantage of the situation but he'd wanted her for so long, he silenced his conscience, pulled her closer and began undoing the buttons on her blouse.

****

Outside Lublin, Eastern Poland

"That's my doll, Raisa! Give her back to me." Felcia stood with her legs apart, hands on her hips and glared at her younger sister.

"Make me!" Raisa squared her tiny shoulders and then thought better of it. She looked around the small yard for help but her father and brothers were working in the fields and her mother was feeding the baby in the back bedroom. She was on her own. She took a step backwards and put the cloth doll behind her back. "I only want to play with her. You can have her back in a minute."

Felcia took a step towards her. Raisa dropped the doll and ran crying loudly towards the kitchen. Felcia sighed, bent down and picked up the cause of the latest argument between the sisters. She couldn't understand why Raisa wanted to play with her dolls all the time. It wasn't as if she didn't have her own toys. Raisa seemed to revel in trying to cause trouble for her and she didn't know why.

"For goodness sake, Felcia, can't you girls play quietly for just half an hour? I'm trying to feed your sister." Felcia looked across at her mother who was standing by the kitchen door with baby Ala leaning over her shoulder crying loudly.

"Raisa took my doll…" She didn't get any further before Raisa burst into even louder tears, her cries mingling with those of Ala.

"You're the oldest, Felcia. I expect you to be better behaved," Magda shouted over the growing din. "Now stop annoying your younger sister and play properly." She glanced down at Raisa just as she stopped crying and a look of satisfaction crossed her face. Magda exploded. She slapped Raisa hard across the back of her legs, catching her daughter by surprise. "Now you've got something to really cry about." She shoved Raisa towards Felcia, pulled Ala into her arms so she could cuddle her properly, turned around and went back in the house, slamming the kitchen door behind her.

Felcia stuck her tongue out and ran off, leaving Raisa staring angrily after her sister's retreating back. After a few moments, Raisa walked towards the narrow lane that led to the fields and wondered if she dared go and find her father. He wouldn't take Felcia's side, she knew he wouldn't, not when she told him how Felcia was always bullying her.

****

Munich, Germany

Karin woke with a headache and an unpleasant taste in her mouth. She opened her eyes and wondered where she was. Then it all came flooding back to her: her mother's murder, Andreas' kindness, the wine and... She stopped her thoughts, shocked at what she'd done. The previous evening was a hazy memory but she could remember him removing her clothes, his hands touching her all over. She blushed as she remembered him squeezing her breasts, his teeth sucking and biting her nipples, then the shock of him inserting his fingers inside her, and giving way to her moans of pleasure. Then he'd climbed on top of her...

"Good morning, darling." Andreas' voice broke into her thoughts and she started. He was lying next to her and she knew she was naked. His hands began touching her again and she opened her mouth to object, then realised it was too late. She had already slept with him; she was no better than a whore. In her mind, she could see her father's face, frowning with disappointment. She was soiled goods, no one would want her now.

"You're beautiful, Karin. I love you so much I really think we should get married, don't you?"

Karin stared at him in astonishment and then burst into tears of relief. Andreas smiled and pulled her closer. It was time he married and had children and who better than a virgin he could mould and train to service his needs. Being married wouldn't curtail his sexual adventures elsewhere, it would give him protection from the girls who thought they could ensnare him by sleeping with him. As a Catholic, he didn't believe in divorce and Karin, who was also a Catholic, wouldn't either. She would be the perfect wife.

He ran his hands down her body until he reached her pubis, his fingers twisting and curling the thick black hair while he whispered softly in her ear. "Let me show you how much I love you, my darling."

Without waiting for an answer he pushed her gently onto her stomach and eased himself inside her.

Karin was too shocked to do anything to stop him. All she could think was that he wanted to marry her. She was saved; she wouldn't rot in hell after all.

****

Berlin

"Bavaria is threatening to separate from the German Republic." Franz read the headlines to Hannah. "General von Lossow is no longer taking orders from Berlin and they look set to declare their independence."

Hannah's shocked expression reflected his own horror. The separatist movement had been growing for several months but they'd both hoped it would die a natural death. "I still don't understand why some of the politicians are supporting him. Why would they want to help the French?"

"I don't think they do." Franz sighed. "They're just hoping the separation of the Rhineland will help them do a deal with the French over reparations."

Hannah frowned. "Is that likely?"

"No, I wouldn't think so. The French hate us and they're determined to have their pound of flesh. They're just stirring things up because, if Bavaria becomes an independent Catholic monarchy, Germany will lose a large part of its industry. That suits the French because, in their opinion, it stops us from recovering and growing strong again. By giving separation serious thought, the Bavarians are playing right into French hands. Unfortunately they are too bloody stupid to see it." He slammed the newspaper down in disgust.

"How much longer will we have to put up with the French making our lives a misery?" Franz could hear the despair in her voice. "The war has been over for years. Will we never be free of them?"

Franz shook his head. "God knows. The British and Americans are furious with the French for paying agitators to stir up trouble but no one seems prepared to do anything about it." As soon as the words were out of his mouth, Franz could have bitten off his tongue. He glanced sideways at her but she didn't seem curious as to the source of his information and he breathed a sigh of relief. He had considered telling Hannah about his meeting with the man from the British Embassy the previous day, but decided at the last moment it would be better to keep it a secret.

"Sorry?" He realised Hannah was speaking.

"I just asked what Germany would do if Bavaria did declare independence?"

Franz's face darkened. "I have no idea. But I fear it will not be a peaceful transition, not with the French pulling the strings, and the last thing we need is another war."

Chapter Four

Munich, Germany

Six weeks later, Hans was in the middle of the estimated three thousand men marching behind Hitler towards the War Ministry in the centre of Munich. It was cold, the air filled with clouds of vapour from the waiting National Socialist supporters. The night before, in the Bürgerbräukeller, the Prime Minister, Dr von Kahr, had started to read the official proclamation of Bavaria's independence but Hitler, Ludendorff and other prominent members of the Nazi party had broken up the meeting. Now they were holding a mass demonstration in favour of national union and Hans and Andreas had rushed to the cause.

It was approaching half past twelve. Andreas was in the line in front of Hans and he turned around briefly to smile at him. Hans was delighted Karin was going to marry Andreas and he was looking forward to the wedding, not because he liked weddings particularly, but because it would mean the responsibility for his sister would pass to Andreas and he could concentrate on other things, like freeing the country from the influence of the Jews. Hans clenched his fists as he always did when he thought about the Jews. His hatred for them was fast becoming an obsession that was taking over most of his waking moments.

The narrow streets were packed solid with marchers and Hans felt a thrill that he was part of such momentous events. He stared straight ahead and enthusiastically joined in the chanting with the men around him, thoughts of his sister's wedding and revenge on the Jews momentarily forgotten.

Eventually they reached Odeonsplatz and prepared to enter the narrow Residenzstrasse, the location of the main building they were planning to occupy. A murmur of excitement rippled through the crowd and Hans felt a brief surge as they thronged forward. Then suddenly the march ground to an abrupt halt. Hans shifted his weight from one foot to the other, veering to either side in an attempt to peer through the men in front of him who were doing the same, their eyes drawn to the activity ahead. The marchers fell silent and stood still and Hans could finally see what the delay was.

Lined up in front of them, blocking the entrance to the forecourt, were about a hundred armed police and soldiers. They were obviously waiting for the protesters.

There was a long pause, Hans could hear muttering all around him while the leaders decided what to do. For a brief moment Hans was concerned the march would turn back and he clenched his fists. He could feel the tension in the crowded street and then the men broke ranks and charged towards the police.

Delighted his companions weren't going to let themselves be intimidated, Hans allowed the momentum to propel him along with the others. They grew closer to the police line and Hans could feel exhilaration course through his body. They were invincible, no one could stop them… He turned to share his thoughts with his companion when suddenly shots rang out. Hans saw the man alongside him fall, he sensed others dropping to the ground but his adrenaline was flowing and, despite the danger, he kept running towards the armed police. Out of the corner of his eye, he thought he saw someone escorting Hitler away, then the police were on him, batons raised, and everything went dark.

Hans regained consciousness on the floor of a police cell, his head throbbing, blood on his face and his ribs aching, but after a quick examination he was sure he did not have any serious injuries. He smiled to himself. If the gutless authorities thought this was the end of the protests, they were very much mistaken.

There was no doubt who was responsible for the Great War and the mess the country was now in. The fault was that of the Jews, no one else, and sooner or later the rest of the country would wake up and realise Hitler was right.

The door opened and another man was thrown into the cell.

"Andreas! So they got you too? What about Hitler?"

Andreas gave a wry smile. "No, he got away." He sighed and the smile faded. "We lost over a dozen men though."

There was silence, then Hans spoke in a low voice. "What's going to happen to us now?"

Andreas shrugged. "I don't know, although I did hear the authorities in Munich are not very happy with Ebert and Stresemann either, so we may get off with light sentences." He closed his eyes. He hoped so. His relationship with Karin was just beginning to get interesting. Now he'd started educating her in exactly the right way to service him, he didn't want her finding someone else while he was locked up.

****

Berlin

Franz put down the newspaper and turned to Hannah, his face alight. He had no time for the extreme right wing, who he considered just as dangerous to the country's future as the Communists. "They've arrested that lunatic Hitler and the other fascists for attempting a coup in Munich. With a bit of luck the courts will send them to prison for a long time." He smiled at Hannah. "Well, at least the coup appears to have put an end to talk of Bavarian separation."

"If Hitler has stopped the Bavarian separation, then perhaps we should be grateful? After all, if that had gone ahead there might have been even more trouble." Hannah sounded thoughtful.

Franz nodded. "Yes I agree, he's probably saved the country from civil war, but Hitler's views are much too extreme to allow him any power. Have you heard the rubbish he spouts about the Jews?"

Hannah nodded. "Yes, I know. He does sound slightly deranged when he speaks. I heard him on the wireless earlier. So do you really think that's the end of the National Socialists and the separatists?"

"Yes, I think so. Things will get better now the French aren't able to stir things up and with the Americans underwriting our loans, we can start to pay off our debts and then the economy will improve. Once that happens, people will have no need of extremists on either side." He pulled her into his arms. "Come on, I think we should go out and celebrate democracy."

Hannah smiled and allowed herself to be cuddled. She wasn't sure things were quite as easy as her husband was making out, but with the separatist issues put to bed and Hitler out of the way, maybe things could finally settle down.

****

Landsberg Jail, Munich, Germany

"Karin, what on earth are you doing here?" Andreas stared at her in astonishment.

"I bribed one of the guards to let me see you." Her face was pale and he could see the strain in her eyes. "You don't mind?" She suddenly looked worried.

He hastened to reassure her. "Of course not. I'm delighted to see you. I was just a little surprised."

"I wanted to make sure you were alright, and Hans too of course."

"Hans is fine. We both are." Andreas wished he could take her hands but the table was too large to reach her and, having been told they couldn't have contact, he didn't want to bring the visit to a sudden end by trying to touch her.

An expression of relief crossed Karin's face. She had been imagining all sorts of things.

"I think we should get married as soon as I get out of here. What do you think?"

Karin's face broke into a huge smile. "Of course. It's a wonderful idea. It will give me something to do while you're locked up. I can organise everything."

"That's what I thought. Do you feel better now?"

Karin nodded, unable to speak for happiness. Her eyes glazed over as she envisaged their future together. Now she didn't need to worry anymore; Andreas would always be hers. He would never leave her like her father had done. She would make sure of that.

Chapter Five
1933

Sportspalast, Berlin

SS Leutnant Hans Kohl stared around the crowded stadium with satisfaction. The arena was full to bursting and Hans was proud to be a part of such an auspicious occasion. He glanced at his watch and then back at the enormous stage behind him. Hitler was due to give his first speech as Chancellor in a few moments and he couldn't wait. Security was very tight, the aisles were lined with sturdy SS men in smart black uniforms, black ties and black caps with the Totenkopf skull and bones on. Hitler's new personal bodyguard, the Führer Schutzkommando, or FSK, founded by Himmler to protect the Führer while he was inside the Bavarian borders, consisted of detectives from the Bavarian police and were also there in force.

A roar went up from the crowd and Hans could hear the frenzied cries of "Sieg Heil!" echoing round the huge stadium as Hitler stepped out onto the podium and stared around the audience with an expression of satisfaction on his face. Hans glanced back, mesmerised to be so close to the great man. He watched while Hitler stared out over the huge cheering crowds and waited a few moments as their adulation swept over him. Hans could hardly contain himself; only the knowledge he was part of the massive security presence prevented him from joining in. Eventually Hitler raised his hand and an expectant hush fell over the watching crowds. Hans felt his stomach knot in anticipation.

It was ten years since he'd cut down his father's body, ten years in which his life had changed completely and it was all thanks to the man standing behind him.

Hans gazed out at the sea of people from his place at the side of the podium, his eyes darting around, checking for threats, but all he could see was devotion and adoration, so he allowed himself to relax and listen while Hitler promised a *Neue Deutsche Reich*.

****

Berlin

The noise from the stadium broadcast through several loud speakers was loud enough to be heard above the evening play on the wireless. Hannah glanced at Franz who frowned, reached over towards the radio and turned up the volume.

"I don't think he's going to go away as easily as that." Her voice was mildly sarcastic and Gerhard looked up sharply. It was unusual for his parents to disagree.

"No, but I don't *have* to listen to him, well not yet anyway, although if that slimy oaf Goebbels has his way, that may change." Franz saw her face and gave a wry smile. "I think we'll have to lie low for a while… see which way the wind is blowing.

Hannah sighed. "And if he gets elected?"

Franz shuddered. "Then our brief flirtation with democracy will be over."

"You can't just give up, Vati." Gerhard was on his feet. "We can't let that madman rule Germany."

"I agree, Gerhard." Franz lowered his voice so Gerhard had to lean towards him to hear. "But the time for overt opposition is probably over." He saw the expression on his son's face and shook his head. The boy was much too hot headed for his own good. "There's more than one way to skin a cat, Gerhard."

"Well he doesn't scare me." Gerhard turned his back on his father and took a step towards the door.

"Then he should do." Franz leapt up from his armchair and travelled the short distance between them in seconds. He grabbed Gerhard's arm, pulling the younger man back to face him. "Keep away from your socialist friends, Gerhard. They will get themselves killed. If you want to fight Hitler, you have to be more cunning."

Gerhard shrugged off his father's grip. "I'm not a coward and no one is going to stop me seeing my friends. Not you and certainly not that jumped up maniac out there."

He stormed out, slamming the door hand behind him.

Hannah stared at the door and then at Franz. She shivered. "I'm scared, Franz." He didn't answer. Instead he walked over and pulled her into his arms. He could feel her fear and, for once, he couldn't think of anything he could say to help. Instead he closed his eyes and prayed for a way to get through Gerhard's stubborn refusal to listen to him before it was too late.

****

Outside Lublin, Eastern Poland

Wiktor heard Magda's footsteps coming towards the back room and, standing up, he hurriedly switched off the wireless, turning towards her just as she entered the room. He forced himself to smile.

"I just came to say dinner's ready…" Her voice tailed off. "What's the matter?"

"Nothing, darling, I was just coming." Wiktor tried to walk past her but she caught his arm.

"You're not fooling me for one instant, Wiktor." Magda's voice was sharp. "What's happened now?"

Wiktor opened his mouth to deny there was anything wrong but, seeing the serious expression on his wife's face, he changed his mind. "Hitler's just made his first speech as Chancellor of Germany…" He fell silent.

Magda frowned. "But he's only Chancellor, isn't he? That other one, Hindenburg isn't it? He's President, surely? And they've got a parliament too. Hitler can't just do whatever he wants."

"No of course not." Franz made an effort to push his misgivings to one side and failed. "I just didn't think Hitler would get this far, not when they didn't get many votes."

Magda shrugged. "The Nazis are just a minor party, Wiktor. I'm sure there's nothing to be concerned about."

Wiktor didn't want to worry her, so he nodded. "I'm sure you're right, Magda." He put his arm around her. "Come on, the dinner will get cold."

Stani and Alek had been on the verge of coming downstairs when they'd heard their parents talking. They exchanged glances and waited on the landing until Viktor and Magda had gone into the kitchen.

"Do you think there'll be a war, Stani?" Alek sounded worried.

Stani smiled back at him, his eyes alight with excitement. "Who knows, little brother. But if there is, we could go and join the army. Just imagine, we could be brave soldiers fighting for our country. What do you think of that?"

Alek nodded with enthusiasm, his concerns of a few moments earlier completely forgotten. "When do we go?"

Stani laughed and patted him on the back. "Not yet, Alek. Let's wait and see what happens, shall we?" They reached the kitchen door and Stani stopped and faced Alek, his expression serious. "Don't say anything to Mama and Tata. They'll only worry."

Alek nodded. Then he grinned. "And they might try and stop us."

****

Hackney, East London

"He's nothing but a jumped up house painter." Rob's father, Bill, a ticket inspector at Liverpool Street Station, threw the paper on the table and reached for his mug of tea.

"But he's taken control, hasn't he?" Rob persisted, his eyes scanning the newspaper headlines as if hoping they would allow him a glimpse into the future.

"Flash in the pan, you mark my words." Bill stood up, drained his tea and indicated the picture of Hitler scornfully. "Come on, we'll be late for work, son."

Rob hesitated and then followed his father to the station where he'd been working as a porter since leaving school two years earlier.

Mike was waiting for him at the barrier, a worried expression on his face. "You seen the paper?" he asked.

Rob nodded. "Yes. Doesn't look good, does it?"

Mike sighed. "My dad thinks he's got no chance of being elected in March, but I'm not so sure. The newsreels of his speech were really scary."

"My dad thinks the same but I agree with you. Unfortunately there's not much we can do about it, is there?"

Mike shook his head. "No. I just hope the German people come to their senses and vote in someone else."

"Are you two lads here to work or chatter all day?" The manager's voice echoed down the platform. After arranging to meet in the pub later, Rob and Mike went their separate ways.

****

Boots the Chemist, Romford High Street, Essex

"Well, she was a miserable cow, wasn't she?" Daisy Harris made sure no one was looking, then stuck out her tongue at the woman's retreating back. Annie hid her laughter behind her hand as she refilled the make-up counter with the latest lipsticks. Annie had been working at Boots for over a year when Daisy had arrived six months earlier, having transferred from another branch. She was a year older than Annie and the two girls had very soon become best friends, spending much of their spare time together.

"Why don't you come home with me tonight, Annie? Then we can go to the pictures from there. You can stay the night, if you want."

Annie thought about it and nodded. "Alright. I'll pop home at lunchtime and tell Mum so she doesn't worry, and get my night clothes. Do you know what's on?"

"No, but we could go with Albert and his friend, Barry."

Annie nodded and smiled, but inwardly gave a silent groan. So that was why Daisy wanted her to come round. Daisy was madly in love with yet another one of her older brother's friends, Barry. Albert had lots of friends and Daisy was always madly in love with one or another of them. Unfortunately Annie and Albert spent an awful lot of time playing gooseberry so that Daisy could date his friends. Annie was surprised Albert went along with it, but he adored his younger sister and would do anything for her. And his friends liked Daisy with her mischievous green eyes, slim figure and relaxed attitude to life.

Annie sighed. She was much more inhibited than her friend and had considerably less confidence. Taller than Daisy, Annie was slim, with long blonde curly hair which was invariably unruly, her grey-green eyes wore an habitually serious expression that suggested an intense approach to life. She was a pretty girl, although she thought her nose was slightly too long and her mouth rather too wide, but these seeming imperfections sat well together, giving her face character and a hidden strength.

Although both girls were quite slim, there the resemblance ended. Daisy's hair was shoulder length and a rich auburn colour that shone in the sun and always appeared effortlessly tidy. Annie secretly envied Daisy's hair which was such a contrast to her own unruly locks, which her mum would often say made her look like she'd been dragged through a hedge backwards. Daisy was nearly always smiling and, although she was not conventionally pretty, her face always appeared animated and she was never short of admirers.

Annie longed to let herself go, but she was too afraid of the consequences of falling for the wrong man so, rather than make a mistake, she turned down most of the invitations she did receive, preferring to play it safe. Deep inside, she knew her knight in shining armour would come along one day and, until then, she was content to wait on the side lines.

In the meantime, she didn't really mind spending her evenings discussing politics with Albert. Annie had never been particularly interested in what was happening in the world until she met Daisy, whose parents and older brother Albert were members of the Independent Labour Party. "I used to have politics with my cornflakes," Daisy would often joke and, to her surprise, Annie was fascinated by something she knew so little about. Fortunately Albert was a more than willing teacher who was happy to answer all her questions.

****

Berlin

The party was in full swing, champagne was flowing, some of his SS friends were singing round the piano and Hans was nowhere to be seen. Andreas wondered where his friend had gone and then spotted him disappearing upstairs with a woman. Andreas watched enviously. He had been married to Hans' sister Karin for nearly ten years now and, although he loved her, he was bored. Most of the time, Karin was a good companion but lately she'd become obsessed by her inability to have children. Andreas wouldn't have minded having a son but he was quite happy with things as they were. Unfortunately, Karin was beginning to drive him away with her constant demands and he no longer had a mistress he could escape to. The latest girl had suddenly stopped meeting him several weeks ago. He had no idea why she'd disappeared, but as he'd tired of her anyway, he hadn't bothered to look for her. It was time to seek out a new conquest. The soiree was the perfect place to meet someone, and in fact he had his eye on a lady already, but speaking to her would not be easy with Karin watching his every move.

"You look fed up. Is everything alright?" Karin snuggled up against him and he resisted the temptation to push her away.

"Yes, of course." He smiled down at her and wondered how he could get rid of her for a while. "You look a little tired, my love. Perhaps you should have an early night?"

Karin stared up at him, her mouth a thin line. She'd seen the looks he'd been giving that red haired woman all evening. However, it wouldn't do to let him know how she felt, so instead she forced herself to smile. "Perhaps you're right. I'll see if I can get a lift home." She leant forward, kissed him on the cheek and was gone before he could say anything.

Andreas watched her move towards a group of men in the corner and frowned. He hadn't expected it to be quite so easy. Feeling guilty, he was about to walk over to her when the red haired girl he'd been surreptitiously watching all evening appeared in front of him.

"Got rid of your wife then?" She was laughing, her heavily mascaraed green eyes sparkling, and he smiled back.

"Yes." His eyes devoured her breasts in the low cut brown dress before returning to her face. "Would you like another drink?"

She handed him her glass and he reached for the champagne bottle on the table nearest to him. After topping up her glass, he stretched out his hand and ran his fingers through her hair. "Let's go upstairs, shall we?"

Karin watched from the corner of the room, her face contorted by rage. He hadn't even waited until she'd left the room. If he thought he could humiliate her, he had better think again. No one made a fool of her and got away with it.

Chapter Six
Autumn 1936

Berlin

Hans frowned. "You can't keep doing this, Karin. Let me take care of him for you."

Karin stared at him in horror. "No. He's my husband and I love him."

Hans sighed. "He obviously doesn't feel the same way, or he wouldn't be screwing every woman he meets."

The slap was loud, echoing around the small corridor outside his office and took Hans by surprise. His face darkened, he clenched his fists, raised his arm and had already taken a step towards her before he regained control. Karin's hand flew to her mouth and she appeared just as shocked. "I'm so sorry. I didn't mean…"

Hans took a deep breath. "It's alright. Don't worry, Karin. I promised you I would always take care of you and I will. I just think you will have to find another way to keep control over Andreas."

"Like what?"

Hans hesitated. "Maybe you should choose the women for him." He saw her outraged expression and hurried on before she could interrupt. "That way you're in charge and you can make sure they just provide him with sex. Elke has only become a threat because he's grown emotionally attached to her."

Karin opened her mouth to say how horrified she was that he could come up with such a suggestion, then she stopped. Her brother was right. She didn't really mind Andreas sleeping with other women as long as he was discreet, although all the time he was with them, her chances of becoming pregnant were diminishing. However, what she wouldn't tolerate was any threat to her position in Berlin. She was married to a high ranking SS officer, and mixed in the highest echelons of their society. She had no intention of allowing anyone to usurp her position, let alone some dirty tart her husband was using to warm his bed.

"Alright. Get rid of Elke and I'll think about it."

Hans breathed a sigh of relief. He reached out and put his arms around his sister. "I'll help if you like. It'll be easier for me to procure them than you."

"You really think this is the answer?" She still sounded unsure.

"I think it's the only way. Providing we stick to girls with low intelligence and obvious attributes, he'll soon grow bored and move onto the next one. Trust me, Karin. I know Andreas."

Karin thought for several more moments before eventually agreeing. Hans breathed a sigh of relief. Karin had nothing to lose by trying his suggestion and if Andreas did become attached to one of them, Hans could always get rid of her, the same as he had been doing for the past few years.

****

Cable Street, East London

The sound of marching feet came closer and closer, their rhythmic pounding echoing ominously on the paved streets. Annie braced herself and glanced sideways at Daisy for reassurance. They were hemmed in amongst a large mass of people at Gardiner's Corner in the East End where they had earlier overturned a tram and built a barricade, blocking the entrance to Cable Street.

"No pasaran!" The shouting of the Spanish Republican civil war chant rang in Annie's ears and she joined in enthusiastically. "They shall not pass," she shouted, the words signifying their determination not to let the fascists pass.

Annie and Daisy were waiting with the thousands of other anti-fascist protesters while they attempted to stop the British Union of Fascists, led by Sir Oswald Mosley, marching though the East End and the predominantly Jewish Cable Street.

Annie had taken little persuasion to join the protesters. Her own innate sense of justice hated any form of discrimination, but her excitement was now tempered by nervousness as the time for the march came ever closer. She glanced at her watch; it was gone half past two and, judging by the increased tension in the crowd, things were about to happen.

****

Berlin

"He's gone." Hannah handed the note to Franz, her hands shaking, tears in her eyes.

His heart sinking, Franz scanned the brief accusatory note.

Mutti, Vati,
I know you won't approve but I can't just sit here while Germany supports Franco against the lawful communist government of Spain. At least this way I can fight the fascists, which you no longer seem interested in doing. I hope you enjoy your new friends and the social position you've gained because of them.
Your son,
Gerhard

Franz lit a match, set fire to the note, dropped it into the metal bin and watched as the paper burned into ashes. Then he pulled Hannah into his arms and shook his head.

"We'll have to socialise with the Nazis even more now."

Hannah stared up at him. "I don't understand."

"Eventually Gerhard will come back home, God willing. When he does, we'll need friends in high places to stop him being arrested, or worse."

Hannah sighed. She hated the Nazis and she was terrified they would eventually see through the lies she and Franz had told them. But she would do anything to protect her son, including supping with the devil.

****

Gardiner's Corner, East London

Rob and Mike were among the large crowd on the corner of Whitechapel High Street and Commercial Road, waiting for the fascists to arrive.

"It's a good turn out." Rob grinned

Mike nodded. "Shame about the police presence, though. I can't believe they're protecting this scum."

Rob shook his head. "It's ridiculous, isn't it? Still, there's enough of us to show them we don't want their kind here."

Mike didn't look convinced. "There's a lot of police too and they've got batons…" Whatever else he was about to say was cut off as a roar went through the surrounding crowd. He peered through the people in front and his face darkened.

Two men wearing distinctive black shirts had arrived and were standing near the wall of the building with several policemen in front, protecting them from the crowd.

Rob and Mike joined in with the rest of the crowd, hurling insults until they heard the sound of a vehicle heading towards them. A large black van drew up and several more blackshirts climbed out. The crowd surged forward and then Rob and Mike found themselves shoved forward as the crowd tried to attack the fascists before the police could intervene.

Rob had little difficulty seeing over the crowd. At six foot in his socks, he was a good head taller than most of them.

"Bastards!" He disappeared into the melee, finding himself facing an equally tall man in a black shirt, his face menacing as he swung his fist in Rob's direction. Rob ducked and the man punched the air above his head. Rob straightened up and plunged his fist towards the man's stomach. The fascist had considerably more weight than Rob and struggled to regain his balance. He was unable to avoid Rob's fist and doubled over. Rob hit him again and then felt someone grab the back of his shirt.

He spun round and found himself face to face with a policeman, his baton raised. Rob ducked, the policeman missed and then someone pulled him down towards the pavement as the baton narrowly missed him again, this time striking his shoulder. Grimacing in pain, he was momentarily unable to move and he waited, helpless, for the next blow. Then he heard the policeman grunt and saw him double up in pain. Before he could react, he felt strong arms pulling him backwards as Mike dragged him away.

****

Outside Lublin, Eastern Poland

"I'm sorry, Mama, but we have to do this." Stani appealed to Wiktor. "You do understand, Tata, don't you?"

"I understand and I know there is nothing we can say to talk you out of it, but that doesn't mean I like it."

Magda put her arms around Stani and Alek, tears streaming down her face. She appealed to Wiktor. "There must be something you can do?"

Wiktor shook his head. "They are grown men, Magda, and we should be proud of them for wanting to fight for our country. Would you prefer them to be cowards?"

"But we're not at war."

"Not yet, but with Germany re-arming and having reintroduced conscription, we can't afford to take the risk, Mama. Not to mention the Soviets who are a constant threat on our eastern border." Alek sounded so grown up, Magda smiled through her tears.

"I know, I know. I just wish you could stay here while someone else's sons joined the army instead."

"Who's joining the army?" There was a brief silence. They were so busy talking, they hadn't heard Felcia who had entered the kitchen, a pail of fresh milk in her hand. Then Felcia's face crumpled as she realised both her brothers were about to leave.

"Come on, sis, wish us luck, eh?" Stani gave her a big hug, followed quickly by Alek. "We'll be fine. You don't need to worry. The bigger the Polish army, the less chance we have of the Germans trying to extend their borders."

Felcia nodded, although her stomach was churning. She watched as her brothers went off to the station and then joined her parents while they broke the news to Raisa and Ala.

****

Cable Street, East London

In the distance, Annie and Daisy could hear the ominous sound of marching feet approaching and, above that, they could clearly hear the sound of the Blackshirts shouting:

"The Yids, the Yids, we're going to get rid of the Yids."

Before Annie could comment, the crowd began booing and hissing loudly, the sound interspersed with shouted insults and obscenities.

In the brief silence between the shouts, they heard the Blackshirts retaliating: "We want Mosley; We want Mosley; We want Mosley!"

As the chant reached the crowd, they responded cheerfully: "So do we, dead or alive!" followed by roars of good natured laughter from the mass of people thronging around the barricade.

"Albert! Albert, over here. What's happening?" Daisy had just spotted her brother fighting his way through the enormous number of people now gathered at the corner.

Albert finally broke through. "The police have cordoned off a lot of the side streets to prevent us getting down them, but they couldn't stop us completely. There might be plenty of police but there's more of us." He took a swig of water from a small flask tucked in the top of his trousers. Annie was amused to see that he looked a lot smarter than usual.

Albert worked in the local paint factory and, although he normally wore overalls, his clothes were often paint splattered and he usually smelt of turpentine and paint thinners. Today he was wearing a pair of smart black trousers and a clean white shirt under his jacket and he smelt faintly of some kind of fragrance, although Annie couldn't identify what it was. Briefly, she wondered why he was all dressed up and then wondered who the lucky girl was before turning her attention back to what he was saying. Having finished his drink and wiped his mouth with the back of his hand, he continued, aware that it was not only the girls who were listening now.

"… 'bout half one, a couple of those black shirted bastards arrived and were told to stand against the wall with half a dozen policemen in front of them to protect them. Typical bullies… can give it out, but don't like to be on the receiving end." There was a murmur of agreement through the crowd, who were hanging on his every word. Seeing Daisy looking impatient and about to interrupt, Albert hurriedly returned to his story. "Then a van arrived; full of the bastards, it was, and they started to get out. Before the police could act, the crowd attacked them and knocked them out. Laid them out cold on the pavement, they did. Ruddy marvellous." He stopped as a small cheer went through the crowd and one of the men in the crowd yelled out:

"So what happened next?"

"The bloody police waded in, baton charges, horses, you name it. But we fought back as hard as we could. Trouble was, they were too strong for us. They kept pushing us back so they could carry on with their march. There wasn't much else I could do up there, so I thought I'd come back here and wait for them. They were all lining up to pay homage to their Führer when I left, so it won't be long… just waiting for the b'stard to arrive." Albert spat disdainfully on the floor.

"How many are there?" The question came from a rather smart looking young man with round glasses perched precariously on the end of his nose. He was wearing a neat brown jacket and matching trousers and looked more like a school teacher or some kind of professor. To Annie, he typified the mixture of people manning the barricades. From dockers to factory workers, builders to teachers, they had all turned out to show their support and she suddenly felt a wave of pride that she was there with them.

"About three thousand, give or take," Albert replied after a few seconds' thought. "The column stretches back about half a mile in all, I suppose. Oh, and they've got a couple of hundred women in the middle of them as well, all wearing their black blouses."

Albert was about to carry on when there was a surge from the crowd behind them and more shouting could be heard in the distance. Insults and obscenities flew backwards and forwards between the marchers and protesters, the crowd laughed and joked and Annie was thoroughly enjoying herself.

But then police activity began to increase and the jocular, good natured mood of the crowd quickly changed to something more menacing.

****

Outside Lublin, Eastern Poland

"I don't understand why they didn't say goodbye to us." The three girls were sitting in their bedroom on the beds. Raisa wore her customary sneer and Felcia resisted the urge to slap her younger sister.

"They didn't want to upset you both. I only found out because I had finished the milking and had gone into the kitchen with a fresh pail. Otherwise they wouldn't have said goodbye to me either."

Raisa didn't look convinced and Felcia lost her temper. "Surely the most important thing is that our brothers have gone to join the army. We should be praying for them, not arguing over nothing."

Ala nodded. "Felcia's right, Raisa. They didn't say goodbye to me and I'm not upset."

"Trust you to side with Felcia." Raisa stormed off, slamming the bedroom door behind her.

Felcia exchanged glances with Ala and sighed. She had no idea why Raisa was so difficult. One of these days her younger sister was going to get them all into trouble if she didn't curb her temper.

****

Cable Street, East London

To Annie it seemed like one minute everyone was laughing and joking and the next, mounted police were racing towards them, wielding their long batons and riot sticks, hitting out at anyone who was unfortunate enough to get in the way. At the same time, the police on the ground charged at those the horses had missed, their batons and truncheons laying into anyone who offered resistance. Forced to retreat from the police onslaught, the crowd surged violently backwards and Annie couldn't prevent herself being dragged along with them. Determined to retaliate, the protesters regrouped, throwing marbles under the feet of the horses and hurling stones, fireworks and anything they could lay their hands on at the police, all the time still chanting loudly, "They shall not pass!"

Annie was caught up in a frantic fleeing mob of people while the police forced back the protesters yet again. Unable to free herself, she turned, panic stricken, to see police charging directly towards where she was standing. From then on everything happened in slow motion. She could see the long batons wielded by the police, their faces snarling, their words unheard in the chaos and noise of the fight, but their meaning clear; she could see the riot sticks of the mounted police flailing through the air and she could hear the hooves of the horses clattering on the road while they came closer and, above it all, the yells and screams of the people as they fled in panic; but she was unable to move, penned in by her fellow protesters.

The first baton charge was followed by more mounted police, their riot sticks and batons raining blows down on the unprotected heads of protesters. Annie found herself unable to either push forward against the attacking police, or escape. She was caught in amongst a swirling, thronging mass of people, some screaming and trying to get away, others struggling to push their way forward to fight the police. She had somehow become separated from Daisy and Albert, and was surrounded by people she didn't know. Her heart pounded with terror while she fought to stay upright, knowing that, if she fell, she would be trampled to death. She tried frantically to escape but it was impossible. The more violent the police action, the more angry the protesters became and the worse the clashes between them. Annie was completely trapped, powerless to move in any direction, dragged back and forth like a rag doll with no will of her own.

Chapter Seven

Cable Street, East London

Cable Street was chaos by the time Rob and Mike reached the barricade. Police were hitting out with batons and riot sticks, horses were charging at the crowd which surged violently back and forth. The two men immediately threw themselves into the battle with enthusiasm, only to be forced back by the police as they mounted another baton charge.

"We'll need to pull back." Mike's shout went unnoticed by Rob who was staring at something in the crowd. Mike grabbed his arm and began tugging.

Rob pulled free and shouted, his voice barely audible above the noise: "Look over there." Mike glanced around to see where Rob was pointing but couldn't see anything through the melee of people. A look of confusion on his face, he turned back only to find Rob had disappeared. Mike peered into the crowd but Rob was nowhere to be seen.

****

Berlin

Andreas stared out of the window, a frown on his face. He had arranged to meet his mistress, Elke earlier that day, but she had failed to turn up. It wasn't like her. She was normally very reliable and it was even more strange that she hadn't sent a message to tell him she couldn't make it.

"Is everything alright, Andreas? You look worried?"

Andreas pulled himself together, spun around and smiled at Karin. He hadn't heard his wife come into the study.

"Yes, darling, everything's fine. I thought you'd gone to the park."

"I'm just about to leave. I thought you might like to come with me, if you're not doing anything else of course?"

Andreas started and he stared at her, but Karin's face was expressionless. He must have imagined the hint of amusement.

"Yes, I'd love to." Andreas suddenly couldn't wait to leave the claustrophobic atmosphere of the study. "Some fresh air will be great."

Karin followed him into the hall, a smirk on her face. Elke would not be keeping her appointment with her husband today or any other day, come to that. Karin had denounced her as a Jew a couple of days earlier and, after Hans had finished interrogating her, she would be on her way to one of the camps especially for Jews. Karin had no idea of Elke's ancestry but these days it made no difference, especially if someone in her position made the accusation. The difficult part was making sure Andreas didn't find out what she had done, but fortunately she could rely on Hans' discretion. He loved her and she knew he would do anything for his little sister.

****

Cable Street, East London

Annie's heart was pounding frantically against her chest, stars appeared in front of her eyes and she started to feel dizzy and lightheaded, only the pressure of the crowd keeping her upright. Then, just when she thought she would never get away, she felt someone grab her arm and pull her violently towards the floor. Instinctively, she put her hands out in front of her to protect her face and then the baton came down on the back of her head and the ground came rushing up to meet her. Almost unconscious from the blow, she was only vaguely aware of strong hands catching her before she hit the floor and then miraculously she was out of the crush, in some open space and gasping for breath. She could hear the sounds of the battle continuing but the mass of people were no longer surrounding her and instead she found herself looking into a pair of concerned, soft blue eyes.

"Are you alright?" The voice was deep and melodic, the eyes boring into hers.

Annie nodded gingerly, unable to speak yet, her voice gone in the terror of the assault, but at least she could breathe again and her dizziness had eased. Her rescuer helped her to a quiet spot on the pavement, away from the fighting which was still continuing unabated, and Annie sat down gratefully, closed her eyes and slowly started to regain her composure. Eventually feeling better, she opened her eyes and looked up to speak to him, but he was gone and she was on her own again, left with a vague memory of kind blue eyes and a handsome face.

****

Berlin

The cellar was cold and dank, the single bulb cast its harsh light on the stone floor and the two occupants. Hans smiled at Elke. She was seated on a wooden chair, her hands tied behind her back and he could see the fear in her eyes.

"I'm not Jewish. It's a lie." Elke was becoming desperate. She'd lost track of time and had no idea how long they'd been holding her. No matter how many times she pleaded with them, no one seemed to believe her. She'd tried asking for Andreas but that only seemed to infuriate her captor. "I'm telling you the truth. Why won't you listen to me?"

Hans laughed and bent down so his face was inches from hers. "Oh, but I do believe you, Elke. Unfortunately I am the only one who knows the truth of why you are here, so you might as well save your breath."

Elke gasped. "I don't understand. Why am I here? I haven't done anything."

Hans shook his head. She could smell the cognac on his breath. "That's not strictly true, is it, Elke? You were fucking my brother-in-law and my sister was not very happy about that… so, here you are."

Elke stared at him in disbelief. "She's had me arrested for having an affair with her husband? That's ridiculous!"

Hans smiled and began undoing his trousers. "Now, why don't you show me what Andreas sees in you? You never know, if you're good enough, I may let you go."

Elke struggled against the rope tying her to the chair but she couldn't move, she was trapped. He grabbed her hair and twisted it around his fist. With his other hand, he pulled out his penis, shoved her head forward until her lips were level with his erection and twisted her hair hard. As Elke gasped, he shoved his penis inside her open mouth and began moving against her.

"That's good, use your tongue." His whispered words echoed around the cellar, mingling with Elke's sobs as he thrust harder and faster.

****

Outside Lublin, Eastern Poland

Raisa threw herself down on the fresh straw in the barn and sobbed noisily for several moments before the anger took over. She was always the last one to be told anything, the one who was excluded. She didn't know why everyone hated her but they did. Even her brothers hadn't bothered to say goodbye to her, although they'd managed to find time to speak to Felcia, her perfect older sister who everybody loved.

Her face contorted with rage while she planned how to get even with them all. Despite her best efforts, she hadn't yet thought up the perfect revenge but thinking about it made her feel better, at least in the short term until something else happened to upset her. Her first plan had been to set fire to the farmhouse when they were all asleep but then she'd have nowhere to live, so she'd quickly discounted that idea. Another thought was to shoot them all with her father's shotgun but then the police would arrest her, so that wasn't much good either, unless… Raisa smiled. An idea had just come to her. Maybe she could make it look like Felcia had gone mad and shot all the others before taking her own life. She could say she'd escaped because Felcia had thought she'd killed her too. Her rage disappeared while she picked at the straw and made her plans.

****

Cable Street, East London

Shakily, Annie picked herself up and put her hand to the back of her head where the baton had hit her. There was no blood on her hand, so although her head hurt, the blow did not appear to have broken the skin. She breathed a sigh of relief. Although she would probably have a large lump and a bruise the next day, she appeared to be relatively unhurt.

All around her the battle raged on; paving stones were pulled up and broken into convenient sizes to be used as missiles, glasses and bottles were smashed to throw under the horses to impede their progress. Other protesters raided a builder's yard and used the contents to add to the overturned lorry, packing cases and carts already utilised in the barricade that was being reinforced quicker than the police could demolish it. All the time the marchers, with the protection of the police, hurled insults and threats while they waited for their leader, who was late. And still the protesters fought on.

Volunteers set up makeshift medical centres to tend to the wounded and runners kept protesters up to date with what was happening elsewhere. Having recovered from her earlier fright, Annie now joined in with those protecting the barricade and, much to her surprise, found herself defending it with stones and anything else she could lay her hands on. Always a supporter of the police, Annie had lost her faith in them completely and, angry she had been attacked for no reason, she fought with as much tenacity as the others.

Eventually the police came back with more reinforcements and, after clearing the street with yet another violent baton charge, leaving several people badly injured, they finally succeeded in removing the barricade. Annie retreated with her new friends further down the street and waited to see what would happen next. She still didn't know where Daisy and Albert were, but for the moment she wasn't too worried as she was still high on the adrenaline of the battle.

Mosley finally arrived in a black sports car with two other officers at about a quarter to four and drove down the ranks of his cheering, Union Jack waving Blackshirts. But after a brief consultation with the police, he was escorted out of Royal Mint Street by thousands of officers. The word quickly reached the protesters that he'd had been told the march couldn't take place because of the threat of disorder. News of their victory spread through the streets and loud cheers went up. The protesters hugged and congratulated each other, unable to believe their success. Annie followed her new companions to a local hall where everyone was congregating, and began to look for her friends. She was exhilarated she had been part of something so momentous and was dying to find Daisy so she could tell her about her exciting rescue by her very own hero.

****

Berlin

"What are you doing?" Hannah watched while Franz picked up the phone.

"I'm inviting some Nazis to an evening soiree." He gave a wry smile at her horrified expression. "We need to insinuate ourselves deeper into the party, Hannah. I don't like it any more than you do but the sooner we start, the better. Don't forget our country is supporting the fascists in Spain and our son has gone to fight against them. That makes him a traitor."

Hannah sighed but didn't argue. "I'll organise some food and hire some extra servants. Have you got a date in mind?"

"Next weekend seems as good a time as any. Can you arrange everything by then?"

Hannah nodded. "Yes, I would think so. I'll see if I can book one of the small orchestras too. If we're going to do this, we might as well do it properly."

Franz smiled and returned his attention to the phone. "My dear Hoffman, we're planning on inviting a select few to an evening soiree next weekend and wondered if you would be interested." He listened for a few moments, pulled a face and said enthusiastically. "Great. We'll look forward to seeing you." He replaced the receiver. "Well that's the first one. With Hoffman coming, the rest should follow." He gave a deep sigh, plastered a smile on his face and picked up the phone again.

Hannah left him to it. She needed to plan menus, organise extra staff and find the entertainment for the evening. At least it would keep her mind occupied and stop her worrying about Gerhard.

****

Cable Street, East London

When Annie did finally find Daisy, her face was burning from the heat inside the very warm hall.

"Am I bright red?" It was at times like this when Annie cursed her fair skin which showed the slightest hint of colour.

Daisy shook her head. It was most unlike Annie to care about her appearance and she wondered why her friend was suddenly concerned. Whatever was going on, she certainly wasn't about to tell Annie that she looked a bit like a beetroot. Anyway, she had her own problems. Her hair was hanging limply and the heel had come off her shoe after someone had trodden on her foot in the scuffle. This had left her with one wet foot where she had stepped in a puddle. "You think you've got problems? Look at my shoe!"

Annie leant forward and was about to answer when someone interrupted.

"Never mind, luv, I'll lend you one of my boots!" The remark, from an attractive dark haired man with deep brown eyes, was greeted with hoots of laughter from those within hearing distance and then appreciative smiles when Daisy joined in.

"Maybe we could swap?" Daisy was gratified to hear even more laughter.

"How about a lift home instead?" This speaker was tall, over six foot, had short fair hair, soft blue eyes with flecks of grey that sparkled when the light hit them and was very good looking. Although the remark was seemingly addressed to Daisy, he was looking at Annie.

His voice struck a chord somewhere deep within her. Annie stared up into his eyes and in moments she was lost. The intensity of his gaze seemed to go right through her, lodging in the pit of her stomach and it was some time before she was able to look away. It was also a while before she realised why the voice sounded so familiar; he was her very own knight in shining armour.

Chapter Eight

Berlin

Franz waited until his wife had left the room before picking up the phone. He dialled quickly and, when the person answered, he arranged to meet them the following day. Having replaced the receiver, he sighed. When he'd first been contacted by John Carstairs back in 1923, he'd felt sure he was doing the right thing. Then things had improved in Germany and contact had been reduced to the odd meeting of old friends in the park. But when Hitler became Chancellor, Franz had made the decision to increase contact, concerned about the future of his country.

A part of him still felt like a traitor. The majority of the Army High Command seemed to be supportive of Hitler; dreams of glory, of a new German Empire, revenge on the French and Poles, spurring them on. But all Franz could see was the thousands of dead bodies of his comrades during the four years of hell the last time his country had been at war. He would do anything to prevent that happening again. Meeting Carstairs and exchanging information was the best thing he could think of doing. It was very dangerous, but given his position in the Army High Command he was hoping he could be of considerable help if things went the way he was expecting.

Unlike most German citizens, Franz had read *Mein Kampf* and he knew what Hitler was planning to do. The other members of the Army High Command had been impressed by the ease with which Hitler had retaken the Rhineland without a shot being fired. There had been virtually no objections from the British, who'd considered the territory belonged to Germany anyway. Only the French had complained, but France was embroiled in political turmoil and there was no will to do anything about it, especially as they had not received any support from either America or Britain. Strangely enough, the biggest threat to Hitler had come from the German Generals. Convinced Hitler was about to drag an unprepared Germany into an ill-judged war by his actions, Franz had heard rumours that several members of the Army High Command had considered removing him, seeing him as dangerous and a threat to the Fatherland. But since his success, his enemies had melted away and Hitler could do no wrong.

Unfortunately, Franz was sure Hitler had no intention of stopping at the Rhineland. He had no idea who Hitler would target first, but German pilots and military advisors were already gaining plenty of experience in Spain, supporting General Franco. As far as he could see it was only a matter of time before Germany was at war with someone. The Fatherland had already begun re-arming and conscription had been reintroduced. Only a fool would ignore the warning signs and Franz was no fool.

****

Cable Street, East London

Normally Annie would have refused the offer of a lift from someone she didn't know, but she didn't fancy walking home after such an exciting afternoon and, in any case, her willpower seemed to have suddenly deserted her. Glancing briefly at Daisy, she surprised herself by replying almost immediately, "Thank you, that would be much appreciated." She gazed up into his face, her eyes fixed on his dazzling smile.

"Rob." He held out his hand. "Robert Davies and this is Mike Jacobs, my best friend." He indicated the man standing slightly to his right.

"Ah the man who wants to borrow my shoes." Daisy laughed as she took the outstretched hand. Introductions completed, there was a moment of awkward silence and then both Annie and Rob went to speak at once.

Rob smiled. "After you; ladies first."

Annie shook her head; suddenly feeling shy and Rob smiled, continuing, "You don't look like a communist."

Annie laughed. "I'm not. Albert, Daisy's brother, is a member of the ILP and he persuaded us to come along and show our support."

"You're not a political person then?" Rob persisted.

Annie shook her head. "No. To be honest I'm very ignorant about politics, or at least I was until recently, but after the things I've seen today, I'm going to take a much greater interest." She spoke with such determination, Rob didn't doubt her sincerity for one moment.

"What about you?" She found it easier to talk to him without looking into his eyes, which seemed to be hypnotising her.

"Mike and I have been worried about the rise of fascism since we watched the newsreels of Hitler coming to power." He hesitated. "Mike's Jewish, so I suppose you could say we have a vested interest in what's happening here today. We feel it's really important to stop people like Mosley before their extreme views take hold here as well."

She could hear the passion in his voice. "Do you think that's likely?"

Rob shrugged. "Not if we make it clear we don't want fascism, but if we all sit back and do nothing, it'll be too late to stop them."

Annie was about to say something else when Daisy interrupted: "Albert's gone off with that girl from the sugar factory, Sandra I think her name is, so he won't be taking us home. We might as well leave, if that's alright?" She glanced at Rob whose gaze was still fixed on Annie.

"This way, ladies." He finally managed to tear his eyes away from Annie and smiled at Daisy. As they walked through the still chaotic streets to where he'd parked his father's Austin Seven, they chatted and Annie listened while Rob told her all about the Spanish Civil War and how he and Mike had thought about volunteering.

"Why don't you come to one of the meetings with me?" Rob stopped suddenly and stared deep into her eyes. Annie wondered if he knew the effect he was having on her. When he looked at her like that, she was unlikely to be able to refuse him anything.

Mutely she nodded and then felt a thrill of excitement course through her body as he put his arm round her and pulled her close

"I'm so glad I met you, Annie." He called out to Mike: "Annie's going to come with us to the meeting tomorrow night, isn't that great?"

Mike glanced at Annie's rapturous face and felt a slight stirring of unease but Rob looked so pleased, he didn't have the heart to say anything, so he just smiled and nodded. "Good on you, Annie. You'll meet some really great people there, you'll see. What about you, Daisy?"

"No thanks. I get enough politics at home!" She smiled to take the sting out of her words. "Although I am open to other offers!"

****

Berlin

Hans finished spurting all over Elke and, breathing heavily, pulled up his trousers. There was no sound from her and he slapped her buttocks to make sure she was still conscious.

Elke whimpered and eased her naked body away from the chair he had forced her over. He waited until she was facing him, then reached out and squeezed one of her nipples until she moaned.

"Well, I'm afraid you haven't passed my test, so get dressed and I'll arrange some transport to one of our brothels further south where you can entertain our new conscripts."

"You can't do this to me." Elke's voice was hoarse from crying and he laughed.

"I can do whatever I like, Elke, unlike you. I think I'll recommend you for special duties, servicing the young soldiers rather than the officers." He turned around and left the cell. Elke sank to her knees, wishing she'd never met Andreas. She wondered briefly if this was his way of getting rid of his women so his wife didn't find out, then she shook her head. Andreas had been a gentleman. She was almost sure he didn't know what was happening to her.

****

En route to Romford, Essex

They eventually reached the place where Rob had left the car and climbed in, Rob and Mike in the front and Annie and Daisy in the back.

"I think you've scored a direct hit there," Daisy whispered as they huddled together on the back seat.

"He's gorgeous, isn't he?" Annie was no good at pretending or lying. Her feelings were written across her face. To Daisy it was perfectly obvious she had fallen under the spell of the tall handsome man who was busy concentrating on driving and avoiding the odd fight that was still going on in the streets of the East End.

She smiled and took Annie's hand. "Just be careful, Annie. You don't know anything about him."

Despite her words, Daisy didn't really think Annie had much to worry about in Rob. Annie was well and truly smitten and, one look at Rob's face told Daisy that he felt the same. He hadn't taken his eyes off Annie since they'd first spoken, and the way his face lit up when he smiled at her gave away his feelings. Daisy frowned. She wasn't used to Annie being the centre of attention when it came to men, and she wasn't sure she liked being sidelined. On the other hand, it might all come to nothing. They had only just met; the relationship could fizzle out in a couple of weeks, although somehow she didn't think so. Perhaps she should try and put a stop to things before they went too far. Most men ran a mile if you mentioned marriage. She squeezed Annie's hand. "So can I be a bridesmaid?" she whispered, quite loudly.

"What was that?" Rob asked. Daisy had chosen her moment well. There had been a lull in his conversation with Mike, and Rob had heard her remark.

"Oh, nothing." Annie was absolutely mortified and a deep red flush spread over her face. "Nothing important."

"She was just telling me about some friends of hers who were getting married and I asked her if she was going to be bridesmaid," Daisy quickly interjected.

"Oh." To Daisy's dismay Rob actually sounded disappointed and his eyes twinkled as they met Annie's in his driving mirror. "I could have sworn you said something else."

Gathering that he was laughing at her, Annie smiled back and decided it was probably safer not to answer and, after finally managing to drag her eyes away from his, she realised with a sense of disappointment they were nearly at her house.

He pulled up outside the small neat terraced house where she directed him and, after Rob arranged to pick her up the following evening, she climbed reluctantly out of the car.

Chapter Nine

Berlin

"What do you mean she's disappeared?" Andreas frowned into the telephone and listened for several moments before replacing the receiver and staring into space. He had returned to his office that evening to make some enquiries about Elke. Her non-appearance was all very strange. If they'd had a row, or it was just Elke who'd suddenly stopped turning up for their assignations, he wouldn't have worried too much, but he'd finally realised she was the latest in a long line. Maybe something had happened to them? He smiled. The idea was ridiculous. Why should his mistresses disappear?

He sighed. He wasn't proud of himself for being unfaithful to Karin, but he had become addicted to the excitement of an affair, the adrenaline of keeping it a secret from his wife, the thrill of a new body writhing under him, pleasuring him in ways he could hardly bring himself to think about, except when he was alone. It was also a relief to be able to enjoy himself without being under pressure to produce an heir.

He closed his eyes and thought back to succession of women he'd slept with since his marriage. Apart from Elke, who he was becoming rather fond of, he'd only seen most of them a few times before moving onto the next one. However, it was very strange he hadn't seen any of the women at all after he'd stopped sleeping with them. He would have expected to have seen them at various functions or even in the street, but it was as if they'd vanished into thin air. Andreas smiled as he recalled the redhead he'd met at the party after Hitler's accession to Chancellor. He couldn't remember her name now but her laughing green eyes and her tongue licking and sucking his penis while his wife was still downstairs and could come up and discover him at any moment was something he would never forget. The danger of Karin catching them in the upstairs bedroom of the country estate had added to the excitement and he had climaxed much too quickly.

The girl had come to his office the following day and he'd shoved her over the desk and fucked her hard until the phone rang and interrupted them. To his horror it was Karin, saying she was coming into his office to pick up some money. His erection had vanished, the girl had dressed quickly and he'd arranged to meet her at a hotel that afternoon. She'd never turned up. He'd assumed she'd lost interest and, because he'd soon found someone else, he'd forgotten all about her.

He pulled some paper towards him and began writing. Although he couldn't remember all their names, he should be able to list enough about the girls to allow him to trace them.

****

Outside Lublin, Eastern Poland

"I'm sure they will be alright, Magda. They're not stupid."

Magda ignored him. Felcia was stirring the stew, Ala was helping her and Raisa was laying the table, for once her normal scowl absent. Magda frowned. Given the noisy slamming of doors earlier, she was surprised Raisa was not in a worse mood. She wondered briefly why her middle daughter was so calm, then put the thought out of her mind. She had more important things to worry about. She still couldn't believe both her sons had gone to join the army. If she'd had some notice, she could have adjusted, but no, they'd made their plans and presented it to their parents as a fait accompli.

"Magda?" Wiktor hated the pleading tone in his voice. He would worry just as much about the boys but they were adults. He had no control over them anymore.

She turned around and his heart sank at her tear-stained cheeks. He reached out and, after a brief hesitation, she allowed him to pull her into his arms. Wiktor stared out across the fields of the farm he was so proud of and sent up a silent prayer for God to keep his sons safe so they could return to home to their inheritance. Although he had reassured Magda, he was deeply worried about the rhetoric coming out of Germany and he knew his boys were right. There was a real threat to Poland now from both the Soviet Union in the east and Germany in the west, and he didn't know who was the more dangerous.

The sun was setting, bathing everything in a rosy red glow. Wiktor sighed. Perhaps he was worrying unnecessarily. Britain and France were unlikely to let the Germans attack their neighbours without doing anything. He was almost sure Hitler wouldn't want to risk another war with Germany's old enemies and he certainly wouldn't want to fight on two fronts. He looked down, tilted Magda's face up to his and kissed her lightly on the lips.

"Everything will be fine, Magda. I promise. Come on, let's have something to eat. I'm starving."

Magda nodded and turned her attention to the stove. Judging by the pungent aroma filling the room, the stew was almost ready. Wiktor was a clever man. If he said there was nothing to worry about, she was sure he was right.

****

Berlin

Hans let himself into his flat and made his way straight to the drinks cabinet. He poured himself a large cognac, walked over to the gramophone and placed his favourite record on the turntable. As the strains of Wagner filled the apartment, he downed his drink and undid the buttons of his uniform jacket. All in all, it had been a satisfactory outcome. The girl was on her way to a camp, Karin was happy again and Andreas… Hans' face darkened.

Andreas was his best friend and he understood perfectly that the man needed something more than Karin, but he couldn't let him keep humiliating his sister. He sighed. Thank goodness Karin had agreed to his suggestion. He already had some girls in mind. He closed his eyes and smiled. Perhaps he would try them out himself first.

****

Outside Lublin, Eastern Poland

Wiktor switched off the wireless, a thoughtful expression on his face. After all the problems with Germany and Danzig the previous year, everything seemed to have settled down. But Wiktor wasn't convinced. As early as 1935, there had been rumours coming out of Germany that they were prepared to go to war over Danzig. After Hitler had taken back the Rhineland in March that year, the tension between them had escalated but subsequent meetings seemed to have resolved the crisis, at least on the surface. Wiktor shivered. Despite his continued reassurances to Magda before dinner, he wasn't entirely sure they were safe from Germany's increasing aggression and he didn't have much faith in Polish politicians either.

"What's the matter, Father?" He'd been so engrossed in his thoughts, he hadn't noticed Felcia had entered the kitchen and was watching him. He made an effort to smile.

"Nothing, Felcia. I was just listening to the news on the wireless. Listening to politicians always makes me cross."

Felcia relaxed. "I'm a bit worried about Raisa."

Wiktor frowned. "Why?"

Felcia looked uncomfortable. "I'm sure she's meeting someone at night… a boyfriend, I mean." She held her breath. She'd never betrayed her sisters before but she couldn't bear the thought that Raisa had a boyfriend and she didn't. She was the oldest, and tradition dictated that she should marry first. Raisa had never been her friend and now her younger sister was trying to usurp her position as first-born daughter.

Wiktor sighed. "I'll look into it, Felcia. Thank you for telling me." There was a long silence and, realising the meeting was at an end, Felcia turned around and went back out into the yard. She was already regretting allowing her jealousy to get the better of her.

****

Romford, Essex

Not wanting her parents to see her dishevelled state, Annie hurried upstairs and disappeared into the bathroom. But her mother was not so easily put off. Within seconds, Ivy was standing outside the door.

"Are you alright, Annie?"

"Yes I'm fine, Mum. I just needed to get out of my clothes and have a quick bath. I got splashed by a bus and my legs are all muddy." She didn't like lying but this was better than them worrying about her.

"You didn't get caught up in the fighting then?" Ivy sounded concerned. "We heard all about it on the news."

"I did, but I'm perfectly alright, honestly, Mum." Not completely satisfied, Ivy went back downstairs to relay Annie's assurances to Harold, who was not entirely convinced either. However, realising they were unlikely to get anything more out of their daughter that night, they resolved to try again the next morning.

Upstairs, Annie ran a bath and climbed gratefully into the warm, rose scented water, closed her eyes and allowed her thoughts free rein to plan her future with Rob.

****

Berlin

Karin was reading by the fire and she smiled up at Andreas when he came in. "You look tired," she said. "Would you like a drink?" She put down her book, stood up and crossed the room to the drinks cabinet.

Andreas didn't answer. He was still preoccupied with his thoughts.

"I said, do you want a cognac?" Karin sounded faintly irritated and he forced himself to smile.

"Sorry, darling, I was miles away. Yes, I'd love a large one, please."

Karin was facing the drinks cabinet, with her back to him, so he couldn't see the furious expression on her face. He was obviously pining for his mistress. Somehow she composed herself and, keeping her expression blank, she turned around, stepped towards him and handed him a large glass. Andreas took the drink and gazed down at her. Thinking about his girlfriends had aroused him.

His wife was still an attractive woman. Her dark hair was shining in the gentle light and he reached out and ran his fingers through the silky curls. "Perhaps we should have an early night." He leant down and kissed her. Karin hesitated briefly, wondering whether he was thinking of Elke. To her astonishment, the thought of Andreas and his mistress did not put her off. Instead, she returned his kiss with a passion that surprised him.

Andreas put down his drink and pulled her towards him. He slid her cardigan off her shoulders with one hand, while his other urgently caressed her breasts. He was expecting her to object at any moment, but instead she eased the cardigan off completely and began undoing the buttons on his jacket.

With practised ease, Andreas reached behind her and undid the buttons on the dress, followed quickly by the catches on her bra, before removing both and dropping them to the floor. He reached greedily for her breasts, her nipples responding instantly to his touch. While she groaned in pleasure Andreas slid his hands down to her black lace knickers, his fingers clenching her buttocks hard, pulling her closer to him. Karin pulled back slightly and wriggled quickly out of her knickers and he pushed two fingers inside her. Andreas gasped. He'd almost forgotten how warm, wet and accommodating his wife could be. He wanted her. Right now. He picked her up, lay her down on the floor and stared down at her naked body while he quickly discarded his jacket and shirt. Karin smiled up at him, opened her legs and began stroking herself. Andreas needed no further encouragement. While Karin opened her legs wider, he knelt down in front of her, his fingers joining hers rubbing and stroking until she was moaning with pleasure.

Moving up, Andreas leant forward and kissed her, Karin placed her arms around his neck and closed her eyes. Maybe this time she would get pregnant. She'd read somewhere that she should remain lying down afterwards to allow the sperm to travel up to where it was meant to go. Andreas stared down at her and mistook her closed eyes for passion. For a brief moment he felt guilty about the other women. He took her arms from around his neck and raised them above her head. Her breasts rose upwards, the nipples erect and he leant his head forward, nipping and biting until she was moaning and writhing with pleasure. He sat back up and quickly undid his trousers. Having escaped confinement, his erection sprang to attention. He gazed down at her, his eyes glazed and began rubbing himself until he could wait no longer. He raised her hips and plunged deep inside her. Karin gasped. She was hot and wet and he could feel her muscles tightening around him. He began to thrust against her, her moans mingled with his own while her fingers snaked down his back, scratching him with her nails and making him groan in pleasure.

Andreas finally reached a noisy climax and collapsed on top of her. Karin held him close and lay still, willing his sperm to impregnate her. "Please, God, this time," she muttered under her breath. Andreas frowned. When he heard her start to speak, he thought she might have been going to say she loved him, but then he heard the muttered prayer. He sighed in disappointment. Even in the height of their passion, all she could think about was having a baby. Karin felt his chest heaving with exertion and gave a grim smile. She wondered where Elke was and marvelled that her husband could be so stupid he hadn't even noticed the disappearance of his women.

****

Ilford, Essex

"Goodnight, Daisy. Are you sure you don't want to come with us tomorrow night?" Rob was leaning across the seat so he could talk to her through the open car door.

Daisy laughed. "Absolutely certain, Rob, but thanks for the lift home." She turned her attention back to Mike and smiled up at him. "As I said, I am open to other invitations though."

Mike grinned. "How about the pictures then? On Saturday?"

Daisy nodded. "As long as it's not a war film or anything political." Her eyes twinkled.

Mike put his hand over his heart and spoke in a solemn voice. "I promise to only take you to fun, happy films. How's that?"

"Perfect." Daisy turned towards her front door. "Night, Mike. See you Saturday."

Mike watched her go through the door before climbing back into the car. Rob grinned. "Well that was unexpected, wasn't it?"

Mike frowned. "What was?"

Rob looked horrified. "Meeting such beautiful women…" He realised Mike was teasing him. "Obviously you're not as smitten as I am."

Mike shook his head. Sometimes Rob could be very irritating. There were so many important things going on in the world and all his friend could think about now was a girl. He decided to ignore Rob's interest in Annie and instead he began talking about the subject closest to his heart: the Spanish Civil War. "So after everything you've seen today, you can see how dangerous things are getting. I really think its time we made up our minds, don't you?"

Rob frowned in confusion, his mind still on Annie.

Mike sighed and tried to hide his frustration. "About volunteering?"

Rob still looked bemused. This time Mike made no attempt to disguise his annoyance. "About us going to fight in Spain, Rob."

"Oh, yes, of course." Rob nodded but he didn't sound very enthusiastic.

"I don't understand. Seeing those bastards today has made me even more determined to fight them. Surely you feel the same?"

"Yes, of course I do." Mike glanced at his friend. Something had changed, but he didn't know what. Surely it couldn't be to do with Annie?

His heart sank as Rob's next words confirmed his fears. Rob took his eyes of the road and stared at Mike, his face alight with enthusiasm. "Isn't she wonderful? I think she's the girl I'm going to marry."

The Austin swerved, the car behind hooted loudly and Rob quickly fixed his eyes back on the road without waiting for Mike's reaction.

Mike opened his mouth to say something funny, thinking Rob must be joking, but one look at his friend's face told him that he was deadly serious. He stared at his friend in alarm. "You've only just met her."

Rob nodded, this time keeping his eyes on the road in front of him, much to Mike's relief. "I know, but I can't help it. It's as if I've always known her."

Mike tried to hide his irritation. Rob was no stranger to acting on a whim, so his behaviour was not that unusual. Mike could count numerous times where he'd had to stop Rob doing something he quite obviously hadn't thought through properly. Unfortunately, he'd never been successful at curbing Rob's impulsiveness where girls were concerned, but he had to try. "You said that about the last girl... Mary, wasn't it? And then there was Jacqueline..." Mike didn't get any further.

"No, this is different. I only *thought* I was in love then, now I *know* I am." Rob gave a superior smile which irritated Mike even more. He bit back his angry retort and stared out of the car window. There was no point arguing with Rob when he was like this. But inside he was seething. They had more or less agreed they were going to Spain. Surely meeting this girl was not going to stop them doing something they'd been planning for ages? Hopefully Annie was just a whim, another passing fancy and, after the meeting the following evening,

Rob would change his mind. Mike glanced across at the set expression on his friend's face and his heart sank.

Chapter Ten

Wannsee Park, Berlin

Franz glanced at his watch then back at his newspaper. Carstairs was late. He would give him a few moments more, then leave. Although he was sure he was not under suspicion, there was no point in taking unnecessary risks.

He was about to go when he felt Carstairs sit down on the bench beside him. "Sorry, I got held up." He spoke out the corner of his mouth as he fiddled with his pipe.

"You weren't followed?" Franz sounded nervous.

"No, nothing like that. What have you got for me?"

"I'll leave it in the newspaper."

There was silence while the Englishman puffed away at his pipe. Franz read to the end of the page, made a big show of folding his newspaper, laid it on the seat and stood up. He stretched, his eyes scanning the area for any danger, but there were few people about and no one appeared to be watching them. He walked off, leaving the paper on the bench.

Carstairs waited a few moments then picked up the newspaper, unfolded it carefully and began reading. The message was on a small piece of paper which slid onto his lap behind the cover of the large periodical. He scanned the contents carefully and frowned. It looked like Churchill was right after all. In the Colonel's opinion, Germany was gearing itself for war, although he wasn't sure yet which country was in the firing line. The army had been given carte blanche to increase its purchase of weapons and the research budgets had grown massively. The costs of suppling the growing army were enormous but the German economy was still weak. The only way the Colonel could see the country being able to afford to pay for the massive rearmament programme was to invade another country and steal their resources. Even more worrying, there were rumours circulating that Hitler had suggested sending envoys to the Soviet Union to make a non-aggression pact. At the moment this was unsubstantiated but the Colonel thought the British should know anyway.

Carstairs screwed up the paper and placed it in his pipe. It smelt and tasted disgusting but, within moments, the incriminating message was no more than tendrils of smoke drifting into the clear October sky.

****

Romford, Essex

"So you're definitely going tonight then?" Daisy searched Annie's face. The shop was finally quiet after a busy morning and this was the first chance she'd had to mention the coming evening.

Annie nodded enthusiastically, a dreamy expression on her face. "Oh yes. I'm sure it will be absolutely fascinating."

"Are you sure you don't mean Rob is 'absolutely fascinating'?"

Annie blushed. "Well yes, but the meeting will be interesting too, of course."

Daisy sighed. "You've only just met him, Annie. You don't know anything about him. You need to watch yourself."

Annie looked surprised. "You don't need to worry, Daisy. I'll be perfectly safe with Rob." She was about to add that he was the one she'd been waiting for all her life when she changed her mind. Daisy didn't believe in the 'one and only', at least not in the same way she did. If she told Daisy how she felt, Daisy would only start giving her dire warnings, and she was much too happy to let her friend spoil things.

Daisy watched the contented expression on Annie's face and bit her tongue. She turned away and busied herself with tidying the creams on the counter in front of her. This obsession Annie had with finding the 'one and only' was bound to end in tears. Still, that wasn't her problem. There were times Daisy found Annie very trying. Why did she have to be so intense? She was much too young to settle for one man. Much better to play the field, have lots of fun and worry about marriage later. With a bit of luck Rob would turn out to be just another boy and then maybe Annie would learn her lesson, that there was no 'one and only'. Just as long as she didn't expect Daisy to pick up the pieces when it all went wrong.

****

Berlin

Karin stared at the red and gold leaves fluttering gently on the trees outside her window in the late autumn sunshine. Her monthly wasn't due for another two weeks, so she would have to wait at least three weeks to know if she was pregnant. She was never late, so if she was overdue by a week, she would know. She hugged herself. She wanted so much to believe that this time she might be lucky, but she was scared to get too excited. She couldn't stand another let down after so many years of allowing her hopes to rise, only to have them dashed every month. Her doctor said there was no reason he could see why she wasn't conceiving. He implied that her anxiety was preventing conception but Karin wondered if the fault lay with Andreas. There had been numerous mistresses and none of them had fallen pregnant, not as far as she knew anyway.

Perhaps she should suggest he go to see a doctor. She shivered. Andreas was a gentle man and, although he had a temper, he had always treated her well. But something told her he would not appreciate his manhood being questioned. It wouldn't go well with his image. No, she would not risk upsetting him. She would just pray a little harder and, maybe this month, she would be lucky.

******

Hackney, East London

Despite his misgivings, Mike made an effort to greet Annie warmly when they drove to her house to pick her up.

"I thought you might have changed your mind." Rob was relieved to see her.

Annie smiled. "Of course not. I've been looking forward to it all day." This wasn't quite the truth. Annie had spent all day longing to see Rob, the meeting was just the means of bringing them both together and allowing her to spend time with him.

Mike glanced at his watch and Rob grinned. "Don't worry, Mike. We've got plenty of time to get there." He glanced in the mirror at Annie who was sitting in the back. "All set?"

She nodded and Rob started the car. Annie looked out of the window, hardly able to believe she was really with the man of her dreams. The only downside was Mike's presence in the front seat. She had expected him to move into the back of the car, allowing her to sit with Rob, but instead he'd remained seated, leaving her no option but to climb in behind them.

The meeting was well attended and, by the end, Mike reluctantly admitted to himself that Annie seemed to be almost as enthusiastic about the cause as he and Rob were. Afterwards, they stayed behind with several other people who were also considering going to Spain and they spent a lively couple of hours discussing what they could do to help. When the caretaker came round to shut the hall, they were finally persuaded to leave and, while they walked back to the car, they discussed their next move.

"I think we should go straight away. There's no time to lose."

Rob frowned. "I don't think we should rush into anything, Mike."

Mike stared at him in disbelief. Rob, the man who never considered the consequences of his decisions and always jumped in with both feet, was now telling *him* to act with caution. He opened his mouth to say something but Annie spoke first.

"I'm sorry, Rob but I think Mike's right. You both believe in fighting the fascists, so why are you hesitating? I wish I could come too. I'd love to go."

Rob and Mike both looked horrified. "That's ridiculous, Annie. What on earth would you do over there except get in the way? Girls can't fight."

"Mike's right." Rob jumped in before she could answer. "You'd be a liability. You're better off over here raising money or something."

Stung by their dismissive attitude, Annie opened her mouth to tell them they were talking rubbish, but then she realised she didn't really know enough about war to argue that she could be useful. "Well, maybe you're right Rob, but if you want to go, you should."

Mike looked at his friend, an expectant expression on his face. However, Rob's enthusiasm had waned and he was no longer sure what he wanted to do. He was torn between supporting his best friend and staying with Annie. Although he'd only just met her, he was already wondering whether she was the girl he was meant to be with for the rest of his life and he didn't want to lose the opportunity to find out by disappearing off to Spain. If he did that, she might find someone else. He knew it was probably too early to say he was in love, but he couldn't help how he felt. He'd never met anyone like Annie before.

Mike watched him for several moments, his heart sinking. He knew Rob well enough to realise he was wasting his time. Although he was disappointed, Mike didn't want to put pressure on his friend, so he took a deep breath and reluctantly offered him a way out. "Look Rob, maybe I should go on my own, just for the moment anyway. You can always come over at a later date."

From the relieved expression on his face, Mike knew he'd said the right thing. On the other hand, Annie looked worried, so he hastened to reassure her: "It's alright, Annie. Going to Spain is a big decision and not one to be taken lightly. Rob's right to take his time. He needs to be absolutely sure. He's never been as convinced as me that we should go and, although it will be really strange not having him by my side, I *can* manage without him."

The last bit was said with a big smile and, on impulse, Annie gave Mike a hug.

"You will take care of yourself, won't you?"

He nodded and hugged her back. "Of course I will." He glanced at Rob but his friend was staring at the pavement. Mike let go of Annie and patted Rob on the back. "I'll be alright, you know. You don't need to worry."

Rob looked up at him, guilt all over his face and Mike sighed. "This is my fight, Rob, and it's time I stood on my own two feet. You can always come over later if you change your mind. I have a feeling it's not going to finish that quickly."

Rob hesitated and then nodded. He still felt guilty, but not enough to make him leave Annie.

****

University City, Madrid

Gerhard gazed around in wonder at the brand new University campus, the pride of the city. He could hardly believe he was in Spain. He felt a moment's guilt about his parents, then brushed it away as he took the foaming beer from the young dark haired lady smiling adoringly at him. The bar was full of young men from mainly Britain, Ireland, the USA and France, although there were a few like him from Germany and Italy who had come to fight the fascists. For the first time since Hitler had come to power, Gerhard finally felt like he was doing something to defeat the Nazis.

"You are all heroes." Camila smiled up at him.

Gerhard leaned forward and kissed her gently. Camila put her arms around his neck and gazed into his eyes. He smiled and pulled her close. He intended to make the most of the few days he had in Madrid before being sent to join his fellow Germans in the Thaelmann Battalion.

There he would train before being sent to fight. The Nationalists were very close to the city, having begun their attack in the first week of October. He made a mental note to write a brief letter to his parents before he left. He would have to be careful what he said or he would cause them problems, but he wanted to let them know he had arrived safely. He also wanted them to know he loved them and no longer felt any animosity. If anything happened to him, he didn't want his last words to his parents to be of anger and bitterness.

****

Boots The Chemist, Romford, Essex

"So how was the meeting?" Although she was dying to ask, Daisy waited until the customers moved away from the counter so no one could overhear them.

Annie smiled, a dreamy look on her face as she thought about Rob. "It was very interesting. The speakers put up a very good case to volunteer." The door opened and two women came in and began browsing the make-up counter.

Daisy misunderstood Annie's expression and stared at her friend in horror. "Surely you're not considering going to Spain?"

"Shh!" Annie glanced around in alarm. In her astonishment, Daisy had forgotten the customers and raised her voice.

Daisy ignored Annie's concern and grabbed her friend's wrist. "Please tell me you're not thinking of joining the volunteers?" This time she lowered her voice so much Annie had to lean closer to hear her. She wriggled free.

"No, of course not. Don't be so stupid." Her denial was much too quick for Daisy's liking. She was sure Annie was lying.

"For goodness sake, Annie, think about it. There's a civil war going on over there. People are being killed. Why on earth would you want to put yourself in danger for people you've never met and a country you've never seen? Not to mention that it's illegal to go to Spain."

Annie rubbed her wrist where Daisy had gripped it and shook her head, an angry expression on her face. "I've just told you, I'm not going to do anything like that." She fell silent.

Daisy stared at her. "And Rob and Mike? Are they going?"

Annie shook her head. It wasn't her place to tell Daisy about Mike. He could get into serious trouble if anyone knew, and Rob had already decided not to go. "No, they aren't." She crossed her fingers behind her back. It was only a half lie after all.

Chapter Eleven

Outside Lublin, Eastern Poland

"Stani!" Magda's face lit up and she rushed across the kitchen and threw her arms around her oldest son, before noticing he had someone with him. She stepped back, ready to greet Alek, then realised the man was a stranger. Magda flushed with embarrassment but Stani didn't appear to have noticed.

"Hello, Mama. This is Iwan, my best friend." Stani saw the disappointment on her face and frowned. "I hope you didn't mind me bringing him home?" He sounded uncertain.

Magda looked mortified. "No, no, of course not." She smiled at the other man. "Forgive me, Iwan. I thought for a moment you were my youngest son, Alek. Come in. You're very welcome."

"Stani!" Felcia came flying through the door, her face flushed from the cold wind, her long blonde hair streaming out behind her. She was closely followed by Raisa and Ala. She stopped dead when she saw Iwan, and the two younger girls ran into her.

"Hello, you must be Felcia." Iwan smiled at her before turning towards Raisa and Ala, and greeting them in turn. "I'm Iwan. A friend of your brother's."

Felcia tried to ignore the thudding of her heart. Iwan was taller than Stani with military cropped black hair, flashing dark eyes and a beaming smile.

"Hello, Iwan." Felcia forced herself to turn away. "Is Alek with you?" Her face fell when Stani shook his head.

"No, he's away doing some training."

Iwan sighed. "I think I'm a bit of a disappointment to your family, Stani. And here was I hoping they would think I was a wonderful friend to you."

Felcia laughed. "I'm sure you are a good friend, Iwan, and you're not a disappointment to us, honestly." She flushed and looked away.

Raisa watched her sister and felt her blood boiling. Obviously Felcia was interested in the soldier and, judging by his reaction to her sister, the attraction was mutual. Apart from his greeting, Iwan hadn't given her or Ala a second glance. Raisa clenched her fists behind her back and wondered why Felcia was getting all the attention as usual.

****

Boots the Chemist, Romford, Essex

"So why didn't you tell me?"

Annie took one look at her friend's angry face and sighed. She'd known something was wrong by the angry looks Daisy had aimed in her direction since she'd arrived at work that morning. "I assume you're talking about Mike?" Daisy nodded and Annie carried on, "Because it wasn't my place to say anything, Daisy. I didn't want to get him into trouble."

Daisy stared at her in astonishment. "And you thought I would go running to the police?"

"No, of course not. But it wasn't my secret to tell." Annie fell silent.

Daisy uncrossed her arms, stopped glaring at Annie and leaned forward onto the counter. "He told me last night. He'll be gone by now. You do think he'll be alright, don't you, Annie?"

Annie breathed a sigh of relief. Daisy was only angry because she liked Mike. She smiled. "I didn't realise you felt that strongly about him, Daisy, or I would have said something, honestly."

Daisy looked surprised. "I don't, not really, but he's a nice man and I wouldn't want him to get killed for nothing."

It was Annie's turn to stare. "Don't you think he's brave to be so determined to fight for what he believes in?"

Daisy shrugged. "Or stupid?" She saw Annie's horrified expression and shook her head. "Honestly, Annie, do you really think Mike going to Spain is going to make much difference?"

Annie opened her mouth to argue then changed her mind. There were times when she couldn't understand Daisy at all.

****

Outside Lublin, Eastern Poland

Wiktor was furious, although he tried not to show it. His neighbour sensed his anger and tried to smile. "I'm sorry, Wiktor, I thought you should know what they're saying about her."

Wiktor nodded. "You were right to tell me. I have to go." He turned abruptly on his heel and strode back to his ancient truck. Climbing inside, he switched on the engine, selected first gear, let out the clutch and put his foot down hard on the accelerator. The truck sped off through the village, dust spraying everywhere. Wiktor didn't notice. The rumours about Raisa were probably true and that was why he was so angry. He had no idea how to control his middle daughter and he often wondered why she was so different from the others.

If she carried on behaving in the same way, he would never be able to marry her off. No one would have her. Wiktor sighed. He'd been wrong all those years ago when he'd said Raisa would get over her jealousy. If anything, she had grown worse.

He reached the track which led to his farm and veered off to the left. His thoughts on his wayward daughter, he was driving so fast he skidded and had to fight to keep the truck on the road. Much as he hated to admit it to himself, he didn't actually like Raisa very much, so perhaps this was all his fault? If only she was more like Felcia.

At the thought of his eldest daughter, Wiktor's anger receded slightly. He liked Iwan and he had already given the young man permission to write to his daughter. He knew Felcia liked Iwan and couldn't wait for his next leave. Wiktor smiled to himself. He knew it was early days but he hoped Iwan would soon ask to marry Felcia. Iwan would make Felcia a good husband and he was sure they would be happy together. But that wasn't the main reason. With Felcia married, tradition would be satisfied and he could begin looking for a husband for Raisa. The sooner she was off his hands and someone else's responsibility, the better. He wished he'd taken more notice of Felcia's warning and checked up on what Raisa was doing but he hadn't and now he was reaping the rewards of his inattention.

****

Berlin

Hans woke with a start. He could feel the sweat on his face and body and he began shivering. It was a long time since he'd had the nightmare. Perhaps all the worry about Karin had stirred up the bad memories. He sat up and stared into the darkness. He tried to hear beyond his ragged breathing, his ears straining into the claustrophobic darkness of his flat. Then he heard it. The sound was faint at first and he wasn't entirely sure he was hearing anything. Then the noise grew louder and more persistent. He put his hands over his ears to block it out but he couldn't. He began to panic and he breathed in sharply, trying to fight the feeling of panic threatening to overwhelm him.

His body jerked violently and he abruptly opened his eyes. The moonlit room was quiet, other than the rhythmic ticking of his clock on the small cupboard beside him. This time he was really awake. He sat up, switched on the bedside light and reached for the half drunk bottle of cognac behind the clock. He drank deeply, his breathing slowly returned to normal and the nightmare gradually receded.

****

Berlin

Karin stared down at the blood and her heart sank. Her monthly was dead on time. Yet again she had failed to become pregnant. She put her head in her hands and began to cry, noisy sobs that filled the expensive bathroom, echoing off the tiled walls.

Eventually she stopped. There was no point crying any more, the hopes of the last two weeks had gone, to be replaced by a black, all-consuming despair. She left the bathroom and went into the bedroom she shared with Andreas. She glared at the picture of him on her dressing table. Andreas stared back at her, resplendent in his black SS Uniform, his eyes confident and secure, a hint of laughter around the mouth. Karin had always loved that photo of him but now she had to resist the temptation to smash it on the floor.

Her inability to have children must be his fault, otherwise at least one of his mistresses would have become pregnant. She was married to a man who was consistently unfaithful to her and the only thing she really wanted from him, he couldn't give her. And there was nothing she could do about it… Except have an affair. Karin frowned and wondered why she hadn't thought about it before. Providing she was very careful, Andreas would never know. It wouldn't occur to him to think she'd been unfaithful to him. In fact he'd probably be grateful she'd finally fallen pregnant. His friends and colleagues must have wondered why he was unable to father children, given his voracious sexual appetite.

The more she thought about it, the better the idea seemed. Now she just had to find someone to father her child and she knew just the man to help her.

Chapter Twelve

Outside Lublin, Eastern Poland

Felcia was sitting down at the kitchen table having a quick cup of coffee after finishing her morning chores, a smile on her face while she read the letter from her brother. The post had just arrived, the only envelope addressed to the three girls.

Felcia had recognised Alek's untidy scrawl immediately and hurriedly ripped open the envelope. Iwan had written only the day before to let her know he would coming to see her at the weekend and she was terrified her brother was writing to tell her Iwan couldn't make it for some reason. She couldn't wait to see the young soldier again and, once she'd satisfied herself there was no bad news about Iwan, she settled down to read her brother's news.

When Iwan had asked her father if he could write to her, she had been sure he would refuse, so she was delighted and not a little surprised when he'd agreed almost immediately. They had been writing to each other every day since Iwan had returned to his regiment and the tone of their correspondence had grown in warmth with every letter.

"Is that from the boys?" Ala came into the kitchen and interrupted her thoughts. "Can I read it after you?"

Felcia nodded. "Of course. Just hang on, I'm nearly finished." Felcia put Iwan firmly out of her mind and re-read the scrawled words in front of her. Alek and Stani both seemed to be enjoying the army and, much to her relief, there was no mention of any fighting.

"Here." Felcia handed Ala the letter just as Raisa came in through the back door. Raisa frowned. Her first thought, that Iwan had written yet another letter, was obviously wrong or Felcia would not have given it to her sister to read. Her jealousy of Felcia's relationship with Iwan was quickly replaced by anger that the letter must be from her brothers.

"I don't understand why they've written to you and not me." Raisa sat down noisily at the table and scowled at her sisters. She was still smarting from the scolding Wiktor had given her. She didn't know why he was so annoyed. She couldn't help it if the village women couldn't keep their men happy. And the men paid very well for the few moments it took to satisfy them. He was probably jealous he didn't have a girl he could go to when he got bored. She smiled to herself. Perhaps he did have someone; maybe that was why he was so cross. She turned her attention back to Felcia, who was speaking in the patient voice she reserved especially for her younger sister.

"The letter's to all of us. I just happened to read it first because I had finished my chores before you."

Raisa pouted and made a grab for the letter. "Well I'm the next oldest, so I should get to read it before Ala." Ala sighed, pulled a face at Felcia and handed the pieces of paper over.

"Here, I've finished anyway."

Raisa began reading but the pleasure had gone. As usual she was the last to find out what was happening in her own family. No wonder she liked meeting the men in the village. At least they paid her some attention and put her first.

****

Berlin

"You are joking I presume?" Hans stared at Karin in disbelief.

Karin shook her head. "No, I'm deadly serious, Hans. You have no idea how hard it is not being able to have a child. It's all I think about."

"I don't understand why you don't talk to Andreas."

"Because I can't. I need your help, Hans. You've never refused to help me before."

"You've never asked me to find you a lover before."

Karin gave a wry smile. "It's no different from the suggestion that you find girls for Andreas and that was your idea." Her expression changed. "I could do this without your help, Hans, but I thought this way would be more discreet."

Hans was about to argue but he could see there was no point. He held up his hands. "Alright, alright. Leave it with me."

Karin leant forward, hugged him and kissed him on the cheek, then whispered, "I knew I could count on you. Thank you, Hans. You won't regret it, I promise."

Hans hugged her back. She was right, he wouldn't regret it because he had no intention of finding his sister a lover. Karin didn't need to know that, of course. He would just lie to her and hope she'd lose interest. He watched her leave and slammed his fist on the desk. He needed some fresh air.

The wide tree-lined streets were surprisingly quiet. Hans strode purposefully along the road looking for a distraction, something to take his mind off his sister. He turned left onto one of the side streets and smiled. A young girl was hurrying along the road towards him, her head down against the wind, her long blonde hair streaming out behind her.

Hans stepped out in front of her. "Your papers!" The girl jumped and began fumbling in her coat. Hans could see her trembling and her fear aroused him. He glanced around but the streets were still deserted. He reached out and pushed her towards a doorway. The terror on her face intensified. Hans shoved her on her knees and began twisting her hair until she raised her head and opened her mouth. With his other hand Hans undid the buttons on his trousers and, before she could struggle anymore, he had forced his penis into her mouth.

Hans could hear her stifled sobs and the sound aroused him even more. With his hands, he forced her face harder into his groin, his penis straining towards the back of her throat, making her gag. Hans ignored her choking sounds and he began thrusting hard against her before finally exploding, all the anger at his sister's request filling her mouth. He held her face against him until he was sure she had swallowed, then he released her. She collapsed on the floor, her sobs becoming noisier by the moment. Hans leant down. "Shut up, or I'll have you arrested." There was no response. "I said SHUT UP!" he screamed, but she continued crying noisily and Hans saw red. He grabbed her by the throat and squeezed hard. He could feel her struggling but he was beyond caring. Eventually she went limp and he removed his hands.

****

Madrid Front Line, Spain

Over the past few weeks, the Nationalists had attacked the north west flank of Madrid's defences and forced a bridgehead over the River Manzanares. Three quarters of University City had fallen to the Nationalists but the poorly armed Republican militias, with help from the International Brigades, had finally managed to halt their advance and now both sides were digging in for the winter.

Gerhard stared across the valley of death, the area between the two front lines and the key to the hill dominating University City. It was cold and damp, although there was no snow. His eyes were drawn to movement on the bullet-swept road in front of him. The German commander and another man were pointing to a large red house that lay beyond their lines.

Gerhard closed his eyes and wondered what his parents were doing. In just over a month it would be Christmas. He hoped they weren't worrying about him too much.

"I need some volunteers. Six in all." Gerhard sprang to attention and raised his hand guiltily. He realised he'd allowed himself to relax when he was supposed to be on sentry duty, but the section leader did not seem to have noticed.

"We're going to check whether La Casa Rosa Grande is still occupied."

Gerhard groaned inwardly. The house had changed hands several times in the intense fighting. The last time he'd looked, it was occupied by Moors, some of the fiercest fascist fighters. Volunteering to take a closer look was probably not a very good idea.

****

Outside Lublin, Eastern Poland

Wiktor breathed a sigh of relief. The rumours about Raisa in the local village appeared to have stopped although he was sure she was still sneaking out at night. He had debated following her but he wasn't sure he really wanted to know what she was doing. Providing there was no scandal, he would turn a blind eye and hope for the best.

Felcia finished feeding the chickens and glanced sideways at Raisa. She was sure her sister was up to something, but as they had never been close, there was little chance of Raisa taking her into her confidence. She shrugged. At least she was easier to live with at the moment than she had been recently. Perhaps she did have a secret boyfriend. Felcia frowned. She wouldn't think any man was crazy enough to take on Raisa, but it would explain her secretive air. She would mention it to Ala and see what she thought.

****

La Casa Rosa Grande, outside University City, Madrid

Gerhard dived for cover as the weird singing sound of another shell flew over them while they crept towards the house. Fortunately it landed several metres away, the ground shaking violently. The men picked themselves up and carried on up the slope towards the large building.

"You three wait here. Keep an eye out. We'll take a look around." The section leader and three others carried on towards the house while Gerhard positioned himself at the corner of the boundary wall to keep watch. He crouched down, his rifle cradled in his arms and prayed the constant machine gun fire pinging off the structure would not hit him. The bricks were already crumbling around him and the ground shook intermittently as both sides shelled the area.

It appeared their intelligence was right. In the distance he could see hundreds of Moors retreating in the direction of their own lines. He was tempted to fire at them but that would only give away their position and draw the enemy's fire, so he resisted.

He was still watching when another shell whistled overhead. This one was much closer and he instinctively threw himself on the ground as it hit the house behind him, the wall next to him smashing into small pieces, bricks and rubble flying everywhere.

****

Berlin

Andreas shook his head as re-read the report in disbelief. He had tried to trace his previous girlfriends and every single one appeared to have been arrested by the Gestapo or the SS. There was no information about what had happened to them afterwards, other than a brief mention of being sent to a camp for re-education. He knew there was little point trying to find them. In any case, after time spent in a camp, he was hardly likely to want to rekindle a relationship with them. He ignored his conscience reminding him that he'd liked these women and enjoyed their company and that he shouldn't just leave them to their fate. He had more important things to think about.

What was really worrying him was the reason given for their arrests. Every file stated that an informer had reported they were Jewish. Andreas didn't believe in co-incidence, so that meant someone must have known or at least guessed about his relationships with them. The question he was trying to answer was whether they'd been targeted because he was under suspicion for some reason, or whether they'd just been arrested because they'd slept with him. Both thoughts were enough to send shivers up his spine.

****

La Casa Rosa Grande, outside University City, Madrid

Gerhard raised his head cautiously. The house had vanished and his heart sank. The men must be dead; they could never have survived that. He was about to check his companions when a movement caught his eyes. He stared in disbelief as the four men crawled out of the wreckage, the section leader grinning, his arms full of weapons.

"Take more than a fascist bomb to kill me!"

Gerhard breathed a sigh of relief and, climbing slowly to his feet, he followed the others back to their own lines.

****

Outside Lublin, Eastern Poland

"I've really enjoyed our evening." Iwan gazed down at Felcia. They had left the theatre in Lublin and were walking back to the car he'd borrowed for the weekend, when he stopped and put his arms around her. She was staring up at him, an expectant expression on her face. The moon shone down, highlighting her upturned nose and the dimples on her cheeks. He could see her full mouth, the lipstick glinting in the light and he was unable to resist leaning towards her. He placed his lips over hers and was gratified to feel her responding. He slid his tongue inside her mouth and felt her body tense. Then she began kissing him back, tentatively at first and then with rising passion.

Eventually he pulled back and smiled down at her. "I suppose I'd better take you home, or your father will stop me writing to you."

Iwan was gratified to see the horrified expression on Felcia's face. "Is it that late?"

Iwan laughed. "No, not yet but it will be if I don't get you home soon. Come on, the car is over there." He pointed down the road and took her hand.

On the way back to the farm, Iwan regaled her with tales of his army life and the journey passed quickly. Before long they were pulling up outside the farmhouse. Iwan glanced at the building and saw the curtains twitching in one of the ground floor windows. Reluctantly, he climbed out of the car, walked around to the other side and, opening the door, he helped Felcia out. She leant towards him but, conscious of someone watching them, he took her hand and led her to the front door.

"Goodnight, Felcia. May I see you tomorrow? I thought we could go for a picnic or take a drive into the country or a walk around Lublin?" He was running out of ideas.

Felcia laughed. "I'd love to see you tomorrow, Iwan, and I don't mind doing any of those things, just as long as it's with you."

He smiled down at her and somehow managed to resist the temptation to kiss her again. Seeing the disappointment in her face, he lowered his voice. "We're being watched by someone in the house, probably your father, or I'd kiss you again."

Felcia stepped away from him, a momentary look of alarm on her face. She held out her hand. "Goodnight, Iwan. I'll see you tomorrow." Her voice carried clear across the farm in the still night air.

Iwan nodded, saluted politely and then turned away. Felcia watched him climb back into the car and drive off, then she let herself into the house.

In the sitting room, Raisa shut the curtains, a scowl on her face. It looked like Felcia was going to see him again the next day, although Iwan didn't seem that keen. He hadn't even kissed her sister goodnight. Her mouth set in a cruel line. Iwan would be much better off with her. Unlike her cold fish of a sister, she knew exactly what to do to keep a man happy. If he was with her, she'd make sure he couldn't keep his hands off her.

****

Romford, Essex

"Rob's very much like his father, isn't he?" Ivy snuggled up to Harold as they walked home. They'd spent the evening in the local pub, *The Greyhound*, with Bill, Rob's father, as Annie and Rob thought it was time they'd met. The evening had been a success and they had all stayed chatting until closing time.

Harold put his arm around her and nodded. "Yes, he is."

Annie was walking just in front and she turned around and laughed. "See, I said you would like him."

Harold smiled. "You did, Annie. I like Rob too; he's very good for you."

Ivy smiled at her daughter. She couldn't be happier. Annie had found a lovely young man and she couldn't wait for them to get married. She wouldn't say anything, because Harold was bound to say it was too soon, but she had a feeling Annie had found her 'one' and that it wouldn't be long before Rob asked Annie to marry him. She could tell by the way the boy looked at her daughter that he loved her.

"Stop making plans," Harold whispered in her ear. "I know exactly what you're thinking."

Ivy blushed in the darkness and whispered back. "I'm right, Harold. You know I am."

"Didn't anyone ever tell you it's rude to whisper?" Annie grinned. She knew exactly what her mother was thinking, but she didn't mind. She couldn't wait to be married to Rob. Then her spirits sank. Her biggest problem was making sure he didn't go rushing off to Spain to be with Mike.

Chapter Thirteen

Outside Lublin, Eastern Poland

Felcia reluctantly finished reading Iwan's latest letter. She always tried to make them last as long as she could and then she re-read them several times. She reached for the previous letter and, opening the top drawer in her dressing table, she pulled out the small bundle of envelopes tied together with a pink ribbon. Now she had a new letter to read, she would add the previous one to the steadily growing pile. Every few weeks she re-read them from beginning to end, marvelling at how quickly their relationship had blossomed. She knew she loved him and she was sure he felt the same.

At night she would lie in bed staring at the stars through the open curtains and plan their future together. Iwan would leave the army and come and work on her father's farm and they would have several children. Of course Iwan might not want to leave the army, which would mean living somewhere else. At first the thought worried her, but eventually Felcia no longer cared. As long as they were together, she didn't mind where they lived.

"Not asked you to marry him yet, then?" Felcia spun around. She hadn't heard the door open or Raisa come in.

"Don't you ever knock?" Felcia snapped at Raisa because she was annoyed her sister had voiced her own thoughts.

"Why? Do you have something to hide?" Raisa's sneer implied that was unlikely and Felcia resisted the temptation to slap her sister. She turned her back, willing Raisa to leave her alone. But her sister wasn't finished yet. "Maybe he's got someone else. For all you know he could have a girl in every town."

Felcia stared at Raisa in disbelief. "I really don't understand why you have to be so nasty all the time. Iwan is a good friend of Alek and Stani. Don't you think they would have told Tata if he did have lots of other girlfriends?"

Raisa shrugged and hid a smile. Whatever Felcia said, Raisa could see she'd succeeded in rattling her. She'd do and say anything to take that smug look off her sister's face. Unfortunately she couldn't think of anything she could do to put Iwan off Felcia. She'd heard her parents talking the previous evening and knew they were expecting him to ask for Felcia's hand at any time. Perhaps it would be more fun to let them get married and then do something to upset the apple cart. She was sure that would be much more enjoyable than any of her other plans, which had come to nothing.

****

Romford, Essex

It was the first time Rob had been apart from Mike for any length of time and more than once in the intervening weeks he'd been on the verge of going to join his friend, but the thought of leaving Annie always held him back.

"You have to decide what you want to do," Annie repeated for what seemed like the umpteenth time. She was fed up with his mood swings and, although she didn't want him to go, she knew that having to decide between staying with her or going to be with Mike was tearing him apart. She snuggled up to him on the sofa hoping they weren't going to spend the whole evening going over the same ground. It wasn't often they had her parents' house to themselves and she was hoping they might spend the evening kissing, cuddling and planning their future, rather than discussing Spain.

Rob sighed. He knew she was right, but he couldn't take the final step which would mean leaving her, and having her remind him wasn't helping.

"I'm perfectly happy here," he snapped.

Annie shook her head. "No, you're not. You feel guilty because you think you should be with Mike. I'm not going anywhere, Rob. If you go to Spain, I'll still be here when you get back." She held her breath and then let it out slowly when he shook his head and pulled her into his arms and kissed her.

"You're all I want, Annie. I'm not going to risk losing you." He kissed her again while his hands snaked down her body until they reached the buttons of her blouse, which he began to undo, hoping she might let him go further now he'd told her how important she was to him. He was disappointed.

"No, Rob." She pushed his hands away. Rob caught a brief glimpse of white flesh while she swiftly redid the buttons. "You know I'm not that sort of girl." Although she loved kissing and cuddling, she was determined not to go any further. Her mother had always impressed on her that nice girls didn't do that sort of thing.

"But you know how I feel about you." Rob's frustration began to show. "I've chosen you over my best friend. Surely that must mean something?"

Annie pulled away and stared at him in disbelief. "How dare you try to blackmail me. What sort of girl do you think I am? If that's all you think of me, you might just as well go to Spain." She was so angry, for a moment she couldn't speak.

"Right, I will." Rob stood up and walked over to the door of the sitting room.

Annie watched him, anguish written all over her face. She stood up, rushed towards him and caught his arm just as he was about to go through the door. "I'm sorry. I didn't mean that. I don't want you to go Rob, please."

Rob turned back towards her, relieved she'd changed her mind. He didn't want to leave Annie either but he had backed himself into a corner. He put his arms around her and began kissing her again. After a very brief hesitation, Annie responded and Rob relaxed. He could feel himself growing hard and, after a few moments, he couldn't resist trying the buttons on her blouse again. He was expecting her to stop him so he was astonished when this time she allowed him to undo them. Annie had been about to object again when she'd had second thoughts. She loved Rob with all her heart and she was reasonably sure he loved her too, but she was still terrified he would decide to leave her and go to Spain. Maybe if she let him go just a bit further, he'd be satisfied.

Completely unaware of Annie's thoughts, Rob was in seventh heaven. He could hardly believe his luck. He rubbed his hands across her breasts, feeling her erect nipples through the lacy material of her bra and had to fight hard to stop himself climaxing. He was tempted to try and undo her bra but he didn't want Annie to stop him again, so he concentrated on enjoying his small victory.

******

Outside Lublin, Eastern Poland

"Well, Iwan. You're looking very well, if a little nervous." Wiktor struggled to hide his amusement. He was reasonably sure Iwan was about to ask for Felcia's hand; at least he hoped he was.

Iwan cleared his throat and took a deep breath. There was no point beating about the bush. "I'd like your permission to marry Felica, sir."

Wiktor smiled. He liked a man who got straight to the point and he was impressed Iwan had asked him outright. A memory of himself asking Magda's father surfaced briefly. He'd been much less confident and he still squirmed to think how he'd stumbled over the request. But then, Magda's father was very stern and not given to making people feel at home. He pushed the memory away and turned his attention back to Iwan.

"I should probably ask you lots of questions about how you are going to care for my daughter, how you see your prospects and so forth, but to be honest the only thing I want to know is how much do you love Felcia?"

Iwan was taken aback. He'd prepared answers to the things he thought Wiktor would ask, but this wasn't one of them. Then he smiled. "I love Felcia with all my heart and soul. The first moment I saw her I knew she was the one for me and I'm so grateful she feels the same about me." He searched around for something else to say. "I respect her as a person and I promise to love and cherish her above everything else to the best of my ability." He fell silent, wondering if he'd said too much and risked a glance at Wiktor. To his relief, Felcia's father had a twinkle in his eye and a broad smile on his face. He held out his hand and Iwan took it gratefully.

"You have my permission, Iwan, providing Felcia agrees of course." There was a brief silence while Iwan finally allowed himself to relax. "Congratulations, Iwan, and welcome to the family. When are you going to ask her?"

"As soon as possible, sir. I can't wait to marry her." Iwan could hardly conceal his excitement. He was almost there. "I have to ask my commanding officer for permission first, but I'm sure he'll say yes. And I'll have to fit it in with any regimental duties and training. I think I'll find out the best time first, then when I ask her, I can suggest some dates." He frowned. "You don't think she'll mind having to fit in with the army, sir?"

Wiktor laughed. "No, Iwan, I'm sure she won't. Felcia is the most accommodating of my daughters and I'm sure she'll be too happy that she's marrying you to worry about such a trivial thing."

Iwan nodded, his eyes shining with excitement. Once he had the army's permission, he only had to ask Felcia and he was almost certain she would say yes.

Raisa leant back against the wall of the house and clenched her fists, her face contorted with rage. She'd watched Iwan arrive and, when he didn't immediately seek out Felcia, her curiosity was aroused and she'd followed him. Standing by the window of the sitting room she'd heard every word. Her fury gradually subsided and she smiled. She would keep out of the way for the time being and, once they were happily married, she would put her plan into action.

****

Madrid

Mike stared around with a mixture of bemusement and despair. "This has to be a joke, surely?"

His companion was dark haired and German and he'd seen a lot more than the Englishman.

Gerhard gave a weary smile. "I've just passed half a dozen men having a siesta and thought that was bad enough, but singing in the meadow over there? What the hell's the matter with them all? We went to speak to some anarchists yesterday and, because it was quiet, they'd all gone into the city to the cinema leaving only a couple of men on duty." He let out a long sigh, took a sip of his water and held out his hand. "Gerhard Emmet."

"Mike Jacobs. Makes you wonder what the hell we're doing here, doesn't it?"

Gerhard grinned, revealing a mouthful of very white teeth. "If you'd come from Germany you wouldn't think that."

Mike looked embarrassed. "You're right, of course. I'm sorry. I just thought they would be more organised."

"You've obviously just arrived on the front line."

Mike nodded. "Yes, I've been training for the past few weeks. I only got here a couple of days ago."

Gerhard laughed. "Well, I agree it would help if they had some idea of what they were doing." He offered Mike a cigarette. "That idiot Caballero broadcast his entire battle plan over the radio last month, apparently. No wonder we took such heavy losses." Gerhard sighed, and not for the first time, wondered if he should go home.

"I heard it failed because the infantry couldn't keep up with the tanks?"

Gerhard grinned. "Well that probably had something to do with it too, but the infantry are so poorly trained, I'm not surprised."

Mike frowned. This wasn't what he'd been expecting at all. Perhaps the German was wrong. Gerhard saw his expression and guessed what he was thinking. He sighed. Mike would soon find out for himself. "Welcome to Spain, Mike. Come on, let's go and get a drink and I'll introduce you to my friends… the ones that are left anyway," he added under his breath.

The city was chaotic, the streets full of peasants and their livestock blocking the way. Mike was just about to comment when there was a commotion further ahead. "What's going on?"

Gerhard gave a wry smile. "The Government is fleeing Madrid. They're expecting it to fall at any moment."

Chapter Fourteen
1937

Madrid

Fears of Madrid falling had proved to be groundless. The Government had been stopped at Tarancón and the Foreign Minister and Under Secretary of War were arrested for desertion in the face of the enemy. The Anarchists, who had previously refused to help the Republicans fight the Nationalists, now rallied the people to fight, their cry, 'Long live Madrid without government' echoing through the beleaguered city, inspiring many acts of bravery. Women and children formed chains passing rocks and stones to help build barricades, trenches were dug on the western side and houses on the south west of the city prepared for hand to hand fighting.

The fighting had reached the southern suburbs and there was mass mobilisation with railwaymen, barbers, tailors and school masters forming themselves into individual battalions. At the same time, the Ritz Hotel was turned into a canteen for the homeless and refugees.

Mike and Gerhard were now part of the 18th Brigade, their role to defend La Marañosa, a seven hundred metre high hill. The rain that had fallen relentlessly through January had finally stopped, as had the ice and mist that had protected them and, when morning broke on the fifth of February, the nationalists opened their attack.

The ground shook with explosions from artillery shells, bullets ricocheted all around them and the air was filled with smoke and cordite. Screams, yells, curses in various languages reached Mike's ears and he knew it wouldn't be long before he finally saw some action.

****

Outside Lublin, Eastern Poland

"I know we haven't known each other very long but I've never been more certain of anything in my life." Iwan took a deep breath. "Will you do me the honour of becoming my wife, Felcia?"

Felcia nodded. She was too overcome to speak. Iwan reached down to kiss her and she found her voice. "What about my father?"

Iwan grinned. "No, I don't want to marry him."

Felcia laughed. "No silly, I meant you should have asked him first." She frowned. What if her father said no?

Iwan took her hand. "I've already asked him, Felcia, before Christmas. He has given his permission, providing you agree of course."

Felcia relaxed. "Then I can't think of anything I want to do more, Iwan."

He breathed a sigh of relief. "Thank goodness for that. You have no idea how nervous I've been."

"Of me or my father?"

He laughed. "Both!" He face grew serious. "I don't want to rush you, Felcia, but my life is not really my own. If the army decides to move me somewhere else, I won't have any option but to go. I want to marry you as soon as possible."

Felcia stared into his eyes and nodded. "I agree." She frowned again. "You said you asked my father before Christmas. That was two months ago."

He nodded. "I had to have my Commanding Officer's permission too and find out when we were likely to be on regimental duties. There are also lots of big training exercises planned for this year, so I thought it was best to do all that, then I could suggest some dates." He looked worried. "Is that alright?"

Felcia laughed. "Of course it is. I know I'm marrying you and the army." Then the reality of what he'd said hit her and her face fell. "The training exercises… for war, you mean?" Iwan nodded, but she didn't give him a chance to answer. "You don't really think there'll be a war, do you?"

Iwan shrugged. "Our neighbours on both the eastern and western borders hate us. We have a strong army now but whether it is enough…" He shook his head. "I don't want to think about that now, Felcia. I want to concentrate on you." He gazed into her eyes and ran his fingers through her hair. "Come on, let's tell your family and then we can make the arrangements."

"Will I be able to live with you once we're married?" Felcia suddenly wasn't sure how she felt about leaving her family.

"Of course. We'll have our own quarters." He frowned. "Unless you prefer to stay here?"

Felcia shook her head, her doubts momentarily forgotten. "No, I want to be wherever you are. I love you."

Iwan pulled her close. "I love you too, my darling."

****

Hackney, East London

Rob pulled Annie closer to him. His father was at the pub and they had the house to themselves. She smelt of soap and perfume and he breathed in her scent. Putting Mike out of his mind, he raised her face towards him and kissed her. Annie responded with passion and, encouraged, his hands inched down towards her breasts.

Other than moaning, Annie made no move to stop him as he slid his hands inside her jumper. He fumbled with the catch of her bra and, once her breasts were free, he began sucking her erect nipples. He could feel her writhing under his touch so he ran his hand up her stockinged leg until he found the gap between the top of the stocking and her panties. His hand snaked purposefully towards her panties and then his fingers were sliding inside her. She groaned and he could feel the warmth as she gripped his fingers. With his other hand he undid his trousers and his penis sprang to attention. He took her hand and placed it around the shaft and she began to masturbate him in the way he'd shown her.

By now he was almost at the point of no return and he began to pull down her panties. Annie stopped and pulled away.

"No."

Rob groaned. "Come on, Annie, we've been going out for ages now. I won't think any less of you. You know how I feel about you."

"For goodness sake, Rob. How many more times?" Annie sounded annoyed. "You know I don't believe in sex before marriage."

Rob sighed. "Alright, I'm sorry. It's just that I want you so much."

There was no answer.

"Don't stop what you were doing, please. I won't try anything, I promise." Rob knew he sounded desperate but he couldn't help it.

There was another silence and then he felt her fingers grasping his penis and she began to manipulate him again.

His orgasm covered her hand and he glanced up, wondering if she would be offended, but she was smiling. "I think I'd better go and wash my hands."

He was out of breath and unable to speak, so he nodded.

When she came back he was dressed again and his thoughts had returned to Mike.

He had received some letters from his friend but the post was intermittent and he often had to wait a long time between correspondence. He also had a feeling the letters didn't tell the true story. The first one had been full of an excitement and enthusiasm which the subsequent letters lacked. Rob sighed. His guilt hadn't lessened; if anything it had grown. He loved Annie but he couldn't just forget all about Mike. If anything happened to his friend, he would never forgive himself for not going with him. But if he went and Annie found someone else, he would be heartbroken.

He let out a massive sigh, leaned back, closed his eyes and wished he could make a firm decision and then stop thinking about it. It wasn't that difficult. Either he left Annie and went to join his friend, or he remained in England with her and made do with second-hand news from Mike.

****

Berlin

Hans watched the woman serving drinks in the bierkeller. Despite telling Karin it would easy to find a whore for her husband, the reality had proved surprisingly difficult. He'd vetted several girls in the intervening weeks but none had been suitable. However, he was reasonably sure this one was perfect for Andreas: long blonde hair and blue eyes, her large breasts spilling over the top of her low cut blouse. His brother-in-law would soon tire of her and move onto the next girl. Hans sighed. He wouldn't normally frequent places like this. He preferred his girls to struggle and fight him, their eyes filled with terror, not hand everything over on a plate. But if he wanted to hire a whore to amuse Andreas, this was probably the best place. At least the girls here were clean. Andreas would never knowingly sleep with a whore and, in any case, he couldn't risk his brother-in-law catching something and giving it to Karin.

Hans raised his hand and beckoned the girl over. To his relief she was just as pretty close up, although much too forward for his liking. He attempted a smile.

"Yes, sir?" She fluttered her eyelids and gave him a beaming smile. Hans hid his revulsion and forced himself to look appreciative. He ordered another beer and waited for her to return before indicating the seat next to him.

"Sit." Briefly forgetting the part he was supposed to be playing, Hans barked out the word and for the first time she looked uncertain, but he was an SS Officer so she did as she was told.

"What's your name?"

"Claudia."

"Well, Claudia, I have a job for you."

An expression of bewilderment crossed her face. Hans patted her leg and her face brightened. She reached across and began to stroke the outline of his penis through his trousers. Hans grabbed her hand and leaned forward.

"Not that kind of job." He tried to calm himself down. He hated whores; they reminded him of his mother. He could see the fear in her eyes and, for the first time since she'd sat down, he felt a momentary surge of sexual desire for her. "I have a friend I want you to amuse. I'll pay you well, but he mustn't know anything about the arrangement. Do you understand?"

The fear left her face and Claudia nodded, relieved to be back on more familiar ground.

"He must think he's picked you up and persuaded you to sleep with him. Can you do that?" She'd forgotten he was still holding her hand and she winced as his grip tightened.

"Yes, sir."

Hans held her gaze for a few seconds more before letting go. He pulled out a picture of Andreas. "This is him. I'll tell you where he is likely to be and you can arrange to be there."

There was silence. Claudia nodded, swallowed nervously and made to stand up. Hans grabbed her arm and pulled her down towards him. His face was inches from hers and he could see the fear on her face. He smiled. He'd been intending to take her address and then leave, but the terror in her eyes had changed his mind. He pulled out his wallet, placed some Reichsmarks on the table and, without giving her a chance to move away, he hurried her towards the door. "We'll go to a hotel and you can show me how good you are."

Claudia tried to pull away but his grip was too tight. She glanced around the cellar but no one was paying any attention and, within seconds, they had reached the door.

****

Outside Lublin, Eastern Poland

Felcia glanced at the clock. It was late now and she was beginning to feel overwhelmed. Her parents and Ala had been delighted for her when Iwan announced their news and even Raisa had seemed happy. Her father had opened some bottles of wine to celebrate and the alcohol was flowing freely. Everyone was talking at once and her mind was spinning with all the arrangements that had to be made and the short time they had to do everything.

Because of Iwan's army commitments, the wedding would take place the following month which meant there was little time to plan. It was either that or wait several months and neither she nor Iwan were prepared to delay any longer than necessary. Wiktor had gone to speak to the local priest so the bans could be read and had just returned, a beaming smile on his face.

Felcia didn't mind a small wedding in the local church, although she knew there would be a certain amount of gossip at the haste in which they were marrying. She would just have to hope she didn't fall for a child too soon after the wedding or people would be pointing the finger and saying she'd only wed because she was pregnant.

"Are you alright, my love? You're very quiet." Iwan sounded concerned.

Felcia smiled up at him. "Yes, I'm just planning my outfit. I think I'd better wear something tight so people don't start talking!"

Iwan looked confused, then the penny dropped and he smiled. "I can't wait to see you in something figure hugging." He rolled his eyes making her blush.

Raisa watched them smiling and joking from under her lashes and somehow managed to keep the false smile plastered on her face.

"It'll be you next, Raisa." She jumped. She hadn't heard Ala approach.

"Yes it will, won't it?" Raisa thought about that and felt a frisson of excitement. Her marriage wouldn't be a small hole in the wall affair like this. For once, she would be the centre of attention and she would make the most of it. She couldn't understand why Felcia was agreeing to such a small wedding, then her smile widened. Perhaps she had to marry in a hurry. The thought that Felcia had been indiscreet made her laugh. She thought it was very unlikely her sister was pregnant – she was much too prudish – but it wouldn't hurt to drop a few hints in the village.

****

Berlin

Claudia hurried out of the hotel room and back to her tiny flat, all the time trying to block out the events of the past couple of hours. The SS man had given her a piece of paper with some addresses and times on and told her not to fail. The expression on his face left her in no doubt as to what would happen to her if she didn't manage to pick up the man called Andreas or if he found out she was being paid to keep him happy.

Claudia shivered and glanced over her shoulder, but the street was silent; he wasn't following her so she gradually slowed down. She could only hope this Andreas wasn't like the SS man who was paying her. She reached the safety of her tiny flat, let herself in and shut the door behind her. Her breathing slowly returned to normal and she began removing her clothes. The mirror was stained and frosted in places but from what she could see, her body was unmarked. She wished she could say the same for her mind.

Hans dressed slowly. The girl had been quite satisfying after all. He would have liked to have been a little rougher but if he'd marked her, she would have been no good for Andreas. He would wait until his brother-in-law had finished with her and then have some more fun when she came to collect her money.

Chapter Fifteen

Jarama, Spain

Mike wiped the sweat from his upper lip and peered ahead. He couldn't see anything moving at all and he cursed. He and Gerhard had been on the front line for a few days now and Mike was becoming increasingly used to the sights, sounds and experience of battle. It seemed ages since he'd finished his basic training, even though it was just a matter of weeks. The training had included the opportunity to fire one round from the ancient Russian rifle he was clutching close to his body. Then he had been told he was ready to fight. Despite the lack of proper training, he was learning very quickly. But that didn't stop terror being his constant companion. The sweat on his lip was not from heat – the temperature was almost freezing – but from fear. Not for the first time he wondered why he had made the reckless decision to come to Spain. The only good thing was that Rob had been sensible enough to stay in England.

****

Boots the Chemist, Romford, Essex

"You're very quiet." Daisy watched the pensive expression on Annie's face.

Annie gave a wry smile. "Sorry, I was thinking about Rob."

"Now there's a surprise." Daisy covered her sarcasm with a laugh.

Annie opened her mouth to explain that she meant about him going to Spain when something made her change her mind. She glanced around the shop but there were no customers near them. "He wants to… well, you know, go all the way."

"Ah." Daisy gave a knowing wink. "Well, it's not surprising, is it? You've been going out for ages, haven't you?"

Annie looked shocked. "But what about getting pregnant and what if that's all he wants?"

Daisy laughed. "If that was all he wanted, he would have given up by now." She quickly checked the few customers in the shop were not within hearing distance before lowering her voice. "I've never found it made any difference, to be honest."

Annie appeared even more shocked. "Do you mean you've *done it?*"

Daisy nodded and, seeing Annie's expression, added in an even lower voice, "And I'm not the only one. Most girls I know have."

There was a long silence. Annie had no idea what to say. She had been brought up to believe that no decent girl slept with a man before they were married and now Daisy had told her something completely different, she didn't know what to think.

****

Berlin

Franz took the letter from Hannah, read it quickly, lit a match and then watched as the paper burst into a brief flame before burning brightly for several seconds. As he let go, it floated gently towards the waste paper bin, before smouldering into nothing.

"I wish we could keep them." Hannah voiced his thoughts.

"It's too dangerous, darling." He put his arm around her. "At least we know he's safe, well he was when he wrote that anyway." He felt Hannah stiffen and cursed himself for speaking the words out loud.

"He's no fool, Hannah. I'm sure he'll come home safe to us."

"And then what?"

Franz sighed. "I don't know, but we'll worry about that when it happens." He glanced at his watch and grimaced. They were due to attend a party hosted by Goebbels in a couple of hours. "Come on, let's get ready for the evening. Much as we both hate these gatherings, this is our best chance of protecting Gerhard." He didn't add that it was also one of his best ways of gathering intelligence on the Nazis which he passed on to John Carstairs. There was no reason to tell his wife what he was doing. She would only worry and, if she didn't know anything, she would at least be safe if he was caught. Franz ignored the niggling voice in his head that suggested he should tell her because, as his wife, Hannah would automatically be presumed guilty, whether she was involved or not.

****

Suburbs of Lublin, Eastern Poland

The man pulled up his trousers, put his hand in his pocket and pulled out a couple of notes.

Raisa stood up, fastened her bra, took the money and put it in her cleavage. The man grinned, his teeth yellow and uneven. "Not the safest place to keep it." He laughed.

Raisa smiled. "Same time next week?"

He glanced around the field. It wouldn't be long before the green shoots of the crops would be bursting through the soil and the hedges brimming with life. He reached out and ran his fingers over her breasts, now safely enclosed in her bra. "Yeah, but we'll use the barn next time. It's a bit safer now spring's on its way, less chance of being seen."

"I thought you found the danger exciting." Raisa leaned forward and rested her hand on his penis. She could feel him growing hard again and she ran her tongue over her lips. "Goodnight."

She turned away and began the long walk back to the farm. The man watched her for several seconds before turning away and walking in the other direction. If he hurried, his tea wouldn't be ruined and his wife wouldn't shout at him for being late.

Raisa waited until he was out of sight before taking out her small flask and rinsing her mouth out. It was dark but the light from the full moon was just enough for her to pull out her small compact and check her face. She touched up her lipstick, glanced at her watch, sprayed herself with some perfume and changed direction. She had one more call to make before heading home.

****

Madrid

The next couple of days blurred into one raging torrent of gunfire, death and destruction. Time stood still for Mike as he and the other Republicans fought tenaciously to hold on to the hill, while the Nationalist assault grew more deadly. Gradually the enemy overcame the defenders, working their way slowly up the incline. In the valley below, Gozquez de Abajo fell and now the fascists were only a kilometre from the River Jarama,

"They've taken San Martín de la Vega and Ciempozuelos." Gerhard was filthy, his face blackened from cordite, his eyes red rimmed from lack of sleep. The battle was still raging and he had to shout to make himself heard.

Mike rubbed his filthy unshaven face with an equally dirty hand before staring at him. "Then we're finished?"

Gerhard nodded. "We need to get out of here." As he spoke, the noise abated and an eerie silence fell.

Mike shook his head and made no attempt to move. "We can't just desert our friends." His voice sounded strange. He had been shouting for so long, he hardly recognised the hoarse sounds coming from his throat.

Gerhard grabbed his arm. "The hill's going to fall soon, Mike. We're outgunned, men are already fleeing. We're no good to the cause if we're dead or prisoners."

Mike looked around and realised Gerhard was right. Most of the defenders were taking the opportunity of the brief lull in the fighting to escape. There was no point throwing his life away in some meaningless gesture. He stood up and hurriedly followed his friend back down the other side of the hill.

Within three days, the Nationalists controlled most of the west bank of the River Jarama and the brigade had lost over thirteen hundred men.

Chapter Sixteen

Berlin

Andreas tried to ignore the rising excitement coursing through his body. The girl was very pretty and she had returned his smile with more than a hint of promise. The Town Hall had been busy when he'd arrived and, with reluctance, he had joined the rather long queue. The girl had fallen in behind him, her perfume gently assailing his nostrils. Unable to resist glancing back, Andreas had been rewarded with another smile which he had returned.

He looked up at the clock as the queue inched slowly forward and made his decision. He turned towards her and held out his hand. "Hello, I'm Andreas. I know we've not really met but I wondered if we could rectify that. Would you like to have lunch with me?"

Claudia hesitated and then nodded. "I'm Claudia. Thank you, that would be very nice." She stared past him at the people waiting in front of them and sighed. "Perhaps I should come back another day. I think I could be here ages."

Andreas smiled. "My thoughts exactly. Where would you like to eat?"

Claudia shook her head. "I don't mind, really. Wherever you would normally go."

Andreas gently took her arm. "You don't mind?" When she shook her head, he smiled. Work could wait. The girl seemed delightful and he could hardly pass up such a golden opportunity. His misgivings about his previous mistresses' disappearances vanished to the back of his mind as he prepared to seduce a new conquest. "We'll go to Haus Vaterland. It's one of my favourites. They do a wonderful Weiner Schnitzel and Spatzel."

Hans watched them discreetly from across the other side of the road. When he'd suggested procuring women for his friend, he'd only done it to help Karin, but it might prove very entertaining after all. He would wait until he knew Andreas was hooked, let Karin know and then check on Claudia when she went home. He couldn't wait to hear all the juicy details.

****

Madrid

Mike watched the swollen River Jarama and breathed a sigh of relief that the winter rain had made the river unfordable. Now the winter was almost over, the water level would soon go down. But it had bought them enough time to allow them to reinforce the Madrid Road and the right bank of the River Manzanares in preparation for the next Nationalist assault.

They were dug in near the Pindoque railway bridge which ran from Vaciamadrid and San Martín de la Vega. Gerhard threw himself into the trench near Mike and took a large swig from his water bottle. "We've placed charges on the bridge so it's ready to blow if they take it."

"Don't you mean 'when'?" Mike was still scanning the area and feeling increasingly uncomfortable at the growing number of troops on the other side of the river.

Gerhard shrugged. "The French are guarding it." He sighed. "They're moving their tanks into the area; let's hope our batteries can hold them off."

There was silence. Mike lit a cigarette and offered one to Gerhard who took it with gratitude. "I'm surprised you've got any left."

"These are the last few. There are rumours the fascists have overrun the factories that manufacture them, so make the most of it!"

The two men smoked in companionable silence for a few moments before Gerhard spoke again. "I need to write to my parents and let them know I'm safe. They must be terrified if the German newspapers are carrying stories of the fascists' victories."

There was another silence. This time it was Mike who broke it. "If we're killed, do you think anyone will notify our parents?"

Gerhard shook his head. "I doubt it, to be honest. Perhaps we should have a pact, you and me. If either of us is killed, the other is duty bound to let his relatives know."

Mike nodded. "That sounds like a good idea to me. I'd hate for my parents to never know what had happened to me. I'll write down their address and you do the same for your parents."

"You'll need to be careful what you write to mine, don't forget." Gerhard warned. "If you say anything about Spain, you could cause them trouble."

Mike nodded. "Don't worry. I'll think of something." He smiled. "Anyway, I won't have to because we're both going to survive."

Gerhard laughed. "Of course we are, Mike." For some reason this made them both laugh. They were still chuckling when the fascist artillery opened up, the shells fortunately landing several metres away. The lull was over.

****

Outside Lublin, EasternPoland

Felcia smiled into Iwan's eyes as he lifted her veil and kissed her. She was finally married to the man of her dreams and she couldn't be happier. They would be going straight to his regiment the following morning to settle into their married quarters and she couldn't help feeling excited at the thought of having her own house. She would miss her family but her new life would be so exciting with lots of new people to meet, she was sure she wouldn't have much time to be miserable.

Magda watched her daughter with tears of pride in her eyes. Her only misgiving was that Iwan was in the army. She wished he'd been a farmer or someone who worked in Lublin. Her eldest daughter would be so far away and if, God forbid, there was a war…

"She looks beautiful, doesn't she?" Magda could hear how proud Wiktor was. He put his arm around her and squeezed her shoulder. "No tears, Magda. Our daughter has married well. Iwan is a good man with excellent prospects in the army. They will have a good income and he loves her. Alek and Stani say he never stops talking about her."

Magda nodded. "I know. I just wish she was living closer and I worry there will be a war."

Wiktor shook his head. "No sad thoughts today, my love. If there is a war, our army is strong enough to defend Poland…" He was about to say more but Felcia and Iwan were already coming back down the aisle. He took Magda's arm and they followed, the rest of the congregation falling in behind them.

Outside, Iwan's fellow cavalry officers were providing a guard of honour, their swords an arch across the pathway through which the happy couple ran. At the end, Felcia stopped, closed her eyes and threw her bouquet behind her.

There was an audible gasp and Felcia spun round. Ala was staring ahead, a look of embarrassment on her face. The flowers had been meant for Raisa but, fed up with all the adulation aimed at Felcia, she had moved away at the last moment. Not knowing this, Felcia had thrown the bouquet to where she thought Raisa was standing, but instead Ala had stepped into the space vacated by Raisa and it was she who had caught the flowers.

****

Berlin

Karin stared at the clock on the wall as it ticked away the evening hours. Andreas should have been home ages ago. Presumably Hans' plan had finally worked and he was with his new mistress. Strangely enough, the idea did not infuriate her as much as she'd expected. At least this way she was in control. Andreas was not humiliating her; if anything it was the other way round. She was controlling him, a bit like a puppet master and she could jerk the strings whenever she felt like it. The idea amused her.

With the problem of Andreas solved, she could turn her attention back to how to get pregnant. Hans had not been very successful in finding her a lover and she wondered whether he was playing for time, hoping she would change her mind. She had given a lot of thought to how she could meet someone herself, but had not come up with any workable ideas. Andreas was a high ranking SS man. The young fit healthy men who were his subordinates would not want to risk his wrath by sleeping with their superior's wife and his contemporaries were all older and she didn't find any of them attractive. Obviously she would have to wait for Hans to find her a suitable man to sire a son. Perhaps she should pay him a visit and remind her brother that he'd promised to help?

Karin reached across and turned on the wireless. Mahler's First Symphony was playing. She smiled. This was one of hers and Hans' favourite. It must be a good omen. She turned up the volume and helped herself to a small cognac. Andreas didn't really like her drinking but the odd one helped to relax her and, anyway, he was no longer in charge of their marriage; she was. Her smile broadened. Of course, there was no reason for him to know that.

****

Berlin

News of the Nationalists' victory in Jarama was all over the newspapers and wireless news. Franz tried to ignore the sinking feeling in his stomach and did his best to comfort Hannah, who was convinced Gerhard was lying dead or injured somewhere.

"If something has happened to him, will we be told?" Hannah voiced his thoughts out loud. Unfortunately he had no idea what the answer was, so there was nothing he could say to allay her fears.

He glanced at his watch. He would have to go out soon or he would miss his meeting with Carstairs. Perhaps he could ask the Englishman if he'd heard anything about casualty lists. Then his heart sank. It was just as illegal for British citizens to be in Spain, so the likelihood was that Carstairs wouldn't know any more than him.

"We'll just have to trust in God and pray for him, Hannah, and do our best to make sure if… when," he corrected himself, "he comes home he will not be in trouble with the regime."

Hannah stared up at him in concern. "This is all our fault, Franz. If we'd not been so vocal in our opposition to the Nazis when he was young, he wouldn't have expected so much from us as he grew older. We brought him up to fight for what he believes in, then to his eyes we've given up and sold out. He should be here with us, Franz, safe and sound."

Franz sighed. Hannah was only repeating what he'd already thought. Unfortunately he couldn't turn back the clock and, quite frankly, he didn't want to. Their son might be risking his life fighting fascism but at least Gerhard was doing something and he, for one, was proud of him, whatever the outcome. Sadly Hannah was a woman and she saw things differently, especially when it came to Gerhard.

Chapter Seventeen

Romford, Essex

"Still nothing?"

Rob shook his head. There had been a big battle in Jarama in February and the Republicans and the International Brigades had sustained heavy casualties. Rob had not heard from Mike for several weeks now and Annie knew he was becoming increasingly concerned for his friend.

Annie sighed. They couldn't go on like this. She was about to say more but the lights in the cinema dimmed and the newsreel came on. After a few moments, a collective gasp of horror spread through the building, then the audience fell quiet. Image after image showing the German aircraft bombing the Basque town of Guernica filled the screen. The sight of over a thousand people dead, most of the town destroyed or in flames, with hardly a building left intact sent shock waves through the audience. Annie felt sick. She couldn't just sit back and do nothing. The planes were even filmed strafing the flocks of sheep in the fields.

No longer interested in the following film, they left the cinema. They had only taken a few steps in shocked silence when Annie stopped, grabbed Rob's arm and faced him.

"Why don't you admit it, Rob? You're eaten up with guilt because you've chosen to stay here with me instead of going to find Mike?" Before he could say anything, she rushed on: "I've got a possible solution. I'm not a trained nurse and I probably wouldn't be much good as a soldier but I am sure there is something I can do and, if you're prepared to risk your life, then so am I. I think you should go to Spain and I should come with you."

She ignored his sceptical expression. "There are plenty of other women going out there, so why do you think I'm not up to it?" Annie tried to fake an anger she didn't really feel but she knew she had to make him listen or he would continue to prevaricate and that was only making them both miserable: "What right have you to tell me that I can't go? Why shouldn't I do my bit too? You keep telling me often enough that if we don't stop fascism, it will come here and then I will be affected anyway, so I have a right to come with you and, if you try to stop me, I'll go on my own." She had absolutely no intention of going without him, but she was counting on the fact he would use her threat as an excuse to finally do what he'd wanted to do all along.

There was silence while he digested her words and then Rob picked her up in his arms and swung her round, whooping for joy. "Looks like we're off to Spain, then," he whispered gleefully in her ear.

Annie held him tight and closed her eyes, gratified he was so happy. She only hoped she wouldn't end up regretting her decision

****

Berlin

Andreas kissed her tenderly on the lips and gave a sigh. "Sorry, my love, I have to go home." He climbed reluctantly out of bed. Claudia rested her head on her elbow and watched him. He could see the outline of her breasts under the thin sheet and he wished he didn't have to go. Although he'd been seeing her for a few weeks now, he wasn't bored with her at all.

"Will I see you again soon?"

He smiled down at her. "Yes, I'll take you for dinner tomorrow at the Café Berlin. Would you like that?"

Claudia gasped. "I thought you were worried about your wife seeing us."

Andreas shrugged. "You let me worry about that." He could feel his heart beating faster as he said the words. It was difficult to believe Karin was guilty of having his previous girlfriends removed but he couldn't find any other explanation, so, after much thought, he'd decided to do something about it.

He had quite a few powerful friends in Berlin and he intended to use that to his advantage. Karin might think she could do what she liked, but before long he would prove to her she couldn't.

****

Romford, Essex

"How on earth do we get to Spain?" Annie had thought of nothing else since the previous evening when she'd thrown caution to the wind and suggested they volunteer. In the cold light of day, she'd begun to wish she hadn't said anything and she was now hoping travelling to the war torn country might be too difficult. Although they were in the park and there was no one around, Annie subconsciously lowered her voice. "It's illegal, isn't it?"

To her chagrin, Rob didn't look particularly concerned. "Yes. We can't get passports to go there, but I've had a word with the local Communist organiser and what we have to do is go to Victoria Station, buy special weekend tickets for Paris, which we don't need passports for, and then get on the train. It's as easy as that." He beamed at her and she tried to smile back.

"What about my parents and your dad?" Annie frantically hunted around for another reason not to go. She cursed herself for acting on impulse and wondered what had come over her. She was normally much more level headed, always thinking things through properly before acting. Of course she could always stay at home but that thought was even worse. She would have no idea what was happening to Rob, or even if he was still alive.

"We can write them a letter, telling them where we've gone and why. They'll understand." Rob sounded so supremely confident, Annie stared at him in disbelief. She was quite sure her parents would not understand at all. They would be horrified and worried sick. She opened her mouth to argue, then realised it was a waste of time. Now he was going to Spain, Rob had a one track mind and nothing she said would make any difference.

****

Berlin

The idea of taking photos had not occurred to Hans before, but they would provide him with a lever if ever Andreas found out what he'd done. The small weaselly man with the round spectacles was not his idea of a private detective but, having searched through the files, Krussman's name had arrived at the top. Krussman had already been arrested for blackmail and murder and was awaiting sentence. It was a simple matter to persuade the man to work for him, under pain of sending him to a trial in which he would definitely be found guilty and sentenced to death. Hans explained in detail exactly what he wanted, watching Krussman's face to ensure he was listening properly.

"You understand your instructions?" Hans' eyes bore into the man.

"Yes, sir. You want me to take photos of this man and any woman he is seen with, apart from his wife. The photos should be explicit, if possible."

Hans nodded and then pulled out a photograph. "Just to make sure there are no mistakes, this is his wife. I don't want to see photos of her. Understood?"

Krussman inclined his head. "Yes, sir."

There was a brief silence then Hans nodded. "Good. Don't let me down." He watched Krussman leave and wondered if he should mention this to Karin. He shook his head. She might not like the idea of his having pictures of her husband with other women, even if they were only for insurance.

****

Outside Lublin, Eastern Poland

Raisa watched the farmer disappear in the direction of his house before leaving the isolated barn and hurrying home. He was proving to be one of her most lucrative clients, although, unlike the rest, he wanted to try things she wasn't prepared to do… not yet anyway. Raisa sighed as she approached the farmhouse. The farmer should count himself lucky he was…

"Where the hell have you been?" Wiktor stepped out of the shadows making Raisa jump.

"I've just been into the village to get some… some material for a new dress." Raisa said the first thing that came into her head.

"Don't lie to me, you whore."

Raisa blanched. "I don't know what you're talking about…" She began to bluster.

"I know what you've been doing and I can't even bear to look at you." Wiktor shook his head and tried to control his temper. "I'm ashamed of you. You're nothing more than a whore; and to think you're my daughter…" He looked away.

"I don't know who's been lying to you, but…" She didn't get any further.

Wiktor slapped her hard across the face. Stunned, she stepped back and stared at her father. He'd never hit her before. She paled and tried to think of some means of talking herself out of trouble but nothing came to mind. Then she started to feel angry. How dare he treat her like this? He wouldn't speak to Felcia or Ala like that.

As if he'd read her mind, Wiktor began yelling at her: "Your sisters would never do anything like this. What the hell is the matter with you?" Raisa opened her mouth to defend herself but she didn't get a chance. "Go and pack your clothes and leave my house. I never want to see you again, do you understand?"

Raisa turned the colour of chalk. "But where can I go?"

"I don't care, just get out of my sight!"

Raisa stared at him for a few seconds longer and then ran into the house and up the stairs to her bedroom. With tears streaming down her face, she began throwing her clothes and anything else she considered a necessity into a suitcase. When the bag was full, she sat on the lid to close it, wiped her eyes and walked slowly back downstairs. Magda was waiting for her. She was almost as white as her daughter. "Go and stay with Felcia for a while until he calms down." She shoved some money and a small piece of paper into Raisa's hand and pulled her into her arms. "Go quickly. Here's the address. I'll let you know when it's safe to come home again."

Raisa hesitated but Magda was already pushing her towards the door. She caught a glimpse of Ala's pale shocked face watching from the shadows by the sitting room, then she was outside and the front door had slammed firmly behind her.

Chapter Eighteen

London

The late May morning of their departure was warm and sunny and, having given in their notice to their respective employers the day before, Annie and Rob crept silently out of their homes.

"Did you leave your letter in the bedroom, like we agreed?" Rob stared at Annie. He knew she was not as enthusiastic as him about going and he couldn't help wondering if she might try to sabotage their plans before they left the country.

Annie nodded. She had been tempted to leave the letter by the fireplace in the front room in the hope her parents would find it and try to stop them, but at the last moment she'd changed her mind. Rob would never forgive her if she let him down, so she'd pushed her misgivings to one side, packed the minimum of clothes and hurried down to the end of the road where he was waiting anxiously.

"Come on then, let's go!"

She could feel his excitement and she forced a smile onto her face.

"Spain, here we come!"

Rob said little on the way to Victoria station, other than to warn her to keep an eye out for anyone who might look like Special Branch. Annie tried to suppress her rising hope that they might yet be stopped, but she was unlucky. There was no one to be seen, apart from other young men and women also buying tickets to Paris.

The train was already on the platform and they hurried aboard, found seats, sat down and held hands while they waited for the train to leave the station.

"This is it, then." Rob turned to face her. His voice was suddenly serious. "Are you absolutely sure you want to come? There's still time for you to stay here. I won't think any less of you, I promise."

Annie squeezed his hand but didn't answer. She would have loved nothing more than to change her mind, get off the train and go back home, but she couldn't carry on watching him tear himself apart as he tried to do what was right for both her and his friend, and she couldn't bear to be apart from him either. This was definitely the best solution for him; she just had to hope and pray the decision was right for her too. She couldn't tell him this or he would start worrying, so she just smiled, kept her fingers crossed and said nothing.

Rob squeezed her hand back and resumed his anxious search of the platform. He was still terrified something would happen to stop them going. Deep down, he also knew Annie was only coming with him because she knew he wouldn't be happy until he went to Spain and joined Mike and this was the only way he could be with her *and* his friend. He didn't know what would happen once he got to Spain but it was unlikely Annie could go with him to the front line, wherever that was. He knew he should warn her that they were likely to be separated when they arrived, but he was unsure how she would react. The whole point of them going was to be together, so if Annie found out they might be separated she might change her mind and decide to stay at home after all, which was the last thing he wanted. If he left her in England she might meet someone else and forget all about him. At least if she was in Spain, she wouldn't be able to forget him because he was the reason she was there. He knew he was being very selfish and irresponsible, but he loved her and couldn't bear the thought of losing her. He pushed his misgivings aside, glanced anxiously at his watch and willed the train to move.

Eventually the engine noise and smoke increased and the train eased slowly out of the station. They were on their way. Rob stared out of the window, his heart soaring. Not long now and they would be across the Channel and on their way.

Annie tried to ignore the nervous pounding of her heart and join in his enthusiasm, but each mile was taking her further away from safety and from those she loved.

****

Bydgoszcz, Northern Poland,

Felcia wandered through the town, her thoughts on her exciting news. She loved living in Bydgoszcz with its beautiful gothic churches, Old Market Square and atmospheric red bricked tenement buildings, their reflections mingling with those of the old chestnut trees shimmering in the rivers of Wyspa Mlynska.

Normally she would have stopped to gaze at the progress of the town's newest church, Saint Vincent de Paul's Basilica, begun in 1925 and still being built, but today she had too much on her mind. She couldn't wait for Iwan to return home from the latest exercises so she could tell him that he was going to be a father. She knew he would be delighted but until he came back later that day, she had no one to share the news with. She wished her family were closer but even if they were, Iwan had the right to know first. At least this way she wouldn't be tempted to tell them before her husband.

"Felcia! Felcia!"

She spun around in astonishment. "Raisa? What on earth are you doing here?"

"I went to the house but you weren't there and your neighbour said you'd come into town, so I thought I'd come and find you." Raisa plastered what she hoped was a friendly smile on her face and wilfully misunderstood Felcia's question.

But her sister was not about to be put off so easily. "No. I mean what are you doing in Bydgoszcz?"

"I came to see you." Raisa kept the smile on her face. It wouldn't do to let Felcia know their father had thrown her out. She was hoping that, after a few weeks away, he would get over his rage and she could go home. Her blood boiled just thinking about it. It wasn't her fault the stupid farmer she'd been seeing had been caught by his wife, who'd then told Wiktor everything. She pushed her angry thoughts aside and tried to greet her sister with enthusiasm.

Felcia frowned. Something wasn't right. "We've never exactly been friends, Raisa. Why would you come all this way?" Her mouth hardened into an angry line. "What have you done?"

Raisa felt her own fury rising again and opened her mouth to protest her innocence. Then she saw the expression on Felcia's face. There was obviously little point lying. She sighed. "Tata has thrown me out." She ignored Felcia's gasp and glanced around. "Perhaps we could talk at your home instead of in the street?"

Felcia stared at her for a few moments without speaking, then nodded. "Come on then." Her voice was grudging and Raisa breathed a sigh of relief. The walk back would give her time to rehearse the sanitised version of the truth she'd prepared, and hopefully it would be enough to satisfy Felcia. As much as she hated her sister, Felcia was her only option at the moment. The money Magda had given her she'd spent on travelling and a few nights in a hotel while she tried to think of somewhere else she could go, rather then throw herself on her Felcia's mercy. Unfortunately she'd not been able to come up with an alternative plan and the money was running out so she needed to get her sister on side somehow.

Felcia headed reluctantly towards the house she shared with Iwan, her earlier excitement forgotten. As usual, Raisa had managed to spoil her day. She wondered what trouble her sister was in and what she was going to do about it. It must be bad if their father had thrown Raisa out, but she could hardly refuse her sister a bed, so it looked like she was stuck with her for the foreseeable future.

****

Berlin

Karin stared at her husband in horror. "You can't do this to me."

Andreas eyed her with contempt. "But you can have innocent women dragged off to concentration camps because I slept with them?"

Karin gave him a haughty stare. "You shouldn't be sleeping with whores."

"I wasn't." Andreas snapped back. He took a deep breath. "As you know I have friends in very high places and, unless you want Hans to disappear, you are going to do exactly as I say. Do I make myself clear?"

"You can't… Hans is your friend."

"He was until he started carrying out your dirty work." He stepped towards her and took her chin in his hand, pulling her closer to him. "This conversation is between us, of course. If you tell him, neither of you will survive the day. You do know I can make that happen, don't you?"

Karin shrank back from the venom in his eyes. Andreas had always treated her with gentleness, courtesy and respect. She didn't recognise the man in front of her. She belatedly realised just how dangerous her husband was and wished she hadn't agreed to Hans' plan. If Andreas ever found out his latest girl was a whore sourced by Hans, he would carry out his threat, she had no doubt about that. She shivered. He was still waiting for an answer. "Yes. Yes I know you can."

Andreas held her gaze for a few seconds and then seemed satisfied. He turned towards the door. "Claudia will be here for supper at ten tonight. Make sure you are dressed in your underwear and on your best behaviour." He didn't wait for an answer. He headed through the front door and reflected how much better he felt now he had taken control of his household again.

Karin stared at the door and wondered what on earth she could do. If she told Hans, she would be signing her brother's death warrant but if she didn't, he would continue to supply Andreas with whores and, sooner or later, Andreas would find out. She would have to think of a reason to stop Hans. Maybe if she said she didn't care any more… She didn't know if Hans would believe her, but she had to try.

****

Boots the Chemist, Romford, Essex

"And you're quite sure you don't know where Miss Parker is or why she's suddenly left without giving the appropriate notice?" The Branch Manager's piggy eyes peered at Daisy over the top of his round metal glasses, while his hand brandished a short hand-written note in her face. Daisy could hear the distain in his voice. Quite obviously he didn't believe her. She didn't blame him, she didn't believe it herself. How could Annie hand in her notice and just leave without telling her first? It didn't make any sense. She tried to pull herself together.

"I have absolutely no idea, Mr. Clark, I swear. She never said anything to me." Even as she said the words, Daisy felt sick. Annie was supposed to be her best friend. How could she humiliate her in front of the manager like this?

"She knows she's supposed to give a week's notice to allow us to fill her position. I must say I'm very disappointed. If I'd known she was this flighty, I would never have employed her. And I'm even more surprised at you, Miss Harris. You don't seriously expect me to believe you knew nothing about this, do you?" Cornelius Clark pursed his thin lips in disapproval. Daisy could feel herself blushing under his scrutiny and she wished the floor would open up and swallow her. She was about to deny any knowledge of Annie's whereabouts again when he turned away and called the junior shop girl over.

"Miss Wilson. Do you know what's going on? Perhaps Miss Parker confided in you?"

Patty Wilson shook her head. "No, sir, but she has been acting a bit strange lately…" She tailed off when she caught Daisy's furious expression.

The manager turned his attention back to Daisy. "Well, Miss Harris? You're her best friend, aren't you? Has Miss Parker been acting 'strangely'?"

Daisy hesitated. She hadn't noticed any difference in Annie's behaviour. But she didn't want to say that because then she would look even more stupid. On the other hand, if she lied and said Annie had been distracted, he would expect her to know the reason why, and she didn't. She was still trying to think of an answer when he interrupted her thoughts.

"I'm waiting, Miss Harris. Surely as her best friend you would know if there's a reason she's left a perfectly good job without any explanation?"

Daisy decided ignorance was probably best. Although she hated being humiliated, Annie certainly wasn't worth getting the sack for. "I don't know anything, sir."

"Really?" She winced at the sarcastic tone. "Then I suggest that if you want to continue working here you find out why your *best friend* has left us all in the lurch. Not now, you daft girl!" He raised his voice as Daisy began walking to the door. "We're already short staffed." He shook his head, unable to believe anyone could be that stupid. "You can go during your lunch break."

Daisy tried to ignore the furious blush spreading across her face. She lowered her head and began tidying the counter. How dare Annie make her look like a complete idiot in front of Mr. Clark and the junior shop girl? She'd better have a good explanation for her disappearance, like… Daisy frowned. Actually she couldn't think of any reason Annie would suddenly pack in her job, but as Annie never acted on impulse, she'd obviously been planning this for some time, which made the fact she hadn't said anything even worse. She would go round to Annie's parents' house at lunchtime, because she had no choice if Mr Clark was to be appeased. But as far as she was concerned, Annie was no longer her friend and Daisy couldn't wait to tell Annie exactly what she thought of her.

****

The English Channel

By late morning, Annie and Rob were on the south coast and waiting to board the cross-Channel steamer to France.

"Looks like we're not the only ones going." Rob indicated the numerous young people hovering around. Their expressions veered from excitement to nervousness and Rob knew exactly how they felt. He couldn't wait to get to Spain, but even he was apprehensive about travelling to a foreign country whose language he didn't speak to fight in a war for which he'd not had any training or experience.

Annie nodded. She was still nervous, but the presence of so many other people was making her feel a little better. "Perhaps we should go and talk to some of them?"

Rob hesitated. They had been told not to draw attention to themselves by travelling together, but he'd never been further than London and this was a big adventure. He nodded and they made their way over to a small group of young men and one woman and began chatting. Annie was relieved not to be the only female and she said so, much to the amusement of the other woman, who was several years older than Annie.

"I'm Christine. I've been a nurse for several years, so I'm sure they can use my help. I can't keep watching the suffering and not do anything about it." She smiled at Annie. "What are you going to do?"

Annie shook her head. "I don't know to be honest, but I'm sure there's something."

"You're not a nurse then?" Christine looked slightly concerned when Annie shook her head but she patted the younger girl's arm. "They'll need all sorts of help and I'm sure they'll find you something to do."

Before Annie could answer, Rob was introducing her to some other people. Christine shook her head and turned back to her companions. Annie seemed so young and innocent. It was obvious by the way her eyes strayed constantly towards her boyfriend that she was only there because of him. Christine shrugged. It wasn't her problem but she hoped the girl would be able to cope when he was sent off to fight. Her friend Janice was already in Spain and her letters home hadn't pulled any punches. That was why she was here: the situation was dire, volunteers were little more than cannon fodder and the Republicans were crying out for help. There was no time or capacity to carry people who weren't useful. She wondered briefly if she should say something, but seeing the love struck expression on Annie's face, she knew she would be wasting her time.

The Channel crossing was smooth and uneventful, the sea calm and gentle. Rob and Annie stood on the deck and held hands while they watched the white cliffs of Dover fade into the sea haze obscuring the coastline.

Rob pulled her close and smiled down at her. Annie could see the excitement in his eyes and she tried to ignore her doubts. The decision was made; she would just have to make the best of it.

****

Berlin

"Hannah? What's the matter?" Franz stared at his wife, his heart in his mouth. She was looking at a letter, tears running down her cheeks.

To his relief she smiled up at him and, before answering, indicated he should shut the door. "It's from Gerhard; he's alright. Well he was when he wrote this."

Franz felt his heart rate fall to normal. "Thank God. Does he say when he's coming home?"

Hannah's face dropped. "Not really, although it might be sooner rather than later." She handed him the brief note.

Liebe Mutti and Vati

Just a brief note to let you know I am well and hope you are too. Not much has changed here, so I think it won't be too long before I return home, although I can't tell you when yet.

Love to you both,

Yours,

Gerhard.

Franz re-read the note and then struck a match and watched it burn slowly before dropping it in the waste paper bin by his desk. He smiled at Hannah. "I think he's had more than enough by the sound of it."

"So why doesn't he come back home now?" Hannah sounded frustrated.

Franz shrugged. "I don't think it's that easy, my love. If everyone just went home when they'd had enough, the fascists would easily win. I have a feeling he might not want to leave his friends, but also it might be more difficult than just deciding to go home." He debated whether he should tell her what he'd heard from Carstairs. He didn't want to worry her even more, but if she understood the difficulties Gerhard might be facing, she wouldn't expect him to walk through the door at any moment.

"I've heard the Russians are shooting deserters."

Hannah gasped. "But they're volunteers…"

Franz shrugged. "I don't think it makes any difference to them."

There was silence while they both thought about the dangers facing their son. Hannah sniffed and wiped her eyes. Franz put his arm around her. "He'll be alright, you'll see." His other hand was behind his back, his fingers crossed, while he sent up a silent prayer that their son would come home safely.

****

Romford, Essex

Having spent the morning stewing on the way she'd been treated, Daisy had wound herself up into a fury and she wasted no time in rushing around to Ivy and Harold's house at lunchtime to confront Annie.

"Annie's not here. She's gone to Spain with that lunatic boyfriend of hers, but then you already know that, don't you?" Harold stood on the doorstep, arms folded, barring her entry, his expression almost as furious as Daisy's.

Daisy stared at him in astonishment. "What? She can't have? I don't believe you. You're lying…"

"Don't play the innocent with me. You and Annie were thick as thieves. You helped her, didn't you?" Harold was almost incandescent with rage.

Daisy stepped back and shook her head. "No, I don't believe you… let me in… I want to give her a piece of my mind. The manager's threatening to sack me…" Daisy faltered. She could see the confusion on Harold's face and, for the first time since she'd banged on the door, her certainty that Annie was hiding in the house began to waver.

Harold stared at her for a moment then shouted over his shoulder. "Ivy, bring me Annie's letter."

Ivy appeared in the hall beside him, her face blotchy and tear stained, and handed him a piece of paper.

"Read it for yourself." Harold thrust the letter under her nose.

Daisy took it and quickly scanned the words. She shook her head. "No, she can't have. She would have told me." She stared up at them. "I had no idea, I swear. I can't believe she planned all this and never said a word."

Harold and Ivy exchanged glances. Daisy looked so shocked they finally believed she was telling the truth. Harold stepped back and invited her in. He waited until they were in the sitting room before answering her. "Well, she did. It's all that bloody boy's fault. She'd never have done anything this stupid on her own." Harold glared at Daisy, the furious expression on his face making it clear he still blamed her. If they hadn't gone to the demonstration, Annie would never have met Rob.

Daisy blanched under his withering gaze. "I'm so sorry. If we hadn't got involved…" She tailed off, not knowing what she could say to put things right. She was absolutely furious Annie hadn't trusted her enough to tell her what she was planning. Not only had Annie made her look like a total idiot at work, she was now humiliated in front of Harold and Ivy. Daisy was supposed to be Annie's best friend, the person Annie confided in. How could Annie keep something as momentous as going to Spain a secret from her best friend? And it wasn't the first time Annie had kept her in the dark. When Mike had decided he was going to Spain, Annie hadn't bothered to tell her, just given her some lame excuse that it wasn't her secret to tell. Well that wouldn't work this time. Annie and Rob had obviously planned this for ages and yet Annie hadn't given her a second thought. Daisy was seething. The way she felt now, if she never saw Annie again it would be too soon.

Ivy mistook Daisy's fury for consternation and took pity on her. "You can't blame yourself, Daisy. Harold's right. This is all because of Rob."

"That and you filling her head with nonsense about the 'one and only man' rubbish. If you hadn't, she might have seen through this madness."

"This is hardly my fault," Ivy retaliated. "You were the one who said how much you liked Rob and how good he was for her." Her face crumpled and she burst into tears.

Daisy stood awkwardly at the sitting room door, not sure whether she should go or stay.

"I'm sorry, Ivy. There's no point us arguing, is there? She's gone and that's that." Harold slumped down in his favourite worn armchair by the window and gazed gloomily through the net curtains.

"We could call the police. Maybe they can get her back?" Daisy suggested hesitantly. It would serve Annie right if she got into trouble.

Harold shook his head. "It's illegal to go to Spain. She won't thank us for getting her arrested."

"Being arrested is better than being dead."

Harold's head shot up and he stared at his wife in horror. "You're right." Suddenly galvanised into action, he stood up, went into the hall, took his hat and coat off the stand and opened the front door. "I'll go to the police station now."

****

Bydgoszcz, Northern Poland

Felcia stared out of the window waiting for Iwan to come home. Raisa had told her some tale about a woman in the village accusing her of having an affair with her husband. Raisa had denied it vehemently, but Felcia had a feeling her sister was lying. A part of her hoped Iwan would say Raisa couldn't stay, then she would be absolved of the responsibility for her but she doubted that would happen. Iwan would probably think Raisa was good company while he was away on exercises. Felcia sighed. She could feel her sister's eyes boring into her back and she turned towards her.

Raisa was sitting at the small kitchen table trying to avoid the temptation to hold her breath. She knew Felcia didn't believe her story. She'd questioned her relentlessly throughout the morning but Raisa was hoping family loyalty would override her sister's antipathy towards her.

"Alright, you can stay if Iwan agrees. But you'll have to get a job in the town; we can't afford to support you and if there's any hint of scandal, you'll be out. I won't let you do anything to affect Iwan's career. Is that clear?"

Raisa let out a slow breath and smiled. "Thank you, Felcia. I won't let you down, I promise." She stood up and gave Felcia a hug. Felcia hesitated and then returned the embrace, stiffly at first and then with more warmth. She didn't trust Raisa, but if she kept an eye on her, there was probably nothing to worry about. Perhaps they could even become friends.

Raisa pulled away and forced a smile again. "Is there anything I can do to help with dinner?" Inside she was seething at having to beg her sister for anything. On the other hand, she'd wanted a way to get back at Felcia and thought her chance had gone when Felcia moved away. But now she was in the perfect place to wreck her spoilt sister's perfect marriage.

****

Paris, France

"I'm not sure how I passed the political evaluation or why I was accepted for nursing so quickly." They were sitting in a small café near the Eiffel Tower and Annie was feeling uneasy again. When the Communist officials had started asking questions, she had stuck to the truth. Her boyfriend wanted to be with his best friend who was already fighting and she had come too, because she couldn't bear to let him go alone. Annie had half hoped they would turn her down, especially as she had no experience of nursing, but instead they had discussed her in low voices, at least she'd assumed that was what they were doing, because she didn't speak Spanish. Then the man in charge had stood up, smiled at her and reached out his hand for Annie to shake.

The interview was over and they told her she would be departing for Spain in the morning, leaving Annie slightly shell-shocked at how easy it had been. Then a horrible thought had crossed her mind. What if they accepted her and not Rob? The next few moments were spent in agony as she contemplated the prospect of being sent to Spain while Rob returned home. Then she realised she was a volunteer. She could still change her mind. She'd breathed a sigh of relief and was busy thinking up her excuses when the door reopened and Rob came out, a broad grin on his face. Her first reaction had been disappointment because he'd obviously been successful so there was no excuse for her to go home, then relief that at least they would still be together.

Rob grinned, his smile bringing her back to the present. "Nor me. The medical was bad enough but when they started asking questions…"

"Perhaps they're so desperate for help that, unless we were obviously fascist, we would have been accepted." She still couldn't quite believe it had been that simple.

Rob nodded. "You're probably right." His face was alight with the almost fanatical excitement she had grown to recognise and Annie tried to join in. She raised her glass of wine.

"To Spain!"

Their glasses clinked and Rob reached across the table to hold her hand. "Thank you so much for supporting me and for coming with me. One day I'll bring you here properly and we'll spend days just walking around seeing the sights. Would you like that?"

If we both survive. Annie's sense of doom increased, but determined not to let him see, she feigned a yawn instead. "I'll look forward to that, Rob, but now I think we should go back to the hotel. I'm sorry but I'm exhausted and tomorrow looks like it could be a long day."

Rob paid the bill and they walked slowly back along the Left Bank of the River Seine. Annie gazed out at the river and tried to ignore the feeling of helplessness that had washed over her. She loved Rob, otherwise she wouldn't be here, but she was terrified of the future and wished with all her heart she could be safely back home.

As if he could read her thoughts, Rob suddenly stopped, turned her face towards him and kissed her passionately. "I love you so much. I do know what you've done for me and I will look after you, I promise."

Before she could answer, he put his arm round her and they continued the long walk back to the hotel. To Annie's relief, they had been given separate rooms which made it much easier to say goodnight at the door. She had a horrible feeling that if they had been sharing a room she would have found it very difficult to resist him and she didn't want to be travelling to a strange land with her only companion not speaking to her because she had spurned his advances. Although Annie wanted him, if they slept together, there was always the risk she would get pregnant. That would have been bad enough in England, but in

Spain, so far from home, with neither of them knowing whether they would even be coming home, it would be a complete disaster and one Annie wasn't prepared to risk.

Chapter Nineteen

Berlin

"I'll get you a drink while we're waiting for Karin to come down." Andreas walked purposefully towards the drinks cabinet. "Why don't you take off your clothes?"

Claudia nodded and began undoing her dress, her eyes on the photographs lining the large ornate sideboard, searching for one of Andreas' wife. It would be nice to know what Karin looked like. "Is this your wife?" She indicated one of the pictures.

Andreas turned around. "Yes, that's Karin and the other man is her brother, Hans."

Claudia was about to comment that Karin was very attractive when she suddenly realised who Hans was. Her face paled and it was all she could do to stop herself gasping. She felt light headed and glanced across at Andreas but fortunately he was pouring the drinks and not looking at her.

She stepped away from the pictures and tried to calm down. She'd thought the SS Officer was some friend of Andreas, not his brother-in-law. What on earth had she got herself into?

****

"There have been some desertions." Mike kept his voice low. They were in a trench and, although he thought they were alone, it didn't do to take risks.

"So I've heard. Although how you can be a deserter to an army into which you've volunteered and which doesn't pay you, I have no idea!" Gerhard slammed his fist disconsolately into the trench wall.

Mike shrugged. "It's the Russians driving it. Any excuse will do for them to shoot you. Apparently one officer only went back for his binoculars and they accused him of deserting and had him shot in double quick time."

Gerhard glanced around. "What about you?"

Mike looked horrified. "I think I'd rather take my chances against the fascists, to be honest. Probably less chance of being shot by them." He sighed. "Ridiculous, isn't it?"

"Well, I suppose they've got to do something, or everyone would pack up and go home, and then they'd be sunk. Casualties are so high the enthusiasm's gone. Discipline was never that great but it's really gone downhill since Jarama."

Mike shook his head. "There'd be fewer casualties if they didn't think it was cowardly to take cover in trenches when the shelling starts. God only knows what idiot told them it was their patriotic duty to stand out in the open when the fascists open up with their machine guns. Anyway, I'm not sure terrorising your own men is the best way to get loyalty. I thought we were fighting against that kind of thing."

Gerhard stared at him for several moments then lowered his voice so much Mike had to lean forward to hear him. "I'm fast coming to the conclusion there's not much difference between the communists and fascists. Maybe the deserters have got it right."

****

Romford, Essex

As Harold made his way to the front door to answer the insistent knocking, he glanced at the clock in the hall. It was just gone ten and he wondered who could be calling at this hour. He was more than surprised to find Bill standing on his door step, his face an angry mottled colour. Before Rob's father could say anything, Harold stepped forward until his face was inches from the other man's, the fury in his eyes evident. "I'm surprised you've got the nerve to show your face round here."

Bill ignored him and launched into his own attack. "You shouldn't have gone to the police. God knows what trouble they'll be in when they come home, thanks to you."

"What do you mean, 'thanks to me'?" Harold could hardly contain his rage. "This is all down to your stupid, brainless son. He's dragged my daughter off to a bloody war zone, where God knows what danger she's in, and all you're worried about is the fucking police!"

"Harold!" Ivy had come out to see what all the shouting was about. She was shocked. She'd never heard him use that word before.

"Stay out of this, Ivy." Harold turned back to Bill, his fists clenched but Ivy grabbed hold of his arm.

"This isn't going to help Annie, Harold. We should be trying to find a way of getting them back, not fighting amongst ourselves."

Harold ignored her. He pulled his arm free of her grasp and was about to hit Bill when she manoeuvred herself in front of him. "No, Harold. Please stop. I'm sure Bill didn't know what Rob was going to do."

Harold stopped, his fist still aimed towards Bill who raised both hands, palms towards him. "I don't want to fight, Harold. Ivy's right. I would never have guessed he would do something this stupid and I want Rob back as much as you want Annie home. He's all I've got left now Sally's dead. I know he's an adult, but if I could get my hands on him I'd give him a right hiding for putting us all through this."

Harold hesitated. He could see Bill was telling the truth. He nodded, took a deep breath and lowered his arm. "You'd better come in." He stood aside and Bill walked past him into the sitting room. Harold was suddenly aware of his neighbours standing on their doorsteps watching. He'd certainly given the gossips something to talk about for the next few weeks. He sighed. That was the least of his worries.

****

Berlin

Karin stared at her robed reflection in the mirror and then turned away. She could hear the low murmur of voices downstairs and she shuddered. She couldn't put it off any longer. She made her way down the winding staircase and hesitated outside the drawing room door. She was just contemplating going back upstairs when the door opened and Andreas grabbed her arm.

"Oh, Karin, I was just about to come and look for you." He pulled her into the room, closed the door firmly behind him and handed her a drink. "This is Claudia… Beautiful, isn't she?"

Karin glanced at the younger woman and nodded. Claudia was only wearing stockings and suspenders, her large breasts naked, the nipples hard. Andreas reached out and squeezed them, making her moan. Then he turned to Karin. "Take off your dressing gown, dear, and let Claudia see you."

Karin shrugged the robe off her shoulders and stared at the floor. She was aware the girl was approaching her and she closed her eyes. To her surprise, the touch, when it came, was gentle and the fragrant aroma of perfume drifted lazily in the air. She opened her eyes. Claudia's face was inches from her own, her eyes drawing Karin in closer. Mesmerised, she made no attempt to resist and then Claudia's tongue was in her mouth and she moaned.

Andreas watched in astonishment. He'd arranged this to humiliate his wife but instead, she seemed to be enjoying herself. Perhaps he should stop Claudia but Karin was now joining in, her hands tentatively exploring his girlfriend's body. Andreas let out a sigh. The sight of the two women caressing each other was too much for him… He forgot all about getting revenge. He couldn't wait to join in.

****

Bydgoszcz, Northern Poland

"Thank you for letting Raisa stay." Felcia snuggled up closer to Iwan. He smiled and put his arm around her. They were lying in bed, the only time they'd had to be alone since he'd come home.

"She's your sister, Felcia. Of course she can stay. This is your home too and your family is welcome whenever they want to come and see you."

Felcia sighed. "I know, but I don't know how long she's going to be here."

"It doesn't matter, darling. Like I said, she's your sister. Anyway enough of her. I've missed my beautiful wife while I've been away." He reached down under the covers and began lifting her nightdress. Felcia stopped him. With the arrival of her sister, she'd forgotten the most important thing that had happened that day.

Iwan frowned. "Felcia?"

"I have some news."

He leant up on one elbow and stared down at her. He could see her smiling in the moonlight that was shining through the half-open curtains. "You're not…?"

"I am. I'm pregnant!"

Iwan leant forward and kissed her. "Oh, darling, I can't believe it. How long have you known? When is it due?"

Felcia laughed. "I found out this morning but I wanted to wait until we were alone before telling you." She didn't want him to know she'd forgotten because of her sister. "It's due at the end of December, maybe around Christmas or the New Year."

"I can hardly believe it. I'm going to be a father!" He shook his head then smiled. His hands reached down under the covers again. "I think we should celebrate."

Felcia stopped him again. "I'm not sure we should. What about the baby?"

Iwan looked surprised. "I'm sure it won't do the baby any harm, darling, but perhaps you should make another appointment to see the doctor tomorrow, just to make sure." He lay back down and put his arm around her again. He would have liked to make love to her to show her how happy he was, but he didn't want to take any chances with the baby.

Felcia lay silently in the dark, her good mood having evaporated the moment Iwan had wanted to make love to her. Her sister was in the next room. How could they do that when the walls were so thin? Raisa would hear them. She would never be able to look at her sister without embarrassment if she thought there was the slightest chance Raisa was listening. They would have to wait until Raisa left before making love again. Fortunately her pregnancy was the perfect excuse.

****

Berlin

Claudia let herself into her flat. She was completely bemused by the sudden turn of events. The last thing she'd expected was to find herself attracted to Andreas' wife. But it was even more astonishing that Karin returned her feelings. Claudia smiled to herself and she wondered if she could see Karin without Andreas. Then her heart sank. Of course she couldn't. It would be much too dangerous and complete madness, and not because of Andreas. He would be furious of course if he found out his mistress was having an affair with his wife and no doubt that would be the end of their relationship. But Andreas was the least of her problems. The real danger came from the SS Officer who'd hired her in the first place. She'd only discovered his identity by chance from seeing those photos of him in Andreas' drawing room, but now she knew who he was, she was terrified of Hans finding out she had slept with his sister, even if it had been at Andreas' insistence. Somehow she didn't think that small detail would make any difference to Hans. He would be horrified, but it would be her he would punish, not Andreas.

Chapter Twenty

En route to Spain

The train to Spain was full of people of various nationalities travelling to fight for the Spanish Republic. What little secrecy there had been soon vanished and, for a while, banners proudly proclaiming 'They shall not pass', were waved optimistically out of the windows. Annie and Rob joined in the chanting, Rob pleased to be part of something so momentous, Annie pretending to be just as excited.

When they grew closer to the Spanish border, a Communist party official stood up. "You must take down the banners now and try to look less like revolutionaries. Keep an eye out for the French border guards. Although most of the time they turn a blind eye to us, occasionally they have a purge and arrest people."

The mood of the volunteers immediately changed from one of excitement to sobriety, while they considered the unhappy prospect of being arrested before they had even managed to reach their destination.

Eventually they arrived at Portbou, a small village nestling at the foot of the Pyrenees. Annie stared out across the shining blue Mediterranean and wished she was on an exotic holiday. If she had been, she could have sat on the beach and listened to the waves lapping gently on the shore, instead of being wracked with fear and anxiety about the future. She glanced at Rob and her heart sank even further. His face wore the fanatical expression she was growing used to and, for the first time, the enormity of what she was doing finally struck home. Once they crossed into Spain, she was trapped. There was still time…

"This way." The official was already leading the way towards a row of houses, behind which the gardens had been turned into a road leading up into the mountains. Annie hesitated briefly then Rob grabbed her hand and they followed the others. Her last chance to escape had gone.

As they walked past the cottages, Annie half expected someone to come out and ask what they were doing, but no one paid them any attention and they slowly began the climb up the side of the mountain. At first the incline was gradual but, as they climbed higher, it grew steeper and Annie could feel the strain on her lungs.

"The custom's shed is back down there." One of the more experienced volunteers, who was going back for the second time, pointed to a building back on the main road. Annie glanced back and tried not to pray someone would come out and stop them, while Rob found himself subconsciously holding his breath as they passed within five hundred yards of the shed. No one challenged them.

Rob squeezed Annie's hand. "Not too long now and we'll be there." He lowered his voice, even though there was no one around.

Annie nodded and held tight to his arm. She was already out of breath and ahead she could see the column weaving their way up an even steeper incline. It was just the beginning. The ancient smuggler's route took them through snow-capped mountain passes five thousand feet above sea level and, before long, the high altitude and lack of fitness began to take its toll. Annie wished she had worn better shoes, but it was too late. All she could do was to keep climbing. The higher they went, the harder it was to breathe and, if it hadn't been for Rob's comforting arm and her fear of travelling home alone, Annie was sure she would have asked to go back.

For the first few hours, while the light gradually faded, they could hear the dogs of the French border guards barking in the distance.

"You must keep absolutely quiet and leave nothing for the guards to find." The whispered instructions were repeated several times. One of the men sighed and, pulling out a crumpled packed of cigarettes, lit one up. The official rushed over to him and knocked it out of his hand, his heel angrily stubbing out the remains on the scree of the mountainside. "There are to be no cigarettes either, in case the smoke gives you away! Understood?"

There were low murmurings of assent and the official, finally satisfied, turned back and began climbing again.

They continued to struggle upwards while darkness fell. Despite the brightness of the full moon highlighting the icy snow caps on the mountains towering thousands of feet above them, visibility was poor. Several times, Annie stubbed her toes on rocks jutting out in the darkness and she wondered if her feet would be red raw by the time they reached their destination.

The night seemed endless. Every time they reached the top of one mountain, there was another in front. The temperature had dropped dramatically. Annie had not come prepared for the extreme change of temperature, nor the hike over the mountains. She was only wearing a light jacket and normal day shoes and soon she could no longer feel her feet because they were so cold. They climbed all night, each step taking them further from France and their old lives and then, as they reached the summit of one particularly high mountain, the dawn began to break.

While they stopped to get their breath and waited for the Spanish guides to take over, the sun finally rose majestically over the mountains. Behind them, in the distance, the blue Mediterranean Sea sparkled, the sunlight playing on the froth-topped waves and the towns and villages dotted along its edge. It was a magnificent sight that would stay with them forever. In front of them lay more white-capped mountains, the snow and ice glistening in the early morning sun, and then Spain.

With renewed determination, they crossed the remaining peaks until they were finally coming down the last of the mountains into a village where trucks were waiting to transport them to a Napoleonic fort at Figueras, the processing town for all volunteers coming from the north. Here Annie and Rob had their first taste of Spanish food; some sardines, bread and tomatoes which they gulped down hungrily, the long climb and lack of food since the previous day increasing their appetites. They finished the meal with their first cigarette since they had left France and, as Rob drew the smoke deep into his lungs, he closed his eyes and put his arm round Annie. He was grateful she was with him but his thoughts had already turned to Mike and how on earth he was going to find him.

****

Romford, Essex

"I'm sorry, sirs, and madam, there's nothing we can do until they come back to this country. Spain is in the middle of a civil war; it would be impossible for us to find them, let alone bring them home."

Harold and Bill exchanged glances. They'd spent a sleepless night waiting for the police to contact them. "So we have to just sit and wait?" Harold was having trouble controlling his temper.

"That's about it, sir." The policeman stood up to go.

Harold stood up too. "I'll see you out." He waited until they were by the front door before asking the other question that was utmost in his mind. He hadn't wanted to ask in front of Ivy because he thought he knew the answer and he wanted to spare his wife even more distress. "Will they be arrested when they come back?"

The policeman shrugged. "To be honest, sir, I don't know. By the time they come home things might be different." He hesitated. "If I were you, sir, I'd stop contacting the police. It'll only serve to keep reminding them that your daughter and her boyfriend have done something illegal. By the time they come home, the police will probably have forgotten all about them. I know it's not what you want to hear, but it's the best advice I can think of to give you."

"Is that what you would do, if they were your children?"

The detective gave a wry smile. "Yes, it is. I'd also be rather proud of them for doing something to fight fascism. Good morning, sir." He tipped his hat and walked down the path, leaving Harold staring after him, a slightly bemused expression on his face.

****

Berlin

Hans stared at Karin. He was sure she was lying to him and he wondered why.

"I don't understand. You were so determined; what's changed your mind?"

Karin squirmed uncomfortably under her brother's intense gaze. "I've decided I don't care what he gets up to any more. He can do whatever he wants. Now I've had time to think about it, I think finding him whores to sleep with is just *so* grubby." She tried to sound disgusted and outraged by the whole idea but, even to her, the words sounded like lies. She kept her head down; she daren't look at Hans. He was bound to guess she was lying. She wondered whether now might be the time to remind him that he was supposed to be finding her a lover so she could get pregnant, but then decided against it. She would give it a week or so and then ask again. There was still time to get pregnant; she was only thirty-one. However each successive month reduced her chances, so she couldn't wait too long. She turned her attention back to her brother.

Hans was shaking his head. "Well obviously it's up to you, Karin. If you're absolutely sure, I'll stop. We'll pretend we never had the other conversation."

There was a long silence. Hans could almost feel his sister's relief and he wondered why she'd suddenly changed her mind. Not that it made any difference of course. Having employed Krussman to spy on Andreas, he didn't intend to stop now. Life in Nazi Germany was all about who your friends were and what information you had on people. The photos he had so far were amusing but not enough to use as leverage if ever the need occurred, so he would keep digging. He frowned. Given Karin's abrupt volte-face, maybe Andreas did have a secret after all…

Karin hurried out of his office, her mind elsewhere, the conversation with her brother already forgotten.

****

Train to Albacete, Spain

Once they had finished their meal, Annie and Rob were taken to the railway station to await another train. The station was unlike anything they had seen in England, the platform full of soldiers saying goodbye to their families and girls giving oranges to the men to take with them. Annie had never seen so much fruit.

"I'd love to go to sleep." Annie yawned loudly. Exhausted from their long climb and with a full stomach, all she could think of was curling up in a nice comfortable bed.

"Me too, but it looks like we're getting on this train." They watched while the engine chugged slowly into the station. Unlike the closed trains they were used to, this one was open and, while Rob helped her aboard, he asked the man in front if he knew where they were going.

"Albacete, the Headquarters of the International Brigades. It's halfway between Madrid and Valencia."

Rob nodded. "Thanks." He turned back to Annie. "Come on, let's see if we can find a seat."

Annie sighed. The train was packed full of soldiers and their packs and she couldn't see any empty places on the uncomfortable wooden seats.

They pushed their way through the mass of soldiers gathered by the door and made their way further into the carriage.

"You are here to fight the fascists?" One of the young Spanish men spoke to them in English.

"Yes, we're going to Albacete," Rob answered before Annie could say anything.

The man and woman stood up and offered them a seat. Rob started to refuse but the girl interrupted him with a stream of Spanish.

"My fiancée is right. To offer you our seats is the least we can do when you come here to fight with us," the young man translated.

Annie and Rob smiled and sank gratefully onto the seats, thanking their fellow travellers profusely. As they set off, Annie longed to enjoy the passing scenery and take in her new surroundings, but she was so completely exhausted that, within moments, the gentle rolling of the train had lulled her into a dreamless sleep. Rob tried to keep awake and make conversation but soon, he too fell into a deep sleep which only seemed to last moments before they were rudely awoken by their arrival in Albacete.

Saying a quick goodbye to the young couple, they climbed off the train and onto the platform where they were met by a tall dark haired man in a rather tatty khaki uniform.

To Annie's horror, the man, who greeted them with a terse "Welcome", wasted no time in separating them. They had a brief moment to say a hasty goodbye and then Rob was taken away with the other men. Annie was on her own.

Chapter Twenty-one

Berlin

Andreas stared at the paperwork on his desk. He wasn't in the mood for work. He couldn't get the memories of the previous night out of his mind. The whole evening had been a complete surprise from the moment his wife and his girlfriend had made love to each other. Just the thought of them writhing on the floor made him hard. He glanced at his watch. It was early but he was entitled to one afternoon off. He would go and visit Claudia. Then he smiled. On the other hand, perhaps he would go home and surprise Karin.

He put the files in the safe, shut and locked the door and hurried in the direction of the stairs.

****

Bydgoszcz, Northern Poland

Raisa eyed Felcia in disbelief. Then she tried to look pleased. "Congratulations, sister. I bet Iwan is excited, isn't he?"

Felcia smiled. "He's over the moon; we both are. Oh, Raisa, I can't wait to see if it's a boy or a girl."

Raisa nodded then she looked worried. "Will it still be alright for me to stay here? I mean, you'll need the other bedroom won't you, when the baby comes?"

Felcia laughed. "Not for ages, Raisa. The baby can sleep in with us once it's born and that won't be until the end of the year. Who knows what will happen by then. You might be back home, or you might even find yourself a husband here."

Raisa joined in. She was relieved there was no danger of being thrown out again, but she was fed up seeing how happy her sister was.

"Won't that cramp your style a bit, having a baby in the bedroom?" Raisa had said the first thing that had come into her head but she was intrigued by Felcia's reaction.

Her sister blushed, looked embarrassed and said quickly, "Honestly, Raisa. There's more to marriage than sex, you know."

Raisa nodded and hunted for a way to keep digging. "Yes, but it's a big part of it, surely?"

Felcia shook her head and snapped. "What would you know about it? Oh, I forgot you were having an affair with a married man, weren't you?"

It was Raisa's turn to shake her head. "You know that's not true, Felcia. His wife made it up because she saw her husband looking at me."

Felcia was about to continue the row when she remembered she was hoping they could become friends. She took a deep breath and sat down at the table with her sister. "Look, Raisa, you're going to be with us for a while and if we're at each other's throats all the time it's not going to be much fun. Can't we put the past behind us and start again? We've got the perfect opportunity to become friends; can we at least try?"

Raisa stared at her sister for a few moments without answering, then nodded. "You're right, Felcia. We haven't always seen eye to eye but, like you say, maybe now's the time to start again."

There was a long silence then Felcia smiled. "Let's go into town and see if there are any jobs going. If you want to, of course?"

Raisa nodded. "Yes, the sooner I can find some work, the sooner I can support myself." While they'd been talking, a glimmer of an idea had come to her. She'd lain awake the previous night wondering if they were discussing her but, after hearing them talking for a while through the thin walls, there was only silence from Felcia and Iwan's bedroom. She would have to listen again tonight. Iwan was a young healthy man. If Felcia was no longer sleeping with her husband because she was pregnant, her plan to break up her sister's precious marriage would be so much easier.

****

Albacete, Spain

Annie was taken to a different part of the camp where she found herself being interrogated by a rather abrupt man whose job, she assumed, was to work out what to do with her. Her fear and anxiety had increased and it was all she could do not to break down and ask to be taken home. But she was determined not to leave Spain without Rob, so she bit her lip and prayed they would soon be reunited, because she had no idea how to find him, especially as she couldn't speak any Spanish.

As if sensing her discomfort, the man suddenly stopped talking and left the room, returning quite quickly with a small pretty girl with dark brown shoulder length curls who smiled at Annie and spoke in halting English.

"It is all strange, no?"

Annie nodded, relieved to be able to understand something at last.

"Juan…" The girl indicated the man who now seemed much less stern. "He want to know what you can do. You not nurse?"

Suddenly terrified they might send her home and then she would never find Rob, Annie shook her head vehemently. "But I can do first aid and help with less serious injuries."

The girl translated quickly and Jean nodded. "Bueno." He smiled at her and then turned back to the girl before continuing, a rapid stream of words which sounded strange to Annie's ears.

The girl nodded then turned back to Annie. "Come. You go to Madrid to help there." She led the way out of the room and then introduced herself. "I am Marie. I come from France and I too will go to Madrid. We can go together, no? We have to hurry, train come soon."

Panic stricken, Annie protested that she needed to say goodbye to her boyfriend. Marie laughed and took her back to the edge of the parade ground where Annie finally spotted Rob, standing with hundreds of other men.

"They learn some basic Spanish, then they go to their Brigades." Marie explained. She glanced at her watch. "You must be quick, we have train to catch."

****

Berlin

Karin closed the front door and smiled at Claudia. "I was hoping you might want this back." Karin handed Claudia the silk scarf she'd left in their sitting room.

Claudia looked relieved. "Thank you. I was worried I'd lost it somewhere on the way home last night. It belonged to my mother, so I'd hate to lose it."

The two women smiled at each other as the tension between them rose. Karin moved towards Claudia, who instinctively stepped back.

Karin stopped abruptly, her smile replaced by uncertainty. "I... I thought after last night..." She searched Claudia's unsmiling face and flushed. "I'm sorry. I've obviously made a mistake."

"No, you haven't." Claudia grabbed Karin's arm and stared into her eyes. "I feel the same, but I'm just scared of what could happen if... if anyone found out."

Karin relaxed. "I am too, but there's no reason for Andreas to know, not if we're careful."

Claudia shivered. It wasn't Andreas she was scared of but she could hardly tell Karin about Hans.

Karin hesitated then added. "We need to make sure my brother doesn't find out either. I'm not sure how he would react."

Claudia somehow managed to hide her shock that Karin had read her thoughts, but she felt slightly better. If Karin was also concerned about Hans at least she would be careful. However, Claudia would still be taking a terrible risk if she became more involved with Karin.

"We don't have to do anything, not if you're really worried?" Despite her assurances, Karin had taken another step towards her so their faces were only inches apart. Claudia swallowed. A sudden burst of lust coursed through her body and she shook her head.

"No I want you too much…"

Karin leaned forward and brushed her lips gently across Claudia's. Claudia closed her eyes and tried to find the will power to push Karin away.

"I'm not scared of Andreas, Claudia. I'll protect you." Her voice was low and intimate and Claudia sighed. If only it was that simple. This was such a bad idea but she could feel Karin's breath on her cheek and her own body responding. Making a determined effort to regain control, Claudia opened her eyes to tell Karin she'd changed her mind. But Karin's eyes were boring into hers, her legs felt weak and she longed to feel Karin's hands touching her.

"Are you absolutely sure this is what you want?" Claudia gave up fighting and wrapped her arms around Karin, pulling her close.

"Oh, yes." Karin began kissing her and Claudia no longer cared about anything, other than the tongue exploring her mouth with increasing passion. "Andreas is at work, he won't be home for ages." Karin suddenly felt shy. She'd never been attracted to another woman before and she didn't really understand why Claudia had such an effect on her.

She was still trying to make sense of the feelings flooding her body when Claudia reached up and stroked her hair, before taking her hand. "Let's go to bed then."

Karin hesitated briefly then followed Claudia to the bedroom where they sat down on the large bed.

Claudia began taking off her clothes. She was just as bemused as Karin with the strange turn of events. She'd never enjoyed sex with other women before. She'd only done it because that's what her clients were paying her for. When Andreas had suggested she seduce his wife, she hadn't had to feign horror; she was genuinely shocked. But he'd told her it was the only way he could get his wife off his back. If she did as he asked, Karin would no longer have any power over him and they could be seen in public whenever they felt like it.

She'd pretended to consider his proposal for some time and then reluctantly agreed. No one could have been more surprised than her by the outcome. She pushed her fears to the back of her mind and watched Karin undress. She would just have to be very, very careful.

****

Albacete, Spain

Rob and the other men had been taken to a large bull ring which was being used as a parade ground. Here they were given a short welcome speech, a uniform of a greenish, khaki colour and then divided into national groups and taught some basic Spanish. Caught up in the excitement of meeting new people who all felt as passionate about the cause as he did, Annie was soon forgotten. So it was a bit of a shock to see her running across the parade ground towards him.

Ignoring the whistles and shouts of appreciation, she flung herself into his arms, catching him by surprise.

"I'm going to Madrid, or at least I think that's where I'm going." He could see the fear in her eyes.

Suddenly worried she was about to make a scene, Rob held her tight for a few seconds and then pulled back and stared into her eyes. "We'll find each other again, don't worry. I promise, alright?" He had no idea how that was going to happen but he wanted to reassure her so she didn't start panicking and make a fool of him in front of his new friends.

It seemed to work because she nodded. Relieved, he hugged her close once again. "I love you and we're always going to be together.

You do believe me, don't you?' He didn't wait for an answer, instead he began kissing her passionately on the mouth to the accompaniment of cheers and lewd comments from the watching men.

As much as he loved her, Rob wanted to get back to his training, so reluctantly he stopped, pulled back and let her go. He stared into her eyes and stroked her hair gently. "Look after yourself, Annie; in no time we'll be together again, you'll see." He gave her one more quick hug and then turned away. Annie waited until Rob was back with the other men before giving him a final wave and allowing Marie to lead her out towards the camp gates and away from him.

Rob watched her go with mixed feelings. Although he was concerned about how she would manage without him, underneath there was a growing sense of excitement that he was really here and soon he would be doing what he'd dreamed about for so long. He knew she would be safe at home if it wasn't for him, but he pushed the guilt away. Annie would be perfectly alright; of course she would. It wasn't like she'd be in any real danger. She'd probably spend most of her time in Madrid, shopping and doing other things girls did. Anyway it wouldn't be long before they were reunited.

Rob watched her for a few more seconds, then put her out of his mind. Turning around, he said goodbye to the volunteers from other countries who had travelled with them. Eventually there were only the British volunteers left and, with a growing sense of excitement, Rob prepared to go to Madrigueras, the Headquarters of the British Brigade.

Chapter Twenty-two

Berlin

Andreas arrived home with a beaming smile on his face. Karin would be surprised to see him, and for the first time in ages he couldn't wait to make love to his wife. He wondered briefly if his wife did genuinely prefer women, then shook his head. Of course she didn't. She was married to him and their sex life had always been good. The only fly in the ointment was her inability to get pregnant. If only she could, life would be so much easier. For a brief moment he wondered if the fault lay with him, then he dismissed it. How could he be the problem? He was healthy and virile. No, there was nothing wrong with him. Karin was obviously at fault, or they were just unlucky.

He frowned. On the other hand, maybe she was right about him spending so much time with his mistresses. Perhaps that was part of the problem. Well, it wouldn't be for much longer, not if she was willing to join in like she had the previous night. He would be quite happy to spend every night at home. He smiled. There was just time to have some practice making babies and then later he would invite Claudia around for dinner and they could have some more fun.

The hall was silent. She must be upstairs. He ran up the winding staircase and hurried towards the bedroom.

****

En route to Madrid

The journey to the front line seemed interminable to Annie, squashed as she was between some burly soldiers and the other women who had volunteered. From the little bits of conversation Annie had managed with them, she had learned they were all trained nurses, although some had considerably more experience than others. She was the only one who was not a nurse and had no experience of caring at all. This put her at a considerable disadvantage for a while, as they at least had something in common to talk about.

There were six of them in all, including her; two from France, her new friend Marie and another dour looking woman by the name of Bernadette. Bernadette seemed much older than the others and, from what Annie could gather, had been a nurse for some years. She was the most experienced nurse there and wasted no time in letting them know that she had been put in charge. Annie tried hard not to take an instant dislike to her but her arrogance, combined with her condescending attitude to Annie, soon left her in no doubt that Bernadette didn't like English people in general and Annie in particular.

Her other companions were Geneve from Belgium, a short, rather stout girl who was about thirty years of age with a pleasant face and relaxed manner. Leila, from Holland, was much nearer Annie's own age, and fortunately spoke quite good English. She had long, ash blonde hair that was currently tied up in plaits that wrapped round her head. Annie liked her immediately. She had an open face with a wide smiling mouth and sparkling blue eyes. She announced her Jewish origins in almost her first sentence and laughed about how she was the most Aryan looking Jew in Europe. The fifth girl, Carla, a German with short dark hair, looked horrified and hastened to add that she had nothing against Jews and that was why she was there, to fight against anti-Semitism. So frantic was she to be forgiven for her German origins that Leila quickly took pity on her and took pains to make her feel at ease.

Annie found herself fascinated by everything she saw in this strange country, from the peasant girls in their bright clothes on all the platforms, giving fruit to the soldiers, to the olive groves and wide open plains she could see from the train. The only thing she wasn't very keen on was the heat. It was sweltering in the train, the only breeze coming through the open windows as they sped through the Spanish countryside. At each station there was a long wait while the train became more crowded and the heat intensified. Annie could feel sweat dripping down her neck and her clothes started to stick to her body but she was unable to move because the train was swollen with more soldiers making their way to the front line. She was struck by how young most of them were and she thought of Rob, soon to be undertaking this journey too. She wondered what had happened to Mike and whether he was still alive and then her thoughts wandered naturally back to Rob and how long it would be before she saw him again.

****

Berlin

Karin had just reached her second climax when Claudia collapsed, panting on the bed next to her. "Your turn." She rolled onto her back and opened her legs invitingly. Karin reached down and began rubbing gently.

"Use your tongue."

Karin moved obediently down the bed and knelt between Claudia's thighs. She ran her hands over Claudia's pubic hair and then bent forward eagerly.

She flicked her tongue gently across her clitoris. Claudia tasted sweet and, as she moaned, Karin moved her tongue quicker.

"Do I taste nice?" Claudia wriggled, pushing her hips closer to Karin's face.

Karin sprung back in horror, her face pale, perspiration glistening on her skin.

"Karin, what on earth's the matter?"

******

Bydgoszcz, Northern Poland

"Never mind. We've left your name and our address at several shops. You might hear something quite soon." Felcia tried to cheer up Raisa. "It's only the first day, after all."

Raisa nodded. She didn't really mind that she hadn't found anything, but it wouldn't do to let Felcia know. She'd seen several young men in the town, many of whom had looked her up and down appreciatively. Of course she'd had to pretend she hadn't noticed, but she was reasonably sure she could make a living here if she wasn't under the constant watchful eye of her sister.

Raisa shrugged. It suited her to be under her sister's roof for the moment. But she would have to hurry up and put her plan into action. If she was successful, she might soon have her own place and then she could earn some real money, and with real money she would be independent of her sister and the rest of her family.

"I said shall we stop for some coffee?" Felcia was smiling at her in the warm sunshine. Raisa smiled and nodded back while she wondered how much longer she was going to have to put up with her patronising sister.

****

Madrigueras, Spain

The journey in the back of the trucks to Madrigueras was surprisingly quick but Rob's relief when they arrived was soon replaced by shock at the poverty he could see all around him. There were no pavements, just dirt tracks down the main streets. At one end of the road he could see a stone column with a lead pipe leading from it. There was a queue of people waiting patiently in front of it.

"That's the only water supply." The voice came from further up the truck and Rob couldn't see the speaker. "We have to queue day and night to make sure we have enough water for cooking and drinking now there are nearly six hundred of us here. There's no point asking the villagers to sell you anything either; they have nothing to spare."

The truck had left the water pipe behind and was now driving past a large bar. "That's the canteen where we can go and have a drink and you will be able to meet the local people."

Rob smiled. That sounded a bit better. It obviously wasn't going to be all training then. A few moments later, they arrived at the camp and were shown to their sleeping quarters. Rob glanced around the worn army hut with its rows of three-tier bunks and, for the first time, felt some misgivings.

"Welcome to Spain!" The speaker jumped off his bunk and came towards Rob. He was short, wiry and had a Manchester accent. "Come on, let's get some food. I'm Henry Muccleburgh, by the way, known to all as Harry."

Rob put down his belongings and shook his hand. "Rob Davies." He glanced around. "I can't believe I'm really here."

Harry grinned. "Nor me, mate. I felt exactly the same when I got here a couple of weeks ago. I can't wait to get stuck in."

"Have you done any training?" Rob asked as they walked towards the door.

"We've done a bit, but not much yet. We've been mainly learning the language and getting used to the heat. But now you lot have arrived, I expect they'll start training us up for some action."

Rob nodded. "Good. My mate's already here. Mike Jacobs, came last year. I only hope I can find him amongst all these people."

"Shouldn't be too hard." Harry thought for a few moments. "I'm sure the officer in charge of us will know how you can go about it." They had reached the army hut which was serving food and Harry tailed off. Rob smiled. He was feeling better already.

His enthusiasm lasted until he sat down with his meal, which consisted of meat so tough the only way he could eat it was to hold it and tear strips off.

"I was hoping the cooking would improve when we got some new recruits, but obviously not," Harry remarked in a loud voice. Rob was about to answer when an unshaven man stood up and introduced himself as Sergeant Valasqueth, who was in charge of their training.

"The camp has strict rules to which you must all conform. Lights are put out at half-nine and you will be awoken at six. After breakfast you will drill until midday. Then we will have short break for lunch followed by siesta."

The idea of sleeping in the afternoon was greeted with a certain amount of amusement which the sergeant ignored. "You will train again in the evening, this time learning to clean, oil, load and unload your weapons in the dark." He pointed behind him and indicated they should help themselves to the rifles. These were either of Russian manufacture or old Great War Lee Enfields. "We have very little ammunition to spare, so firing will be kept to a minimum, although you should all have fired about fifteen rounds before you go to the front. We will also teach you map reading, to speak Spanish and carry out field manoeuvres." He glanced at his watch. "Time for siesta. Enjoy the rest of the day and be ready for tomorrow. Buenos días." He saluted and left the men staring at each other in consternation.

"Surely we need to fire more than fifteen rounds?" Rob was horrified.

Harry shrugged, but he too looked worried. Perhaps that was why they hadn't done much training yet. "Nah. He's probably exaggerating."

"Given those weapons, I shouldn't think so." The speaker was tall and thin with a nasally voice. Rob glanced down at the small pile of old, rather rusty Lee Enfields in the corner of the room and felt uneasy for the first time since he'd left England. No wonder Mike had not sounded very enthusiastic in his later letters if this was all they had to train with.

Chapter Twenty-three

Berlin

Andreas flung open the bedroom door and stared. There was no one there. Feeling deflated, he sat down on the edge of the bed and wondered where Karin was. Perhaps she'd gone shopping. Maybe he should go and see Claudia instead. Except, for some reason, it was his wife he wanted. Well, she would probably be back soon. He'd wait for her.

He undressed slowly, climbed onto the bed and closed his eyes. While he was waiting, he would replay the previous evening's entertainment, just to get in the mood.

****

En route to Madrid

To take her mind of the stifling heat, Annie stared out of the open window at the tiny hamlets and villages and the vast empty open spaces of the plains. In the fields she could see the peasants dressed all in black and she wondered how they coped with the heat. The women wore black shawls round their shoulders and black skirts with belts tied round the middles and canvass shoes, the men black capes, trousers and jackets. She watched as they walked in between the villages and the fields, the men riding on their donkeys or mules, the women walking behind carrying skins full of water. Annie thought how bleak their lives seemed and how empty this part of Spain appeared to be. Other than the peasants toiling in the fields and the odd cloud of dust thrown up from a cart moving on a track in the distance, everything was still. It was so hot she could see the heat shimmering and she was grateful for the fan Leila had given her. She began to doze, the movement of the train and the intense heat lulling her into sleep, the thought passing through her mind that it was hard to believe there was a war going on.

No sooner had this thought entered her head than everything suddenly erupted into chaos. The train stopped abruptly and she opened her eyes in time to see everyone throwing themselves onto the floor.

****

Berlin

"I'm sorry. I can't talk about it." Karin hugged her knees to her chest and tried to ignore the racing of her heart.

Claudia put her arms around her. "Don't worry. It doesn't matter. I don't want to upset you, Karin."

"You didn't, honestly." Karin sighed and wished the memories would return to the box at the back of her mind where she'd hidden them. "It's just something that happened… a long time ago."

"Well, if you ever want to talk, I'm here." Claudia glanced at the bedside clock. "But I think you'd better go now, it's getting late. Won't Andreas be home soon?"

Karin looked at the clock and jumped up. "Goodness! I didn't realise it was that time already." She began pulling on her clothes. She put on her coat and she turned to Claudia, who was still sitting on the bed, her long blonde hair framing her naked shoulders.

"Can I come again?"

"Of course." Claudia looked relieved. "I was frightened you wouldn't want to." She stood up, leaned forward and kissed Karin on the lips. Karin forgot her hurry and returned the kiss.

Claudia pulled away reluctantly. "You'd better go."

Karin grinned. "Until next time then."

As she hurried down the road, an idea came to her. She was tempted to go back and suggest it, but it was late and she didn't want Andreas asking questions. She would think about it and then talk it over with Claudia the next time she saw her.

Claudia hugged her knees to her breasts and wondered what on earth had possessed her. She must be completely barmy to risk Hans' wrath by having an affair with his sister, but for some reason, she couldn't help herself.

****

Madrigueras, Spain

The heat of the Spanish summer afternoon took them by surprise and, after a few moments, they were grateful to be sent to their bunks to rest. The journey was beginning to catch up with him and Rob fell onto his bunk in relief and dozed while the sun beat down mercilessly above them.

"We're being sent to join 15th Brigade." Harry interrupted his nap. He'd been wandering around the camp and had overheard two of the Spanish sergeants talking. Having been in Spain for two weeks, his Spanish was already quite good.

Rob perked up. He was sure Mike had said he was in the 15th Brigade.

Harry saw his expression and nodded. "I thought you'd like to know, or I wouldn't have woken you. Your friend is likely to be there because the battalion we're being sent to is a combined British and American one."

Len, the tall thin man with the nasally voice, joined in: "What's left of them after Jarama, from what I've been told."

Rob's spirits fell. He'd been so sure he would find Mike, now he started to have doubts again. Maybe he hadn't survived the battle? His thoughts turned to Annie and he wondered what she was doing. He hoped she was enjoying herself. He smiled as he imagined her shopping with the other girls and having fun. At least he knew she was safe and not in any danger.

****

En route to Madrid

Caught by surprise, Annie and her new companions looked on in amazement until one of the soldiers pulled her roughly off the seat and onto what was left of the space on the floor, throwing his arm round her, covering her body partly with his own and shoving her face-down onto the wooden floor. Before she could object or react in any way, there was a tremendous crash, followed by another and another, each one seemingly coming closer. The train shook more with each explosion and, hearing the roaring sound of aircraft overhead, she belatedly realised they were being bombed. The bombs were followed by the sound of bullets zinging along the carriages, sending sparks skyward when they hit the metal rails and pitting the train with holes that showered everyone with shards of splintered wood. Annie lay there absolutely terrified; she no longer cared about the soldier's body on top of her, instead she was immensely grateful for his quick reaction. At least she had the illusion of safety.

The attack seemed to last forever and she squeezed her eyes shut, praying she would survive. Then, as suddenly as the bombing had started, the planes flew off. The passengers got to their feet, dusted themselves down and the train jolted slowly back into life. Miraculously, no one had been injured in their carriage and it seemed the bombers had failed to hit the train, although she later found out that a few people in other carriages had suffered shrapnel and bullet wounds. The soldier who had pulled her onto the floor helped her back into her seat and she gave him a shaky smile.

"Thank you… I mean gracias." She belatedly remembered the Spanish.

He smiled and then said something that was too quick for her to understand. Leila immediately answered for her, an answer which seemed to please the soldiers and other civilians who all started smiling at her and talking at once.

Seeing Annie's confusion, Leila translated quickly: "He asked if we have come to help them fight the fascists and I said yes."

Annie nodded and tried to smile back. She was still shaken, although she was determined not to show it, especially since everyone else seemed to be taking the bombing in their stride.

They drew closer to Madrid and were soon under attack again. Each time a bomb dropped, the train rocked and clouds of dust came in through the open window space. They finally reached the outskirts of Madrid and then came under intermittent artillery fire, the shells landing perilously close. Annie began to wonder whether she would ever reach her destination.

When the bombs and shells weren't falling, she tried to distract herself by looking out through the open window. The scenery had changed, the ring of factories giving way to wide tree-lined boulevards, the giant Bullring with its Moorish architecture, dusky brown arches with decoratively coloured tiles and columns. But Annie was unable to really appreciate the beauty of the city because she was terrified that every thought would be her last. Wondering if the journey would ever end and wishing she was safely at home in England, she was relieved when they pulled into a station and she climbed out gratefully. However, there was no time to stop and think, no time to change her mind before they were ushered into some trucks and transported a short distance to a large building that was being used as a hospital.

****

Berlin

"You look a little flustered." Andreas was waiting for her when she finally arrived home. He'd grown bored waiting in bed, so had dressed and come downstairs. "Is everything alright?"

Karin nodded. "I went for a long walk in the park. I didn't realise what the time was." She had a feeling she sounded agitated but he had caught her unawares. She hadn't expected him to be there, even though she'd not hurried home from Claudia's flat. "I'll put my coat in the wardrobe." She headed towards the stairs. She had to get away from him before she did or said something to make him suspicious.

Andreas watched her disappear upstairs and briefly considered following her. But the urge had long since left him. He was now more curious about what she was so obviously hiding. Then he remembered the fate of his other girlfriends and he paled. Surely she wouldn't dare do anything… Andreas leapt up, grabbed his coat and rushed out of the house.

****

Romford, Essex

"I came round to see if you'd heard anything." Daisy stood on the door step and shifted from one foot to the other under Harold's steely glare.

He shook his head. "Nothing. I take it you haven't either?"

Daisy sighed. At least she wasn't the only one Annie was ignoring. "No, not a word." It wouldn't do to fall out with Annie's parents, not if she wanted to know when Annie came back, so she tried to sound encouraging. "But they've only been gone a short time. I'm sure they'll be alright. Mike's been over in Spain since last year and…" She fell silent as she realised she hadn't heard from Mike for weeks either.

"And what?" Harold stared at her.

"Oh nothing, I was just thinking… that is…" she improvised quickly. "The last letter I had from Mike said he was well and they were winning." Daisy crossed her fingers behind her back. She was sure he'd actually said they were being hammered and he was glad Rob hadn't gone with him, but she could hardly repeat that to Annie's father, not without upsetting him.

"Humph!" Harold snorted. "That's not what the papers and the BBC have been saying about it."

"Well perhaps they're wrong." Daisy was wishing she'd hadn't come round now and she turned to go. She was also feeling slightly guilty. Perhaps she should have shown Rob Mike's letter, then he and Annie might not have gone. Then she shrugged. It was hardly her fault both Mike and Rob were stupid. But she had credited Annie with more sense, even if she was always banging on about 'the one and only'. And look where that had got her. It just went to show how wrong you could be about people.

Daisy sniffed her disapproval. She was sure Annie would be perfectly alright, they'd hardly have women fighting on the front line. But it would be a long while before she forgave Annie for making her look stupid. It was also very inconsiderate. Now Daisy would have to find someone else to go with to parties and the cinema.

****

Berlin

Andreas hurried round to Claudia's flat after his strange conversation with Karin, terrified she would have disappeared. But to his relief she was safe and well.

"Is everything alright, Andreas? You look a bit worried?" Claudia stared at him in concern.

"No, I just missed you." Andreas kissed her and, after a brief hesitation, Claudia responded.

"You'd better come in." She broke away and smiled up at him.

Andreas laughed and followed her into the apartment. Claudia led the way into her bedroom, relieved she'd made the bed again after Karin had left. She joined in their love making with enthusiasm and, by the time he left, Andreas had forgotten all about his earlier worries.

Claudia breathed a sigh of relief. He'd caught her off guard but fortunately he didn't appear to have noticed her discomfort and, by the time they'd finished making love, she had recovered her wits. Obviously he didn't suspect there was anything going on between her and Karin. She would just have to make sure she did nothing at all that would make him suspicious.

Chapter Twenty-four

Madrid

There was no time to be frightened any more. Annie found herself thrown into something that reminded her of a picture she'd seen called *Dante's Inferno*. The hospital was quite large but only some of the wards were being used, because many had mould growing in them and others were little more than repositories for bodies. There were hundreds of patients lying on filthy beds with virtually no bedding, and equally as many lying on the floors. There was little equipment and limited staff; supplies of medicines were almost non-existent and hygiene was primitive, with instruments being sterilised in boiling water perched precariously on primus stoves. Other instruments were being flamed, which involved pouring burning alcohol over them. For Annie and the others, there was no time to change out of their clothes, or even to find something to eat or drink.

Wounded soldiers were arriving all the time in trucks, ambulances, carts, anything that had wheels. Most were not on stretchers and only had a blanket over them. Some had very few clothes and those that did were often full of lice. When they arrived, they were laid out on the floor in the large reception area, hundreds of them, moaning and screaming in pain, while the doctor walked between them deciding who to treat. With such limited supplies, they had to concentrate on those they could save, so many were just left to die. Those who were not too badly wounded were also left to the few nurses to treat. Although Annie had no nursing training at all, she found herself learning very quickly. From sterilising instruments, she quickly progressed to bathing wounds and bandaging, to stitching and from there to giving injections. She had to learn by watching and asking the others, and from listening to their conversations. Bernadette had long since disappeared, as had most of the other girls she had travelled with on the train. Only Leila remained and she quickly became Annie's closest companion, helping, encouraging and teaching her. Without Leila, Annie would have given up and gone home, unable to believe what was happening all around her.

The operating theatre was even more chaotic, as limbs were amputated one after another. With limited resources, tough decisions had to be taken quickly. There was no time to save limbs, only lives, and if the only way to do that was to amputate, then that was what happened.

****

Madrigueras, Spain

Rob's training had intensified. There were more night time manoeuvres so they could learn to cross the Spanish countryside in darkness without getting lost, and form up in the dark. However, the food had not improved and dried fish, known as *bacalao*, now accounted for quite a few meals once it had been soaked to take out the salt. But the biggest problem was the shortage of cigarettes, because the tobacco came from the areas now controlled by the fascists.

"We're off!" Harry rushed into the bunk house where Rob had just flung himself onto his bed after another exhausting night-long march. He sat up.

"Are you sure?"

Harry nodded. "There's going to be a big Republican assault on the fascists at Brunete where they are controlling the western approaches to Madrid."

Rob looked surprised. "Are we supposed to know that?"

Harry grinned. "You know how good the Republicans are at keeping secrets."

Rob sighed, then enthusiasm took over. "Go on then, tell us more. I can see you're dying to."

Harry was about to continue when Sergeant Valasqueth arrived. He pulled out a dog-eared map, called all the men together and began addressing them. "We are going to pull out later tonight. Our objective is Brunete, which is situated at the crossroads of a minor road system on the Castilian plain between the Perales and Guadarrama Rivers." He pointed to a small spot on the map. "The attack is part of the offensive to relieve the pressure on Madrid. From what I can gather, our first objective is to seize the Heights and Brunete; that way we can push the Nationalist artillery back out of range of Madrid."

Rob nodded. "Sounds simple, Sarge. What's the catch?"

The Sergeant frowned and shook his head. "There isn't one. From what I've heard, we have a massive advantage. Sixty thousand men, over a hundred planes, twenty artillery batteries and a hundred plus tanks."

Rob looked sceptical. They had very little knowledge of what else was going on in the war but he was pretty sure most of what they were told was propaganda to keep up their morale. "Are you sure?

The sergeant looked offended. "The fascists are really stretched there, only a few divisions and static brigades to guard the whole of the line from the French border to the Straits of Gibraltar. Even better, they're only supported by about thirty Italian aircraft and a Spanish reconnaissance squadron."

"A walk in the park then," Rob whispered.

Harry grinned. "Let's hope so. I can't wait to get stuck in."

"'Bout bloody time too." Len sounded as enthusiastic as Harry, and Rob tried to keep his misgivings to himself.

He began packing up his meagre possessions but he couldn't shake off the butterflies in his stomach and the general feeling of unease. However, like the others, he allowed himself to be carried along on the crest of righteous fervour that permeated the rest of the international fighters. As they travelled the two hundred and seventy two kilometres to Brunete, by train and by foot, he sang along with them, their voices carrying poignantly across the hot, dry, dusty, Spanish countryside.

****

Berlin

Krussman stared in astonishment at the images emerging in the developing fluid. The photographs were quite clear and showed two naked women making love. His first reaction was to smile. The other woman was Andreas' wife. He recognised her from the photograph Kohl had shown him. But he'd found out since that Andreas' wife was actually Kohl's sister which was presumably why Kohl was paying him to spy on his brother-in-law. Well, well. When he'd first put the camera into Claudia's flat, he'd not really expected to see anything other than her and the man he'd been told to follow.

He'd followed Andreas to work again that morning and, realising he would probably be there for a while, he'd decided to take the opportunity to go back to the girl's flat and see if he could retrieve the film from the camera he'd hidden in the bedroom a couple of weeks earlier. He'd tried several times to do this but, every time he'd gone around there, the girl had been in and he couldn't hang around for too long or he would look suspicious. To start with it looked like he was going to be unlucky again. He was about to leave when he saw Andreas' wife arriving at the flat. The fact that she'd let herself in didn't register until much later. Surprised to see her, he'd presumed she'd found out about her husband's affair but when she didn't emerge fairly quickly, his curiosity had been aroused, so he had taken a chance and remained there. Fortunately for him both women had then left the apartment so he'd let himself in and retrieved the film, replacing it with another one.

Seeing Andreas' wife in bed with the girl was a complete surprise. Then he remembered that she'd opened the door with her own key which meant the affair must have been going on for some time. He frowned. Kohl would not be very happy if he gave him these pictures. Most men would be horrified but Kohl was likely to react violently, especially as he'd specifically told Krussman he didn't want to see pictures of Andreas' wife. In fact, Kohl might decide Krussman knew too much about his family and that was a good enough reason to get rid of him.

Krussman shivered. Kohl was the only reason he wasn't rotting in a camp or swinging from the end of a rope. If the SS officer realised he had seen pictures of his sister naked and in bed with another woman, there was no telling what his reaction might be. Krussman knew a dangerous man when he saw one. Perhaps he should keep these to himself. He wouldn't throw them away, because they might just come in useful in the future. In the meantime, he had better take some photos of Andreas or he would have nothing to give Kohl at their next meeting and the last thing he wanted to do was to make the SS man suspicious.

****

Madrid

"There's someone been asking about you." Gerhard flung himself down in the trench near Mike. He had another man with him, tall well built with a shock of dark curly hair. "This is Helmut. He's German too."

Mike nodded to Helmut then realised what Gerhard had said. He stared up at them both in astonishment. "Really?" His spirits rose. Perhaps Rob had come out after all. "Do you know who and where he is?"

"Madrigueras, from what I can gather." Gerhard answered before speaking rapidly to his companion in German.

Helmut nodded a couple of times then spoke to Mike. "I did not get his name." He shrugged. "He was looking for Englishman; it means nothing to me until I meet Gerhard and he tells me your name."

Mike sighed. Madrigueras might as well be the moon. He could hardly go and find out. If he went without asking, he'd be shot as a deserter and, given they were preparing for a massive offensive, he was unlikely to get permission.

Gerhard saw his expression. "Perhaps we could ask for some leave after the next battle, take a trip there and see if we can find this mysterious man."

Mike gave a wry smile. "It must be my mate Rob, the one who was going to come over with me."

"Ahh the one who fell in love instead." Gerhard laughed.

Mike nodded. "I can't think of anyone else, to be honest."

"Unless it's the boyfriend or husband of one of those señoritas you were enjoying so much the last time we were in the city." Gerhard glanced sideways at him. There had been more than one girl in Mike's life since he'd been in Spain. Not that Gerhard was judging him; he'd had a fair few women himself. "Perhaps you left her with a little more than money!"

Mike blanched. He hoped not. He had no intention of being forced to get married in Spain. All thoughts of returning to Madrigueras vanished. "Perhaps it's a good thing we're off to Brunete after all."

****

Bydgoszcz, Northern Poland

"This is very nice, Raisa. I didn't know you could cook." Iwan smiled at his sister-in-law, who had just dished up a very tasty cabbage, potato and bacon casserole. Raisa smiled back, peering at him from under her long eyelashes.

"Until I find some work and can support myself, I thought I would help Felcia as much as possible, especially now she's going to have a baby. You must be so excited." She sat down and began helping herself to some of the food.

Iwan nodded. "I can't wait to be a father." He reached across the table for Felcia's hand and squeezed it, then turned his attention back to Raisa. "What kind of work are you looking for? I have lots of friends, maybe they know of something."

Raisa shrugged "Anything really. We called in at all the shops again today but there still weren't any vacancies."

There was silence while they ate. Iwan hesitated. "This may not be exactly what you want, but there is a vacancy on the camp for a secretarial assistant in the accounts office. I could ask, if you want?"

Raisa's face lit up. "That would be wonderful, wouldn't it, Felcia?" She glanced at her sister just in time to see an expression of concern on her face that vanished almost immediately.

Felcia nodded. "Yes definitely, Iwan. The money would be better than in a shop as well, so you'd soon be back on your feet."

"Right, I'll ask tomorrow then." Iwan stood up and headed towards the ornate sideboard in the corner. The furniture had been a gift from his mother and took up the whole of the back wall. He took out some glasses and returned to the table. "I think we should raise a toast to our baby and a job for Raisa. New beginnings!" He reached for his bottle of beer, poured them both a small amount and they clinked their glasses against his bottle before drinking.

Chapter Twenty-five

Madrid

Working till she was exhausted and living on black coffee and cigarettes had become normal, and Annie could barely remember what life had been like before she had arrived in Spain. She was just finishing another long shift when she was summoned to one of the corridors where Leila was waiting with two other girls she didn't know.

"What's going on?" Annie glanced around, a wary expression on her face.

"We've been selected for something, apparently," one of the girls she didn't know piped up before yawning loudly.

"There's an emergency hospital been set up on the front line near Brunete. We're going there." The answer came from a rather harassed looking doctor who had appeared from one of the doors off the corridor. He gave Annie a weary smile. "We're going to launch a big offensive apparently."

Annie felt her stomach squirm. She hadn't heard anything from Rob since they'd parted. If there was a big battle planned, he might be involved.

The doctor misread her expression and tried to reassure her. "I'm sure we won't be too near the front line."

Annie blushed, horrified to realise he thought she was afraid. "No, it wasn't that. My boyfriend is with the International Brigade. I was scared he might be involved in the attack."

"Ah." The doctor smiled. "Was that why you came over here?"

Annie nodded. "He wanted to come and fight the fascists and find his best friend who came over last year. I couldn't let him come alone."

"Well, I am sure our patients are very pleased you're here, whatever your reasons."

Annie opened her mouth to defend herself, thinking he was criticising her, but before she could speak, they began moving towards the ambulances.

****

En route to Brunete, fifteen miles north-west of Madrid

After three days' travelling, Rob and the rest of the brigade had arrived at the edge of the plain. Here they stopped to await orders. Preparations for the coming battle were going on all around them and he was feeling increasingly nervous.

"I hope they've had more training than we have," Rob muttered.

Harry frowned. "I doubt it. Doesn't look like they've got better weapons either."

"They haven't." Len pointed to some infantrymen lying up in the bushes close to them. "I just had a chat with them. They reckon most have only got one shot, bolt action rifles. Some have got five shot Soviet rifles and the really lucky ones have machine guns, although they don't have much ammunition."

"And what happened to all the artillery they were boasting about? All I can see is infantry." Rob sighed. He'd been looking forward to finally getting involved in the fight but he'd expected to at least have some chance against the enemy.

"We'll be alright." Harry shrugged and lay back, staring up at the sky.

Rob stared at him. "The last I heard, the fascist army is highly trained and experienced. Italy have given them light tanks which have got machine guns and the Germans have supplied them with Panzer I and II light tanks which have got cannons as well as machine guns. What have we got to fight against them?"

"I did see some T25 tanks back on the road, although I don't know where they are now." Len grinned. "And of course there's always our wonderful Russian rifles."

Harry glanced around. "You wanna be careful who you say that to, Len. I've heard some rumours the Ruskies don't like their equipment being criticised."

Len shrugged. "Should give us some decent stuff then, if they want us to win."

"We've got plenty of 'planes." Harry spoke loudly. He was suddenly aware they had an audience. Seeing Len about to argue, he kicked him hard on the shins.

"Oy!"

"Shut up you idiot, or you'll get us all shot." Harry's nervousness was infectious and Rob was starting to feel uncomfortable.

"Yeah, he's right. I've heard we normally control the skies."

Len stared at him in astonishment and shook his head. They might have more aeroplanes, but they all knew the Russian aircraft were vastly inferior to those of the German Condor Legions.

"Of course we do." A communist official suddenly appeared from behind them. "Our artillery and weapons are vastly superior to anything the fascists can produce." He stared at the men, daring them to argue.

Harry and Rob nodded immediately, followed a few seconds later by Len, who belatedly realised it would not be wise to upset the Russian. Satisfied by their answer, the official saluted and headed off. The men breathed a sigh of relief.

"I thought we was out here to fight bloody dictators like him," Len muttered under his breath. Ron and Harry exchanged glances. Sometimes it was hard to tell the difference between the enemy and their own side.

****

Berlin

"Are these all the pictures you have?" Hans was furious and Krussman winced at his tone.

"Yes. They don't seem to be meeting there very much lately. Perhaps he's bored with her, although I can't find any evidence that he's seeing anyone else." He held his breath, wondering whether Kohl would believe him. "I do have some other photos of the man, though." He handed Hans the envelope with pictures of Andreas at various places in the city. He didn't think they were of any use but then he didn't know what the SS officer was looking for.

Hans took the envelope and handed over the money. "Keep changing the film in the flat and watching him to check if he's seeing anyone else. Don't let me down, or I might forget our arrangement and you wouldn't want that, would you?"

The menace in his face made Krussman shiver and he shook his head. "No, sir."

Hans stared at him for a few seconds. "Well? What are you waiting for? Get out and do you're the job I'm paying you for."

Krussman didn't need telling twice. The photos of Kohl's sister were in a safe place, together with a letter to Krussman's cousin, the editor of one of Berlin's numerous newspapers. If anything happened to him, he'd arranged for his cousin to receive the letter and the photos. It wasn't the ideal insurance, but it was the best he could come up with at the moment.

****

Brunete, Spain

Rob had no time to reflect on the political similarities between the two forces before they were on the move again and, by late evening on the following day, they had almost reached their objective. As they marched past La Solana de Torrel Christophenes hospital, an old house situated between two hills on the junction of the roads from Madrid to El

Escorial and Brunete, their voices echoed off the hills while they sang their own national songs and then stopped for a brief halt.

Rob took the opportunity to ask for Mike but there was not enough time to search properly. Once darkness fell, they began crossing the plain, their objective to reach the road to Brunete, which ran along the crest of a low broad ridge situated between the shallow valleys of the Perales and the Guadarrama. The plain was intersected by numerous deep gullies, rivers and streams that restricted their movement and, once the men were safely across these hurdles, they had a steep climb to reach the top of the ridge.

Eventually, by early morning, they were in position. Rob crouched down in his hastily dug trench, licked his lips nervously and waited for orders to advance. He was disappointed not to have been able to find Mike and, once again, he wondered if perhaps his friend was dead. He thought of Annie for a moment and smiled, imagining her enjoying herself in Madrid, then he allowed his thoughts to drift back to when he would be able to continue his search for his friend.

While Rob stared into the darkness, the sky began to lighten and, as dawn rose on the sixth of July, the Republicans launched a massive artillery and aerial bombardment. The battle for Brunete had begun.

Chapter Twenty-six

Brunete, Spain

To Annie's relief the long journey in the back of ambulances slotted in amongst trucks full of soldiers was reasonably uneventful and they arrived without incident. Fortunately it only occurred to her afterwards that many of the trucks in the convoy were carrying ammunition and, if a bomb or artillery shell had hit them, the ambulance they were travelling in would have been destroyed as well.

The emergency hospital had been set up in an outbuilding on the edge of a small village not far from Brunete. There was no running water or electricity and it was left to the medical staff to devise a means of using the engines of the ambulances to run the lights. Water arrived each day in large barrels on a cart and they filled every spare container in the hope of securing enough for the day's use. If conditions in Madrid had been bad, this was indescribable. But Annie had no opportunity to think about that. The first casualties were already arriving.

****

The Battle of Brunete, Spain

As the bombardment raged around Rob, the men were ordered forward, out of their trenches, up the hill and straight into the oncoming fire. Within a few moments, Harry and Len had succumbed, limbs and torso ripped apart by the ferocity of the machine gun fire, their blood soaking into the brown dried soil of the Basque scrubland. Rob threw himself flat on the ground, wishing he was still in the trench he had spent so long digging the previous night. His head was already reeling from the continual noise, his throat hurt from the smell of cordite and, to his horror, he was trembling. He tried frantically not to look at Harry or Len, their bodies lying at unnatural angles. They'd come all this way to be cut down within minutes of beginning to fight; how could Mike possibly have survived anything like this?

Bullets zipped around where he was lying, missing him by inches and Rob knew he would have to move or he too would be dead. Rolling over a couple of times, he spotted a small copse of bushes and a short stubby tree to his left. Anything was better than lying out in the open, so he offered up a prayer and made a dash for it, expecting at any moment to hear the murderous zinging of machine gun bullets as they ripped through the earth behind him. But Rob was lucky and, having reached the relative safety of the bushes, he came to a decision. He had come here to fight; at least two of his friends were dead and here was he hiding behind some bushes. It was time to do something. Taking a deep breath, and then wishing he hadn't as his lungs filled with acrid foul smelling smoke, he rolled over and peered cautiously round the side of the bushes. If he kept low and used the bushes as cover, he could possibly make his way forward towards the machine gun post that was causing such massive casualties. He had a couple of grenades, but he needed to get close enough to use them. The machine gunners' attention was on the mass of men moving towards them, not on him, so if luck was on his side, he should be able to reach it.

****

Villanueva de la Cañada, north of Brunete, Spain

The village was being shelled by two pieces of artillery and Mike could see the cavalry charging around on the flat ground outside the small settlement. The order was given to advance and they made their way down the slope and into the dry river bed of the valley until they reached a ridge about six miles from the village where they were pinned down. Above the defenders, the blue sky was cloudless and the scorching sun beat down. Mike and Gerhard sipped the remains of their water and kept their heads down. The snipers were very accurate and, after a couple of hours, several men were dead.

"Anyone got any water left?" The soldier was younger than Mike, one of the replacements. Mike shook his head and glanced at Gerhard. The German also shook his head. There was silence, other than the intermittent shelling and occasional plane dropping bombs.

"Perhaps we should try and get to the village. There must be water there," Mike suggested. Gerhard hesitated and then nodded.

"I'll let the sergeant know what we're going to do." Without waiting for an answer, he crawled on his stomach towards the section leader. Mike leaned forward to watch and then a machine gun opened up and he threw himself flat, heart pounding, as the bullets whizzed past his head.

******

Brunete, Spain

To start with there were fewer wounded than expected at the hospital, but then, as the fascist counter offensive intensified, the casualties flooded in. The conditions were made worse by the number of civilians who also arrived at the doors of the hospital, their feet cut and bleeding as they had scrambled over rocks in the dark to get to the hospital. Most had wounds caused by the bombing and strafing, bullets, shrapnel, limbs hanging by threads, but others needed operations for more routine things. Most people in Spain were too poor to be able to pay for medical treatment, so the field hospitals had become the nearest they could get to a doctor. Annie and the other staff at the makeshift hospital treated everyone to the best of their ability, whether civilian or military and, despite the shortages and impossibility of the situation, saved many lives which otherwise would have been lost.

Annie found treating the injured children by far the worst thing she had to do. She could not understand why planes would target children playing in the fields, or their mothers toiling along tracks carrying their day's water rations. The planes would even strafe the sheep in the fields and the hens and chickens.

At first, while the wounded poured in, she would try to check every casualty to make sure it wasn't Rob or Mike but, before long, she was just too busy; there were too many casualties and not enough time.

******

The Battle of Brunete, Spain

Using all the available cover, Rob gradually crept forward on his stomach. The machine gun was still firing at the attacking troops, its bullets raking the earth in an arc, backwards and forwards, and men were falling like ninepins. Rob felt sick. Turning his attention back to the machine gunners, he realised he was almost on the edge of the arc of fire. Providing they didn't spot him, he was now in a position to get close enough to use his grenades.

He was scarcely aware he was no longer scared, all his concentration on stopping the deadly machine gun while he crept closer and closer. He felt like hours had passed, but in reality it had only been a few moments. But in that brief time, tens of men had died and Rob's only thought was to stop the carnage.

Pulling the pin, he counted to four, raised his head, took careful aim and threw the grenade with all his strength in the direction of the gunners. The explosion was almost instant, deafening him for several seconds and, when he finally raised his head, he could see nothing through the thick black smoke drifting in his direction. He rubbed his eyes and was busy peering through the slowly moving haze when he was startled to feel a hand on his arm. Throwing it off, he grabbed for his rifle before realising it was one of the Brigade Sergeants.

"Well done, lad." Rob was surprised to hear the sergeant was English, but before he could react, the man had gone into the smoke and beyond the first defensive line of the fascists. Rob hesitated and then followed, to find they had broken through the outer defence and the village lay before them. But the fighting wasn't over. Within minutes, Rob found himself in hand-to-hand fighting with one of Franco's Spaniards. Other than vaguely recognising they were of a similar age, Rob was too busy fighting for his life to take much notice, as one after another came at him. The fighting became a blur of blood, noise and chaos and seemed to go on forever until the last of the defending Nationalists was dead or captured and they finally held the village.

By now it was midday and the hundred degree heat of the July day was beginning to take its toll on the men of both sides, but it was far worse for those from temperate climates who were unused to the searing temperatures. Rob began to wonder how he could possibly survive the first day, let alone a whole campaign. His head was pounding from dehydration, his throat so dry and sore from thirst and from the toxic smoke and cordite wafting unchecked across the landscape, that he was struggling to breathe.

****

Villanueva de la Cañada, North west of Madrid, Spain

Mike and Gerhard crept along the top of the ridge over to the right of the battalion and eventually reached a dyke that ran alongside the road into the village. Everything was quiet until they reached a bend in the road and almost immediately came under fire from the settlement. Turning around, they hurried back to the bend, but their position had been spotted by the machine gun firing at the ridge.

"Looks like we're stuck." Mike threw himself flat in the small dip in the dyke while bullets whipped up the soil all around him. Gerhard followed, his body crashing down next to Mike's, a hail of machine gun fire narrowly missing him.

"We'll wait until dark and then try and get back to the others."

Mike nodded but he was beginning to wonder if their luck had finally run out.

Chapter Twenty-seven

HQ, Pomorska Cavalry Brigade, Bydgoszcz, Northern Poland

Raisa stared around the small office in satisfaction. The job wasn't very exciting but it was easy and the location was perfect. She was in the middle of the army camp, surrounded by men. She'd been delighted to find the secretary was older than her by several years, and very overweight. As the only woman under thirty, she would have been the centre of attention anyway, but Raisa was also attractive. Her long brown hair was tied back, exposing her classic high cheek bones, deep brown eyes and full mouth. Unlike Felcia, who took after Magda with blonde hair and green eyes, Raisa's colouring resembled her father's side of the family. But she had Magda's features and this, combined with her own flirtatious, knowing smile made the accounts office in the Headquarters building a magnet for the officers and men who spent hours trying to think of excuses to visit her.

To start with, Raisa was tempted to accept some of the offers but she quickly realised word would get out if she slept with any of the men who asked, and that wouldn't suit her plans at all.

Iwan brought her to work in his car every morning and took her home every evening, giving her the perfect opportunity to get to know him. Despite her father's accusations, Iwan seemed to consider her an innocent girl and, realising it was Felcia's innocence that had attracted him in the first place, Raisa took pains to cultivate that image in herself.

****

Brunete, Spain

Annie was exhausted. She couldn't remember the last time she'd slept for more than an hour or two, and breaks were few and far between while they struggled to cope with the overwhelming numbers of injured streaming through the doors.

She wanted to write to her parents but she couldn't think what to say to them, other than to apologise profusely for the pain and concern she knew they must be experiencing, thanks to her selfishness. There was nothing good to say and she didn't want to give them even more to worry about. She thought about writing to Daisy but she felt guilty about not telling her friend that she was going to Spain, so eventually she gave up on the idea of writing any letters at all and concentrated on treating the increasing number of patients. Perhaps when this battle was over she'd be able to think of something positive to tell her parents and she would find the right words to explain her actions to Daisy, but until then it was probably better to say nothing at all.

****

Berlin

"A very good party, Franz." Andreas shook his hand and bowed to Hannah who smiled back at him. She'd learned to hide her feelings quite well and at least Andreas was one of the nicer men she and Franz had to kowtow to.

"Is your wife with you?"

Andreas smiled and, turning slightly, indicated Karin. She was standing with her brother, their heads close together. Andreas wondered what they were plotting. Then he remembered his hosts and returned his attention to Hannah. "She's over there with Hans. Did you want to speak to her?"

Hannah shook her head, slightly too quickly and Andreas hid a smile. He didn't blame Hannah. He wouldn't chose to talk to his wife either, the way he felt at the moment. He was still curious about what she was hiding but at least this time it didn't appear to have anything to do with his mistress. Claudia was alive and well and he was due to go round to see her once he left the party. He glanced at his watch. Another half an hour and he would ask Hans to see Karin home.

Franz watched the members of the Nazi Party circulating happily in his house, drinking his alcohol, eating his food and availing themselves of the girls he'd arranged, and wondered what they would say if they knew the truth. When Gerhard arrived home, he would have enough information about his illustrious guests to ensure his son's safety. He had no idea whether the information he passed to Carstairs was of any use, but he would do whatever he could to prevent another war.

He watched Andreas approach Karin and her brother. A brief conversation ensued and then Andreas left. Franz was fascinated by the expression on Karin's face but even more so by that on her brother's. While she was staring after Andreas with a mixture of longing and something he couldn't identify, Hans was watching his sister with disgust.

Franz made a mental note to find out what was going on between the three of them. There might be something he could use in the future. Then Kurt Daluege, his guest of honour, began speaking to him. Daluege was chief of the Ordnungspolizei, known as Orpo, which gave him administrative authority over most of the uniformed police in Germany. This made him a very important person and Franz gave the SS man his full attention. Andreas, Karin and Hans were temporarily forgotten.

****

Bydgoszcz, Northern Poland

"So you're enjoying the job?" Iwan manoeuvred the car carefully through the camp gates. They were late leaving because Iwan had been summoned by his Commanding Officer at the last moment. The meeting had only just finished but Iwan was feeling rather pleased with himself, having been recommended for promotion to Wachmistrz. He would have to go on a course first but, providing he passed it, he would soon be a Sergeant of Horse. He was dying to tell someone but he knew Felcia should be the first one to know, so he restrained himself by asking Raisa questions instead.

Raisa nodded with enthusiasm. "Yes, it's very interesting."

Iwan glanced at her, amusement on his face. "I don't think it is, but it must be very nice being the talk of the camp… in the nicest way of course," he added hastily.

Raisa smiled. "Well, everyone is friendly and they've all made me very welcome."

Iwan laughed and wondered whether he should say something about protecting her reputation. She was his sister-in-law and unmarried and he was responsible for her while she was under their roof, so he supposed he should warn her, even though it was a little embarrassing.

He cleared his throat. "Just watch the men, Raisa. You don't want to get a reputation for… for…" He couldn't think of a way to put it without upsetting her.

Raisa debated whether to act offended, then decided that would be a little too much. Instead she turned towards him and gave him the full benefit of her smile. "Its alright, Iwan. I will only go out with one of them if I really like him."

Iwan glanced sideways at her and found himself momentarily dazzled. Confused by his own reaction, he turned back to watch the road and nodded. "Good. Good."

There was silence. Raisa stared out of the side window, an amused smile on her face. Iwan stared ahead but he was no longer concentrating on his driving. He was suddenly intensely aware of the young woman sitting next to him. Perhaps he should make alternative arrangements for her to get to and from work. He shook his head mentally. That was ridiculous. She was Felcia's sister. He was obviously imagining the tension between them.

****

Berlin

"Are you quite sure you don't want me to do something about her?" Hans leant close to his sister and whispered in her ear.

Karin looked horrified. "No, Hans, honestly. Please don't. It doesn't matter anymore. Please just leave it."

Hans frowned. He wished he knew what was going on in his sister's head. He'd seen the longing in her face, which told him she still loved Andreas. So why was she suddenly adamant she didn't want him to interfere?

He glanced around the room and hid a grimace. He hated these events but had no option other than to attend, his job to listen to those colleagues who might be indiscreet after too much alcohol. He frowned while he thought about those of his comrades who couldn't keep their mouths shut after a few beers. Of course they were nothing compared to those who were guilty of pillow talk. Hans smiled. The idea had come to him after he'd dealt with Karin's problem and found a whore to satisfy Andreas. His eyes scanned the room, searching for his girls, the half dozen prostitutes he'd infiltrated into the room with specific men to target. To his satisfaction, all the girls were with the right men. He almost rubbed his hands together but stopped himself in time. He was looking forward to the following morning when he met them to get their reports. That was always the best part.

****

Romford, Essex

"I'm sure she'll be alright, Ivy." Harold spoke with confidence although he didn't really believe it himself.

"Yes, Harold's right," Bill joined in. The three of them had become good friends and often spent the evenings together, worrying about Rob and Annie.

"So why hasn't she written at all since she left?" Ivy wiped her eyes. "Even Daisy hasn't heard from her."

"There could be all sorts of reasons." Harold looked to Bill for support.

"It might be hard to get letters out, or she's not in a place where there's any post." Bill fell silent. They had been over this several times and he wasn't sure he was helping very much.

"She might just be scared to write, not knowing what we'll say," Harold chipped in.

"But she'll know we'll be worrying and, even if we're furious with her, she must know we still want to know she's alright." Ivy twisted the handkerchief in her hands and stared down at her lap. She would give anything to hear from Annie, just to know she was alive and safe.

Bill said nothing. He was worried about Rob but he was also furious with him, not only for going somewhere so dangerous and taking Annie with him, but for not bothering to write himself. He hadn't said anything to Harold, although he was sure Annie's father must have considered that the reason they hadn't heard anything was that their children weren't safe. He couldn't bring himself to even think they were dead, but if they didn't hear anything soon, they might have to consider that possibility.

****

Bydgoszcz, Northern Poland

"Congratulations, darling." Felcia leaned over him and kissed his mouth. "When are you likely to find out if you've been accepted on the course?"

"In the next few weeks, I think." He reached out for her nipple. He was in the mood to celebrate.

Felcia pushed Iwan's hand away from her breast. "You know the doctor said we should wait until the pregnancy is much further on to be absolutely sure it's safe." Felcia kept her voice low, conscious of Raisa in the next room. She was totally unprepared for Iwan's reaction.

"For goodness sake, Felcia. Can't you be more specific? How much longer do I have to wait?" Iwan's furious whisper sounded very loud and she winced, imagining her sister could hear every word.

Felcia wondered briefly what had suddenly changed. Iwan had never been so insistent before. He'd seemingly accepted her reluctance to make love until she was further into the pregnancy, so his attitude took her by surprise.

"Perhaps I should speak to the doctor. Maybe you've misunderstood."

Felcia blanched. She was grateful the room was dark and Iwan couldn't see her face. She reached out tentatively and placed her arm on his stomach. She had to stop him going to the doctor's or he would know she was lying. "We agreed to wait a bit longer." She whispered back. "Another week or so." Perhaps she could persuade her parents to take Raisa back by then.

There was a long silence and Felcia began to relax, her eyes closed and she began to doze. Then Iwan gave a loud sigh. "Alright, just do it to me."

Felcia started awake. "What do you mean?"

Iwan took her hand and placed it on his erect penis. Felcia tried to pull away but he ignored her and began moving her hand up and down faster and faster. Felcia was shocked but made no further effort to stop him.

Once he was sure she wasn't going to stop, Iwan closed his eyes and, with his other hand, lifted her nightdress. Felcia let go of him and tried to push him away.

"I'm not going to fuck you, just lie still." Felcia was too shocked to say anything. Iwan had never spoken to her like that before. She lay motionless as he knelt over her, his penis in one hand, his eyes closed. She could hear him muttering to himself but she couldn't understand what he was saying. He pushed her legs apart, then leant closer so he could see better. Felcia looked away, totally embarrassed, as he masturbated harder then showered her in warm liquid before collapsing back on the bed beside her.

Felcia didn't move. She could hear him panting beside her but she had never felt so far away from him. She no longer felt like his wife. Instead she felt like some whore he'd paid to open her legs. She felt tears forming in her eyes and her nose became blocked. She tried not to sniff or draw attention to herself. Iwan seemed totally unaware of her discomfort. He rolled over and put his arm around her.

"You see, there's lots of things we can do that won't put the baby in danger. Thank you, darling, that was wonderful." He closed his eyes, relieved his wife hadn't been able to read his thoughts while he was experiencing one of the best orgasms of his life.

****

Villaneuva de la Canada, Spain

It was dark, when the armed men came upon them from the undergrowth. The enemy appeared so swiftly there was no time to defend themselves. Their only option was to surrender.

"Hands up!" The harsh voice spoke in Spanish with an accent and Mike's heart sank. His biggest fear had come true. They had been captured by the fascists. If they were very lucky, they would spend the rest of the war as prisoners, but more likely…

He shut off his thoughts and carefully laid down his weapon. Gerhard did the same and both men raised their hands and stood up slowly.

"Who are you?"

Mike gave the number of his battalion and the name of the commander and waited for the inevitable bullet. Rumours of atrocities were rife and he fully expected to be shot. He heard the men question Gerhard and then one of the soldiers pushed them both forward towards the village.

Mike glanced around, wondering whether he could escape, but they were surrounded by the small group of soldiers. He tried to be optimistic. Perhaps the fascists would put them in a prison camp and then send them home when the war was over. Then he remembered Gerhard was German. What would happen to his friend once these men knew that? He tried to ignore his squirming stomach and was grateful for once that he'd had virtually nothing to eat. At least he wouldn't disgrace himself.

They entered through the small gate which led into the village and relief flooded through his body. There was enough light from the moon to see that the men refreshing themselves in the water trough, were from his battalion. The Republicans had taken the village; they hadn't been captured by the fascists: they were free. The men turned around in surprise and, recognising them, rushed over to greet their friends. Mike and Gerhard ducked their heads in the cool water. They'd survived another day.

****

Bydgoszcz, Northern Poland

Felcia plastered a smile on her face and kissed Iwan goodbye.

"Goodbye, darling. Look after yourself and our little one." Iwan patted Felcia's stomach before turning to Raisa. "Ready?"

Raisa looked awkward. "Yes, Iwan. I'm ready." She hesitated. "I do appreciate you driving me every day. I could walk if you prefer?"

Iwan shook his head. "Don't be silly. We're going in the same direction; it would be daft you having to walk, wouldn't it, Felcia?"

Felcia nodded. "Of course it would. I'll see you both later." She watched as they walked to the car then turned away. She was still wondering about the sex the previous night, she couldn't call it 'love making' because there had not been any love involved. She hoped it was just a one off and that her husband would not want a repeat. Of course, she could always let him make love to her, but all the time her sister was in the next room, she couldn't bring herself to do that. She tried to put the previous night out of her mind and concentrate on the housework but her doubts and worries continued to hover at the back of her mind.

Iwan tried to ignore the rising sexual tension in the car. He'd been convinced he was imagining it the previous evening but now he wasn't so sure. He risked a glance at Raisa but she was looking out of the side window and not paying him any attention.

He shifted uncomfortably in the seat and wished they would hurry up and reach the camp so he could drop her off. After he'd imagined fucking Raisa while he masturbated over his wife, Iwan had felt guilty enough to consider finding an alternative to driving Raisa, but he'd been so enthusiastic about it before, he wasn't sure what he could say to Felcia that would explain his sudden change of heart. And now Raisa had suggested she walk and he'd laughed it off, he had been backed into a corner. He would just have to try and think of something else while she was around him.

Raisa stared at the passing countryside and smirked. She knew exactly what Iwan was thinking. She'd seen the expression on his face the previous evening and knew it was only a matter of time. She shifted position, slipping her cardigan down her shoulders slightly and leaned towards him. "Felcia is so lucky to have you. I hope I'm as fortunate when my time comes."

Iwan glanced across to answer her and caught a glimpse of her breasts through the buttons of her blouse. Feeling himself grow hard, he stared back through the windscreen and tried to think of something to say that wouldn't get him into trouble. His mouth was dry and his head full of images he couldn't eradicate.

****

Berlin

Karin waited until Andreas had left for work before hurrying around to Claudia's flat. She'd spent the rest of the evening at the party in agony, imagining her husband making love to her girlfriend. The irony of the situation didn't escape her. She used to envy the time and attention Andreas lavished on his mistresses but now she couldn't care less about him; it was Claudia she wanted to be with and any time her friend spent with her husband was time away from her. She also wanted to ask Claudia to help her. She'd given it a lot of thought and she was sure this was the best way to resolve her problem.

"Karin!" Claudia looked up in surprise from the sofa in the sitting room. "You must be more careful or people will see you coming here." She stared at Karin and her heart melted. She reached out her hand and began stroking Karin's hair. "I missed you last night. I was so disappointed when Andreas turned up here on his own."

Karin gave a wry smile. "I wanted to come with him but it was impossible." She took hold of Claudia's hand and stared into her eyes. There was a long silence then Claudia leaned forward and kissed her. Karin forgot all about her request and instead gave in to the surge of passion racing through her body.

****

Berlin

"Good morning, ladies. I hope you've all got something to tell me?" Hans raised an eyebrow and stared at the girls in front of him. "So, who's first?" His eyes roved over them, searching for the one who appeared the most scared.

"Helga. Let's start with you."

The tall redhead licked her lips nervously and stepped forward. Hans ran his hands over her breasts before ripping the blouse apart. "Go ahead." Helga began talking, her eyes fixed on the wall behind him like she'd been told to do. Hans continued his exploration of her body, eventually raising her skirt and shoving her legs apart before inserting the handle of his dagger inside her. Helga cried out in pain and he slapped her across the face.

He leant forward. "Keep talking. I haven't finished yet."

Helga continued her report while he moved the handle back and forth, making her gasp. Eventually she finished and, shaking violently, she stared at him in fear. But he smiled and removed the handle. "Good girl, you've done well. Come back in a week and I'll give you a new target."

Helga stepped away in relief while he turned his attention to the remaining girls. To his delight, they all looked terrified now. His eyes scanned them before making his decision. The blonde reminded him of Claudia. He gave a wintry smile.

"Petra! Your turn. Why don't you come over here and tell me all about your evening."

Chapter Twenty-eight

The Battle of Brunete, Spain

For the next four days, the Republicans advanced steadily. They took Brunete, but failed to take Mosquito ridge, the heights overlooking the River Guadarrama and the villages of Romanillos and Boadilla Del Monte. This was a turning point. The advance came to a standstill. Although Rob had no idea of the bigger battle raging around him, even he recognised that, from moving forwards, they were now on the defensive.

The fighting continued relentlessly into the night and the next day, as the Republicans desperately tried to hold on to the captured territory, their aircraft still just managing to control the skies. But when the Condor Legion's Messerschmitt Bf-109s appeared, closely followed by the Heinkel He 111 bombers, everything changed.

Rob was no longer really aware of what he was doing, he just knew he had to keep going, or he would die. Totally exhausted, his eyes red rimmed and sore, he couldn't hear anything other than the noise of battle, so he was astonished when the man who was fighting next to him suddenly grabbed him and shoved him hard onto the ground. About to retaliate, he noticed everyone around him was holding their heads in their hands and trying to bury themselves deeper into the trench they had just captured.

The first bomb caught him by surprise, then he realised why they were all trying to disappear into the ground. Each time the bombs dropped, the ground shook and clouds of earth went skyward, showering them all in stones, plants and hard dry soil. Bullets zinged along the sun baked ground throwing up clouds of dust and soil, followed by bombs which left massive craters in their wake. There was nowhere to go and Rob could only pray the enemy fire would miss him and that he would survive.

After what seemed like hours but in reality was a few minutes, the planes were gone and the Nationalist artillery opened up, bombarding them relentlessly. It soon became apparent they couldn't hold their ground much longer and the order was finally given to withdraw. While some stayed to provide covering fire, Rob joined the others in a headlong retreat back down to the valley where they regrouped and again tried to open up the Boadilla Road, but without air support they were even more vulnerable to air attack from the Condor Legions.

****

Berlin

"Did you notice the strange atmosphere between Hans Kohl, Karin and Andreas the other evening?" Franz had just spotted Andreas hurrying past the window and the expression on his face had reminded him.

"No, to be honest Hans and Karin are very odd anyway. He makes me shudder and she… well, she's very…" Hannah searched around for the right word to describe her.

"Intense?" Franz suggested.

Hannah nodded. "Yes, that's a very good description. So what was the atmosphere?"

Franz thought for a few moments. "I'm not sure, to be honest. I just got the feeling that everything wasn't as it should be."

Hannah shrugged. "They're all Nazis, so nothing would surprise me." She gave a wry smile at the worried expression on Franz's face. "The last time I looked there weren't any listening devices in here."

"This is not a game, Hannah. There's too much at stake." Franz had lowered his voice automatically and she took his hand.

"I'm sorry. I just get so frustrated at having to be nice to them."

He squeezed her hand. "I know, but just think of Gerhard. We're doing this for him."

Hannah's face grew serious. "I wish he'd hurry up and come home, Franz. You do think he's alright, don't you?"

He put his arm around her. "Yes, of course he is. I'm sure we'll get another letter soon. He's just being careful. He knows how dangerous it is contacting us." He hoped he was right. They hadn't heard anything since he'd talked about coming home and, although Franz was trying to be optimistic, the longer time went on without any word, the more concerned he was becoming.

****

The Battle of Brunete, Spain

Sheltering once more in a hastily dug trench, while the latest bombardment shattered the air around him, Rob began to wonder what on earth he was doing there. He still hadn't found Mike and he was beginning to think his friend was dead or badly wounded. They seemed to have achieved precisely nothing over the past few days, despite the dead and dying bodies of his comrades lying all over the battlefield. Morale was at rock bottom and then, while the sun rose higher in the sky, more orders arrived.

Rob dragged himself wearily out of the relative safety of the trench and followed the others in yet another hastily ordered, ill prepared retreat. While the bombs and bullets rained around him, Rob was sure he could vaguely remember reading that withdrawal was one of the most dangerous times in a battle and that it should be planned properly to ensure minimum casualties. This was not a planned withdrawal, it was nothing more than a rout and the bodies of his comrades bore witness to this.

****

Bydgsozcz, Northern Poland

Iwan was no longer sure whether he dreaded the journeys with Raisa or looked forward to them. It was probably a combination of both. He still wasn't certain whether she was aware of his feelings, so he spent the time in the car staring rigidly out of the window. He could still remember the white of her breasts through the open buttons of her gaping blouse and he daren't look at her long shapely legs stretched out in front of her as she changed position several times on their journey. If it had been anyone but Raisa, he would have guessed the movements were deliberate but he couldn't bring himself to believe his wife's younger sister was purposefully trying to seduce him. It was all in his mind, so he would have to just put up with the guilt.

He sighed inwardly. He knew he wasn't being fair to Felcia but he had to have some kind of sexual release or he was likely to pounce on Raisa. So night after night, he masturbated over his wife while thinking about her sister. His only consolation was that at least he was only being unfaithful in his mind, although he had a feeling that was probably almost as bad as being physically unfaithful.

Raisa shifted position again, this time ensuring the top of her stocking was visible, and glanced sideways at Iwan. She could see his erection though his uniform trousers and she smiled. They were approaching the small wooded area just before the small housing estate where they lived. It was time to take a chance. She reached across and rubbed her hand over his trousers.

****

The Battle of Brunete, Spain

"I think we've had it." Mike drank sparingly from his water bottle and surveyed the carnage in front of him. They had been sent on ahead to survey the land and see what was happening in the valley. Since reaching Mosquito Ridge the battalion had been frantically trying to hang onto the small gains they had made, but the fascists were gradually pushing them back.

Gerhard nodded. Shells were falling all around and the machine gunners were becoming more accurate with every burst. The area was swarming with fascists and it wouldn't be long before the rest of the battalion, sheltering in the trenches, were overrun. "Let's head back and give them the bad news."

Mike sighed and the two men began to make their way down. They hadn't gone very far when he saw movement ahead. Mike stared in disbelief. Below them the men were leaving the trenches and falling back down the hill. There was no attempt to protect the rear of the column and the machine gunners soon found their range.

"For fuck's sake…" he began then he frowned. Something about one of the men seemed vaguely familiar. "Quick, give me your glasses."

Gerhard handed them over, struck by the urgency in Mike's voice. "What is it?"

Mike didn't answer for a moment, then he sighed. "I knew it. That's Rob, I'm sure it is." He handed back the glasses to Gerhard and began scrambling down the mountainside, ignoring the bullets zipping around him. "Come on, we need to hurry or he'll be dead."

Gerhard hesitated, then shaking his head at his friend's foolhardiness, he reluctantly followed.

****

Bydgoszcz, Northern Poland

"What the hell are you doing?" Shocked to feel the warmth of her hand caressing him through his trousers, Iwan swerved the car.

Raisa didn't answer. Instead she began undoing his buttons. Iwan put his foot on the brake and the car shuddered to a halt. There was no one in sight. He reached across and pushed up her skirt until he could see black lacy knickers. "Get out of the car. There's no room in here." His words were muffled, but Raisa immediately obeyed.

Outside the car, he shoved her quickly towards the trees and, as soon as he was sure they couldn't be seen from the road, he stopped and forced her to her knees, intending to enter her from behind. But Raisa had other ideas and she was in control. She was already undoing the rest of his buttons and, before he could say anything, she was licking and sucking his penis. His climax was almost instant, filling her mouth with hot sour liquid. Raisa swallowed and licked her lips. She smiled up at him.

Iwan was still panting, his hands resting on the tree behind her. He looked down at her and groaned. "Oh God, what have I done?"

Raisa shrugged. "There's no reason for Felcia to know, is there? It'll be just between us." She licked her lips again and, leaning forward, began licking him once more.

Iwan's efforts to push her away were ineffectual and she sucked harder. "No, we can't do this again…"

Raisa pulled away, lay back on the ground and opened her legs. "Are you sure?"

Iwan groaned again. She smiled, pulled her knickers aside and slid her finger inside. Iwan held his breath while she brought her finger up to her mouth, licked it and smiled. "Want some?"

Iwan was lost. He shoved her back, straddled her and forced himself inside. To his astonishment, he couldn't get all the way in. Horror struck, his erection vanished and he pulled out. "You're a virgin?"

Raisa shrugged. She was furious he'd stopped. That wasn't part of her plan. "What difference does that make?"

Iwan shook his head. "No, I'm not taking your virginity." He took a deep breath, turned away and tried to regain some control over his body.

"I don't understand what…?"

"You're Felcia's sister. We can't do this. Get dressed."

Raisa stared at him in dismay. This wasn't going the way she'd envisaged it. If he didn't make love to her, she couldn't claim he'd raped her. Felcia was bound to make her see a doctor to prove what she was saying.

Iwan was still staring in the opposite direction and trying to work out what to do. They'd already gone too far; he could never look at Raisa in the same way again. Even as he tried to think about something else, he could feel himself growing hard again.

"Get in the car." He risked turning around and then wished he hadn't. Raisa was still lying on the ground, her legs open. Iwan gave up fighting his conscience.

"Turn over."

Raisa smiled. She could see his erection. She did as he asked and felt him kneel down behind her. He pushed up her skirt, swiftly removed her knickers, lifted her up on her knees and, the next moment, she felt his penis pushing against her bottom.

Raisa began to struggle. "You're in the wrong place…" she began but he ignored her.

"You wanted me to fuck you, didn't you? Well this is the only way I'm going to, so enjoy it. At least there'll be no danger of you getting pregnant." He shoved harder until he finally managed to enter her.

****

The Battle of Brunete, Spain

Eventually, seeking shade from the merciless sun, an exhausted Rob crawled behind some bushes and, with the last vestiges of his strength, dug himself a small shell scrape, hoping to protect himself from the strafing and bombing still going on all around him. His face and arms were red raw and burning from the sun but at least the sweat that had persistently run into his eyes, making them sting while he was fighting had stopped from lack of fluid. His lips were so parched and burned the skin was peeling off, his voice hoarse and sore when he tried to talk. In fact, it was so painful to speak he had given up trying, even if there had been someone left to talk to.

Desperate for water, Rob checked his flask again, although he knew it was empty. Despite the artillery bombardment going on around him, the dehydration began to take its toll. He was struggling to concentrate and, although he knew he needed to find water or he would die, his eyelids felt heavy and he couldn't prevent them closing while his body sought to preserve what little energy he had left. He drifted in and out of consciousness, no longer able to react to the bullets that were ricocheting all around him. It was almost with a sense of peace, he finally let himself drift off, the sound of the battle faded into the distance and he was sure he could see his grandmother smiling at him.

****

Brunete, Spain

Annie wiped her hand across her weary face. Casualties were pouring in faster than the nurses and doctors were able to deal with them. Some had died before they even reached the assessment stage and their bodies were piling up outside, decomposing quickly, their stench attracting swarms of flies in the intense heat.

The doctors trying to assess the steady flow of injured men finally noticed. "You lot?" One of them pointed to some men who weren't seriously wounded. "Get some shovels and start burying the bodies before we end up with a typhus epidemic."

The men grumbled amongst themselves but the threat of typhoid was more than enough to galvanise them into action and they started digging large pits into which they pitched the hundreds of bodies.

****

Bydgoszcz, Northern Poland

Raisa pulled on her clothes and stared at Iwan in fear. He was watching her, a speculative expression on his face and she wished she was anywhere but in a deserted wood with him. She'd planned on letting him taking her virginity and then telling Felcia her husband had raped her. But she couldn't tell anyone what he'd done to her. It was too horrific.

Iwan was struggling to control his rage. He couldn't believe he'd been stupid enough to fall for Raisa's tricks. Now he was using his brain again, he could see Raisa had planned to use his infidelity to hurt Felcia and, because he was so weak, he'd given her all the ammunition she needed. Or perhaps not… From the look on her face she'd obviously not been expecting him to do what he'd done. Maybe he could use that to his advantage and take back control of the situation.

"Obviously you won't be telling Felcia about this? 'Just between us,' I think you said?" Somehow he managed to inject some irony into his voice and she could hear the sarcasm.

Raisa shook her head. "No, I won't tell Felcia, or anyone." She shuddered at the very thought of having to articulate what he'd done to her and tried to stop the tears falling. "I don't understand why… how… how could you do that to me?"

Iwan stared at her in amusement. "I thought I explained while I was fucking you." He glanced down at his penis which, much to his surprise, was growing hard again at the memory. He reached down and touched himself. "I could show you again, if you like?"

Raisa shrank away in fear. Iwan breathed a sigh of relief. His main concern was to protect his wife. On the other hand, she still didn't want sex, so he might as well make the most of her sister's kind offer. He grinned. "I think we should make this a regular thing, don't you?" He ignored her gasp of horror. "I'll help you get a small apartment in the main town, then I can visit whenever I feel like something different. That way we both get what we want. We'll have a look tomorrow night on the way home from work. You can tell Felcia tonight that you've got an advance on your wages and I'm going to help you find somewhere tomorrow." He glanced at his watch. "Now get in the car. We're going to be late and I don't want Felcia to worry about us."

Raisa stared at him and didn't move. He took a step towards her and she turned and hurried back to the car. She couldn't work out how everything had suddenly gone so terribly wrong and she had no idea what she could do to take back control. Iwan stared through the windscreen and wondered what on earth he'd done. He'd only suggested finding her somewhere to live to get his own back on her, but now he thought about it, getting Raisa out of the house as soon as possible would be the best way of making sure she didn't have the chance to ruin his marriage.

****

The Battle of Brunete, Spain

The voice close to Rob's ear made him start violently and his heart began to pound wildly against his chest.

"Come on, Rob, you have to drink, mate. No point coming all this way to go and die, is there?"

Rob struggled to open his eyes, wondering if he was dreaming.

The water again trickled between his parched lips and gradually he began to feel slightly better. His head was still pounding but his brain seemed to be working again. He opened his eyes properly and looked at the filthy, dishevelled, unshaven face staring anxiously into his own.

"Mike?" His voice was hoarse and so quiet, even he couldn't hear it, so he repeated the question.

Mike nodded, relieved he appeared to have got there just in time. "What on earth are you doing here?" He didn't give Rob a chance to answer. "I heard someone was asking for me."

"I thought you might need a hand." Rob gave a wry smile. His voice sounded nothing like normal. He cleared his throat and tried again. "Has it been like this ever since you got here?" he indicated the devastation all around

"No, this started off well. We were actually winning." Rob could hear the cynicism in his voice. Mike smiled and changed the subject. "I'm really pleased to see you, Rob, although you've only just caught me as I was thinking of going home."

The irony of Mike's words hit Rob and he began to laugh hysterically, not stopping until he started to cough violently. Seeing Mike's shocked look, he attempted a smile

"It's alright, I'm not mad, not yet anyway. I'm just pleased to see you."

Mike nodded, although he didn't look too convinced. When he had first seen Rob lying prone on the ground, he had thought he was too late. The tall man with dirty blond hair and cloudy blue eyes standing next to him spoke quickly to him and Mike nodded before turning his attention back to Rob.

"This is Gerhard. Come on, we need to get out of the firing line or those bastards'll get us."

****

Bydgoszcz, Northern Poland

Felcia watched her sister and husband and wondered what was wrong. There was definitely an atmosphere between them.

"Is everything alright?"

Iwan looked confused. "Of course, darling. Why?"

Felcia shrugged. "I don't know. I thought maybe you and Raisa might have had a row?"

Iwan laughed. "I can't think what's given you that idea, can you, Raisa?"

Raisa shook her head and forced herself to smile. "No, Felcia. There's nothing wrong, honestly. I'm just a bit tired." She stepped closer and lowered her voice, whispering, "The time of the month."

"Oh." Felcia nodded, a knowing expression on her face. One of the lovely things about being pregnant was not having to go through that every month. "Why don't you have an early night?"

Raisa gave a sigh of relief. She wasn't sure she could bear to sit there all evening and pretend everything was fine. "Yes, I think I will."

She turned around and started to head towards the door when Iwan spoke. "You've forgotten your good news."

For a moment Raisa didn't know what he was talking about. All she could think of was how he'd abused her. Then she remembered. She took a deep breath and turned back towards Felcia. "Iwan's right. I was feeling so ill, I'd forgotten all about it. I've been given an advance on my wages, so I'm going into town to look for a flat of my own after work tomorrow. Iwan said he would help. I was hoping you'd like to come too? We could pick you up after work and all go together." Raisa kept her eyes on her sister. At least if Felcia came she would be safe. She didn't dare look at Iwan, guessing he would be furious.

"That's a very good idea, Raisa. What do you think, Felcia?" Iwan hid his anger well.

Felcia glanced from one to the other and smiled. "I'd love to. We can have a meal out. It'll be lovely."

Raisa leaned across and kissed her sister. "Goodnight. I'll see you in the morning."

"Goodnight. I hope you feel better." Felcia was already much happier. With Raisa in her own place, she and Iwan could get back to normal and he would stop treating her like some kind of prostitute.

Iwan moved aside to let Raisa pass. With Felcia watching them there was no opportunity to say anything to her. Never mind, he'd remind her who was in charge tomorrow.

****

Berlin

Karin lay still waiting for Andreas to finish. He'd come home early and insisted they go to bed. The irony almost made her smile. She'd waited years for him to show her more attention and now he was, she was no longer interested. On the other hand, there was a chance he might make her pregnant, so she'd tried to pretend a passion that wasn't there any more. She still hadn't told Claudia her plan, because every time they met they ended up enjoying themselves so much the idea always slipped her mind. She was sure Claudia would agree but she didn't want to risk spoiling things between them.

Andreas finally grunted and rolled off her, panting loudly. He patted her arm, rolled over, closed his eyes and almost immediately fell asleep. Within moments, his loud snores filled the room.

Karin didn't move. She wanted the toilet but she knew she should try and lay still for as long as possible to maximise her chances of becoming pregnant. Her thoughts turned to Claudia and a smile crossed her lips. She was still having trouble accepting that, not only was she was madly in love, but she was in love with a woman. The biggest danger was Andreas or Hans finding out. She shivered. Andreas would just stop her seeing Claudia, especially if he knew what she was planning. Hans on the other hand… Her brother would never understand. She would just have to make sure he never found out.

****

The Battle of Brunete, Spain

Mike and Gerhard had helped Rob up onto his feet and half dragged, half supported him towards the relative safety of their trench where he'd collapsed gratefully and drunk some more water. He was starting to feel a little better.

"I can't believe I've actually found you, well you've found me. I was beginning to think I had no chance. When Annie suggested we come over here so I could look for you, I was over the moon. I never dreamt it would be so difficult though, or I might have had second thoughts."

Mike was staring at him in disbelief. Perhaps he'd misheard.

"Did you say 'when Annie said we should come over'?"

Rob nodded. "Yes, sorry, didn't I say? Annie's over here too. She came with me."

Mike shook his head, unable to believe his friend had been so thoughtless. "You have to be joking. What the hell were you thinking of?" He clenched his fists and struggled to resist the temptation to grab Rob by the throat. He was still recovering after all. He took a deep breath. "Where is she?"

"I don't know." Rob shrugged. "The last time I saw her, she said she was going to help with the nursing. I think she was going to Madrid…" He tailed off when he saw the exchange of glances between Mike and Gerhard and, for the first time since he'd left Annie, he felt uneasy. He sat up and grabbed his friend's shirt. "What's the matter?" He was suddenly panic stricken something might have happened to Annie.

Mike hesitated. "Some of the doctors came out to visit us with a couple of the nurses. Their truck took a direct hit on its way back to the village they were using as a front line emergency hospital." He saw the expression on Rob's face and, although he was still angry, he hastened to reassure him. "There's no reason to suppose it was her. She's probably fine, but… it's not been a picnic for them out here, you know. The fascists regularly target the hospitals; several women have been killed." Mike didn't want to cause his friend unnecessary pain but he was furious Rob had so carelessly risked Annie's life by bringing her out to a war zone.

Rob stared at his friend in horror. He was beside himself with worry. He had given little thought to Annie over the past few weeks, assuming she was safe behind the lines doing whatever it was the women did, wiping a few brows, holding men's hands, something like that. Now he had to face the fact that he didn't know where she was, or even if she was still alive. Together with the fear and worry was a growing sense of guilt and self-loathing that, if anything had happened to her, he would be to blame. He knew she had only offered to come because he was too weak to make a decision, but he'd ignored that and let her put her life at risk, because it was easier for him than having to choose.

****

Brunete, Spain

Annie stared at the latest casualties and wondered whether it would ever end. She was so tired, she could no longer think clearly and she spent most of her time tending to the wounded in a kind of daze.

Whenever an English casualty came in, she always asked whether they knew Rob or Mike but no one ever did and she began to despair of ever seeing either of them again.

"There's lots of dead, miss, all over the battle grounds without graves and no one knows who they are." The injured man was in too much pain to think much about what he was saying. He was still in shock and unaware of the horror his words were having on the young woman nursing him.

Annie gasped and tried to concentrate on cleaning the blood from his wound so the doctor could remove the bullet. But all she could think of was Rob lying dead in a field somewhere and tears streamed down her cheeks.

"Annie, are you alright?" Leila was by her side, concern on her face.

Annie sniffed and then nodded. "Yes, sorry. I'm just tired, that's all." She couldn't bear to repeat what the man had said, in case it made it happen.

"Do you want to take a break?" Leila glanced around at the growing number of casualties, wondering how they would cope if Annie stopped for any length of time.

Annie shook her head. "No, I'm fine, honestly. I'll carry on and have a rest when the wounded stop coming in."

Leila breathed a sigh of relief and went back to her own patient. Annie pushed thoughts of Rob out of her mind and began chatting to the next casualty. He was French and, after a brief glance at his wounds, she realised they were too bad to treat. It was only a matter of time before he died. She knew he couldn't understand a word she said, but hopefully the sound of her voice was comforting while he left the world of pain behind.

****

The Battle of Brunete, Spain

Rob sipped the remains of his water, pressed himself back up against the rocks in the faint hope of finding some shade and stared over the edge of the shallow trench in desperation. They had been retreating for over three weeks and it was obvious the Republic was going to suffer a massive defeat. The sweat was dripping off him, stinging his eyes; his face and arms were burning from the constant sun.

"Here, I've managed to get hold of some more water." Mike handed him a couple of water bottles. Rob shook them, delighted to feel the liquid moving around inside, then he frowned. "Where did you get them?"

"Do you really want me to tell you?" Mike was already sipping from one of the bottles, his back to Rob.

Rob shook his head. "No, no I don't." He closed his eyes. The heat was so horrendous, it had already driven some of the men mad with dehydration and sunstroke. He, Mike and Gerhard had been lucky so far. "What's happening out there?" It had been Mike's turn to forage for water while he kept a watch for the ever advancing fascists. Gerhard had gone off in the other direction searching for ammunition and weapons they could use.

"It's total chaos. I found some bodies over there." He indicated vaguely in the direction from which he'd come. "Looked like they killed themselves rather than surrender." Mike sighed and wiped the sweat from his face before continuing, "One of the men I did speak to says there are mutinies in several of the brigades and those who tried to run away were mown down by their own machine guns."

There was silence while Mike recalled the dreadful sight that had met him when he'd approached the battlefield stealthily earlier that day. The dead and the dying of both sides were strewn across the battlefield as far as he could see, the screams and cries of the injured gradually fading as they died where they had fallen. He'd been about to crawl forward on his stomach to try and reach some of the wounded who were quite close when the fascist tanks had appeared over the hill.

Mike had ducked back down and withdrawn to the nearest cover, some sparse trees several metres away from the battlefield. He'd waited until the tanks had gone through before venturing back to the field again and then wished he hadn't. The wounded were no longer crying out; they had been run over by the fascist tanks that had powered their way across the battlefield in search of Republican survivors.

He was about to tell Rob what he'd seen when Gerhard slithered down into the trench beside them.

"We have to go now." Gerhard was adamant.

Mike and Rob exchanged glances. "We've not been told to withdraw," Mike said as bullets began bouncing off the arid ground in front of the trench.

Rob interrupted: "We've got no chance here. Gerhard's right. If we stay we'll be massacred."

Mike opened his mouth to argue then, remembering what he'd seen and heard, he changed his mind. They waited for a lull in the machine gun fire before following Gerhard up the steep hill towards some bushes, where they collapsed, panting in the heat.

"There's no time to stop, we have to keep going." Gerhard was already heading towards the surrounding hills. The ground around them was now shaking with explosions and bullets were ricocheting off the hard earth in front of them. Mike and Rob staggered to their feet and, heads down, they began to run, expecting at any moment to be cut down by the vicious machine guns they could hear, or the indiscriminate shelling from the artillery of both sides.

Eventually they reached the relative safety of some thicker shrubs and crouched down behind them. They were safe for the moment.

****

Brunete, Spain

Annie finished her cigarette and stared out at the disturbed ground in front of the hospital. The only indication of the hundreds of men in the unmarked graves in front of her was the increase in flies hovering in the air and the constant smell of rotting flesh that permeated the stifling, shimmering heat of the Spanish summer. She hoped Rob and Mike weren't also buried in unmarked graves somewhere. If they were, she'd never find them.

Food was running out and they were existing on a diet of mouldy bread, coffee and cigarettes. She'd heard that morning that the water cart was unable to get through anymore and they had started to run out of sterilised instruments and, an hour ago, word had reached them the Republicans were in headlong retreat.

Chapter Twenty-nine

Bydgoszcz, Northern Poland

Raisa stared round the apartment in the centre of town and tried to feel happy. She had her independence at last, a reasonably well paid job and her own place, but she had lost control. The plan to ruin her sister's perfect life had failed miserably so far. Iwan came and went when it suited him and she shuddered at the memories.

She had no idea what to say to get rid of him. Her only way out was to tell Felcia what he was doing, but she couldn't do that. Her original plan had always been to play the victim so that Felcia would throw Iwan out and take her sister's side. But if she said anything now, Felcia would want to know why she'd not spoken out earlier. She would never believe Iwan had forced himself on Raisa repeatedly, not for several weeks. She would assume Raisa was having an affair with him and tell her parents. Then Raisa would never be able to go home. She wasn't sure if she wanted to go back, but she did want the choice.

She stared out of the window and tried to summon up the energy to go to work. There were several nice men on the camp, one in particular she liked a lot, but all the time Iwan was visiting her, she couldn't even have a boyfriend. Not only did she never know when he was likely to turn up, he had made it quite clear he had no intention of sharing her with any men from the army camp. She was reasonably sure it wasn't because he was jealous, it was more likely he didn't want anyone finding out about their relationship. She scowled. It hardly qualified as a relationship. She was little more than his possession to do with as he pleased. And what it made it worse was that this was all her own fault.

Her heart sank. She had hoped he would soon lose interest in her but Felcia was nearly five months pregnant now and the baby was beginning to show. Raisa had a horrible feeling Iwan would be coming round even more frequently as her sister grew bigger.

****

Berlin

"Sorry I'm late. And, before you ask, there's nothing wrong, unless you count the antics of the previous king." Carstairs sat down heavily on the park bench, pulled out his pipe and made a big show of cleaning and then filling it.

Franz frowned. "I'm sorry?"

Carstairs sighed. "Hitler's rapturous welcome for Edward and his wife, the former Mrs Simpson, is upsetting quite a few people. Since his abdication, the government is very sensitive to his activities and his unofficial visit to Germany has not gone down very well at all."

Franz nodded. He'd just been looking at pictures of the Windsors in his newspaper. "I would imagine photographs of the ex-king making the Nazi salute haven't helped?"

Carstairs shook his head. "No, they haven't. He's never concealed his admiration for Hitler. The man's an egotistical fool." He fell silent.

Franz was about to say he had little information for the Englishman when Carstairs forestalled him. "I've got a favour to ask." He hurried on before Franz could answer: "Can you hold one of your evenings and invite the Windsors along? We think Hitler and his cronies are planning something and Edward is either too stupid to see it, or arrogant enough to go along with it."

Franz stared at the pictures of the pair in the newspaper and nodded. "I'll do my best. Do you know what's being planned?"

Carstairs shook his head. "No, but Edward is a loose cannon. He doesn't really have a position any more, so he could be open to any suggestions about reinstating him."

Franz couldn't keep the astonishment off his face. "But the British wouldn't allow that…" He let out a big sigh. "Ah… you mean if there's another war?" The question of another war was a frequent topic of conversation between the two men.

Carstairs nodded. "Since Hitler got away with re-arming the Rhineland with little opposition, there is a school of thought that it's only a matter of time before he tries something else."

Franz nodded. "I agree, but my money is on Czechoslovakia. He's already complaining about the treatment of the German population in the Sudetenland."

"But will the rest of the world let him walk over the Czechs?" The question hung in the air between the two men before Carstairs banged his pipe on the bench to settle the tobacco and then struggled to light it in the wind. Finally succeeding, he stood up and walked off, leaving Franz staring at the newspaper and wondering who he knew who could either get him an invitation to meet the British ex-King and his wife, or convey his invitation to them to attend an evening at his house.

****

Santander, Spain

"We can't keep this up much longer." Mike threw down his useless rifle and stared up at the cloudless skies above him.

"I think we need to accept the fascists are going to win." Gerhard sounded dispirited, his eyes closed, his face filthy from weeks of fighting.

Rob sighed. He knew Gerhard was right. The Republicans were too busy fighting amongst themselves and lacked the equipment to ever defeat the fascists. He was already sickened by the rumours that had reached them of atrocities by both sides after the Battle of Brunete. According to the stories, three hundred Republican soldiers who'd been surrounded and taken prisoner had been found dead with their legs cut off, and four hundred Moroccan soldiers who'd been fighting with the fascists had been taken prisoner and shot.

The Republicans had little time to recover before the Nationalists began a new offensive in the north at Santander. Rob, Mike and Gerhard had been fighting a defensive battle for over ten days and the writing was on the wall. All the passion and determination in the world was not going to help the Republicans hold out much longer.

"So what do we do?"

The question went unanswered for a few minutes until Rob spoke up first: "I can't leave without finding Annie and my best chance of finding her is to stay and fight."

Mike nodded. "Same goes for me, I suppose. I can hardly go home without you both, not when you've come all this way to find me."

"Thanks Mike, but this is my mess. You didn't bring Annie over, I did. I'll quite understand if you want to go back."

Mike shook his head. "No chance. You'd never manage without me anyway!"

Rob grinned and tried hard not to show his relief that Mike was not going to leave him on his own.

Gerhard smiled. "I've nothing to hurry back to. The bastards are running my country, so I'm probably safer here."

Rob was about to express his gratitude when a shell landed in front of their trench showering them in clods of hard earth and filling the air around them with choking dust. The conversation forgotten, the three men peered through the clouds of smoke and began firing at the shapes running towards them.

****

Berlin

"I wanted to ask for your help." Karin felt unaccountably nervous. She'd been seeing Claudia for several months now, but it had taken her this long to pluck up her courage.

Claudia stared at her in surprise. Karin sound anxious. "What is it, Karin? You know you can ask me anything?"

Karin took a deep breath. "I want a child, but I can't get pregnant. We've been trying for years." She stood up and walked over to the side of the large window. She was careful not to stand in front of it in case she was seen. "I wondered… that is, I was hoping you could get pregnant and then I could adopt the child." She risked a glance around and then breathed a sigh of relief. Claudia was smiling.

"Of course, Karin." She frowned. "But I've been sleeping with Andreas for months and not fallen. Perhaps the fault is with him?"

Karin nodded. "I think it might be but I can't say that to him, can I?"

Claudia stood up and put her arms around Karin. "You poor thing. It must be terrible for you. I take it you've been to the doctors?"

Karin nodded. "Yes. To start with he said there was absolutely nothing wrong with me and it was probably my anxiety that was preventing me. Then he stopped saying anything. Even he wasn't prepared to say it might be Andreas' fault."

Claudia thought for a few moments. "What if I can't get pregnant either?"

Karin shrugged. "I don't know. I suppose I'll have to give up." She sighed. "I was going to have an affair to see if I could get pregnant that way." She felt Claudia gasp. "But then I met you and I couldn't face it."

"Well, leave it with me for a while and let's see what happens. We don't know which one of you it is, so I'll make sure to time things right for a couple of months and then we can have a re-think if necessary."

Karin breathed a sigh of relief. "Thank you. I knew you'd understand. I should have asked before."

Claudia hugged her, her mind elsewhere. Despite what she'd said to Karin, Claudia had never really bothered about dates and precautions in the past. From what Karin had said, though, there was little doubt Andreas couldn't have children, but maybe Hans could. He was still seeing her intermittently, although he was always careful not to risk impregnating her. In fact he'd made it very clear that, if she got pregnant, he would make sure she disappeared into one of the correction camps. The threat was enough to terrify her. She didn't doubt for one moment that he would keep his word. She wondered briefly why he was so opposed to having children: most SS men wanted to father as many as possible to show how virile they were. Maybe he just didn't want one with her.

Claudia gave a mental shrug. If Andreas couldn't get her pregnant she would have to try Hans, whatever the risk. She loved Karin and would do almost anything for her. But at the thought of fooling Hans, her heart skipped a beat and she felt cold. Then she pulled herself together. There was no reason for Hans or Karin to ever know the child was his, if she was careful with her dates. Andreas would probably be delighted to think he'd fathered a child and at least he or she would come from the same family.

****

Berlin

"You've done an amazing job." Franz kissed Hannah quickly on the forehead. "I never thought you'd pull it off in such a short time."

Hannah sighed. "It wasn't easy but I'm glad you're pleased." She frowned. She'd been watching and listening to the Windsors while they met various high-ranking Nazis and she was quite disappointed. "I heard she was supposed to be very witty and sophisticated but, to be honest, I think she's just very full of herself."

Franz didn't have to ask who she meant. He shrugged. He'd actually found the Duchess quite interesting, but he was a man. She had a reputation and was quite flirtatious, something that wasn't endearing her to the majority of the women in the room. He didn't want to upset his wife though, not when she'd gone to all this trouble for him. "Well if you're married to a king and he's given up his throne for you, I suppose you're bound to be a little arrogant." He lowered his voice.

"They fit in very well, don't they? Hitler must be over the moon about this little propaganda coup."

"Shhh!" Hannah glanced around in alarm but no one was within earshot. She was about to ask why Franz had been so determined to host the Windsors when she changed her mind. She had a feeling Franz wasn't just trying to ensure their son's safety. Several times she had caught the end of strange conversations which Franz didn't explain to her satisfaction. She always knew when he was lying to her but, for once, she didn't mind too much. It was probably safer not to know.

"Your Highness." She realised Edward was standing in front of her.

"I just wanted to thank you again for such a lovely party. It was very kind of you to invite us." He gave her the full benefit of his charm and Hannah found herself responding.

Franz hid a smile. His wife obviously wasn't completely immune to the charms of royalty then. He left his wife talking to the Duke and wandered off to refresh his drink, his mind on other things. Andreas and his wife and her brother were talking to the Duchess, who was flirting outrageously with Andreas. Franz watched Karin for a few moments, surprised she didn't seem bothered by the obvious attentions of the Duchess, but she was staring into the distance, a thoughtful expression on her face. Only a few months earlier, Karin would have been seething with jealousy. He wondered what had changed. He frowned. Talking of change, he wondered if there was any truth to the rumours he'd heard that morning. He only hoped that was all they were.

****

Bydgoszcz, Northern Poland

Iwan drove through the light snow shower, arrived at Raisa's apartment and let himself in. He'd intended to find her somewhere to live and then leave her alone. His main reason for finding her alternative accommodation had been to get her away from Felcia so she couldn't ruin his marriage. But something about sneaking into town to see her was addictive, that and the sex which was completely unlike the love making he had with Felcia. Then, as Felcia had grown bigger and had less interest in making love with him, his visits to her sister had increased.

Raisa came out of the bedroom, pulling her dressing gown around her as she shivered in the cold unheated hallway. She glared at him. "What if Felcia's taken ill while you're here?"

Iwan shrugged. "It's not like you to worry about your sister. Don't tell me you're developing a conscience?"

Raisa sighed and began undoing the dressing gown. Iwan smiled. "That's better. You should be pleased to see me, you must get bored here on your own all the time."

She turned to go back in the bedroom but he grabbed her arm. "No, I think we'll do it here tonight. Take off your clothes and kneel down."

Raisa hesitated then quickly did as he asked. She knelt down and reached for the buttons on his trousers but he pushed her hands away. Instead he picked up her dressing gown and pulled off the cord. He took her hands and then shoved them behind her back and tied them together. He took her chin in one hand and stroked her hair with the other. She really was very beautiful with her high cheek bones, flushed cheeks and generous mouth. Felcia was also beautiful but in a more innocent way. His enduring fantasy since the first time with Raisa was to have them both together. He could feel his penis straining uncomfortably against his trousers and he undid the buttons himself, his eyes on her face. As he reached the last button he pulled her closer so when his erection sprung free, his penis hit her in the face.

Raisa opened her mouth and begun sucking. Maybe she could make him climax in her mouth instead, then he wouldn't want to do the other thing.

Iwan closed his eyes and smiled. He knew what she was trying to do and he had no intention of missing out. He'd finally persuaded Felcia to suck his penis, although he had to admit Raisa was much better than her sister, who only performed under protest. He wondered what it would be like to have them both together and then pushed the thought away. He didn't want to get there too quickly. No, he was here because he'd become addicted to anal sex and that was one thing he couldn't get at home.

****

Front line outside Madrid

As the weather changed and winter arrived, Annie found herself moved from hospital to hospital, outpost to outpost. The names of the villages changed but the streams of wounded, the inadequate facilities and ever present stench of the dead and dying didn't. It was like her very own hell and, having witnessed so much death and destruction, she no longer realistically expected to see or hear from Rob and Mike again, although she couldn't quite bring herself to believe they were dead.

She thought about home a lot and wondered how her parents were. She knew she should have written to them but she'd kept waiting until she could tell them something nice. Unfortunately there was never a good time; things just became worse and, the longer she left it, the harder it was to pick up a pen and write.

There was also a part of her that didn't want to admit that coming to Spain had been a catastrophic mistake. She should have listened to her instincts but instead she'd allowed her love for Rob to influence her into making a disastrous decision. If Rob was dead it would be her fault. If she'd said nothing, they would probably still be at home enjoying life instead of experiencing this never-ending hell on earth.

Annie sighed heavily and stared out at more approaching casualties streaming in from yet another battlefield. She finished her cigarette, ground out the remains on the earth and wished she could just pack up her few belongings and go home, but she couldn't bring herself to leave her friends or the numerous wounded men that kept pouring in and, in any case, going home would have been tantamount to admitting Rob and Mike were definitely dead. All the time she was in Spain, there was some hope, however remote, so she stayed, always hopeful that today would be the day when Rob would finally appear and take her home.

Chapter Thirty
1938

Bydgoszcz, Northern Poland

Iwan stared down at his baby son, cradled in his arms and gave a smile of relief and happiness. "He's so beautiful, Felcia. He looks just like you." He'd been concerned by the screams coming from the bedroom and the length of time the birth was taking and, for a little while, he wondered if he was to be punished for his affair with her sister. The baby was a couple of weeks late as well, which had added to his worries, even though Felcia had assured him that the doctor had said first babies often went beyond their term.

Felcia gave a tired smile in return. The labour had been difficult and she was exhausted, but she'd finally given birth to a boy. She reached out for Iwan's hand and squeezed it. Then she looked for Raisa. "Thank you, Raisa. I couldn't have done it without you."

Raisa looked embarrassed but she leant forward and kissed Felcia before moving towards the door. "The midwife did most of it. He's lovely, Felcia. I hope you'll all be very happy."

She placed her hand on the door handle and then turned back. Iwan was gazing at his son, one hand holding Felcia's. She was forgotten.

"I'll go and telephone our parents." She didn't wait for an answer. She was hoping the good news and the passage of time would help Wiktor to forgive her and that he would let her return home. It was the only way she could think of to escape Iwan.

****

River Alfambra, Spain

"I've written home." Mike took a deep drag of his last cigarette. They were sitting in a deep trench trying to ignore the shelling and intermittent rifle fire echoing around the hills. It was bitterly cold and they knew it wouldn't be long before they were given the order to withdraw yet again. The Republicans had been forced from the city of Teruel by the Nationalist army and Rob, Mike and Gerhard were part of the final defensive line along the right bank of the River Alfambra.

Rob looked horrified. "Did you say anything about Annie?"

Mike nodded. "They have a right to know, Rob. My parents will tell your dad and he'll notify Annie's parents."

"But you'll only worry them unnecessarily. We're bound to find her. It would have been better to wait until we do, then you could have written home." Rob clenched his fists. He couldn't believe Mike had gone behind his back.

"I'm sorry you don't agree, Rob, but I'm not sorry for writing to them." He sighed. "I hadn't written for ages, and I couldn't not tell them I'd found you and then I had to say something about Annie."

Rob was silent. He was still annoyed but he knew that was mainly because he felt so guilty about bringing Annie with him in the first place. It was his fault she was missing, possibly dead and although he would have to live with that, he had been hoping they would find her before he needed to worry her parents even more than they must already be.

"Perhaps you should write to Annie's parents as well?" Mike suggested tentatively.

Rob blanched and he shook his head. "Let's keep looking. If we haven't found her in the next few months, then I'll consider writing to them."

Mike shrugged. He thought Rob was wrong but he could understand why his friend didn't want to write to Annie's parents. In his shoes he wouldn't either.

****

Berlin

"Another letter from the Duke and Duchess? Should I be jealous?" Franz laughed as he handed Hannah the envelope with the royal seal that had just arrived.

Hannah gave a wry smile. "For some reason they seem to like me. It would be very rude not to write back. To be honest, I thought the first one was just a polite letter thanking us for inviting them to that party, but after I replied she kept writing." Hannah laughed. "The letters are from the Duchess, not the Duke, so you don't have anything to be worried about…" She hesitated. "This may sound stupid but I get the impression she's quite lonely really."

Franz snorted. "I doubt she's short of friends, not with all her money."

"Yes, but are they real friends? Let's be honest, Franz," she glanced around to check no one was in earshot, "we've got lots of acquaintances but I wouldn't call any of them friends, would you?"

Franz was about to argue when he realised she was right. None of the numerous people he knew were really friends and he certainly wouldn't trust any of them. He gave a wry smile. "You're right. Well, carry on writing to her. You never know, it might come in useful."

Hannah laughed. "I doubt it, but as I feel sorry for her – yes I know that sounds really stupid but I do, and its only a few moments out of my day – I will keep up the correspondence."

****

Vienna, Austria

Hans and Andreas watched the cheering crowds waving their Swastikas while the German army swept through the city. Andreas and other members of the SS had arrived a few days earlier to ensure there was no visible opposition to Hitler's annexation of Austria.

Hans had been in Vienna for several weeks helping to escalate the tension between the Nazis and other citizens. He scanned the large crowds and then the shops and cafés behind them. Several were closed, their windows broken and the word '*Jude*' scrawled across the brickwork. His men had done well, he was proud of the speed and enthusiasm they had shown while closing up premises owned by Jews and arresting any they found in situ. They had received considerable support from many of the citizens of Vienna in their quest to identify the Jews who lived there and he already had a sizeable list of addresses. He had earmarked several places to visit first and would make a start after the parade finished. In the meantime his job, like that of the other SS present, was to identify members of the crowd who didn't seem rapturously happy at the arrival of the German army. So far he couldn't see any dissenting faces but the day was young and the parade had only just started.

****

Outside Lublin, Eastern Poland

"Does this mean there's going to be another war?" Magda stared at Wiktor with fear in her eyes. It wasn't only her sons she feared for. Felcia had just had a baby; if there was a war, Iwan would also have to go and fight.

Wiktor shook his head, although he looked concerned. "I doubt it. Britain and France aren't interested in fighting another war, but they probably won't put up with Hitler attacking us either, so Germany won't try anything. Hitler is going for easy targets; the Rhineland, Austria, places he knows the British aren't going to argue about too much." He fell silent. Even though he was reasonably sure Britain and France would protect Poland, he couldn't be one hundred percent certain.

"I'm missing our daughters, Wiktor. Can't you forgive Raisa now and let her come home?" Magda had asked him several times and his answer had always been no. "She's behaved herself in Bydgoszcz, and with the news this bad…"

Wiktor sighed. He was enjoying the peace of not having a sulky Raisa at home but he knew Magda was lonely with Felcia living so far away. "Alright, you can tell her to come home. But she has to behave herself. I don't want any more rumours about her. Is that clear?"

Magda beamed at him, the bad news on the wireless temporarily forgotten. "Yes, yes of course. I'll go and write straightaway."

Wiktor watched her hurry out of the room but his mind was not on her or his daughters. He was trying to ignore the uneasy feeling in the pit of his stomach telling him things were going to get much worse.

****

Berlin

"It looks like you were right then." Carstairs spoke out of the corner of his mouth, his eyes constantly scanning the park for signs they were being watched.

"I first heard the rumours back in the summer last year but I wasn't sure how true they were. I wish I'd said something earlier." Franz sounded fed up.

Carstairs hastened to reassure him. "It wouldn't have made any difference, Franz. There's no political will to do anything about Hitler. Most of the British government thought of Austria as a part of Germany anyway, so they were never going to intervene. Hitler is running rings around politicians in Europe and America. Many of them admire him because of the way the German economy had rallied, but they don't see the real picture because they don't want to. No one has the stomach for another war, so Hitler can pretty much do what he wants."

"A depressing thought." Franz sighed. "The situation for Jews is becoming almost intolerable, made worse because the governments of other countries won't take them in. That just validates the Nazis' view of Jews, because they can say everyone else agrees with them."

Carstairs was silent for a few moments. "The camps… are they really as brutal as I've heard?"

Franz shrugged. "Probably worse but no one speaks out because no one wants to end up inside one, me included." He glanced around nervously and cleared his throat. "I think we should find another way of communicating."

"What did you have in mind?" Carstairs wasn't surprised. He'd been wondering the same thing himself.

"Somewhere less public, perhaps?"

He nodded. "I'll give it some thought and then contact you." He hesitated. "I'll make that the last time I telephone you too." He folded his newspaper, stood up and walked off.

Franz breathed a sigh of relief and turned his attention back to his own newspaper. After a few moments he'd had enough of the propaganda and his mind began to wander to other things. It was months since he'd heard from Gerhard and, although he spent much of his time reassuring Hannah their son was alright, he was seriously worried. The winter had not brought the Republicans any success and, even reading between the lines of propaganda, any fool could see that it was only a matter of time before the fascists won. Then what would happen to his son and all the other foreign fighters? He would like to think Franco would let them all go home, but given the way the Nazis behaved in Germany towards those they considered their enemies, he was terrified that wouldn't happen.

****

Outside Lublin, Eastern Poland

Raisa climbed out of her father's ancient truck and breathed a sigh of relief. When she'd received her mother's letter, she'd packed immediately and handed in her notice at work, telling them there was a family emergency. She'd hurried to Felcia's, knowing Iwan was at work and told her she was leaving to return home. To her surprise,

Felcia had looked genuinely sad and Raisa felt a twinge of remorse for her plans to wreck her sister's marriage, but then she remembered what Iwan was doing to her and her guilt vanished. For a brief moment she'd been tempted to tell Felcia what had been going on, but if she did that Felcia would tell her parents and she wouldn't be able to go home and, more than anything, she wanted to get away from her brother-in-law.

From there she went home, collected her belongings and then rushed to the station. She needed to be out of Bydgoszcz before Iwan found out that she was leaving.

Her father had met her in Lublin at the station and, to her relief, had actually seemed pleased to see her.

"Raisa!" Ala came running out, closely followed by Magda. Raisa allowed them to engulf her in their arms and resisted the temptation to cry. She was finally safe.

****

Bydgoszcz, Northern Poland

Iwan flung open the door and strode into the house. Felcia smiled and then frowned at the expression on his face.

"Raisa's handed in her notice. Something about a family emergency?"

Felcia relaxed. Obviously Iwan was worried something had happened to her family and was concerned for her. "There's no emergency; she was just homesick and Tata said she could go home."

Iwan fought to hide the fury flooding his body and forced himself to smile. "Oh, I rushed home because I thought…" He sighed. "Well, as long as everyone's alright." He took a deep breath. "How's my little Mariusz?"

Felcia smiled. "He's asleep, but he'll soon be awake and ready for his feed." On cue, Mariusz began to cry and she sighed.

"Don't move, I'll get him." Iwan headed out of the room and up the stairs. Felcia sat back and waited for him to come back down.

Strangely enough, she was actually missing Raisa. The realisation surprised her and she felt sad. They'd become a lot closer and, although Raisa would never be her best friend, she was glad they had buried the animosity that had always plagued their relationship.

Iwan picked up his baby son and held him close. He was sensible enough to realise it was a good thing Raisa had gone home. They could not have kept their relationship a secret from Felcia indefinitely and he loved his wife and son. Raisa was only ever a temporary diversion. He was just annoyed because she'd made the decision to go and he'd not had any control over it.

Chapter Thirty-one

Berlin

Hans watched Claudia, a speculative expression on his face. "So, are you missing Andreas?" It was early May and he'd returned home to Berlin for a couple of days to sort out some paperwork and, while Andreas was in Austria, he'd taken the opportunity to visit Claudia. It had been a while since he'd seen her, so he was looking forward to taking advantage of Andreas' absence.

Claudia shrugged. "Of course." She kept her eyes lowered, not wanting Hans to read anything in her face that would annoy him. This was the first time she'd been alone with him in ages. It was months since Karin had asked her to get pregnant and, if she was going to get Hans to impregnate her, this was her best chance. She'd tried with Andreas before he left for Austria but without any success, so she could only assume he was infertile, unless it was her of course. But now she had no choice but to try Hans instead. She only hoped Karin would appreciate the sacrifice she was making for her.

"Take off your clothes."

Claudia began to undo the buttons on her blouse.

"Wait!" Hans stepped towards her and she winced. He reached out and ripped her blouse apart before pulling out his dagger.

Claudia blanched and he smiled at the fear on her face. He leaned forward and slit the straps of her bra before running the tip of the blade down her body. Claudia held her breath.

"Turn round and bend over."

Heart pounding, she did as he ordered. Hans lifted her skirt, cut off her knickers with one easy movement and stared at her buttocks. He would have liked nothing better than to use his whip on her but he couldn't afford to mark her. He sighed and looked around for something to beat her with that wouldn't leave any lasting trace. His eyes alighted on her slippers and he picked one up.

Claudia was still bent double, waiting for him to do something. Hans raised the slipper and began pounding her hard. Claudia yelled out in surprise, exciting him even more and he hit her harder until her buttocks were red raw and he could see traces of blood.

Finally satisfied, he forced himself inside her and climaxed almost instantly. Claudia held her breath. She could hear Hans panting heavily, her buttocks were stinging painfully but she didn't care, not as long as she was pregnant.

****

River Ebro, Spain

By late May Rob, Mike and Gerhard found themselves on the move to the River Ebro. Although they had looked for Annie continuously after Brunete, their paths had never crossed and Rob was beginning to despair of ever finding her. The icy cold winter had turned slowly into spring and they were beginning to run out of places to look and people to ask.

Because most of the volunteers did not wear any kind of identification, it was very hard to find out exactly who had been killed. The Spanish battlefields were strewn with the dead of various countries no one had been able to identify and Rob began to fear Annie might be amongst them, lying somewhere in an unmarked grave, never to be found. Every time they passed nurses or doctors, Rob or Mike would ask about her, but to no avail. It was as if she had vanished into thin air.

"We'll find her." Mike patted Rob on the back.

Rob nodded but didn't answer. His guilt over bringing her to Spain was killing him. If only he could find her, he'd ignore the risks of being shot as a deserter, take her home and never let her out of his sight again. He frowned. Perhaps there was another reason they couldn't find her. "Maybe she's gone home already?" The idea had only just occurred to Rob and he stared at Mike.

Mike shrugged. "If she has, there's no way we can find out without going home ourselves and if we do that we won't be able to come back again."

Rob sighed. "Then what do we do?"

"We keep looking." Gerhard joined in the conversation. "The war can't last much longer, so all the time we're still fighting, we keep searching."

"And when we lose?" Even though he was sure they were on their own, Rob had given a wary glance around him before speaking to make sure there were no Soviets present.

"Then we'll probably have no option but to go home." *If we're lucky,* Mike added to himself.

****

Berlin

Andreas let himself into Claudia's flat. He had forty eight hours leave, so he thought he'd surprise her first before going home to Karin. He crept into the bedroom and climbed into bed beside her. Claudia yelled out in terror.

"It's only me. I thought you might be pleased to see me."

"For Christ's sake, Andreas. You nearly gave me a heart attack." Claudia took a deep breath to calm herself down and tried to look pleased.

Andreas sighed. "I'm sorry. I couldn't wait to see you but I suppose it might have been better if I'd woken you first before climbing in."

Claudia grinned. Her heart rate had almost returned to normal. "It's alright, I was just frightened. But I *am* pleased to see you, even if you did try and scare me to death. I've missed you so much. How long do you have?"

Andreas sighed, his hands already pushing the straps of her nightdress off her shoulders. "Only a couple of days…" He kissed her and Claudia relaxed. Now she'd recovered from the shock, this was better than she could possibly have hoped for. Her period was almost a week overdue and she was never normally late so she might already be pregnant. If she was, Andreas probably wouldn't notice the dates and, more importantly, neither would Karin.

****

River Ebro, Spain

A month later the Nationalists had finally broken through the Republican defences and reached the sea. With Franco and the fascists now moving towards Valencia and trying to encircle Madrid, the Republicans prepared for yet another counter attack, this time across the River Ebro. In response to the expected casualties, Annie found herself heading towards the hospital. Much to her surprise, this turned out to be a large cave which at least lessened the danger of being bombed. But the conditions were no better than anywhere else and, after two weeks, they had almost run out of supplies, so the majority of the staff and patients were told to prepare for evacuation across the main bridge over the River Ebro before it was blown up.

Annie and the other nurses were just packing up when a doctor came into the small treatment area.

"We need to get some medical supplies and staff to the other side of the river. There are several wounded men stranded over there. The Germans and Italians are constantly bombarding the pontoon bridges but we have to try. I need some volunteers." The doctor's eyes were bloodshot and red rimmed. He ran a hand over his unshaven face. "I won't pretend it isn't dangerous but…" He shrugged and indicated the shelling carrying on all around them.

"I'll come." Annie spoke without really thinking. She was almost convinced Rob was not coming back, so she had nothing to lose really.

"Me too." Leila raised her hand. Others followed suit and the doctor looked relieved.

"Thank you. We leave at one in the morning. Hopefully they won't see us in the dark. Let's load up what medical supplies we have left now so we're ready to go."

****

Romford, Essex

"Is Ivy in?"

Harold shook his head and stepped back to let Bill come in. He closed the door. "She's gone down the road. Why? Have you heard something?"

Bill shook his head. "Not from Rob, but Mike's dad has had a letter. It's taken a while to get here." He hesitated. "Rob and Mike have somehow survived so far. At least they were okay when the letter was written at the beginning of the year, but…"

"But what?" Harold's heart was pounding… he couldn't lose his little girl. He began praying. *Please God don't let it be bad news*.

Bill took a deep breath. "There's no easy way to say this, Harold. Rob and Annie were separated when they got to Spain. Rob was sent off to join the men and Annie went with the other women to Madrid to nurse in the hospital there."

Harold breathed a little easier. Nursing didn't sound that dangerous and he was sure Madrid hadn't fallen to the fascists. Bill took another breath. "They haven't been able to find her. They've asked everywhere, but no one knows where she is. Mike said she might have been transferred to one of the front line ambulance stations, but so far they've found no sign of her." Bill fell silent. He reached out a hand and placed it on Harold's shoulder. "They won't be coming home until they find her, Harold, or at least find out what's happened to her. Mike was quite clear about that. He was furious with Rob for taking Annie to Spain with him." He stopped. He could see Harold wasn't really listening and Mike's anger was irrelevant: the damage was done.

Harold let out a slow breath. "What do I say to Ivy?"

Bill shrugged. "It's up to you, but it might be better to say nothing. Annie could be perfectly alright."

"And if she's not and I don't warn Ivy…?" Harold leaned back against the wall and closed his eyes.

****

River Ebro, Spain

After a few hours' break in which Annie dozed restlessly, her dreams punctuated by images of Rob calling her, they climbed aboard the ambulances. The doctor checked all the supplies were on board and then gave the order to move out. Although she'd had some sleep, Annie was still exhausted and she was also confused by her dreams.

"Do you think it means Rob is alive after all and looking for me?"

Leila hesitated and Annie gave a wry smile. "It's alright, I'm not serious. I'd like it to mean that, obviously…" She tailed off.

Leila squeezed her hand. "I'm sure he's alive, Annie. Don't give up hope."

Annie nodded but she knew her friend was just being kind.

They left promptly at one, with headlights off, using the light of the moon to see the rough road and, for a short while, made good progress. They had just crossed the river when they heard the sound of a plane above them. The drivers hastened towards some trees and pulled up. Annie and Leila held hands and prayed they hadn't been seen.

"It's alright, it's only a spotter plane," the driver yelled after a few moments.

"If they saw us, they'll be back." One of the other drivers shouted back. "We'd better get out of here."

They speeded up and the ambulances careered around the sharp bends on the rock strewn road, rolling and jolting dangerously at the unaccustomed speed. Taken by surprise, Annie was flung to the floor, banging her leg on one of the empty stretchers.

"Are you hurt?"

Annie shook her head. "No, nothing broken, only bruised. Can you help me up? I think we should hang onto something before the driver kills us both!"

Leila helped her up and the two girls grabbed the straps on either side of the vehicle and closed their eyes. The evasive manoeuvres were to no avail. Twenty-five minutes later, they heard the ominous droning of several aircraft. Annie peered out of the ambulance window nearest her into the dark night sky and, to her horror, saw a dozen bombers outlined against the stars. The aeroplanes were heading in their direction.

The drivers had also seen them. The ambulances braked and they pulled hurriedly into the nearest olive grove. Annie and the other nurses climbed out quickly and helped to camouflage the ambulances. Once they'd finished, they threw themselves under the trees and bushes. They were only just in time. The bombers dived towards them and began repeatedly bombing and strafing the area where they were hiding. Annie put her hands over her head and prayed they would survive the relentless onslaught.

The shelling continued for some time as the aeroplanes bombed the river, the road and the crossroads, anywhere they thought the ambulances might be hiding. Annie tried to think of something else but the noise was so awful she couldn't concentrate.

Eventually the planes flew away and there was silence. Annie and Leila crept slowly out into the open, relieved to find no one was hurt.

"We might as well eat." The doctor indicated the small clearing and Annie sat down next to her friend and began eating her share of the bully beef and bread which was all that was left of their supplies. Eating suddenly reminded her of the oranges she had seen the young girls giving the soldiers at the station just after she'd arrived. She shook her head. That day seemed such a long time ago now and, in terms of experience, was another lifetime. She could hardly remember the young naive girl she had been then.

"Everyone finished?"

There were murmurs of assent and then they all climbed back aboard the ambulances. It would be light soon and they wanted to put as much distance between them and the river as they could. Hopefully the pilots would forget all about them, or decide they were probably a long way away.

They finally reached Santa Magdalen in the early afternoon and began to set up the hospital in a white hermitage set high up in the hills. It was late evening before they finished and, almost instantly, the wounded started to stream in, both civilians and soldiers, many suffering from injuries they had received days ago.

****

Outside Lublin, Eastern Poland

"I'm worried about Raisa."

Wiktor glanced up from his newspaper and stared at his wife. "Why?"

"Haven't you noticed that she's barely left the house since she came home?"

Wiktor shrugged. "I'm glad she's learned her lesson. She's probably just worried we might change our minds and send her away if we think she's up to her old tricks again."

Magda shook her head. "I don't think that's the problem at all. Well, it might be some of it, but there's something else. Maybe something happened while she was in Bydgoszcz."

Wiktor frowned. "Like what? I'm sure Felcia would have told us if there were any problems. I think you're worrying about nothing." He turned the page of his newspaper and carried on reading. Magda sighed. The conversation was obviously over, but she was sure Wiktor was wrong.

Chapter Thirty-two

En route to Flix, Spain

For several days they worked flat out in the hospital while the fascists bombed all the roads and bridges around them, preventing any further supplies getting through. Food, medicines and water were desperately short and they had no means of sterilising and sharpening their instruments. Operations had to be carried out with blunt implements and under local anaesthetic, yet still they persevered. Then the artillery turned their guns towards them and began pounding the hospital with shells. Eventually, after days of intermittent shelling, the decision was finally made to evacuate.

The staff and wounded left the hospital in total darkness and drove for ten kilometres without any lights because the road was under constant artillery fire. The shelling and bombing was so commonplace now that, other than ducking and occasionally covering her ears, Annie more or less ignored it, worried more about her patients than her own safety.

"It won't be long now…" She wiped the brow of one of her patients, a young man with serious leg wounds who whimpered with pain every time the ambulance swerved to avoid a shell. He gave her a grateful smile and opened his mouth to reply when the ground suddenly shook, an enormous explosion rent the air, the ambulance swerved violently and came to a shuddering halt.

****

River Ebro, Spain

The fighting was more intense than ever, the fascists gradually pushing them back towards the river where they would be trapped.

"They've given the order to withdraw." Mike had to yell to make himself heard. They'd spent much of the morning cowering in the trench hoping not to be hit by the continual bombing raids. The fascist Condor Legion had almost complete control of the skies now and every day the Republicans lost more ground.

Rob needed no urging to withdraw, his enthusiasm for fighting had long since gone. If it hadn't been for Annie, he would have risked being shot as a deserter and tried to go home. But Annie had come to Spain because of him, he couldn't just abandon her. He knew there was an increasing likelihood that she was dead but until he knew for certain, he was stuck. He'd suggested several times that Mike and Gerhard should go, but neither would leave without him. Much as he appreciated their support, and being here without them would have been even worse, their loyalty was only adding to his guilt.

****

En route to Flix, Spain

Annie climbed up off the floor, made sure she was not injured at all, automatically checked her patient was still strapped in and then edged gingerly towards the back doors of the ambulance. Pushing them open, she climbed down the step onto the road. At first she couldn't see anything; everything behind her seemed undamaged. She moved around the door and stared ahead. Her hand flew to her mouth and then she was rushing forward. "Leila! Leila!"

The ambulance in front was burning fiercely. Even as she ran towards it, she knew everyone inside would be dead but she still carried on screaming.

"There's nothing you can do." The hand gripped her arm, preventing her from going any closer.

"No, you don't understand, my friend… my friend…" She sobbed loudly while struggling against whoever was holding her.

"She wouldn't have known anything. It was too quick." The voice continued to try and offer her comfort but Annie was distraught. Leila had been by her side since she'd arrived in Spain.

"She can't be dead, she can't be." She kept repeating the words as if that would make them true.

"I'm so sorry, Annie, but she is and if we stay here much longer, we will be too. We have to move and you have to go back to your patients." He released his grip and Annie stared up into the weary face of the young doctor who'd asked for volunteers. She was vaguely surprised he knew her first name and she was about to say so when she heard the ominous drone of aircraft in the distance. Her face paled and, turning away, she rushed back to her own ambulance which was just starting up.

****

Outside Lublin, Eastern Poland

"Is anything the matter, Raisa?" Magda sat down on her daughter's bed and stared up at her.

Raisa shook her head. "No, why?"

"You just seem very quiet." Magda couldn't think of any other way of putting it.

Raisa shrugged. "I'm fine, Mama, honestly. Actually I thought I'd go into Lublin tomorrow to see if there's any work."

Magda breathed a sigh of relief. Perhaps Wiktor was right after all.

"Good. Why don't you take Ala with you?"

"I was going to ask her if she'd like to come with me." Raisa smiled at her mother and hoped she sounded convincing. The last thing she needed was her mother writing to Felcia and asking if something had happened while she was in Bydgoszcz.

"Is there anything you'd like to send to Felcia. I'm thinking of going to visit her and Mariusz in the next few days."

Raisa somehow managed to remain expressionless. "Oh, that's good. I was thinking of getting a teddy bear for Mariusz tomorrow when I'm in Lublin. I was going to post it but if you're visiting, could you take it with you?"

Magda smiled. "Of course I can. Remind me in the morning and I'll give you some money towards it."

****

Flix, Spain

They approached Flix as dawn finally broke and the sun rose majestically into a clear blue sky, lighting up the surrounding hills and fields. Annie stared out of the ambulance window but the view failed to register. Her young patient had died a few moments earlier and she could still hear bombs dropping and see the burning ambulance Leila was in.

"What about that?" The doctor was already climbing out of the ambulance in front and running over to take a look at something. Annie watched him with little interest.

"This'll do." His voice carried clearly in the early morning air. Annie focused on him and sighed. It was a large tunnel. She shrugged and began to unpack her supplies. At least they would be safe from the bombing. She informed the doctor that her patient had died and then joined the others as they stumbled over the derelict railway lines trying to find the best place to set up an operating theatre.

There was no time to mourn her friend. They didn't even stop to eat or to rest. Cold, hungry and tired, they dug, scrubbed and scraped away the years of accumulated soot and grime from the walls. Eventually satisfied, they sat down and ate what was left of their mouldy bread and drank the remains of the very weak coffee. Before they had even finished eating, the wounded began to arrive.

Annie wondered briefly how the casualties always seemed to know the field hospital was there within minutes of their arrival, then she was too busy to think as all her attention was needed for her new patients. Of all the primitive facilities Annie had worked in over the past few months, this tunnel was the most basic. There was no lighting system and only one oil lamp which had to light three operating tables. After two days, the few remaining candles ran out and so did the oil lamp. Further operations, injections and all other procedures were done by the light of matches.

The only thing they did have in abundance was water, which at least meant they could wash daily. Keeping clean went some way to restoring Annie's morale, ridding her of the head and body lice that had been driving her mad. But she didn't remain clean for long, because every time a bomb dropped directly on top of the tunnel, she was showered in soot and dust from the roof and walls of the tunnel.

It was another night in which the bombs had dropped relentlessly and the stream of wounded seemed never ending. As dawn broke, Annie emerged exhausted into the sunlight and walked the short distance to the river. The fascist aeroplanes were often absent in the early morning and she was looking forward to soaking in the fresh clean water of the river. She undressed down to her underwear, left her clothes on the bank and slipped into the cool inviting water. The river washed over her, cleansing and relaxing and she closed her eyes and wondered whether she would ever see Rob or Mike again, or even if she would survive another day.

Chapter Thirty-three

Berlin

The early morning July sun shone brightly through the apartment window but Karin had a feeling it was more than the advent of summer that was putting the smile on her lover's face. "I have some news for you." Despite her elation, Claudia still glanced around nervously, even though the flat was empty, apart from Karin.

"You're pregnant?" Karin's eyes lit up.

Claudia smiled. "It's very early days, Karin, but yes, I am."

Karin nodded, leaned forward and hugged her lover. She could hardly believe it. "When is the baby due?"

"Not until late January, early February."

Karin sighed and Claudia laughed. "It's not that long, Karin. I was going to wait until I was further along but I wanted you to know."

Karin shook her head. "Its not that, Claudia." She fell silent.

"What's the matter? I thought you'd be pleased." Claudia sounded worried.

Karin shook her head. "I am. You've no idea how happy. But this proves the problem lies with me, not Andreas."

****

Vienna, Austria

Hans grinned at Andreas. They were seated at a table by the window in one of the city's bars looking out at the population hurrying about their business in the summer sunshine. Andreas struggled to hide his boredom. He would rather be in Berlin with Claudia, who'd just told him she was pregnant. He was over the moon that he'd finally managed to make one of his women pregnant but he was wondering how to tell Karin. He knew she blamed him for her inability to have a child, so this would come as a shock to her. Andreas didn't want to upset Karin unnecessarily, but secretly he was delighted that he was finally vindicated. He would just have to make sure he hid his real feelings and didn't let her see the triumph he felt. He wondered how she would take the news. She seemed to quite like Claudia, so perhaps she wouldn't take it too badly. He glanced sideways at Hans who was clearly relishing his power over a subjugated people. He had a feeling his brother-in-law might not be very happy to hear Andreas had got his mistress pregnant. A few years ago, this wouldn't have worried him, but Hans was a rising star in the SS and it might not be a very good idea to upset him too much.

Andreas was about to suggest they should leave when Hans frowned and began staring out of the window.

"What is it?" Andreas twisted around in his seat to see what had caught his friend's attention but Hans had already stood up and was striding towards the door.

Curious, Andreas followed him.

"You! Jew! What are you doing walking on the pavement?"

The man turned slowly towards him. Andreas took in the long beard and glasses and the fear in the man's eyes. He sighed. He couldn't really see the point of hounding Jews, even though it was official Nazi policy.

"I'm sorry, sir." The man stepped into the road and turned back to continue on his way, but that wasn't enough for Hans.

"Come back here."

"Me, sir?" The man took a tentative step towards Hans.

Andreas could hear the terror in the man's voice and felt sick. He touched his friend's arm. "Come on, Hans, let's go back to our drinks."

Hans shrugged off his hand and leant towards the man. "Your name?"

"Doctor Saul Liebovitz."

"Well, Herr Doctor, you know you aren't supposed to walk on the pavements, don't you?"

The doctor lowered his head. "I'm sorry, sir. I forgot."

Hans shook his head and leant forward. "Not good enough, Doctor. Give me your glasses."

The doctor shook his head. "Sir, I'm sorry but if you take my glasses I won't be able to see."

"If you don't hand them over to me straight away, you won't be needing them." Hans held out his hand.

Terrified, the doctor removed them carefully and placed them in the SS officer's outstretched hand.

Hans clenched his fist until there was the sound of breaking glass, then he opened his fingers, dropped the remains of the spectacles on the ground and trod hard on them with his boot.

"Get on your knees and eat them."

Andreas gasped. "Hans…"

"Shut up, Andreas, unless you want me to report you for helping Jewish scum."

Andreas was about to protest when he realised there was nothing he could do. If he continued, Hans would have him arrested and carry on torturing the Jewish doctor anyway. He turned away. Behind him he heard the sound of a struggle then choking. He spun back in time to see blood running from the doctor's mouth while he tried to comply with Hans' order.

"Eat faster!"

The man was choking, his face contorted as the glass stuck in his throat.

Andreas pulled out his revolver and fired.

Hans stared at him in disbelief. "What did you do that for? I was enjoying myself."

Andreas shrugged. "My drink's getting warm and anyway I didn't want him spluttering blood all over my clean boots." He held his breath, hoping he'd managed to find the right disinterested tone.

Hans stared down at the body of the dead Jew and scowled. "You could have stepped further back out of the way." He glared at Andreas, sighed and shook his head. His brother-in-law was too soft on Germany's enemies. If he wasn't married to Karin, Hans would have had him arrested.

****

Berlin

"Have you heard when Andreas is due back?" Claudia was resting on her bed.

Karin smiled. "No, thank goodness. With a bit of luck he'll be in Austria for a while longer."

Claudia breathed a sigh of relief. She hadn't heard anything either and she was enjoying the peace. With both Andreas and Hans away, her life was much less complicated and she was enjoying spending time with Karin while they planned for the baby.

"So do you think it's a girl or a boy?" Karin reached out and placed her hand on Claudia's flat stomach. There was no sign of the baby yet and Karin had to resist the temptation to pinch herself to make sure the pregnancy was real.

Claudia shrugged. "I'm not sure, to be honest. Sometimes I feel it's a girl, at other times I'm just as sure it's a boy."

"Well I don't mind a boy or a girl, just as long as the baby is healthy." She lifted her eyes to Claudia's face and gazed tenderly at her friend. "Are you sure you won't mind giving him or her up to me to look after?"

Claudia shook her head. "Definitely not. I'm not the slightest bit interested in being a full-time mother, although I will expect to have 'auntie' rights – you know take them out from time to time, if that's alright of course?"

"You know it is. I'm just so grateful to you."

"You don't have to be, Karin. I love you and I would do anything for you."

Karin suddenly felt her eyes fill with tears. No one had ever said that to her before, not with so much love anyway. She sighed. They weren't there yet. Claudia had only just told Andreas about the baby. Now she had to wait for Andreas to inform her his mistress was pregnant and then she had to hope he would try to persuade her to bring up the child. Karin wished he would hurry up.

****

Near Flix, Spain

The bullets were coming from all directions, zinging along the dry dusty soil which deflected them dangerously close to where Rob, Mike and Gerhard were cowering in a shallow trench. The contested ground ahead of them shimmered in the summer sunshine and the dismembered bodies littering the boulders and rocks of the bare scrub could be seen swelling and bloating in the heat. Rob tried to lick his dry, parched lips but even his saliva had dried up. He had very little water left so he resisted the impulse to pour the remains of his flask down his throat. He closed his eyes for a moment to shut out the view in front of him but at that moment the guns fell momentarily silent, a silence punctuated by the sound of flies.

"Rob? You alright?" Gerhard's voice sounded hoarse and loud in the sudden quiet.

Rob opened his eyes. Gerhard looked awful, his blond hair filthy, his eyes bloodshot in his grime stained face. "Nothing a few pints of water wouldn't cure." He attempted a smile. "They're getting closer, aren't they?"

Gerhard nodded. "I think we should get away."

"What about the Ruskies?" Mike had to shout above the guns which had started up again. Gerhard was about to answer when there was a terrific explosion a few feet just in front of them. The ground vanished as a massive hole appeared, sand and dry soil flew everywhere, briefly blinding them.

"They won't be anywhere near the front lines." Gerhard was already checking out the area behind them. Having satisfied himself there were no Commissars around, he crawled out of the trench, got to his feet and began running full pelt towards a clump of bushes. Rob and Mike exchanged weary smiles and were about to follow him when a rifle shot rang out and Gerhard collapsed face-down in the dirt.

****

Berlin

"Andreas! I wasn't expecting you." Karin tried to ignore the frantic thudding of her heart. She'd planned to stay the night at Claudia's but some instinct had suggested it would be safer to go home, so she'd left early for a change. She was grateful she'd listened. She turned her attention back to Andreas who had made his way into the living room and was pouring himself a drink.

"Is something the matter?"

Andreas downed his cognac and seemed about to say something. Karin waited, an expectant expression on her face but then he shook his head, turned back to the drinks table and poured himself another brandy.

"Are you sure there's nothing wrong?"

Andreas shook his head. His original plan had been to go straight to Claudia's flat. He couldn't wait to see her. But as delighted as he was about the baby, Andreas knew he wouldn't be able to relax completely until he'd told Karin, so on his way home from Austria, he'd changed his mind. He would go home first and tell Karin about Claudia. She was his wife, she'd just have to accept it and not make a fuss. Unfortunately the problem with that plan was Hans. Andreas couldn't rid his head of the image of his brother-in-law forcing the elderly Jew in Vienna to eat glass for no reason other than that he was Jewish. If Hans could behave like that with a stranger, what on earth would he do to someone who hurt his precious sister? There had to be another solution, if only he could think of it.

"How was Austria?"

Andreas shrugged. "Boring, to be honest." He shook his head to try and clear his mind. Hans' obsession with Jews had become progressively worse while they were in Vienna. He had picked on them at every opportunity and Andreas had seen a sadistic side of him he'd never noticed before. Yes, they'd beaten up a few Jews after his mother's murder but that was nothing like his behaviour in Austria.

Karin watched him for a moment or two. It was quite amusing to know the truth and to see Andreas struggling. He was obviously trying to find a way to tell her that Claudia was pregnant.

"I'll go and have a bath then."

Andreas nodded but didn't turn around. Instead he stared at the picture above the fireplace as if that would provide the answer to all his problems. It didn't and he resisted the temptation to throw his glass at the wall. Instead he finished his drink and decided he wouldn't wait until the following day to visit Claudia. He would go there now.

The idea came to Andreas while he was making his way to Claudia's flat. What if he suggested to her that he and Karin brought up the child as their own? Karin and Claudia could go away for a few months to Bavaria or somewhere and then Karin could come back with the baby. He could tell Hans that his sister was pregnant once she'd left, and that would keep him happy. As he walked he thought about it and the more he thought, the better the idea seemed.

He was so engrossed in his thoughts, he failed to notice the man following him.

Having been told by Hans to watch Claudia while Andreas was in Austria, Krussman had become bored quite quickly. At first he'd found it quite amusing that Hans' sister was a sapphist but then he'd realised the danger he was in. Although his cousin had the photos, the longer he was watching Claudia the more chance there was of Hans finding out the truth, so he was pleased when Andreas reappeared. At least if he was following Andreas, there was a chance of taking some pictures that would interest Hans and keep him from growing suspicious at the lack of any other photographs.

****

Bydgoszcz, Northern Poland

"Thank you for looking after Raisa for me." Magda took Mariusz from Felcia, delighted to have the opportunity to give her grandson a cuddle.

Felcia was pleased Magda wasn't watching her face so didn't see the guilt there. "I didn't really do that much." She hesitated, remembering how irritated she had been when Raisa had arrived, wanting to stay. "To be honest, Iwan was more help than I was. I wasn't that happy when Raisa turned up. We've never exactly been best friends and I was worried Iwan wouldn't want her here which would put me in an awkward position. But fortunately, Iwan and Raisa got on very well. They spent quite a lot of time together and it was Iwan who found Raisa the job in the barracks and he even helped her get a flat in Bydgoszcz."

"Really? That was kind of him." Magda was watching Felcia carefully now but her eldest daughter was smiling and didn't seem to realise the implications of what she'd just said. Magda felt sick. She only hoped she was wrong but, given Raisa's reputation and the animosity between the two sisters...

Mariusz wriggled in her arms and she pushed her suspicions to the back of her mind and turned her attention to him.

"He looks just like Alek did at that age." Magda smiled down at her grandson with pride. At nearly eight months old, Mariusz had Felcia's blond hair and green eyes but many of his expressions were Iwan's. The door opened and Iwan came in. He smiled at Magda and kissed Felcia and then his son.

"Mama was just saying how much like my brother he is."

Iwan laughed. "He changes daily. Sometimes I can see Felcia in him, other times it's a bit like looking in a mirror." He gave a proud smile, encompassing both his wife and son and Magda felt her concerns dissipating. It was obvious from Iwan's face that he loved Felcia and Mariusz. Something else must have upset Raisa.

Felcia watched her mother cuddling her son and winked at Iwan. "Well, now you're here Mama, I thought we'd take the opportunity to have an evening out."

Magda nodded, her eyes still on her baby grandson. "That's an excellent idea. It will be good for you to have some time to yourselves and it will give me a chance to get to know my grandson."

Felcia grinned. She'd only been joking but an evening on their own without numerous interruptions sounded wonderful.

Iwan put his arm around her shoulders. "Go and get ready and we'll go out for a meal and maybe some dancing afterwards. Thanks, Magda. It's very kind of you."

Magda smiled up at him. "I know what it's like to have babies and young children in the house. Although husbands are delighted to be fathers, they often feel neglected." She ignored his protests. "Go out and pretend it's your first date."

Iwan nodded. Magda was right. He had been feeling neglected. Felcia was usually too tired to let him make love to her and now Raisa had gone back to Lublin, he'd become increasingly frustrated. Fortunately they'd been on exercise recently in a town several miles away and he'd taken the opportunity to visit a couple of prostitutes while he was there. But it wasn't the same and he'd left both feeling strangely dissatisfied.

"How's Raisa?" he asked.

Magda nodded. "She's well, thank you. She's got a new job in Lublin and a boyfriend too. He's a nice young man called Vada, I don't think it's very serious but she seems much happier." She glanced sideways and was shocked to see an expression of fury on Iwan's face. She turned to face him properly but by then Iwan was wearing his normal pleasant expression and, for a moment, she wondered if she was imagining things. Then her heart sank. Perhaps she'd been right after all. The question was, what to do about it.

****

Berlin

"I don't understand." Claudia was struggling to conceal her joy, so she'd turned her back to him.

"It's the best solution, darling. Karin has always wanted a child and this way she gets what she wants and we can continue to see each other."

"And we couldn't do that any other way?"

Andreas covered the short distance between them and put his arms around her. "Not if her brother finds out. He's really not very nice and he adores Karin. He'd do anything for her. If we upset him, I have no idea what he might do. If Karin's happy he will be too, then we'll be safe."

Claudia wanted to say 'yes' straight away but she didn't want him to become suspicious. She had to let him persuade her.

"I don't know. I might change my mind once the baby's born, I might want to keep it."

"But just think how a baby will interfere with our lives, darling and there are lots of advantages to the baby seeming legitimate."

Claudia nodded slowly then looked puzzled. "But how can we pretend the baby's Karin's. She doesn't look pregnant."

Andreas took her hands and stared into her eyes. He sensed she was weakening. "You and Karin will go somewhere away from here, maybe Southern Germany or even France and you'll have the baby there. Once you've left, I'll tell Hans Karin has just found out she's pregnant and because she's worried about losing it, she doesn't want to travel back until the baby is born. Then you'll both come home with Karin playing the proud mother." He took a breath and watched her face. "What do you think?"

Claudia looked down at her hands entwined in his and decided to put him out of his misery. "It's alright with me, but obviously Karin has to agree… and what if Hans decides to visit his sister?"

Andreas' face fell, then he shrugged. "We'll worry about that if it happens." He breathed a sigh of relief. With one obstacle overcome, now he just had to persuade Karin.

Chapter Thirty-four

Flix, Spain

To Mike and Rob's relief, Gerhard was not seriously wounded, the impact of the bullet hitting his leg had knocked him down but the injury itself was little more than a deep scratch. Unfortunately, after a few days the wound didn't seem to be healing. The gash had turned an angry red colour and there was a faint line heading up his leg. Mike stared at his friend for a long time then turned to Rob and lowered his voice. "I don't like the look of his leg. Out here, the heat causes infections really quickly."

"I'll go and speak to the medics, see if there's anything else we can do."

Mike nodded. "Thanks, Rob." He watched Rob leave the tent and then turned his attention back to Gerhard. He was very pale and sweating profusely. He washed the wound again with the little water he had and wished he had some alcohol, anything to try and fight the infection he was sure had set in to the wound.

"Apparently there's an emergency hospital still operating in a tunnel near Flix." Rob rushed back in to the tent as Mike was replacing the bandage on Gerhard's leg.

He looked up at Rob and frowned. "Are you sure? I would have thought they'd all gone with the amount of bombing over there."

Rob shrugged. "That's what the medic said. Come on let's take him there."

"We need permission…" Mike started to say.

Rob shook his head. "I've got it. That's why they told me about the emergency hospital." He was already helping Gerhard onto a stretcher. Mike hastened to help and they set off towards Flix.

****

Berlin

"She's pregnant?" Karin somehow managed to look furious. "You've got your whore pregnant?" she repeated, raising her voice. "Why are you telling me? Oh, I suppose so you can rub it in that I can't have children?"

"No, of course not." Andreas reached out a hand to her but she brushed it away. "Karin, listen to me, please…" It had taken him a couple of days to pluck up the courage to make his suggestion.

"Why should I? How could you be so cruel?"

"But Claudia doesn't want the baby and I was hoping we could pretend it's yours."

Karin stared at him as if he was mad. "How on earth could we do that? Even if I wanted to?"

Andreas hastened to explain, his carefully prepared speech vanishing as the words tumbled out.

Karin said nothing, mainly because she was having trouble not bursting into laughter at Andreas' panicked explanation. Eventually he fell silent, his heart pounding as he feared the worst. Karin turned her back to him and began counting to ten. If she gave in too quickly he might become suspicious.

Eventually, judging she'd waited long enough, she spoke. "If I was to say yes, would Claudia want to see her baby?"

Andreas breathed a sigh of relief. She was obviously coming round to the idea. "I don't know. She'll do whatever you want, I promise."

Having got her emotions back under control, Karin turned towards him. Andreas waited on tenterhooks. Karin could see the strain in his face and, much as she wanted to punish him further, she didn't want to risk him changing his mind.

"Let me think about it."

Andreas nodded. "Of course. Yes, you should think about it." He fell silent.

Karin allowed herself a small smile. It looked like she was going to finally be a mother.

****

Flix, Spain

They eventually found the hospital which was well hidden in a tunnel underground, but after a good look around they were horrified by how basic it appeared. There was no electricity or anything else as far as they could see. Rob and Mike exchanged glances.

"Is it safe to leave him here?" Mike looked doubtful.

Rob shrugged. "What else are we going to do with him? We can't take him back with us."

Mike still didn't seem convinced. "I don't know. It looks like a breeding ground for Typhoid if you ask me."

"And who did ask you?" They spun around at the sound of a disembodied voice speaking angrily in English from inside the tunnel. "If you think you can do better, then please be my guest."

Rob turned to apologise and almost dropped the stretcher. "Oh my God. Annie? Annie, is that you?"

The figure standing in the open mouth of the tunnel, her hair covered in soot was painfully thin and, for a moment, he wasn't entirely sure. Then she smiled and any doubts disappeared instantly.

"Rob? Oh goodness, Rob! Is it really you? And Mike. Mike?"

Exhausted as she was, Annie launched herself at Rob nearly knocking him off his feet and dislodging the stretcher from his hands. Realising they had an injured man with them, she pulled out of his arms and quickly examined Gerhard's leg which looked like it was already infected.

"We need to get him inside now." She called out something rapidly in Spanish and led them into the makeshift hospital.

Once she had handed Gerhard over to the doctor, she took them back outside and then turned to Rob.

Expecting her to hug and kiss him, he was totally taken aback when she launched a fierce assault on him, her fists pounding his chest relentlessly. Eventually managing to grab her wrists, Rob was about to ask her why she was attacking him when he realised tears were streaming down her cheeks and she was sobbing noisily.

"I thought you were dead, you bastard," she repeated over and over.

Rob felt sick. This was all his stupid fault. He had no idea what she'd been through while he'd barely given her a thought, presuming she was safe in the city. "It's alright, Annie. I'm here and I'm perfectly alright. I've come to take you home, darling. I'm so sorry. I should never have brought you here. Please forgive me." He put his arms around her and held her tight. He could feel her body shaking and he hugged her close until she finally began to relax.

Rob continued to hold her, wondering how on earth he could have been so selfish as to have risked her life to satisfy his own whim. He swore to himself he would never put her through anything like this again. In future he would always put her first.

****

Outside Lublin, Eastern Poland

Wiktor switched off the wireless, sighed heavily and put his head in his hands.

"What on earth's the matter?"

Wiktor jumped. His attention had been focused on what he'd just heard on the radio and he hadn't heard Magda come in.

"Britain and France have handed over the Sudetenland to Germany. They've just caved in completely"

Magda stared at him. "But I thought they'd insisted on a plebiscite and Hitler had agreed?"

Wiktor nodded. "They had."

Magda was quiet for a moment then her heart sank. What if Poland had declared war on Germany anyway and Wiktor didn't know how to tell her? She could hardly bear to ask the question but she had to know. "You said Britain and France hadn't argued about it, what about Poland?"

Wiktor slammed his hand on the small occasional table making her jump. "Our politicians have behaved despicably. They made it quite clear to Britain and France that they had no intention of going to war over the Sudetenland." Wiktor was so angry he missed Magda's sigh of relief. "That's probably one of the reasons they backed down. But to make matters worse, we've demanded the Czechs leave Teschen as well. We're as bad as the Germans!"

Magda was so relieved her sons wouldn't be in a war, she didn't answer for a few moments. Then she realised what he'd said. "But if we start behaving like the Germans, the French and British may stop supporting us…"

"Exactly. The report I just switched off stated that if the Czechs ignore our demands, we will cross the border and occupy Teschen."

Magda's hand flew to her mouth and she gasped. "What about Stani, Alek and Iwan?"

Wiktor shrugged. "I've no idea. They didn't say which units would be sent." He gave a huge sigh. "I'm just worrying where this is all going to end. Our politicians are behaving just like that raving lunatic in Germany, and Britain and France have shown they have no appetite for war. How do we know they'll keep their word if Hitler starts sabre rattling in our direction?"

Magda paled. "But you said they'd guaranteed our borders and we had nothing to worry about."

Wiktor stood up and stepped towards her. He reached out and put his arms around her. "That was before. Maybe I was being too optimistic. I think we should suggest Felcia and Mariusz come back here for a while, until we know which way the wind is blowing."

****

Flix, Spain

By the end of October Gerhard was sufficiently recovered for Mike, Rob and Annie to consider leaving Spain. "You're positive he's going to be alright?" Mike glanced at Annie and then down at his friend who looked much better than he had done when they'd brought him to the hospital several weeks earlier.

Before Annie could answer, Gerhard spoke. "I'll be back on my feet in no time. You really should go home now. I'm going to. There's nothing to stay for. The fascists have all but won."

Rob nodded. "He's right, Mike. The sooner we get back home the better."

Mike frowned. He'd spent so much time with Gerhard it would be strange just walking away from him. "But what about you?"

Gerhard smiled. "Stop feeling guilty, Mike. There's no reason for you to stay here. Like I said, once I'm fit enough, I'm going home. There's no point you sitting around waiting for me. You might as well get going."

"Is it safe for you to go back to Germany?" Mike still wasn't convinced he should leave his friend. "Perhaps you should come home with us."

"And do what?" Gerhard shook his head. "I need to go back to my parents, Mike."

"But what about the Nazis?"

Gerhard shrugged. "There's no reason for them to know I've been here and, even if they do, my parents have lots of friends. I'll be alright."

There was a long silence. "Well if you're sure?" Mike was still hesitant.

Gerhard smiled. "I am. Go home, Mike, and enjoy your life."

Mike sighed, trying to think of a good reason not to leave. Eventually he gave up. "Well goodbye then, Gerhard. You've got my address. Keep in touch if you can." There was an awkward silence, then the two men shook hands and Mike turned away.

"I can't believe we're finally going home." Annie had said a tearful goodbye to the rest of the nursing staff earlier. All that was left for them now was to leave the tunnel and make their way to Barcelona, then the French border.

"Won't be long now." Rob sounded more optimistic than he felt. Although they were leaving, the war wasn't over. They would have to be very careful, or risk being shot by some over-zealous communist official as deserters.

"I think we should travel at night and keep away from villages and towns as much as possible." Mike lowered his voice so Annie couldn't hear.

"We'll need to get food and water though." Rob sounded worried.

Mike shrugged. "We'll manage."

"I wonder what kind of reception we'll get at home." Annie was speaking her thoughts out loud.

"Well, the police might want to question us, I suppose." Rob thought about it.

"No, I meant our families." Annie snapped. "Sorry, I'm just worried about how angry they'll be."

Mike and Rob exchanged glances.

"What is it?" Annie stopped and stared at the two men. "What aren't you telling me?"

Mike sighed. "I wrote home while we were looking for you. I told my parents that Rob was alright so they could let his father know, but I also told them that we didn't know where you were."

Annie was aghast. She glared at Mike. "But Rob's dad's bound to go and see my parents. They'll think I'm dead. How could you be so bloody stupid?"

****

Bydgoszcz, Northern Poland

"There's no reason to go back to your family, Felcia." Iwan scowled at her across the dinner table. "Your father is worrying about nothing. There's not going to be a war. Everything has settled down now, so there's no reason for panic any more." Iwan had no idea whether things had really quietened down but he didn't want Felcia going home in case Raisa said anything.

Felcia stared down at her plate and sighed. "But I would like to see my family, Iwan, and this is as good an excuse as any."

Iwan took a deep breath and tried to think of a really good reason to stop her going. He could forbid it. Felcia was his wife and she had to obey him, but that was a last resort. "I'd really miss you, darling. Why don't you wait until I'm away on exercise again?"

Felcia nodded. She didn't want to argue with him and everything did appear to be quieter now, so perhaps he was right. She could always go nearer Christmas or in the New Year, depending on when Iwan was next away.

****

Berlin

"What on earth is going on?" Karin peered cautiously out of the window. She looked terrified. Sounds of shooting, windows smashing, screaming and shouting echoed through the streets, the noise amplified by the clear frosty November air.

Andreas shook his head. "Some Polish Jew shot a German diplomat in Paris a couple of days ago and now he's died. The SS have been ordered to destroy all Jewish property in retaliation."

Karin started. "Isn't that a little extreme?"

Andreas shrugged. "You know what the party is like; your brother is a prime example." He stopped talking and cursed under his breath. The last thing he needed to do now was to run Hans down to Karin.

Karin didn't appear to notice. She shrugged. "Well, if the Jews have declared war on Germany they can hardly complain when we retaliate."

"No, of course not. You're absolutely right." Andreas hastened to agree.

Karin smiled. She couldn't care less about the Jews but it was fun to make Andreas squirm. She changed the subject. "I've packed all my things ready to go. Claudia and I will leave first thing in the morning…" She hesitated. "If it's safe, of course."

Andreas frowned. "Perhaps I should go round and make sure Claudia is alright?"

Karin was about to object when a better idea came to her. "Why don't you take me there with you now, then we can leave early tomorrow. That way neither of us has to be on our own tonight with all this going on."

Andreas tried to think of a good reason why he should visit his mistress on his own and failed. He gave in with a good grace. "Perfect. Go and get your bags while I start the car."

****

Bydgoszcz, Northern Poland

"I'm still not very happy about you going home. Can't you wait until after Christmas?" They were in the kitchen, Felcia was making dinner and Mariusz was sitting on a rug in the front room playing with his favourite teddy bear, his present from Raisa. The toy was beginning to look rather tatty and one of the ears was hanging off, but Mariusz loved it and wouldn't go to sleep without Patek or 'Patta' as he called him. Outside the snow was falling steadily and Iwan was searching frantically for a reason to delay Felcia's visit to her parents.

"Well, Tata is still worried about the Germans, especially after Kristallnacht."

Iwan gave a dismissive snort. "Kristallnacht was over two weeks ago and it was nothing to do with us; that was against the Jews. And the

Germans got what they wanted back in September and they've been quiet since then, so there's no reason to think they're going to bother us. In any case we're more than capable of protecting ourselves and, don't forget, the French and British have guaranteed our borders now."

Felcia opened her mouth to argue that wasn't what her father thought, then decided not to bother. Iwan rarely listened to her views about politics and, given the option between him and her father, she knew who she was more likely to listen to. She changed tack. "I don't see why you're so adamant that I should stay here. You're away over Christmas so I'd be on my own. I know that's not your fault but it's not very fair. This is Mariusz's first Christmas, don't you think he deserves a bit more than being stuck here with just me. We'll be much happier with my family and, as soon as you're back and everything calms down, I'll come home."

Iwan forced himself to give a grudging smile. He could hardly object to her going home to see her family or to spending Christmas with them while he was away and he couldn't tell her the real reason he didn't want her going home. "Alright, just don't go away for too long. I'll miss you." He would just have to hope Raisa kept quiet.

Chapter Thirty-five
1939

Barcelona, Spain

Having eventually made their way to Barcelona, Annie, Rob and Mike were surprised to find the remnants of the International Brigades were also there. They'd had to lie low for several weeks, nervous about being spotted by the fascists who would either arrest them if they were lucky, or more likely shoot them on sight. They were in just as much danger from their own side, as many republican communists were likely to consider them deserters. They were astonished and saddened to hear that all the rest of the International Brigades had been expelled from Spain.

Mike finished his glass of beer and gave a dispirited shrug. "I can't say I'm surprised. We knew it was only a matter of time before Franco won."

"It just seems such a waste of life." Rob sighed. "And the bastards are growing in strength. Who knows where this is going to stop?"

Annie squeezed his hand. "At least we tried."

Rob scowled. "But it wasn't good enough, was it?"

Annie and Mike exchanged glances. "There wasn't anything else we could have done, Rob."

There was a long silence then he nodded. "I know you're right, but I just feel so useless."

"If it's any consolation, I don't think this is going to be the last chance we have of fighting the fascists." Mike handed Rob the local paper.

"Oh my God!" Rob read the headlines with dismay.

"What is it, Rob?" Although Annie could speak Spanish she struggled when asked to read it.

"The Germans are planning to invade the Netherlands in February, their aim being to use Dutch airfields to launch a strategic bombing offensive against Britain."

Annie went pale. "But that's outrageous. What's the government said?" She swallowed nervously and didn't give Rob a chance to answer. "We need to get home straight away. I have to see my parents…"

Mike patted her shoulder. "It's alright, Annie, we're leaving in a few hours. Although I think it's unlikely that Germany will really invade the Netherlands."

Annie looked confused. "Then why say so?"

Mike shrugged. "Sabre rattling to see what reaction they get. Maybe they're hoping to scare Britain into pulling out of their agreement to guarantee Poland's borders."

Rob put down the newspaper. "Let's hope you're right." He stood up. "Shall we make our way to the rendezvous? The French are busy imprisoning everyone who doesn't have a passport, so the only way back is to let the Commies smuggle us across the border and then make our own way to the Channel coast."

Annie sighed but didn't say anything. The thought of making the long trek back across the mountains in the dead of winter terrified her, but she'd thought at least they would be out of danger once they crossed the border into France. Now it looked like they wouldn't be safe until they reached England.

****

Outside Lublin, Eastern Poland

"I should probably go home soon." Felcia smiled at Magda. She'd enjoyed spending Christmas with her family but she was missing Iwan and she wanted to be home when he returned from his posting on the German-Polish border.

Magda's face fell. She was loving having Felcia and Mariusz staying with them. "Maybe you should stay a little longer? Your father is still concerned there will be another war."

Felcia shrugged. "Iwan thinks Tata's worrying about nothing." She saw her mother's expression and gave a wry smile. "Yes, I know what Tata thinks about Iwan's opinions, but I'm stuck in the middle and I miss my husband."

"If Iwan was right and there's nothing to be concerned about, why have your brothers and Iwan spent Christmas guarding the German border?" Magda shot back.

Felcia spoke patiently. "I'm not saying you're not right, Mama, but I can't stay here indefinitely. If anything happens, I promise I'll come back."

"You're going home?" Raisa came in just in time to hear Felcia.

Felcia smiled at her sister. "Yes, I'll probably go back next week. I need to speak to Iwan first to make sure he's home, so it might be the week after."

Raisa nodded but said nothing. Unlike Iwan, she was sure her father was right. War was coming, but whether it was with Germany or the Soviet Union she wasn't sure.

"I was just saying how much we'll miss her and Mariusz." Magda addressed her comments to Raisa.

"Yes, we will."

Felcia looked slightly surprised. Although she and Raisa were getting on much better, she didn't think her sister would really worry too much if she went home. "Well you could always come and visit again."

A look of horror flashed across Raisa's face and was quickly replaced by a smile. "Yes, of course. That would be nice." She turned away and began laying the table, praying Felcia and her mother couldn't see her hands were shaking and her legs trembling. She would rather die than put herself voluntarily back under Iwan's roof again.

****

Berlin

"Hans, it's good to see you. When did you get back?" Andreas licked his lips nervously and hoped Hans wouldn't see how flustered he was. Thank God Karin and Claudia were safely in Baden.

Fortunately Hans was looking around for his sister and didn't appear to have noticed his friend's reaction. "I've just arrived. I couldn't wait to see Karin… and you, of course."

Andreas had recovered his poise and he indicated the sitting room. "I'll make us both a drink. I have some good news for you. I was going to telephone you but then I thought I would wait a little longer in the hope of telling you myself." He poured two glasses of cognac and handed one to Hans. "I'd like you to drink a toast, Hans, to the imminent birth of your nephew or niece."

Hans stared at him in surprise, then downed a large portion of his drink. "Goodness, Andreas, I was beginning to think you'd never have children."

Andreas gave a wry smile. "Me too."

Hans glanced around "Where's Karin?"

Andreas laughed. "She and her friend had just gone to Baden in Switzerland to take the waters of the spa when she realised she was pregnant. She'd spent so many years childless, she'd ignored all the symptoms, thinking they were just a sign she was growing old. That was the reason for the holiday, because she felt ill." Andreas knew he was babbling but he hoped Hans would think it was through excitement. "When she did have the pregnancy confirmed, she was worried about travelling and the doctor there agreed, so she decided to stay in Baden until the baby is born. I went down to see her last week, Hans. She looks wonderful… glowing. I can't wait, to be honest."

Hans still looked shocked but he managed a smile. "Congratulations, Andreas." He drank some more and sighed. "I'm sorry to have missed her but, as you say, there's no point taking any chances. When's the baby due?"

Andreas let out a slow breath. It looked like Hans believed him. "Any time now, although the doctor can't be a hundred percent sure, especially with a first baby. Apparently they're often late." He finished his drink.

"Perhaps I should go and see her?" Hans was thinking out loud, his eyes on his glass. Andreas was searching frantically for a reason he shouldn't when Hans changed his mind. "No, it's probably better to wait until she's had the baby. Plenty of time to see her when she comes back."

"Yes, yes, you're probably right." Andreas tried to conceal his relief.

Hans stared at Andreas and wondered what he was hiding. He was definitely nervous. Then he gave a mental shrug. Knowing Andreas, he probably had Claudia upstairs. Satisfied that this would explain his friend's anxious behaviour, Hans wondered if he should make his friend squirm a little longer, then he relented. Karin was in another country, so Andreas spending time in her house with Claudia wouldn't affect her. He downed the rest of his drink. "Well, I'll bid you goodnight then. Perhaps you could let me have a phone number for Karin and I can give her a ring."

Andreas breathed a sigh of relief and showed Hans to the door.

****

En route to England

After the perilous journey across the Pyrenees, Annie, Rob and Mike made the long trek back through France to the Channel coast. They had to avoid the direct trains because they were regularly inspected by police and rail officials, so they walked and hitched lifts on trucks and in private cars where they could.

On arrival in Boulogne, they looked for a channel steamer back to England. Annie expected to be arrested at any moment, so she was quite surprised when they were allowed to board the ship without difficulty.

"Obviously the French aren't interested in us now." Mike smiled.

Annie began to relax. Maybe they were finally safe.

"The French probably think it's the British police's responsibility. It's much better to get rid of us and let our own police deal with the matter." Rob shrugged, then he saw Annie's expression. "But we've got nothing to hide, so don't worry, Annie. If we're questioned, just tell the truth."

Rob was right. Police and MI5 officers met every ferry from France and, on their arrival at Dover, they were immediately arrested and questioned. The interrogations went on for hours and, only once they were finally cleared of being a threat to the country's security, were they allowed to leave. Exhausted but relieved that the rules regarding fighting for the Republicans in the Spanish Civil War had been relaxed because of the growing threat from Germany, the three friends headed wearily back to London.

****

Berlin

Gerhard stared up at his parents' house and smiled. Nothing appeared to have changed since he'd left. Unfortunately he had no idea how much trouble he was likely to be in. He took a deep breath and raised his hand to knock on the door.

"Gerhard!" Hannah flung open the door and pulled him into her arms. Franz was standing behind her, relief written all over his face. He stepped forward.

"Come in, boy. Let's shut the door before anyone sees you." Franz waited until they were in the hallway before slamming the door closed and taking a proper look at his son. The expression in Gerhard's eyes reminded him of the faces of the men in the trenches on the Western Front and he sighed. Hannah was already commenting on how thin he was and hurrying him towards the kitchen. Franz followed at a distance. His mind was racing. Although he'd mentally prepared for this moment for several months, now Gerhard was home, he wasn't sure what to do for the best.

****

Romford, Essex

"Annie? Annie, is it really you?" Harold opened his arms and engulfed her in a bear hug. "Thank God, thank God." He muttered several times, blinking away tears of relief, before taking a deep breath and calling over her shoulder. "Ivy! Ivy! Come quick."

Ivy rushed into the hall from the kitchen, her heart pounding, then pulled up abruptly. "Annie?" She was so shocked, her voice was little more than a whisper.

"Mum!" Annie disentangled herself from her father and flung herself into her mother's arms. Tears were streaming down her cheeks and, for a few moments, she couldn't speak.

Eventually Ivy pulled back and stared at her. "You've lost weight."

Annie gave a wry smile. "There wasn't much food, Mum."

Ivy hugged her again, horrified to feel how thin her daughter was. "Is Rob alright too?" Ivy ignored Harold's snort of derision.

Annie smiled. "Yes, both he and Mike are fine. We arrived back in the country this morning. I came straight here; they've gone home too." She lowered her eyes. "I'm so sorry for what I've put you through."

There was silence then Harold patted her on the shoulder. "Never mind, Annie. You're home safe and sound. That's the most important thing."

Annie nodded, relieved they hadn't asked any more questions. She was exhausted from the long journey home.

"I'd love a long soak in the bath, Mum."

Ivy pulled herself together. She was shocked by her daughter's appearance but at least she was home. "Come on, I'll run you a bath and then make you a nice shepherd's pie."

Annie smiled. All she really wanted was a bath and bed but she couldn't bring herself to upset her parents any more. She only hoped they wouldn't ask any questions, because she wanted to forget the things she'd seen, not try to explain them to people who wouldn't have a clue what she was talking about.

****

Bydgoszcz, Northern Poland

"I've missed you, darling." Iwan had hardly been able to wait until Mariusz was in bed before taking Felcia in his arms and kissing her passionately. In the end Felcia had had to wait a little longer than she'd planned to go home, because Iwan's tour of duty had been extended.

"Good. I've missed you too." Felcia stopped talking and allowed him to lead her into the bedroom. She began undressing but Iwan pushed her gently back onto the bed and lifted her skirt. Felcia laughed and eased her bottom off the bed so he could remove her knickers. Within seconds he was inside her and thrusting hard. Felcia moved against him, trying to match his rhythm and in minutes he'd reached a climax. Panting, he collapsed on the bed beside her. "Too many weeks of waiting for you," he gasped in between breaths.

Felcia laughed. "Can I get undressed now then?"

Iwan rolled over and kissed her. "Yes, but don't rush. I want to watch."

Felcia stared at him in surprise and blushed.

"You don't have to do anything you don't want to, but I love your body and I haven't seen it for ages. I want to make sure nothing's changed."

Felcia nodded, stood up and began undressing. Iwan watched in silence. A sudden vision of Raisa doing the same thing came unbidden into his head. Obviously she hadn't said anything, or Felcia wouldn't have come back. He breathed a sigh of relief and returned his concentration to his wife. Her head was lowered as she removed her bra and then she peered at him from under her lashes. Iwan was struck by just how beautiful she still was and he suddenly felt very guilty. What on earth was he doing thinking about Raisa when he loved Felcia so much?

Chapter Thirty-six

Hackney, East London

"Feeling better?"

Rob nodded. He'd had a long bath and was busy tucking into the fish and chips Bill had been out and bought for their dinner.

"I'm sorry, Dad. I should have told you…"

Bill interrupted him before he could say anything else and shook his head. "No matter now, son. You're all home, that's the only thing I care about." He soaked up the vinegar with some bread and changed the subject. "Do you want me to see if I can get you a job back on the railway again, or have you got something else planned?"

Rob frowned. He hadn't really thought about what he was going to do. Everything seemed very strange at the moment. He would have liked to talk about the things he'd seen, but his father obviously wasn't interested.

An aeroplane flew over and Rob threw himself under the table, trembling in fear. The plane continued on its way and silence resumed, apart from the sound of the traffic outside the window.

Rob crawled out from under the table and gave a sheepish smile. "Sorry. Looks like I'll have to get used to life here again."

Bill was watching him, a concerned expression on his face. He'd been totally bemused by Rob's reaction, but seeing his son's fear, he rapidly hunted around for something to change the subject.

"I expect Annie's parents will be over the moon to see her, safe and sound."

Rob made an effort to forget his fear and concentrate on the conversation. He nodded. "Yes, I'm sure they will. I said I'd pop round to see her tomorrow morning."

Bill frowned and cleared his throat nervously. "They might not be very pleased to see you. They blame you for putting Annie in danger."

Rob sighed. "I expected that, to be honest, but I can't avoid seeing them forever. Best to get it over with."

"Would you like me to come with you?"

Rob gave his first genuine smile since he'd been home. He could just imagine what Annie's parents would think if he turned up with his father to protect him. "No thanks, Dad. I'm a big boy now. This is something I have to do on my own."

****

Berlin

"Hans?" Franz stepped back to allow him in. He'd spent most of the previous day trying to decide how best to protect his son and, as he hadn't yet come up with a sensible plan, Hans' arrival early in the morning was an unwelcome interruption. Franz licked his lips nervously and wondered what the SS man wanted.

"I don't want to beat about the bush, Franz. You and Hannah have always been very kind to Karin and myself. I understand your son has been fighting in Spain with the Republicans and has now returned home."

Franz was shocked they had found out so quickly. He swallowed and opened his mouth to try and explain, but Hans shook his head. "It's alright, Franz. I know you're not responsible for your son's behaviour. I only came to say that, normally Gerhard would be arrested and sentenced to a period of time in a correction camp, or he'd be shot as a traitor." He ignored Franz's gasp of horror. "However, you are a good friend to the Fatherland, so it has been decided to offer Gerhard an alternative."

Franz found his voice. "What sort of alternative?"

"If he joins the army, nothing else will be said. His past record will be wiped and he will be free of any punishment. After all, he's an experienced fighter and, if the army can benefit from that experience, then he won't be deemed guilty of treason."

There was a long silence, then Franz nodded. Gerhard had got off lightly really. He wouldn't have to stay in the army forever and he might even enjoy it.

"For how long?"

"Five years."

Franz closed his eyes. He could just imagine Hannah's reaction. He only hoped he could persuade Gerhard to do what they asked.

Hans leaned forward. "If he refuses he will be arrested, Franz, and there won't be anything I or anyone else can do about it."

Franz nodded. "I understand. Thank you."

Hans shrugged. "Make sure he doesn't refuse, Franz. Your friends wouldn't like to see you in trouble because of him." Hans turned around and walked out through the still open door.

Franz stared at his retreating back and sighed. At least he no longer had to make a decision. Now he just had to convince Gerhard.

****

Baden, Switzerland

"She's beautiful." Karin couldn't stop staring at Claudia's daughter. They'd been together when Claudia had given birth and, much to her surprise, she had fallen in love with the baby instantly. Claudia had recognised the resemblance to Karin the moment her friend handed her the newborn baby but, to her relief, Karin did not appear to have noticed.

"What are you going to call her?" Claudia had been terrified she might have had strong maternal feelings but she felt nothing at all for the baby. She wondered briefly whether that was because she knew who the father was and the memory of the conception was a scar she doubted would ever leave her.

"I think Heidi suits her, don't you?"

Claudia nodded and put her misgivings to one side. She was delighted to see her lover so happy. The only dark cloud on the horizon was their imminent return to Berlin.

"I suppose we'll have to go home now." Karin voiced her thoughts and sighed audibly.

"We can probably delay for another few days."

Karin nodded. "Yes. I'll tell Andreas we need to wait until you are fully recovered or people might guess. Have you thought any more about my suggestion?"

Claudia smiled, hoping Karin couldn't read her thoughts. "Yes. Are you sure it will work? If we are living in the same house, won't Andreas get suspicious?"

Karin shook her head. "Not if we're careful. It's the perfect solution. With you as the baby's nanny, you won't be separated from Heidi and we won't have to go to such lengths to see each other."

Claudia tried to ignore the niggling feeling in the pit of her stomach and nodded. "You're right, of course." She closed her eyes and wondered what she was going to do about Hans. It had been very fortunate that he'd been stationed in Vienna through most of her pregnancy or their plan would not have worked. But Karin had mentioned he was back home now. She shuddered. So many secrets… Where would it all end?

****

Romford, Essex

"Mike!" Daisy was shocked by his appearance but she gave him a hug anyway. Her parents were away for the week, so she had the house to herself for a change. "When did you get back?" She stood to one side and let him in. Thank goodness she'd had a row with her latest boyfriend, Dick, and he'd stormed out earlier in a huff because she'd turned down his proposal of marriage. She'd made it very clear that marriage was off the cards and that if he wanted to stick around, then he'd better forget it. She was only interested in having a good time. She turned her attention back to Mike. He looked very thin and his eyes had lost their sparkle. She slammed the door shut and Mike spun around, arms out as if he was holding a rifle. Realising it was just the door closing and seeing the astonished expression on Daisy's face, he lowered his hands and gave a sheepish smile.

"Sorry… force of habit." He pulled himself together. "You didn't mind me coming round to see you?" Mike sounded so unsure, nothing like his previous confident self, that Daisy felt sorry for him.

"Of course not, Mike. I'm so pleased you're safe." She hesitated. "Is Annie back too? And Rob?"

Mike nodded. "Yes, they're both at home… their own homes, that is." He shook his head. "Rob should never have taken her over there. God only knows what he was thinking."

Daisy sighed. Her fury with Annie for making her look a fool had not faded. If anything it had increased, mainly because Annie had not even bothered to write to her. "I think it would have been difficult to stop Annie going if she'd made up her mind, Mike. I'm sure it wasn't all Rob's fault."

Mike nodded. "Yes, you're probably right." There was silence. Daisy was conscious of his presence close to her and she had a sudden urge to comfort him. She thought quickly. She hadn't changed the sheets upstairs and she could hardly take him into the same bed Dick had just jumped out of. On the other hand, her parents had changed their bed before they went away…

"Shall we go for a drink? Or do you just want to sit quietly and listen to the wireless. There's probably some music on, or a comedy programme?"

Mike breathed a sigh of relief. For a moment he thought she was going to suggest they went to bed. It wasn't that he didn't want to, but he was still disorientated from being back in England and he'd always liked Daisy so he didn't want to rush things. He wanted to get to know her again first. "A drink sounds like a good idea."

Daisy nodded and reached for her coat. "*The Dog and Gun* has music on tonight. We'll go there."

****

Berlin

Andreas stared down at his tiny daughter and smiled to himself. She was beautiful, although strangely enough she resembled Karin rather than Claudia. Andreas frowned. He hadn't been very pleased about Claudia moving in with them as the baby's nanny, but he'd been unable to think of a really good reason why she shouldn't, and he was so pleased he'd finally fathered a child, he decided to give in without too much of a fuss. He was even less pleased about the closeness between his wife and Claudia, but again he'd not really known what to do about it. After all, if they hadn't been friends, Karin was unlikely to have agreed to taking the child. The situation was very strange but it seemed to work, so he ignored his misgivings and tried to make the most of his time in the capital. He had a feeling it wouldn't be long before there was a war and then he would have to go away, so perhaps it was a good thing both his women and his daughter were together. He smiled again as he thought back to the previous evening. It certainly made his love life much easier with both of them under the same roof.

"She's lovely, isn't she?" Karin reached into the cot and adjusted the blankets.

"Yes, she is." He hesitated. "I'm glad you're happy."

Karin smiled up at him. "Yes. It's strange, but things have worked out very well."

Andreas glanced at his watch. "I'd better go or I'll be late. Say goodbye to Claudia for me."

Karin nodded. "I will." She heard his footsteps disappear down the corridor, then the door adjoining the nursery opened and Claudia appeared. "Has he gone?"

Karin nodded. Claudia smiled and stepped towards her. "I can't believe he hasn't guessed."

Karin grinned. "He's too arrogant to think of anyone but himself." She laughed. "Thank goodness!"

****

Boots the Chemist, Romford, Essex

Annie debated whether to go inside but she didn't want to get Daisy into trouble, so she paced up and down outside until the shop closed and Daisy came out.

"Annie?"

"Hello, Daisy."

There was a long silence while Daisy took in Annie's thin frame and the distant look in her eyes. "You're back then." It wasn't a question. Daisy sounded annoyed and Annie reached out her hand.

"I'm so sorry for not telling you I was going."

Daisy ignored Annie's hand and shrugged. "You did what you had to do I suppose. I saw Mike last night. He looked pretty awful too."

Annie gave a wry smile. "Thanks, Daisy."

Daisy gave a loud sigh and shook her head. "I'm not sure we can go back to being best friends Annie. You didn't trust me enough to tell me where you were going. That really hurt."

Annie flushed. "I'm sorry. We were told not to say anything…"

"And you couldn't have left me a letter or a note?"

Annie stared at her friend in consternation and didn't answer. She could hardly say the idea hadn't occurred to her. It had been hard enough writing to her parents.

"And when you were in Spain?" Daisy continued. "I know there was a war going on but Mike managed to write home. We all thought you were dead."

Annie sighed. "I don't know what to say, Daisy. If I could turn the clock back…"

"But you can't." Daisy glanced at her watch. "I'm meeting Mike later. I'd better go."

"Are you seeing him again?" Annie looked pleased.

Daisy shrugged. "Well, we're going for a drink, but I'm not sure if there's anything else at the moment. You all hid your plans from me. I don't know if I can forgive that." She spun on her heel and walked away. She hadn't really intended to see Mike as anything other than a friend but she was bored and Annie had inadvertently given her an idea. Dick had come back and apologised for being an idiot after their row so Daisy had reluctantly agreed to carry on seeing him. But he was so eager to please he was beginning to remind her of a puppy, always staring at her with that ridiculous devoted expression. What she needed was a some excitement and having two boyfriends on the go might be just what she needed to restore her damaged ego.

"Wait, Daisy. We can't leave it like this. We were such good friends. I know I should have told you what we were planning and I'm really sorry. Can we please start again?"

Daisy stopped and stared up the road. She wanted to walk away but that wouldn't make up for all the pain and heartache Annie had put her through. She still squirmed with embarrassment when she thought about what a fool she'd been made to look in front of everyone. She gathered from Mike that Rob was always impulsive, but Daisy knew Annie wasn't, so she must have been thinking about going to Spain for ages before she actually went and yet she hadn't said a word. It was bad enough Daisy knowing Annie didn't trust her, but she was absolutely mortified that everyone else also knew. Daisy didn't care about most things but she did have her pride or she had done until Annie had plotted behind her back and made her look less than trustworthy. Daisy was still seething but perhaps she should just pretend she had forgiven Annie and wait for an opportunity to get her own back.

"You're obviously not still cross with Mike, so why are you angry with me?" Annie persisted.

Daisy shrugged, took a deep breath and turned back. "You're right. I'm being silly." She plastered a smile on her face. "I am pleased to see you, Annie. I've really missed you."

Annie relaxed. "I missed you too, Daisy. Thank you." She glanced at her own watch. "You'd better go or you'll be late for your date, but perhaps we can get together for a drink one night, just the two of us?"

Daisy nodded. "Are you sure Rob will let you out of his sight?"

Annie stared at Daisy, an uncertain expression on her face. "I don't…"

Daisy laughed. "I'm joking, Annie." She changed the subject. "Have you got a job yet?"

Annie shook her head.

"We've got a vacancy, on the make-up counter funnily enough. I could ask for you, if you like?"

Annie's face brightened. "Would you really?"

Daisy knocked on the door. "I'll do it right now." If she was going to get her own back on Annie, she had to keep her close.

Annie smiled and breathed a sigh of relief.

****

Outside Lublin, Eastern Poland

"We can't agree to this." Wiktor stared at Stani and Alek who were home for a couple of days' leave. The wireless had just reported the latest demands from the Germans, which included the return of territory in the Polish Corridor, cessation of Polish rights in Danzig, and annexation of the Free City to Germany.

"No, the Germans know that. They're just doing what they did in Czechoslovakia. Start by taking a small piece of the territory and then, when they've got a foothold, they'll just march in."

"Then it will be war?" Wiktor stared at his sons.

"Yes, although it has at least encouraged the French and British to say they will definitely guarantee our borders."

"But will that be enough?"

Alek and Stani exchanged glances. "One of the reasons we came home is that we don't know when we'll next be able to get leave. We've been told we're being mobilised. But it's a secret… you mustn't tell anyone."

Wiktor shook his head. "What about Iwan?"

"He's not received his orders yet, Tata, although its probably only a matter of time."

"What will happen to Felcia and Mariusz?" Wiktor looked worried.

"I expect they'll come home if things get worse," Stani answered. "At the moment he's staying where he is, but if things deteriorate…" He shrugged.

"I know it's supposed to be secret, but have you told your mother?"

Both boys smiled. "We thought we'd let you do that, Tata."

Wiktor gave a wry smile. "Come on then." He stood up. Magda would be terrified for her sons but he couldn't keep her in the dark; she had the right to say goodbye.

Chapter Thirty-seven

Hackney, East London

Britain seemed like another world and it took Annie, Rob and Mike weeks to adjust, not only to the abundance of food and the seeming irrelevance of everyday life, but to the fact that the skies above them were safe and the planes that flew over were not trying to kill them. Loud noises made them dive for cover, to the consternation of passers-by, and everything felt unreal. Annie was now working back in Boots, but she found it increasingly difficult to cope with what she saw as pointless, unnecessary queries by customers in whom she had no interest whatsoever.

"You've changed, Annie." Daisy was watching her friend with amusement and a certain amount of satisfaction. She'd end up getting the sack if she wasn't careful. "You'd never have spoken to customers like that before you went to Spain."

Annie sighed. "I can't help it, Daisy. I've seen so much poverty and suffering…" She saw the expression on Daisy's face and stopped. "Sorry, I'm sure you don't want to hear this again."

Daisy shrugged. "To be honest, Annie, you've become very intense, a bit like my brother on a bad day." She shrugged. "I know it's been awful, but you're back home now. That part of your life is over."

Annie shook her head and tried to keep her temper. "Is it? Don't you ever watch the news, Daisy? That maniac is busy carving himself an empire in Europe and, sooner or later, people are going to say 'enough'. Then what do you think will happen? There'll be another bloody war and this time it will be us who are fighting it, because if we don't, fascism will be here. The only question is, whether we'll be fighting the bastards in Europe or on our own streets!" She fell silent. She was wasting her time. Daisy could never understand the terrible things she'd seen because she hadn't been there and it wasn't fair to take out her anger on her best friend.

Daisy smiled to herself. She wouldn't need to do anything to get her own back on Annie at this rate. Her friend seemed hell bent on self-destruction.

****

Berlin

Gerhard stared into the mirror; the sight of himself in a German army uniform filled him with dismay. He couldn't believe he'd allowed his parents to talk him into joining the Wehrmacht. He'd only agreed because he knew they would be in trouble if he didn't. Gerhard had no idea how he was going to pretend to be a Nazi. He would just have to grit his teeth and hope no one noticed his insincerity.

He stared a few moments longer then clicked his heels together and raised his right hand. "Heil Hitler!" He looked and felt ridiculous.

"Needs a bit more practice." Gerhard spun around to see Franz watching him, an expression of amusement on his face.

He gave a wry smile. "I thought I'd better get used to it; the others will all have been in the Hitler Youth, so it will be second nature to them."

Franz nodded. "I'm sorry about this, Gerhard, but it's better than being in one of their camps."

Gerhard nodded. "Unless Hitler decides to start another war somewhere."

Franz frowned. "Don't even think about it." He sighed, wondering if he should tell his son the rumours he'd heard. Then he realised it would be safer for both of them if he didn't mention anything that wasn't already public. He cleared his throat. "Good luck, son."

Gerhard smiled. "I'm probably going to need it, Vati." He shook his father's hand. The two men stared at each other for a moment then Franz hugged his son before pulling back.

"You'd better go and say goodbye to your mother." His voice was gruff as he tried to hide his emotions.

Gerhard nodded and headed downstairs. Franz closed his eyes and tried to ignore his misgivings, then sighing heavily he followed his son.

****

Hackney, East London

Rob and Mike had found some temporary work labouring and helping to build street shelters, but they found it even harder than Annie to settle. Rob was woken every night by nightmares and the lack of proper sleep was making him very short tempered. Mike found it hard to even get to sleep. As soon as he closed his eyes he could see the bodies of his colleagues in the fields after they'd been crushed by fascist tanks.

"If that bastard calls me a fucking hero one more time, I swear I'll hit him." Rob's fists were clenched, anger and frustration written across his face.

"He's not worth it, Rob…" But Mike didn't get any further. Rob had crossed the short space between him and his tormentor and knocked the man on his back. The other labourers stopped work and stepped towards Rob. Mike sighed and moved in between Rob and the men.

"This isn't your fight."

"Really, Jacobs? If he can't take a joke…"

Mike lost his temper. He moved forward and shoved the man up against the nearest wall. "You don't have any idea what we saw in Spain and, God willing, you won't ever need to, but you mark my words: the fascists aren't defeated. They are growing stronger every day and, sooner or later, you and the rest of these comedians will have to fight them. When you've done that, you come back and tell me how funny war is!" Mike was about to say more when he felt someone trying to pull his hands away from the man's throat. He struggled against them.

"Like you said, Mike, they're not worth it."

Recognising Rob's voice, Mike slowly relaxed his grip. The man pulled away, rubbing his throat and muttering loudly about 'maniacs'.

Mike took a deep breath and tried to calm himself down. "I think we should get another job."

Rob nodded. He was still furious that people were treating the fascists as if they were some kind of joke.

****

Bydgoszcz, Northern Poland

"I'm not sure going to your parents' is the safest place." Iwan put his head in his hands and tried to think. "Is there anywhere else you could go? Further way from the German border?"

Felcia paled. "You really think there's going to be war, don't you?"

Iwan was about to shake his head, not wanting to worry her. Then he changed his mind. "Yes, the fact we're mobilising and moving to the German border is bad enough but now Hitler's signed this pact with Stalin…"

"But the French and British have promised to guarantee our borders…" Felcia waited for him to reassure her. He didn't. She sighed. "I have an aunt in Lvov – my mother's sister. She has a grocer's shop. I could possibly go there?"

Iwan breathed a sigh of relief. Lvov was a long way from the Germans. They'd never get that far inland. He ignored the niggling voice in the back of his mind adding that, if she went to her aunt's, there was less chance of Raisa telling her about them. Although she hadn't said anything at Christmas, Iwan was still terrified she would if there was a war and he was away for ages leaving the sisters together for a long time. "That seems like a good idea. Can you contact her and make the arrangements?"

Felcia nodded. Her face was ashen. "I don't want to leave you, Iwan."

He put his arms around her and held her close. "You don't have any choice, my love. Our orders are to be gone from here by the end of the week."

****

Hackney, East London

"I think I'm in love." Mike leaned up on his elbow and gazed down at Daisy. Her normally tidy hair was dishevelled, her face flushed from their love making.

"No you're not, you just think you are." Daisy reached up and kissed him. "We agreed nothing too serious, didn't we? I'm having lots of fun, aren't you?"

Mike hid a sigh and smiled down at her. "Yes, of course I am. I was only joking, Daisy. I've got no intention of falling in love with anyone until the fascists are defeated."

It was Daisy's turn to sigh. "Honestly, Mike, don't you ever think of anything else? You've done your bit. Can't you just forget about war for one evening. It's not very romantic." She reached down for his penis and began stroking it.

Mike wished he could be angry with her for not caring but the rising tide of sensations in his body were too strong to be ignored. She was right. It wouldn't hurt to forget the war for just a little longer.

Daisy breathed a sigh of relief. She liked Mike, but she didn't love him and she had no intention of being tied down to any man yet. Not when she was having so much fun seeing Dick as well. Her biggest problem was making sure they didn't find out about each other, well not until she wanted them to anyway. She was young and she just wanted to enjoy herself. She'd trained Dick to accept that; she'd just have to do the same with Mike, because if he kept on about love, she'd have to end it. Daisy sighed. She hoped it wouldn't come to that just yet because Mike was very good in bed and he knew exactly which buttons to press. As she thought the words, his fingers slid inside her and all thoughts of love vanished as her body responded to his touch.

****

Outside Lublin, Eastern Poland

Wiktor re-read the newspaper, then folded it neatly, stood up and walked over to the window. The crops were almost ready to be harvested and he wished he could feel the pleasure and excitement he usually felt knowing the growing season had been successful. Instead, all he could think about was impending doom. He was still staring out across the fields when he heard Magda come into the room. She stepped towards him and took his arm. Wiktor reached across and squeezed her hand.

"Do you think there will definitely be a war?" Magda spoke quietly and Wiktor could hear the fear in her voice.

"Yes, I think it's inevitable."

There was silence.

"How long have we got?"

Wiktor shrugged. "I don't know." He gave a sigh. "The German demands are farcical. They know we can't agree to them. They are deliberately goading us." Wiktor thought back to the newspaper report. The Germans wanted Danzig and the Polish corridor back as well as any other territory where more than three quarters of the population were German. They were also demanding rail and road access across the corridor between Germany and East Prussia.

"Maybe the League of Nations can negotiate something?" Magda tried not to sound desperate but she was terrified at the thought of a war in which her sons and son-in-law would be involved. She hadn't forgotten her suspicions about Iwan, but he was Felcia's husband and her daughter had a small child. They needed him. She realised Wiktor was talking and pushed her thoughts to the back of her mind. "Sorry, Wiktor, I didn't catch that?"

Wiktor squeezed her hand again and sighed. "I just said the Polish government will never agree to Hitler's demands. Even if they did, he would just come back with something else. He didn't stop in the Sudetenland, did he? No, I'm sorry Magda but the question is not *if* there is going to be a war, but *when*."

****

Romford, Essex

"We can't go on like this." Rob was pacing up and down on the path by the park bench. His nightmares were getting worse and he was almost becoming too scared to go to sleep.

"I agree." Annie exchanged glances with Mike who was sitting on the iron bench next to Daisy who was in the middle. She was fed up watching every word she said so she didn't upset Rob, who flew off the handle at the slightest thing. Annie was also concerned about her own very short fuse. She was snapping at everyone with very little reason and she seemed to have no control over her temper. If they carried on as they were, she and Rob would probably break up and she couldn't bear for that to happen. "I don't think I can put up with yet another day of answering stupid questions about which shade of eye shadow is best or whether this cream will stop some middle aged woman getting wrinkles." She gave a loud sigh. "But what *are* we going to do?"

"Changing jobs to something equally irrelevant will be just as bad." Mike stared across the park, a thoughtful expression on his face. There was a long silence. Rob kicked the grass border of the path and stared moodily at the ground. He'd thought of a possible solution but he didn't know how Mike would take it. He hadn't mentioned his bad nights to Mike so he didn't know if his friend was also suffering. His idea might make things worse, although he had a feeling that knowing he was doing something useful instead of burying his head in the sand and pretending war wasn't going to happen, might just help.

"I think we need to join the army, Mike."

Annie and Daisy gasped and Mike stared at Rob in astonishment. That was the last thing he'd expected Rob to come out with and he was about to say so when he stopped and thought about it.

"Haven't you had enough fighting?" Daisy stared at Rob as if he was mad.

Rob was about to answer when Mike interrupted, nodding, "Yes, I've seen enough to last me a lifetime and I'm sure Rob and Annie think the same. But that's not got anything to do with it. Rob's right. If we join the army we're doing something, we've taken control again, we're not just sitting back and waiting for the inevitable."

"Well I think you're both barmy. You…"

She didn't get any further.

"War is coming, Daisy. You can't keep ignoring it. We can't keep wasting our time doing pointless things. We have to do something constructive," Annie snapped then fell silent while she tried to think what she could do.

"We *are* doing something constructive and we're still pissed off." Mike grinned at his own joke then his face darkened. "Sadly, I can't think of anything else other than joining the army."

Annie sighed. "I don't ever want to see the things I saw when I was nursing in Spain, so I couldn't do that." She thought hard and then her face suddenly brightened. "I saw some adverts for the ATS the other day. Perhaps I'll see if I can join them, see if I can use my driving skills."

Rob stared at her in astonishment. Annie smiled. "I was taught how to drive an ambulance in case of emergencies. I never needed to, but I haven't forgotten how, although I might need a bit of a refresher course. The Spanish drivers also taught us the basics of how to fix engines, change tyres and that kind of thing, in case we needed to take over." She blushed at the admiration on his face and quickly changed the subject. "We'll tell our parents first this time. Try and get their support."

Rob snorted. "I don't think my dad's going to be very happy." He saw the set expression on Annie's face and nodded. "It's alright, Annie. I wouldn't join up without telling him. I'm just not looking forward to it very much. What about you, Mike?"

Mike gave a wry smile. "I'll enlist with you of course. You'll need me to look after you anyway." He was quiet for a moment. "My parents won't be very happy either, but given that we're Jewish, they'll understand."

"Well, I think you're all bonkers." Daisy glared at them. If they all joined the Armed Forces, how could she get her revenge on Annie for making her look stupid? They would be scattered all over the country. "You don't know for certain that there's going to be a war. You're just guessing."

"Let's just hope you're right." Annie glared at her. "You could always join the ATS too, Daisy. Just think how nice you'd look in the uniform." Her sarcasm was lost on Daisy, who suddenly looked thoughtful.

"Maybe it's not such a bad idea after all. I could come with you, Annie. We could join up together…"

Annie stared at her friend in disbelief. Apart from the fact the ATS didn't have a uniform, only an armband, the thought of Daisy being shouted at by big burly drill sergeants or being ordered about at the double almost rendered her speechless. Mike hid a smile, shook his head at Annie over Daisy's shoulder and put his arm around her protectively. "I think it's an excellent plan." He ignored Rob and Annie's shocked expressions and frowned. "Now all we've got to do is to tell our parents."

****

Berlin

"So we're off to the Polish border?" Andreas re-read his orders and looked for confirmation to Hans, who was now his superior officer.

Hans nodded. "Yes. I'm sorry we have to leave Karin and Heidi but it won't be for long, I'm sure."

"Do you think we're going to war with the Poles?"

Hans shrugged. "No idea, Andreas." Something about his tone made Andreas look up but Hans' face was expressionless. He glanced down at his papers again and then back at Andreas. This time he gave a cold smile. "But first we have to make a little detour."

"Oh?"

"All in good time, my friend!"

Andreas sighed. The more power Hans had, the worse he became. Hans saw his expression and grinned. "This is top secret, alright?"

Andreas nodded.

Hans hesitated, wondering how much to tell his friend. He knew he shouldn't say anything but the temptation to show how high he'd risen in the party was too much to resist. He checked again that the door was closed and then lowered his voice.

"It's no secret that Polish soldiers have repeatedly crossed the border and carried out acts of sabotage in Germany. This has been going on for months and, despite diplomatic attempts by the Führer to stop this, he has finally lost patience. So he has given orders to do something about it."

Andreas paled. "We're going to attack Poland? But what about the French and British…?"

Hans interrupted him. "Not exactly."

A look of bewilderment crossed Andreas' face. "Then what…" He didn't get any further.

Hans leaned closer and lowered his voice even more. "The Poles are going to attack us. That way the French and British won't support them."

****

Romford, Essex

Annie, Rob, Mike and Daisy sat at the pub table with Harold, Ivy and Bill. So far they had managed to avoid talking about the international situation but after several swallows of her gin and tonic to give herself courage, Annie exchanged glances with Rob and took a deep breath.

"Now Hitler has signed that Non-Intervention Pact with Stalin, we think we should be doing more to help the country prepare for war." Annie looked down at the pub table while she spoke. She heard her mother gasp and Harold started to argue. Annie looked up, and ignoring their horrified expressions, interrupted him: "We're only fooling ourselves if we think war is not coming closer. I can't run away or sit around and pretend nothing is happening. I want to do something to help. I've been looking at joining the ATS. I learnt to drive in Spain, and I could be very useful."

"Annie's right." Rob joined in before anyone could else could speak. "Mike and I are going to join the army."

It was Bill's turn to look horrified. "Rob, I'm not sure that's a very good idea…" He'd heard Rob calling out in his sleep night after night and the thought of his son enduring any more horror was too much to contemplate.

"We can't do nothing, Dad. I don't want to fight any more but war is coming whether we like it or not."

Bill sighed and searched frantically for a way to stop him. While he was thinking, Daisy chipped in. "I'm going to join the ATS too. I can't let Annie have all the fun." She gave a cheerful smile.

Bill exchanged a withering glance with Harold. He'd only met Daisy once before and he'd soon decided she was shallow and self-centred. Thank goodness Rob had chosen Annie. He couldn't understand what Mike saw in Daisy, other than the obvious. "What on earth are you going to do in the ATS? Annie's done nursing and she can drive. There's not much call for make up and nail polish in the army." Bill knew he sounded harsh but he was worried about Rob, and this vacuous girl seemed to think the whole thing was some kind of joke.

Daisy frowned and, although she was furious at being belittled in front of everyone, she managed to just look bemused. She turned to Annie for help. Annie sighed. "They also run the canteens and there are bound to be administrative jobs available."

Ivy shook her head. "I wish you'd stay at Boots, Annie. It's a really good job with excellent prospects..."

"And completely irrelevant!" Annie snapped. She took a deep breath. "I'm sorry, Mum. If I stay there much longer I'll get the sack. Much better that I leave before that happens."

"She has become very short tempered..." Daisy felt the full force of Ivy's disapproval and fell silent. She picked up her gin and tonic and took a large mouthful which made her cough. No one was paying her any attention except Mike who gave her what he hoped was a supportive smile.

Harold reached for Ivy's hand and squeezed it. "At least you've told us this time. I suppose you want our blessing?"

Annie relaxed and smiled at her father. "Yes please, Dad."

He gave a wry smile. "As I know you'd probably go ahead and do it, with or without our approval, it would seem sensible to agree. Just don't volunteer for anything!"

Annie laughed, relieved her parents had been so understanding. She glanced at Bill and gave an inward sigh. She could see he was still struggling with Rob's decision. Annie was about to say something when Bill transferred his gaze to Mike.

"What do your parents say?"

Mike shrugged and looked vaguely uncomfortable. "They'd rather I didn't join the army but, given we're Jewish, they can appreciate that we can hardly sit back and let everyone fight for us."

There was silence. Then Bill had an idea. "How about joining the Queen Victoria Rifles?"

Rob frowned. "They're a territorial battalion."

Bill shrugged. "Won't make any difference if there's a war. Last time the Territorials fought alongside the regulars."

Rob and Mike exchanged glances. Rob had a feeling his father had only suggested the Queen Vics because he was hoping they wouldn't be sent abroad as quickly as the regulars. But if he was honest, he wasn't in a great hurry to start fighting again and at least this way he would be doing something. "What do you think, Mike?"

Relieved Bill was coming round to the idea, Mike relaxed. "Sounds alright to me. We'll go and sign up tomorrow."

Chapter Thirty-eight

Outside Lublin, Eastern Poland

"I don't understand why she's not coming home." Magda shook her head.

Wiktor sighed. "Iwan thinks she'll be safer further inland."

"Do you think he's right?"

Wiktor shrugged. "I don't know, to be honest. Alek and Stani agree with him, so maybe he is. Perhaps you, Raisa and Ala should go to your sister's too?"

"I don't want to leave you, Wiktor."

He smiled. "I don't want you to go either, but I do want you to be safe. If the army is that convinced war with Germany is coming, who am I to argue?"

Magda shook her head. "I'm not leaving you, Wiktor, but I will talk to the girls and see what they want to do."

Wiktor reached out and put his arms around her. He could feel her shaking and knew she was crying but there was nothing he could say to comfort her.

****

Berlin

"You're sure about this?" Carstairs glanced sideways at Franz and wished he could take back the stupid question. The request for a meeting in the park had come as a surprise. They had not met face to face for a long time. Obviously Franz would not have suddenly requested an urgent rendezvous if he wasn't convinced the intelligence was genuine.

"Yes. I have a very reliable old friend in the German High Command. The supposed Polish attacks on ethnic Germans reported on the German newsreels are just propaganda to give us an excuse to attack them. For what it's worth, not everyone in the upper echelons of the army thinks it's a good idea."

Carstairs was silent for a few moments. "When is it likely to happen?"

Franz shook his head. "I don't know, but very soon."

"This will mean war, Franz. The British and the French won't sit back and let Hitler continue to carve up Europe much longer."

"I know. I've thought of nothing else." He sighed. "I imagine you won't be able to stay in Berlin much longer if things continue as they are. Do you have a reliable, trustworthy contact at the American Embassy I can talk to?"

Carstairs stared at him for several seconds without speaking. He could see the strain in Franz's eyes. "I'll sort something out and leave the details via the dead drop." He reached out his hand. "Goodbye, my friend. Take care of yourself and don't do anything too reckless, will you?"

Franz smiled. "I'll try not to. You look after yourself too and hopefully we will see each other again."

Carstairs nodded, turned away and began walking towards the park exit. Franz watched him for several moments to make sure no one was following and then turned and walked in the opposite direction. He'd taken a terrible risk meeting Carstairs but, apart from the severity of the intelligence, he also wanted to say goodbye. It was unlikely they would ever meet again.

****

London

Having seen each other virtually every day since they had come back from Spain, it was a shock to Annie and Rob to be suddenly separated. The Queen Victoria Rifles' trucks and motorcycles were lined up outside battalion headquarters in London ready to leave.

"It's just for two weeks, darling, and I'll only be at the camp at Tidworth."

Annie sighed. "I know, Rob. Don't take any notice of me, I'm just being silly. I'll miss you." She stood on tiptoes so she could kiss him goodbye. Wolf whistles and cat calls erupted around them and Annie jumped back, blushing furiously.

Rob ignored the banter and held onto her hand. "I'll miss you too, darling, but the time will rush by, you'll see, and then I'll be home again."

"Come on, Rob, or we'll be in trouble before we even get there," Mike yelled from the truck.

"Yeah, come on, Rob, put her down. She'll still be here when you get back!"

Rob grinned as several other men joined in, but this time he let her go and climbed in to the passenger seat next to Mike who sighed theatrically, put the truck into first gear and pulled away. Annie watched from the pavement until they were out of sight and then turned away.

****

Outside Lublin, Eastern Poland

"What do you think we should do, Mama?" Ala looked from her mother to Raisa and then back again.

"I'm going to stay with your father but you should make up your own minds. I'm sure Felcia would welcome your company and your support, with Iwan away. I've spoken to my sister and she is happy for you both to go there, although it might be a bit crowded and you'd probably have to share a room."

"I think I'll stay and take my chances here." Raisa sounded decisive. The thought of being confined in a room with Felcia, listening to her spouting the virtues of her husband was too much to contemplate. "I have a job I like in Lublin and the Germans may not come anyway. No, I'm staying here."

Magda nodded and turned her attention to Ala. Her youngest daughter thought about it for several moments. She loved Felcia and it was ages since she'd seen her. "I think I'll go to Lvov, for a while at least. If the Germans don't invade, then I'll come back. I just think it'll be nice for Felcia to have someone with her. I know she'll have Aunt Halina but it's not the same, is it?"

Magda smiled at Ala. "I'm going to miss you, Ala, but I know Felcia will be so pleased to have you with her."

Raisa watched her mother and gave an inward sigh. Everyone made such a fuss over Felcia and her son. No one really cared about her. Nothing had changed.

****

Tidworth, Wiltshire

Rob had spent the first Saturday afternoon and all day Sunday learning about the role of a motorcycle battalion in a division. The following two weeks were filled with rifle and Bren gun training on the firing ranges, map reading, driving lessons and field exercises. But the evenings were spent wondering what Annie was doing and whether she was missing him as much as he was missing her. He couldn't wait for the training to be over so he could go back home. It might only be fourteen days but it seemed like a lifetime.

"Sorry?" He suddenly realised Mike was talking to him.

"You look like you're miles away."

Rob grinned. "I was just thinking…"

"About Annie." Mike finished with a broad smile "Why don't you just put her out of her misery, not to mention all of us, and ask her to marry you?"

"But what if she says no?"

"Like that's gonna happen, you pillock!" Andrew 'Marty' Martins, like most of the others, was already bored with Rob's love life, having been subjected to Rob's continual whinging about his separation from Annie since their arrival. It had been bad enough during the evening training sessions when Rob spent most of his time looking at his watch, waiting for the time to pass so he could go and telephone Annie. "We all saw the way she looked at you when you left her. God knows, we waited long enough for you to say goodbye. The poor girl probably can't understand why you haven't asked her."

Rob looked at Mike for confirmation.

"If I thought there was any chance she would turn you down, I'd tell you. Honestly, Rob, you're made for each other and if you don't do it soon, you might not get the chance." Mike's tone was sombre.

Finally convinced, Rob nodded. He closed his eyes and began planning how he would ask her. Mike grinned at Marty and they wandered off to play cards, leaving Rob alone with his thoughts.

"What about you and that Daisy?" Marty asked as they sat down at a table and he prepared to deal the cards.

Mike shrugged. "I'm not sure she would say yes, even if I wanted her to. It's not that serious." Since he'd declared his love for Daisy and she'd mocked him, he'd made an effort to keep his feelings to himself. He was sure that all he had to do was to bide his time and eventually he would wear her down and she would finally admit she did love him. In the meantime he would just have to be satisfied with a relationship based purely on sex and having fun. But he wasn't about to tell anyone else that.

He changed the subject. "Anyway, what's this rush to turn us all into married men? Just because you like having someone to run around after you and cater to your every whim!"

Marty grinned. "Just trying to do my bit to spread a little happiness." His mood darkened. "You've done all this, haven't you… the fighting, I mean?"

Mike nodded. "And you want to know what it's like?"

"No. Well, not really." Marty hesitated. "I think it's probably best not to, if you see what I mean." Mike nodded. He understood completely. If he'd had any idea of what Spain was going to be like, he'd never have gone. He waited for Marty to say what was on his mind.

"I really wondered how you get over feeling frightened. I mean how do you stop it getting to you?"

Mike didn't respond for a moment. "Anyone who tells you they aren't frightened is lying or just bloody stupid. You just do what you've been trained to do, really. Often cowering in a trench is more dangerous than getting out and fighting, and at least you'll be properly trained. In Spain we had minimal training and very little practice with ammunition."

"We had hardly any bloody training; we had absolutely no idea what to expect." Rob's voice took them both by surprise. Having reached his decision, he'd come to ask Mike to be his Best Man and had overheard the end of the conversation. "At least this time we've been taught how to fight, although the Krauts won't be such a walkover as everyone seems to think. Take it from me, I've seen them in action and they're ruthless. Anything goes, however awful, as long as they win."

There was silence while Marty digested this. Realising the depressing effect his words were having, Rob changed the subject.

"Anyway, Mike. I was wondering whether you would do me the honour of being my Best Man?"

Mike grinned, stood up and shook Rob's hand. "About time too, mate. Of course I will, I'll be delighted. So when are you going to ask her?"

"When I get home." Rob was excited, but also nervous. It was unlikely Annie would turn him down but the possibility did exist, so he would have to try and not count his chickens before they hatched.

Chapter Thirty-nine

Gleiwitz, Germany

"We're going to shoot our own people?" Andreas whispered.

Hans nodded. They were dressed in Polish uniforms and hidden in the undergrowth not far from the German radio station at Gleiwitz.

"But if we kill them all, how is anyone going to know it was the Poles?" Andreas shook his head, but there was no time for Hans to answer. Instead he gave the order to advance.

Hans, Andreas and the rest of the SS commando unit rushed into the radio station and began shooting the few occupants. The action was over in minutes and then one of their members, who was Polish, picked up the microphone and began reading out a communique in Polish and German. Andreas nodded. Obviously that was how the world would know they'd been attacked. Then he frowned. But anyone could say they were Polish. He was still pondering this when the man finished, ending with the words, "Long Live Poland."

Hans stepped forward and smiled at the man. "Well done." Before the man could answer, Hans shot him.

Andreas stared in disbelief. Hans gave him an exasperated look. "How else can we prove it was the Poles? Don't worry he wasn't one of us. Come on, let's go. The broadcast should be playing over the airwaves in Berlin by now." He clapped Andreas on the back, a manic glint in his eye. "Won't be long and we'll be at war. Then we can rid Europe of the Jews." He turned around so he didn't see the horror on Andreas' face.

****

Outside Lublin, Eastern Poland

"Do you really believe our troops attacked Germany?" Magda listened to the wireless in confusion.

"I doubt it." Wiktor slammed his hand on the table in frustration. "No one with any brains is going to believe we managed to get five kilometres into Germany without being detected to make a broadcast that was so weak it could only be heard locally. This is Himmler's attempt to stop the French and British supporting us."

"Do you think it will work?"

Wiktor glanced at Raisa who had just stepped into the room. He shrugged and tried to smile. "No, I'm sure it won't. They aren't that stupid."

Magda stared at her husband and her heart sank. She knew when Wiktor was lying.

****

Hyde Park, London

They were walking in the park enjoying the late summer sunshine. Annie was quiet, dreading the prospect of being separated from Rob when he was mobilised or sent away for more training. She was also worried about why he was so very quiet. She wondered if something was worrying him or whether it was just the thought of being away from her that was troubling him. As they approached the lake, Rob decided it was now or never.

"Annie?"

Annie turned to look at him, concerned by the tone of his voice. Whatever it was, it sounded very serious

"Yes, darling." Her voice trembled, betraying her nervousness.

"Will you marry me?" He suddenly remembered he was supposed to be on one knee, so he quickly dropped down, to the amusement of several passers-by.

Annie stared at him in total amazement. She had waited so long for him to ask her, she had almost given up. This was the last thing she'd expected as they had strolled through the crowds of people in the park, all making the most of what everyone now believed to be the last few days of peace.

"Yes, of course, yes…" She stopped, unable to think of anything else to say. He stood up and, when she flung her arms around him, Rob kissed her until the sound of clapping and a couple of cheers made him stop. He looked around to see a small number of people who were watching.

Unable to contain his joy, he gave a deep theatrical bow and Annie, following his lead, curtseyed gracefully, making the crowd laugh even more.

****

Berlin

"So that's it then?" Hannah stared out of the window into the garden. The late summer sunshine cast long shadows and she shivered. They seemed like an omen of things to come.

"Yes, I'm very much afraid it is, my love." Franz sighed. Even the Wehrmacht war crimes investigators sent to examine the scene at Gleiwitz didn't believe the Poles had attacked the radio station. Unfortunately, no one in Germany was prepared to say so publicly, and the nation had already been well primed with repeated propaganda reports of Polish attacks on Germans, so had no trouble accepting the party line. "I think it's just a matter of time."

"And Gerhard?"

Franz shook his head. The last he'd heard, his son and the rest of the 26th Infantry Regiment had been moved to Flensburg before the assault at Gleiwitz. He reached out his hand and placed it on Hannah's shoulder. He wished he could say something to comfort her but he couldn't think of anything, so he stared out at the lengthening shadows and wondered if there was more he could have done. Deep down, he knew there wasn't, but he still couldn't help feeling guilty.

****

Berlin

Karin switched off the wireless and smiled at Claudia. "Well that's good news, isn't it?"

Claudia stared at her in surprise. "We're at war, Karin. How can that be good news?"

"If we're at war, Andreas will be busy… too busy to check up on us. With a bit of luck, he'll be sent to Poland for a while and we'll have some peace."

Claudia was about to argue when she realised Karin was right. Hopefully Hans would also be sent somewhere else, then she would feel safe for a while. She grinned. "I think we should celebrate with a small drink." She had already crossed the room and was pouring them both a small glass from Andreas' favourite bottle of cognac. Karin came over to stand next to her, her arm on the other girl's waist. Claudia handed her the drink and raised her own glass. "Here's to war and to Andreas being very busy somewhere else for a long time."

Both women downed their drinks and Claudia reached out, put her arm around Karin and pulled her close. "Perhaps we should have an early night?"

Karin smiled. "That sounds like a wonderful idea." She leaned forward and kissed Claudia on the lips. Claudia responded, inserting her tongue inside Karin's mouth, her hands gently tugging Karin's dress up until it was around her waist. Claudia grasped Karin's buttocks through her lace knickers and squeezed.

Karin pulled away. "Let's take the bottle upstairs, Andreas won't be needing it and we can always replace it before he comes home."

****

German-Polish border

The 26th Infantry Regiment had crossed the German-Polish border at five in the morning on the third of September. As the day progressed, Gerhard stared out at the abandoned villages, mined bridges and dry yellow sand through which the trucks struggled to advance. Horses soon tired and those on bicycles had to carry them for long periods. He watched the civilians fleeing towards them, bedding, bicycles and small children piled high on Panjewagen pulled by single horses, the poverty and misery reminding him poignantly of Spain.

On the outskirts of Kalisz, they came under attack for the first time. Having taken cover, they returned fire, eventually using artillery to take out the ancient Polish machine gun in a disused factory before setting the building alight. He watched a dozen civilians herded out of the building and listened to his colleagues muttering about snipers. Gerhard joined in but, underneath the camaraderie, his animosity towards his comrades was becoming harder to hide.

****

Polish-German border

Iwan waited for the order to attack. They were hiding in the bushes not far from where one of the infantry battalions of the German 20th Motorised Division were setting up camp. The 18th Lancers had been heading towards the border when they'd come across their enemy and their commander had pulled them up ready to mount a sabre charge. Under him, Iwan could feel his horse moving restlessly. He knew the animals could feel the tension in the air, their nostrils flared, eyes rolling, heads nodding, desperate to be off. In the distance, he could hear the sounds of the infantry battalion making camp. He patted the neck of his horse and leant forward, muttering soothing words. His horse sighed gently and Iwan smiled to himself.

"Charge!"

He had no need to encourage his horse and Iwan and the rest of the Polish 18th Lancer Regiment charged towards the camp. They were there in minutes, catching the Germans by surprise. They raced through the camp, sending soldiers fleeing in all directions.

To start with, there was little opposition. They had caught the Germans unawares and many were dead before they had time to even reach for their weapons. Iwan lost count of the number of men he killed and he started to feel more optimistic. Maybe they could hold back the Germans long enough for the British and French to come to their aid. If only the French hadn't stopped their mobilisation two days earlier, there would have been more troops on the border but the French had threatened to withdraw their support if the Poles antagonised the Germans.

He was still pondering the irony of that when he realised the Germans were actually retreating. Although some were now firing back, the majority were on the back foot. Iwan could feel the occasional bullet rushing past but he paid no heed to the danger. He threw himself forward over the neck of his horse, his lance extended as he slew any German in his path.

"We've got them on the run." He vaguely heard the shouts of his comrades and he fought even harder. To his astonishment, it seemed his fellow lancers were correct, the Germans were pulling back. He thought briefly of Felcia and Mariusz, and smiled. This was for them.

Iwan never saw the hail of bullets that hit him as a group of German armoured cars arrived and opened fire. His last thought as his body crashed to the ground was regret that he wouldn't see his son grow up.

Chapter Forty

Regent's Park, London

Life in Britain changed rapidly after war was declared. Rob's part-time voluntary service became full-time and permanent as did Annie and Daisy's ATS employment. Now under military orders, Annie and Rob found themselves apart again for much of the time and Annie was relieved she was busy, because it stopped her missing Rob too much. Her parents and Rob's father were delighted they had decided to get married. Fortunately Rob's late mother's cousin was the local vicar and he had agreed to marry them on Saturday 23rd September. That would give sufficient time for the bans to be read. While Ivy was busy rushing around arranging the dress and food for the day, Bill and Harold were trying to find somewhere that wasn't booked up for Annie and Rob's reception.

Rob was billeted with the others in the splendour of the Georgian mansions overlooking Regent's Park. The billets were very much the luck of the draw and, whilst some found themselves in large spacious rooms with luxury bathrooms on every floor, others found themselves in the house next door to that previously occupied by the Duchess of Windsor. Rob and Mike were not so fortunate. They ended up sleeping on the floor of a large ballroom without any palliasses, and the packs they were using for pillows slipped and slid across the highly polished surface.

Across the road, Regent's Park provided the ideal place for the compulsory pre-breakfast, early morning runs. Normally hated, the beautiful surroundings soon endeared themselves to the majority and the dreaded runs became quite popular. Other soldiers were based in Wimpole Street and trained in Hyde Park.

"Well at least you're still in London at the moment so we can still meet reasonably regularly." Annie laughed as she listened to Rob moaning yet again about drawing the short straw regarding accommodation.

Rob gave a theatrical sigh down the phone making her laugh even more. "I know. We should make the most of it, my darling."

"We will. When do you next have some leave?"

"I can get a couple of hours off tomorrow, what about you?"

"Yes, that's no problem. I'll see you at Selfridges at about three." She was about to say more when the pips went. There was just time to say goodbye and the line went dead. Annie sighed, replaced the receiver and went back to the canteen where she'd been working for the past few weeks.

****

Lvov, Poland

"Stani, it's so good to see you. Is Iwan with you?" Felcia hugged her brother, at the same time peering over his shoulder to see if Iwan was with him.

Stani eased her gently away from his body and leant towards her. "Shall we go inside?"

Felcia paled and shook her head. She pulled herself free of his arms. "No, please, Stani? Iwan? He's alright, isn't he? Please tell me he's alright?"

Stani shook his head. "I'm so sorry, Felcia." He took her hands but she pulled away from him.

"Is he wounded?" She searched his face for some hope. "He's wounded, isn't he Stani? But he'll be alright, won't he?"

"What's going... Stani!" Ala flung her arms around her brother, then realised something was wrong. "Alek?"

"No, Alek is fine, well he was when I left him. It's Iwan. He was killed defending the border over a week ago." Stani was relieved to finally say the words. He turned his attention back to Felcia who was leaning against the door post, staring into the distance as if she expected Iwan to appear at any moment. "Felcia?"

There was no response. Stani glanced at Ala and indicated they should go inside. She looked shocked but immediately took her sister's arm and led her gently back into the house.

"Felcia, Ala?" Halina came rushing out of the shop and into the hallway. She saw Stani and the expressions on her nieces' faces and her heart sank.

"Hello, Aunt Halina." Stani nodded. "I've bought sad news, I'm afraid…"

"Iwan's dead," Felcia interrupted, her voice flat and unemotional. Halina gasped and hurried towards her.

"Oh, my poor girl…" Felcia stared at her and then the sympathy in her aunt's voice broke through the shock and she crumpled onto the floor, her body wracked by heart-wrenching sobs.

****

Poland

Gerhard lay on his stomach in a shallow hole he had hastily scraped out of the hard ground and stared across at the battle raging in front of him. Stuck on the north bank of the Vistula, the 30th Infantry Division was under heavy attack. Gerhard and just over a hundred of his comrades were tasked with shielding an artillery position behind them but had been told to hold their fire until the enemy was only three hundred metres away. Gerhard licked his lips and resisted the temptation to wipe the sweat from his upper lip. Stretched over a thirty kilometre defensive line, while the 8th Army was thundering towards Warsaw, he could see the Polish infantry inching closer.

"Fire!" The order came as a relief and Gerhard aimed, fired and then reloaded, his actions almost mechanical, as if he were still on the barrack's square. Bullets whistled all around him, he could hear the screams of the wounded on both sides and, for the first time since he'd joined the army, Gerhard forgot his animosity towards the Third Reich and began fighting for his life.

****

Berlin

"Is that a letter from Andreas?" Claudia had just finished putting Heidi down for her afternoon sleep. She sat down at the table and helped herself to some bread, cold sausage and tomatoes while she watched Karin open the envelope and begin skimming through the words.

Karin nodded, her attention on the paper. "Yes. It looks like he won't be back for a while." She read some more and smiled. "Hans won't be either." She looked across the lunch table at Claudia and handed her the letter. "Here, read for yourself. There's no mention of them coming home at all." She leaned back and rested her head on her arms.

Karin could honestly say she'd never been happier. Claudia was the perfect lover, companion and nanny to Heidi and, as for her daughter… Karin's smile broadened. She automatically thought of Heidi as her own daughter now and it was only very rarely she remembered that Claudia was Heidi's real mother. In fact, Heidi didn't look anything like Claudia. Strangely enough, she resembled Karin, which had made life so much easier. Karin didn't know why Heidi should look like her and she didn't really care. Perhaps it was fate's way of showing her she and Claudia had done the right thing.

"Is everything alright?" Claudia was leaning towards her, an expression of concern on her face.

Karin smiled. "Yes, I was just thinking how lucky I am… or we are." She reached out and took Claudia's hand.

Claudia squeezed it and nodded. "Yes, we are. We should make sure we enjoy every moment, Karin."

Karin frowned. "What a strange thing to say. Is there something wrong?"

Claudia shook her head. "No, of course not. But nothing lasts forever, Karin, that's all."

****

Lyons Corner House, London

"How much longer do you think you'll be based in London?" Annie poured them both some tea from the dainty china teapot into the matching cups.

Rob stirred in some more sugar and shrugged. "I don't know. We're all pretty fit now, so I don't think it will be too much longer before they move us out." He sighed. He didn't want to think about being in a camp miles away from Annie. The British Expeditionary Force were already in France and, as he was in a territorial unit, the chance of him being sent overseas was very slim, certainly in the short term. In any case there was very little happening in western Europe at the moment, so with a bit of luck he would be based in England on home duties. He changed the subject. "I can't wait for Saturday."

Annie's face lit up. "Me too. Eleven o'clock, don't forget."

Rob grinned. "As if I would."

"Are you still able to get some leave afterwards for the honeymoon?"

Rob nodded. "Yes." He hesitated. "We might have to change things if I get sent away though…"

Annie's face fell. "Do you think that's very likely?"

Rob shrugged. "Who knows? There's a war on, anything can happen." Seeing her disappointed expression, Rob shook his head. "I'm sure that won't happen, so don't worry, Annie. You aren't going to get away that easily…" He reached out, took her hand and thought about how the other men in the regiment couldn't wait to go to France. He knew they were only impatient because they'd had no experience of fighting. As far as he was concerned, every day they spent in England was a bonus. He was in no hurry to go anywhere.

Annie watched him across the table. She sensed his growing despondency and wished there was something she could do to help. She knew it was only a matter of time before he was sent away from London and she was dreading the moment they would be separated.

****

Berlin

Franz re-read the letter from Gerhard that Hannah had just handed him and breathed a sigh of relief. His son appeared to still be in one piece. Hannah was watching him and he could see the tears in her eyes. He reached across the kitchen table and took her hand. "He's alive and well Hannah. Just be grateful for that."

Hannah nodded. "I know. It's just the thought of having to go through all that again: the not knowing, the worrying…" She fell silent.

"At least this time we don't have to pretend." Franz gave a wry smile. "Or cosy up to odious party officials just so we can protect him." He frowned, wondering whether he'd actually succeeded after all. Perhaps his son would have been safer in a correction camp than in the army. He was still pondering that when Hannah spoke again.

"How long do you think the fighting will go on?" Hannah watched him carefully.

Franz shrugged. "With Poland? Probably not very long. But Britain and France won't be so easy." He fell silent. Europe was about to be engulfed in another war. Franz sighed and offered up a silent prayer that God would look after his son.

****

Regent's Park, London

"We've got our orders!" Marty ran through the ballroom whooping with delight. Rob and Mike exchanged glances.

"Where are we going, then?" Mike asked eventually.

Marty shrugged. "Don't know, but it's got to be overseas, hasn't it? I'll go and see what else I can find out." He disappeared back through the door.

Rob turned over on the hard floor and tried to ignore the churning sensation in his stomach. This was the news he'd been dreading. He would have to contact Annie and put off the wedding, unless they weren't going immediately. He hoped he would at least have time to say goodbye to her before they left.

"It might not be overseas." Mike spoke in a low voice. Most of the other men were celebrating the news and he didn't want to dampen their enthusiasm.

"No, let's hope not." Rob couldn't bring himself to tell Mike about the nightmares that had begun again since the likelihood of their being mobilised had increased.

Mike fell silent. He wasn't looking forward to fighting again either, but as far as he was concerned, there was no choice.

"Excitement over." Marty reappeared and flung himself down next to them, disappointment etched across his face. "Looks like we're only going to Kent."

Rob breathed a sigh of relief. The wedding could go ahead after all. Feeling slightly happier, he rolled over onto his back and stared up at the ornate ceiling. He could hear Marty complaining about the lack of action and Mike making suitably sympathetic noises. He smiled to himself. He knew Mike was likely to be just as delighted as he was that they'd had a reprieve.

Chapter Forty-one

Forest of Kampinos, Poland

"We need to make a run for it!" Stani had to shout to make himself heard above the German artillery bombardment and the relentless bombing of the Heinkels, which were busy setting ablaze the woods that were their only protection.

Alek was about to argue when a shell landed a few metres away, throwing him off his horse and deafening him completely. He was vaguely aware of his brother pulling him upright, his vision blurred, head still spinning from the force of the explosion.

"I said, are you injured?" Stani yelled for the third time. This time Alek heard him and shook his head, then immediately wished he hadn't as a sick, dizzy feeling swept over him. Seeing him stagger, Stani grabbed his arm and Alek's horse's reins and pulled them both into the woods, away from the advancing Germans.

Although the woods were deeper here, they weren't safe yet. They could still hear the aeroplanes above them and, every now and then, craters appeared as stray shells landed nearby.

"Where are we going?" Alek was finally beginning to regain his senses.

"The rest of the Poznan Army has gone to defend Warsaw. I think we should try and join them."

Alek nodded. "Good idea. We'll never turn them back here." He sighed. "I think the bastards are going to win, Stani."

Stani stared at his brother for a few moments. "I think you're probably right, but we have to keep trying."

Alek gave a wry smile. "Come on then. Let's go and defeat the rest of the German army." He and Stani climbed back up onto their horses, ducking as more shells landed.

Stani sighed. "They're getting closer…"

****

Beltring, outside Paddock Wood, Kent

"I don't think much of this."

"Christ almighty, they can't be serious. I wouldn't expect my dog to sleep in this."

"Surely they don't really want us to live here?"

"Right bloody tip!"

Rob exchanged glances with Mike and they both grinned as the chorus of complaints reached their ears. They'd been billeted in several large hop houses, which had never been designed for habitation, and given straw mattresses to sleep on. After their previously luxurious accommodation, their new surroundings came as a bit of a shock to most of the men, but Rob and Mike were delighted. Anything was better than being sent overseas and, after their experiences in Spain, the hop houses were more than comfortable enough. Rob was most concerned that after the wedding, for the first time since Spain, he and Annie would be apart for more than a couple of weeks.

"Never mind. You'll be able to get the odd weekend pass and we should get leave at Christmas." Mike tried to cheer him up. Rob shrugged.

"It's not the same though, is it?

"Well at least you're in the same country. It could be worse. Come on, let's get settled in."

Rob tried to put his depression aside and followed his friend into the nearest hop house.

****

Poland

"It looks like the bastards are beaten. Won't be long before they surrender."

Manfried Adelchi smirked. He was one of the more rabid Nazis in the Regiment and Gerhard usually took care to avoid him. Unfortunately only he, Gerhard and half a dozen others had survived the assault a few days earlier when they had finally been relieved by another division and some tanks. The survivors had stayed together, so Gerhard was stuck with Manfried. Still, he was grateful to be alive and he was only likely to remain that way if they defeated the Polish army who were using the wood opposite them for protection.

The Germans had now encircled the Polish army and were pounding them relentlessly with heavy artillery shells while their aircraft bombed every inch of the woods the Poles were using for cover.

"You fought well." The words caught him by surprise and he jumped smartly to attention before he recognised the SS man facing him.

"Yes, sir. Thank you, sir." Gerhard remembered just in time what his father had said about Hans Kohl. He stared ahead, wondering why the man had singled him out.

Hans smiled and, leaning forward, he lowered his voice so only Gerhard could hear him. "When I told your father to make you join the army, I half expected you to refuse, but you surprised me then and you have done again. I've heard nothing but excellent reports about you. Obviously you are putting your experience in Spain to good use." He straightened up and spoke normally. "How would you like a change of uniform?"

Gerhard forgot all about not looking the man in the eye. "Sir?"

"We need good men like you. I'll arrange a transfer to the SS. I'm sure your parents will be delighted." He saluted and walked off, leaving Gerhard staring after him with a mixture of horror and disbelief.

****

Romford, Essex

The guests stood and clinked glasses and Rob looked deeply into the eyes of his wife. They had been married just over two hours now and he could still hardly believe it.

"I love you so much," he whispered softly in her ear, his voice barely audible above the toast to the bride and groom.

"I love you too." Annie was also struggling to believe they were finally married and that this handsome young soldier was really her husband. Although they had known each other for just under three years, it hardly seemed five minutes since they had met. He had changed her life completely and, despite the incredible highs and lows, the times she'd thought he was dead and she would never see him again, she knew she would not have changed anything.

Rob had quite literally swept her off her feet. She couldn't really remember a time when she hadn't known him, when he hadn't been a part of her life. Despite her strong belief that one day she would meet 'the one', her all consuming passion for him had taken her completely by surprise. But now they were finally married and she felt secure.

She glanced around at all the people gathered to celebrate the occasion and smiled. Given the rush to arrange everything, her mother had performed a miracle. The trestle tables were overflowing with sandwiches, sausage rolls, cheese and salad, trifle and cakes. Although she knew Ivy would have preferred Annie resplendent in long flowing white dress and veil, Annie was perfectly happy marrying in the church in a smart day dress and matching coat. Because of the short notice, the reception was being held in Harold's local pub, *The Greyhound*. The large back room of the pub had been decorated with banners and balloons and an area cleared of tables and chairs so they could dance.

Rob looked impeccable in his uniform and she thought again how lucky she was to have found him. Then she remembered that he might soon be leaving to fight and she felt a cold shadow cross her heart, making her shiver, despite the warmth of the early autumn day.

Resolutely she pushed the thought out of her mind and, as they took to floor to dance the first waltz, she relaxed into his arms.

"I can't believe we're finally married," she whispered softly in his ear.

Annie danced with Rob for the next two songs before reluctantly allowing Harold to claim a dance. He was followed swiftly by Bill and then Mike and, much as she enjoyed dancing with them, she couldn't wait for the music to finish so she could be back in Rob's arms again. Eventually, her duty done, she was able to rejoin him. Annie relaxed, closed her eyes and wished the moment could go on forever. If only there wasn't a war… Feeling a gentle tug at her elbow, Annie started, brought out of her reverie by Daisy. She glanced round and realised some time had elapsed while she'd been dancing with Rob and the floor was now filled with the other members of the wedding party.

"Sorry, I didn't mean to make you jump." Daisy was grinning at the startled expression on her friend's face. "I was just coming to ask when you were leaving, as I know you wanted to get an early start."

"Right now, I think?" Annie glanced at Rob, who nodded enthusiastically.

In a flurry of kisses, hugs and good wishes, they said goodbye to everyone and then she threw her bouquet over her shoulder. Turning round to see who had caught it, she was delighted to see it was Daisy, although her friend looked horrified. Annie glanced at Mike. He was watching Daisy with such longing, Annie felt sorry for him.

Annie stepped towards her. "You look petrified!"

Daisy shrugged. "You know me. I've no intention of getting serious about anyone. Even you throwing your bouquet at me is not going to change that." She was pleased to see that Annie looked disappointed.

"So there's no chance for Mike then?"

Daisy took her hand. "No, Annie, none at all and he knows it too, so stop matchmaking and go and enjoy your honeymoon."

"I've seen the way he looks at you when he thinks no one's watching." Annie couldn't leave it there. She liked Mike and she knew he still liked Daisy.

Daisy shrugged. "There's nothing I can do about that, Annie. I just don't feel the same and that isn't going to alter, however much you might want it to." She changed the subject and began talking about Annie's honeymoon. "I think Potter Heigham sounds delightful. So romantic!"

Annie laughed and gave up. She would work on Daisy again when she came back.

"I thought it was going to be difficult to arrange at the last moment, especially as so many people are getting married or taking holidays, in case…" Annie fell silent as she thought about the danger Rob was likely to be in soon.

Daisy smiled to herself. Although she hadn't meant to upset Annie, just stop her asking questions about Mike, it looked like she'd unintentionally managed to hit a nerve. She'd told Annie the truth, well sort of. She'd finally broken off the relationship with Dick because he had started talking about marriage again, but that didn't mean she was getting serious about Mike. She liked Mike but she had no intention of tying herself down to him, not when there were so many other men out there she hadn't met yet. She realised Annie was talking again.

"Fortunately the hotel had a last minute cancellation, so Norfolk here we come!"

****

Forest of Kampinos, Poland

"Have you any idea where we are?" They had been walking for days and Alek was sure they'd already covered this part of the forest. So far they'd managed to avoid the bogs and marshland but the shelling was unceasing and, although they'd filled their water bottles from one of the rivers and found some stale bread and cheese in an abandoned house, he was feeling weak from lack of food. The horses were also tired and hungry, so they'd stopped riding and were walking them instead.

Stani shook his head. "No, I'll search the next dead German we come across and see if he's got any maps of the area."

"Let's hope he's also carrying some ammo and food. My stomach thinks my throat's been cut."

Stani gave a wry smile. "Mine too." He was about to say more when he spotted a break in the trees in front of them. He motioned to Alek to stay where he was, handed him the reins of his horse and crawled forward on his stomach. He could see a village but it was at least a mile away, across open ground. On the steep bank of the Vistula, he could see German artillery. The position allowed them to dominate the region. Stani sighed. If the horses were fresh they might make it, but they weren't. He was still thinking about what to do when the Germans opened fire, showering the road with a formidable barrage. Alek tied the horses to the nearest tree and crawled forward to where Stani was concealed.

"How the fuck are we going to get across there?" Alek stared in horror.

Stani shook his head. "I have no idea, Alek. We can't go back, we have to go forward."

"We'll never make it."

Stani was silent. Then he looked at his brother. "We have to. Either that or we surrender."

****

Potter Heigham, Norfolk Broads

The hotel was on the banks of the river not far from the low bridge. The countryside was lush and green from the autumn rains and Annie fell in love almost immediately with the wide open fields, interwoven with numerous rivers and the large lakes known as the Broads. As they drove through the countryside, Annie found herself wishing she could sit in the car enjoying the scenery for a lot longer. This was partly because she was enjoying the freedom of having nothing to do other than to enjoy herself with the man she loved, but more to do with the fact that she was trying to put off the moment when they would consummate their marriage. She kept telling herself that it was ridiculous to be nervous… this was Rob after all. This was the man who she had been tempted to sleep with so many times over the past few years. She had refrained because of her fear of becoming pregnant and the conventional wisdom that he would leave her immediately he'd 'got what he wanted'. Now there was nothing to stop them, she was faced with unaccountable nerves.

She wondered whether Rob felt the same, but looking at his calm unruffled exterior, she dismissed it as unlikely. He seemed quite his normal self and not in the least worried about what was to come. Fleetingly she wondered if he'd ever slept with anyone else, perhaps before he'd met her or maybe when he was in Spain, when they'd been apart for so long and when neither had known whether the other was still alive. That would explain his lack of nerves, or maybe it was just because he'd had to wait and now it wasn't going to be much longer. Goodness, the thought suddenly struck her, what if she was a disappointment to him and he regretted marrying her. As her thoughts began to descend into anxiety, she was suddenly aware that Rob had stopped the car.

"What's the matter?" She was so engrossed by her anxious thoughts, she initially thought he was going to tell her he'd made a mistake.

"I just wanted to kiss my wife and tell her how much I love her, how happy she has made me by becoming my wife and how I will always love her, no matter what happens in the future and whatever the world throws at us."

He gave her no chance to answer as his lips met hers and his arms held her close. Feeling her fears melt away, Annie began to respond and, as she felt her body begin to flood with desire, her earlier worries disappeared as if they had never existed.

"Come on, let's get to the hotel and settle in." Rob reluctantly pulled away, knowing if he continued to kiss her he would not be able to stop. Trying frantically to think of something else because it was almost too uncomfortable to drive, he turned his thoughts to the war, a subject always guaranteed to dampen any desire.

Unaware of his reflections, Annie smiled. She was feeling more relaxed now and when, after another half an hour, they arrived in the village, her earlier fears had almost completely disappeared.

****

Czeczotki, Poland

"I can't believe we made it." Alek was panting almost as much as his horse.

Stani was about to answer him when the Germans started shelling again. He stared back at the forest and began to pray. He could see numerous men on horses charging full speed across the open ground, German shells and bullets flying all around them. Several men and horses were hit and then the German firing stopped suddenly. Stani stared hard at the raised ground behind the charging horses but all was quiet.

"Why have they stopped?" Alek was standing by his side.

Stani shrugged. He was still watching the horsemen who were almost upon them now. To his relief, he could see that the majority had made it. He stepped forward as the survivors skidded to a halt not far from where he was standing.

"Fuck, that was close." The officer nearest Stani grinned at him, slid to the ground and patted his sweating horse. "Any idea why they stopped firing at us?"

Stani shook his head. "No, none at all." He gave a weary smile. "Perhaps we should just be grateful for small mercies. I'm Captain Stanislav Sosnkowski, 18th Polish Lancers or what's left of them. This is my brother Aleksander, of the same."

"Captain Klemens Rudnicki. We're all that remains of the 7th Mounted Light Infantry. The *Szkop* have taken thousands of prisoners." He fell silent remembering all his dead men, then turned his attention back to Stani. "We're going to make for Warsaw. What about you?"

Stani nodded. "That's where we were heading. We'll go with you."

"Good." Klemens looked down at his map and glanced round to get his bearings before climbing back up on his horse, patting him gently and tugging on the reins. He pointed towards some fields to their left. "That would seem to be the quickest way, although we may need to detour if we run into too many *Szkop*. There's no time to waste. Let's go."

Stani and Alek were already mounting up and, within moments, they were riding across the fields.

****

Berlin

"It's so peaceful without Andreas here." Karin propped herself up on her elbow, stared down at Claudia and leaned forward to kiss her. They were both in bed, the door firmly closed. Karin's servants were both out for the evening, Heidi was asleep and they had gone to bed early intending to make the most of their time together.

"Mmm. It is, isn't it?" Claudia returned her kiss and reached for Karin's breast, then Heidi began crying. Karin grinned and sat up.

"Looks like someone has other ideas." She climbed out of bed, opened the door, hurried along to the nursery and picked up Heidi. Her daughter immediately stopped crying and smiled instead. Karin laughed, took her back to the bedroom, put her in the bed and climbed back in so Heidi was between them.

Karin gazed down at her daughter and reached out for Claudia's hand. "I can never thank you enough, Claudia."

Claudia smiled. "It was a pleasure, Karin, especially as we pulled the wool over Andreas' eyes as well."

Karin nodded. She reached out and gently stroked Heidi's head.

Claudia watched them for a few moments. She loved seeing Karin so happy. "Shall I go and make some coffee?"

Karin nodded. "That would be nice. Bring the cognac upstairs too. We can have some with our coffee." Claudia nodded and was about to climb out of bed when downstairs the front door banged loudly.

"Karin!"

Claudia and Karin stared at each other in horror before leaping out of bed. Claudia hid her underwear under the bed and dressed quickly in her dress and cardigan while Karin pulled her dressing gown on and hurried to the bedroom door.

"Andreas?"

"Of course! Who else would it be?" She heard him laugh. "Don't come down, I'll come up." He began bounding up the stairs before she could answer. There wasn't time for Claudia to get back to her own room, so she picked up Heidi and walked over to the window, her heart pounding, her throat dry with fear.

Andreas kissed Karin at the door and slid past her into the bedroom. He stopped. "Oh, hello Claudia. I didn't know you were in here…"

"Heidi woke, so I brought her in here while I fed her."

"I like to be a part of all her life," Karin chipped in.

Andreas glanced from one to the other and wondered what was going on. Something was definitely not right. Karin was flushed, her hair disheveled and she was undressed. If it had been anyone else but Karin, he might have wondered if she had been hiding a man in the room but that was ridiculous. In any case, Claudia had been here. Andreas frowned as the thought crossed his mind that maybe they had been in bed together. Then he relaxed. Claudia was fully dressed and, in any case, Karin wouldn't do anything so degrading. He'd probably just startled her.

He turned his attention to Claudia, staring at her until she finally took the hint. "Sorry. You want to be alone, don't you… I'll take Heidi back to the nursery. Goodnight Karin, Andreas." She looked quickly at Karin who nodded imperceptibly and headed through the door before he could say anything else.

Andreas was still watching his wife. She definitely looked uneasy for some reason. He stepped towards her. "I'm sorry if I frightened you. I got a week's leave at the last moment, so I thought I'd come home and see my wife and daughter."

Karin forced herself to smile. "It's a lovely surprise." She undid her dressing gown and reached out for him. She couldn't afford for Andreas to become suspicious, not when everything was so perfect. "I've missed you, Andreas."

Andreas put his arms around her and pushed his misgivings to one side. Perhaps he was imagining things.

****

Potter Heigham, Norfolk

The hotel was quite small with only three guest rooms but was so homely, Annie wished they could stay there forever, safe from the outside world. The owners, a small bald man with a rather large pot belly, a big smile and an almost incomprehensible accent, and his equally rotund wife, made them very welcome. Fortunately she spoke much slower and more clearly than her husband, her soft country burr explaining what time dinner and breakfast were and where they could find clean towels. Then she took them up to their room.

As they went up the winding narrow stairs to their room overlooking the river, Annie suddenly felt shy again and her earlier anxieties resurfaced. The large comfortable double bed in the middle of the room seemed almost threatening. Glancing at Rob, she realised for the first time that he felt the same and she relaxed slightly. Rob could sense her nerves and it was affecting him too. The last thing he actually wanted to do now was to go to bed.

"Come on let's have a quick wash and some dinner." He was relieved when Annie nodded. This struck him as rather ironic, given the number of times they had almost 'gone all the way' and how frustrated he had been when he'd had to pull back at the last moment.

Their hosts had made a special effort for them, their table lit by a solitary candle. There were also two complimentary glasses of wine.

Dinner was roast chicken with roast potatoes, stuffing and a selection of vegetables, something Annie normally loved but she had suddenly lost her appetite and she pushed the food around her plate listlessly.

"We can always just go to bed and sleep, you know." Rob picked up on her mood.

"Wouldn't you mind?" Annie felt even more stupid.

"We've got our whole lives ahead of us, of course I don't." Rob gave a rueful smile. "I love you. I'm quite happy to wait until you're ready. I just want you to be happy."

Annie began to relax, knowing he meant what he said. She tucked into her food with renewed appetite and ordered second helpings of the homemade rhubarb crumble and custard.

Rob watched her with some amusement. His offer hadn't been entirely altruistic. He too was becoming increasingly nervous, and offering to wait had taken some of the pressure away from him. The first time they made love was so important, especially after they had waited so long. But having never slept with anyone before, he was worried he would be a disappointment.

Unfortunately, making love to Annie was all he could think of and he wondered whether it would have been easier if they had just given into their passion earlier, when making love would have been a natural progression. All this preparation was making the whole thing seem rather clinical and adding to his anxiety about his ability to perform. It was one thing talking about it in the barracks with his mates, most of whom were probably lying about their experiences anyway; it was something completely different when you wanted to make it perfect with the woman of your dreams. Mike hadn't been much help either, just telling him it would all come naturally and to stop worrying.

"I can't eat another thing." Annie finished her third glass of wine and stared across the table at him. Rob reached out and took her hand. Rather reluctantly, they left the dining room and climbed slowly up the narrow stairs to the bedroom.

The minute they entered the room, Annie grabbed her long cream silk nightdress and dressing gown, bought especially for the occasion, and disappeared into the bathroom where she was gone so long, Rob began to worry. Having cleaned her teeth twice and washed the more intimate parts of her body several times, she eventually reappeared and, before he could say anything, she discarded her dressing gown on the floor and disappeared quickly under the bed covers.

Rob went into the bathroom and stood there for several moments trying to calm himself down. Although he had only caught a glimpse of the undulating curves of her body through the silk of the negligee, it had been enough to still his fears about being able to rise to the occasion; his main worry now was that he was so excited, it would be over before it began. He undressed quickly, took one last look in the mirror, returned to the bedroom and climbed in beside her. Sensing she might be more comfortable in semi darkness, he switched off the light and got up again to open the blackout curtain, leaving the room flooded with moonlight. Annie stared at the outline of his naked body silhouetted in the moonlight and smiled.

They lay there for a couple of moments, the tension rising silently between them and then Rob turned and awkwardly put his arm round her. "Why don't you take your nightdress off?"

Annie hesitated, then she sat up and quickly discarded the silk gown before lying down again and pulling the covers over her naked body, snuggling up to him. Unable to wait any longer, Rob kissed her, his tongue probing and teasing as he gently ran his hands over her body, sending shivers up and down her spine. Annie moaned softly as the familiar sensation of desire flooded through her and gradually her shyness began to disappear in a haze of pleasure as his hands explored her body in the way she knew so well. Only this time she didn't have to say no or try to stop him.

Listening to her moaning and writhing with pleasure, Rob could wait no longer. He lifted himself up until he was poised above her. He stared into her eyes and eased himself inside her.

After the initial discomfort of him entering her, Annie suddenly found her body reacting to his thrusts. Within minutes, she had lost herself to the waves of passion engulfing her, and her gasps and moans filled his ears as he moved gently backwards and forwards. Her cries were enough to tip him over the edge and, unable to restrain himself any longer, he finally allowed himself to release the pent up tension that had been building in him all day. The depth of his climax when it did come took him completely by surprise and left him panting with exertion.

Finally spent, he lay back down on the bed, his first reaction relief that he had not climaxed too soon or been unable to perform at all. His second reaction, coming almost instantly on the heels of the first, was that he had just experienced paradise and that nothing else in his life could ever match such an incredible feeling. Within seconds he had regained his breath enough to speak and he looked at Annie anxiously, worried that he might have hurt her or that she hadn't enjoyed it.

"Are you alright?" He kept his voice low, suddenly conscious they might have been making rather a lot of noise.

Annie smiled back at him, a dreamy look in her half closed eyes, her face flushed with the aftermath of her passion. "Mmm. I didn't think it would be like that. Mum always gave the impression it was something women had to endure rather than being…' She stopped, unable to describe how she felt and, turning on her side towards him, she reached out her arm and lay it gently across his chest.

Rob closed his eyes, wondering if he would ever feel better in his life than he did right at this moment and then, feeling totally complete, he quickly fell into a deep sleep. Annie smiled contentedly and, snuggling up to him, lay listening to his breathing for some time until she too began to doze.

Chapter Forty-two

Berlin

Andreas sat sipping his coffee in the kitchen and wondered why he felt like a stranger in his own home. The relationship between Karin and Claudia seemed even closer than when he'd gone away and, while he didn't mind them being friends, they both appeared to have forgotten he was the master of the house. It was nothing he could put his finger on, just a feeling they had secrets he wasn't privy to. Several times he'd entered a room and the conversation had ceased abruptly; at other times he was sure they'd changed the subject the moment he'd come near them.

"You look thoughtful. Is anything the matter?" Karin tried to sound solicitous although her heart was beating faster. She wished Andreas would hurry up and go back to Poland. All the time he was there, she was terrified he would suspect something.

Andreas smiled. "No, not really…" He was about to mention his concerns when he decided against it. He was leaving later that day and he probably wouldn't be back for while, so why cause problems. Given the circumstances of Heidi's birth, things would be much worse if his mistress and his wife hated each other. Maybe he should be grateful, instead of trying to find problems.

****

En route back to London

"I can't believe it's been a week." Annie sighed. "I don't want to go home."

Rob squeezed her hand. "Nor do I, but unfortunately we have to."

Even the weather had been kind to them, bathing each day in unseasonably warm sunshine and gentle breezes. They had spent the days wandering the countryside, stopping by rivers and streams to eat the picnics packed by their genial hosts. The nights were mild with cloudless skies, ideal for walking in the moonlight through the quiet country village and looking up at the stars. When they returned to their room they would make love and then lie in each other's arms listening to the gentle lapping of the river on the shore or the poignant sound of the rigging on the yachts rattling in the wind.

On the day they were due to leave they drove home and stopped off in Thetford Forest. Neither of them wanted to hurry, so they lingered as long as they could, watching the squirrels and rabbits at play while they wandered through the trees and listened to the cheerful singing of the birds, revelling at the peace and serenity surrounding them. Eventually, unable to delay any longer, they climbed back into the car and headed silently towards London.

****

Berlin

Franz read the latest letter from Gerhard and tried to hide his misgivings from Hannah. He couldn't think of any reason Hans would recommend a transfer to the SS for Gerhard, unless it was an unspoken threat to him. Maybe Hans suspected him of leaking information to the British. Franz shook his head and told himself not to be so dramatic. There was no reason to suppose anyone suspected. Perhaps Hans really did think Gerhard was worthy of promotion.

"What's the matter? Is Gerhard alright?" Hannah was pale, her hand to her mouth. She had seen the post arrive but by the time she got there, Franz was already reading the letter, an expression of concern on his face.

"No, Gerhard's fine Hannah, honestly." He sighed and handed her the piece of Feldpost paper. "Apparently Hans is in Poland as well and has recommended Gerhard for a transfer to the SS."

Hannah stared at him in disbelief, then down at the letter to see if he was joking. She glanced back up at him. "I hoped you were teasing me but you're not."

Franz shook his head. "No."

"Why would he do that?"

Franz gave a wintery smile. "That's a very good question, Hannah. I wish I knew the answer."

****

En route back to London

As they neared the capital, Rob stopped on the outskirts and found a fish and chip shop, more to delay the inevitable than because he was hungry. Having bought them both some cod and chips, they looked around for somewhere to sit and eat and then saw a bench just inside the local park. In the far corner there were some boys playing football, their voices carrying on the breeze and a group of younger children were playing on the swings. As they sat eating their meal out of newspaper, Annie licked the salt and vinegar off her lips and smiled. "Don't you wish you could eat fish and chips every day?"

Rob laughed. "I think you'd get very bored." He loved seeing her enjoying herself. Whenever he thought back to how close he had come to losing her in Spain, he felt cold. He put out his arm and pulled her close, loving the feel of her body next to his. They sat for a while in silence, enjoying each other's company while the clouds gradually gathered overhead, first hiding the sun and then growing darker until Rob felt the first spots of rain on his head

"Come on, let's go home." He suddenly needed to feel the warmth of her body next to his for one last night. He was due to return to Kent the next day, back to the other world; the one that was at war and which threatened his future happiness; but this was still part of his honeymoon and he wanted to make the most of every minute.

As the rain descended in sheets, Annie raced him back to the car, jumping over puddles and narrowly missing a car in the gloom. Although they were both soaked by the time they reached the car, it didn't seem to matter. Even the smell of their clothing drying while they drove through the winding lanes in the evening light, was something to be savoured.

Rob sighed. He had something he needed to discuss with Annie but he didn't know how to broach it. He knew that eventually he would be going to fight and there was a possibility he might not come back but, knowing Annie would do anything to avoid the conversation and not wanting to spoil their honeymoon, he had decided to wait until they were in the car on the way home. He was now running out of time, London was fast approaching and he still hadn't said anything.

****

Lvov, Eastern Poland

"The Soviets have crossed the border." Aunt Halina rushed into the small bedroom Felcia was sharing with Ala and Mariusz. There had been a brief lull in the shelling and they had emerged from the street shelter to try and get some rest. The Germans had been bombarding Lvov for days, the defenders' job made more difficult by the help the enemy was receiving from local Ukranian-Polish citizens. They were busy informing the Germans of the Polish positions and the Poles were taking very heavy casualties.

For the first time since she'd heard about Iwan's death, Felcia showed interest in something other than Mariusz. She sat up and stared at Halina in alarm. "Are you sure?"

Halina nodded. "They've just said so on the wireless. They're here to help us fight the Nazis apparently."

Felcia didn't answer for a moment. She exchanged glances with Ala and then turned back to Halina. "That doesn't sound like the Russians. I thought they'd signed a pact with the Germans not to fight them."

Halina nodded. "That's what the news reader said."

"So what do we do?" Felcia gazed down at Mariusz playing happily on the floor with his toy cars and tried to fight back the tears that threatened to fall every time she looked at her son and remembered that his father would never see him growing up. "Iwan wanted us to come here because he thought we'd be safer. If he'd known how quickly the Germans would advance, he would probably have suggested we go home to my parents instead. Now we'd have trouble getting to them without going through the German lines. But if we stay here…"

"Well, we don't know the Russians mean us harm," Ala interrupted. "They might really be here to help us." She saw her sister's face and fell silent.

Halina nodded. "Alright, but I don't think we should leave it too long. I wouldn't trust the Ruskies any further than I could throw them. I'd rather take my chances with the Germans."

But Felcia shrugged. "Ala is right. We don't know anything for certain, so perhaps we should stay here and wait and see what happens before making any decisions."

Felcia sighed. Deep down she felt the same as Halina. If only Iwan was here to ask, but he wasn't. She was on her own now and she had her son to look after. More than anything, she would love to go home but she had to make sure she made the right decision.

****

Romford, Essex

Rob pulled up outside her parents' house where they were staying the night and, reaching across the seat, he took her hands. "Before you get out, we have to talk."

Annie stared at him, her heart in her mouth. She made an attempt to joke. "That sounds serious."

Rob didn't smile. "I don't know when I'll be going overseas but it will happen eventually."

There was silence, then Annie gave a tremulous smile. "I know, although I was hoping the war might end or something…" She tailed off.

Rob sighed. That had been the easy part. "I know you don't want to think that anything might happen to me but… no, please let me finish, darling." He was determined not to let her interrupt. "This isn't easy for me either, but I have to say it, just in case. If anything happens to me, you must find someone else and get on with your life."

Annie gasped and opened her mouth to argue. Rob ignored her. "I couldn't bear it if I was sitting up there on a cloud in heaven playing my harp, watching you being miserable down here." His attempt to lighten the mood failed miserably. Annie just glared at him. He tried again. "Annie, we have to be realistic and, if the positions were reversed, you wouldn't want me to live on my own for the rest of my life, would you?"

Annie was silent. She would never expect him to live on his own if anything happened to her, but that was different. She would never fall in love again if Rob didn't come back. Even in her thoughts she couldn't say 'was killed', in case that jinxed him and made it happen.

Knowing he wouldn't leave the conversation there if she didn't agree, she gave a reluctant nod. "Let's not talk about it anymore." She squeezed his hand.

Rob shook his head. "You have to promise me, Annie."

Annie stared at him in horror. But even as she searched frantically for some argument that would make him change his mind, she knew nothing she could say would make any difference. She blinked away her tears. "I promise." Her voice was so low, he could hardly hear her, but it was enough. Rob knew she would keep her word. "The same goes for you." Her softly added words made him smile. He would never want anyone else; Annie was the only girl for him, but he nodded anyway.

"Yes, I promise too."

He pulled her into his arms and hugged her close, relieved the words that had been floating around his head for so long were now in the open. "Thank you, darling. I didn't want to upset you but we did need to talk about it so there was no doubt." Rob didn't add that he couldn't bear the thought of her being with anyone else because he didn't want her going back on her promise. He loved her so much he just wanted to be sure she would be happy. He had no right to expect her to live out the rest of her life on her own. If he wasn't there to help her enjoy life, then it was important that someone else did.

Chapter Forty-three

Warsaw

Warsaw was in chaos by the time they arrived. The Germans had reached the outskirts of the city weeks earlier but the defenders, over a hundred and fifty thousand civilians led by a small defence force under the command of General Walerian Czuma, had constructed barricades from overturned trams, furniture and removal vans and managed to stop the 35th Panzer Regiment in the suburbs of Ochota and Rakowiec.

"They're trying to get through Praga," a harassed officer yelled at Stani and Klemens on their arrival. "It's an eastern suburb." He pointed roughly in the direction they should go, after seeing the confusion on Klemens' face.

Stani nodded. "We're on our way. Can we get some supplies first? We're low on ammunition and the horses haven't eaten."

The officer gave a harsh laugh. "If you can find something, you're welcome to it." He turned back to yell at his men who were busy reinforcing a barricade. As he did so, bullets ricocheted around them and he fell to the floor. Stani, Alek and Klemens ducked their heads, kicked their horses and rode towards a damaged building. They were followed by the rest of the men. Sliding down from their horses, they found some cover and began firing in the general direction of the German infantry who were fighting their way through the streets towards them.

"Christ, look at that!" Alek pointed in amazement. Burning beds and mattresses were falling from the tenement buildings on top of the advancing Germans. Despite the noise, he could hear the horrific screams of the enemy as burning oil lamps were hurled at them, adding to the fierce cacophony of noise. Flames, smoke, snipers firing relentlessly from the roofs of the surrounding properties soon took their toll and, after a short violent fight, the Germans began to retreat.

****

Romford, Essex

Annie sat on the bed and watched Rob pack. Breakfast had been a quiet sombre affair, despite his attempt to raise the mood. Annie had made an effort to be cheerful but she struggled to ignore the relentless ticking of the wall clock, bringing their last moments together ever closer. She made an effort and pushed the dark thoughts from her mind. If only he hadn't insisted on talking about her remarrying if anything happened to him. *But he's only going back to Kent, stop imagining the worst.* Annie gave a wry smile at the sensible voice in her mind and wished she could block out the other one, the niggling voice that said if he went overseas he wouldn't come back to her.

Eventually he was ready and she walked downstairs with him, out of the front door and into the street. "I think we should say goodbye here, Annie. I don't think I can bear you coming to the station with me… all those strangers…"

Annie was about to argue, then she nodded. "You're right. I don't think I could either." She fell silent, willing the tears to wait until he'd gone.

Rob turned to face her. "Well, this is it then." He reached out and stroked her hair.

"Yes." Annie stared up into his eyes and struggled to fight back the tears. "You will take care of yourself, won't you?"

"Of course I will." Rob pulled her into his arms and hugged her tight. "I love you, Annie. Never forget that."

"I love you too, darling." Annie could hardly say the words. She clung to him and it was only with a supreme effort that he managed to pull himself away.

"I have to go, Annie, or I'll miss my train." He stepped away, not giving her time to say anything and strode off towards the station. Annie watched him until he reached the end of the road. He turned briefly, waved and was gone.

****

Lvov, Poland

"The Germans have asked us to surrender." Halina was pale and Felcia could see the strain on her face.

"Do you think we will?"

Halina shrugged. "I don't know. I wouldn't think so."

There was silence and Felcia exchanged glances with Ala. "Maybe we should try and get home while there's no fighting going on."

Ala blanched. "We'd never make it with Mariusz, Felcia. It's much too far. It's not like we even have any transport."

"But if we stay and the Germans over-run the city, we could be stuck here." Felcia stared at her aunt and Ala and wished she knew what to do for the best. "If only Iwan was here." She could feel tears pricking her eyes and she quickly wiped them away. "Or Stani and Alek."

"Do you think they're alright?" Ala voiced her own fears. Felcia reached out for her sister's hand.

"Yes, I'm sure they are. We have to believe that anyway."

Ala nodded and tried to ignore the pounding of her heart.

****

London

To start with, Annie didn't have much time to miss Rob; she was too busy now the ATS was on a war footing. She and Daisy had been billeted together and they were both working in a canteen, much to Annie's irritation.

"Are you still going to volunteer for something else?" Daisy was admiring her new skirt suit in the mirror. "I think this colour goes well with the armband, don't you?"

Annie looked up from her bed and sighed. Daisy's shallow outlook on life never ceased to amaze her. "Well, having learnt to drive in Spain, I thought I would volunteer to be a driver. It's got to be more use than serving food." *Which any idiot can do*, she added to herself.

Daisy laughed. "Good luck with that. You know what the men in charge are like. They think us little women aren't capable of doing much more than cooking and cleaning."

"According to the woman who recruited me, the ATS are grudgingly accepting women drivers. I wouldn't have joined otherwise." Annie bristled. "I'm as good as most of the men when it comes to driving and I even know the basics of how to fix an engine when it goes wrong, which a lot of them don't."

Daisy shrugged and kept her voice expressionless. "Don't have a go at me, Annie. God forbid anyone should tell you not to something you've set your mind to."

Annie gave a rueful smile. "It would be stupid of them to waste my skills and experience, especially with so many men having been mobilised."

Daisy said nothing but she smiled to herself. She had a feeling Annie might have to fight with more than words to get the ATS to take her seriously as a driver.

****

Outside Warsaw

Gerhard stood to attention in the large army tent and wondered what Hans wanted from him.

"Well, Gerhard, the uniform suits you. I'm sure you're pleased to be away from the fighting."

Gerhard hesitated. What on earth was he supposed to answer to that?

"I'm pleased to be of service to the Reich in whatever capacity I'm needed," he replied eventually.

Hans roared with laughter. "I see you've inherited your father's tact and diplomacy. Good answer." He glanced down at the file in front of him and then back up at Gerhard. "I have a job for you."

"Yes, sir."

"This is top secret." Hans was standing now, his face inches from Gerhard's. "We're taking heavy casualties, so we need to recruit some more men. Some of the Poles we've captured are of German origin; others might be persuaded to fight for us." He ignored Gerhard's gasp of surprise. "You'd be surprised how many men would prefer to do that than be a prisoner. We've already recruited several. Your job will be to investigate those who have volunteered. We need to make sure there are no spies among them. Understood?"

Gerhard nodded then remembered where he was. "Yes, sir."

Hans smiled. "Good. You can start with this pile here." He indicated a small number of files by the side of his desk. "I'll have a desk brought in here. You can work with me."

"Yes, sir." Gerhard was bemused and he wondered why Kohl was being so friendly. He had a feeling there was another agenda, but he had no idea what it was.

****

London

As Daisy had anticipated, becoming a driver with the ATS was not as easy as Annie had expected. Although she requested a transfer to the driving pool, no one took any notice. Instead she was still stuck in an extremely hot kitchen from early morning to late at night.

"I've got no intention of spending the war in a bloody kitchen. I'm not going to give up arguing with them." Annie threw herself down on her bed and sighed loudly.

"Good for you." Daisy was sitting on her bed busy reading the latest *Woman* magazine and wasn't that interested. Working in the canteen was the perfect place to meet some very nice young men and she loved every minute of it. "I'm quite happy where I am. It's much better than working in Boots."

"Only because you can flirt with all the men." Annie shook her head. "Honestly, Daisy, sometimes you're so shallow."

Daisy looked hurt. "I didn't ask for a war, so I might as well try and enjoy it while I can. And anyway, I'm helping to keep up the men's morale."

Annie grinned, her earlier bad humour temporarily forgotten. "Only you could say that."

Daisy glanced up from her magazine. "Talking of keeping up morale, there's a dance tomorrow night in the Mess. Do you want to come?"

Annie hesitated then shook her head. "No, I don't think so. It doesn't seem right to be out enjoying myself when Rob could be getting ready to go overseas."

Daisy sighed. Annie's love for Rob had always bordered on obsession and Daisy was becoming really fed up with Annie's determination to feel sorry for herself. God knows what she would do if anything happened to Rob; she would never cope. Daisy wasn't sure how she felt about that. She didn't want Rob to be hurt but she did want Annie to know how it felt to suffer like she had when Annie had gone to Spain and not bothered to tell her. Even now Daisy could hear the spiteful words and disdainful expression of the Branch Manager as he belittled her for not knowing where her 'best friend' was, the humiliation that Annie, Rob and Mike had plotted behind her back, the disbelieving expression on Harold and Ivy's faces that she really hadn't known what their daughter was planning. Even worse was the knowledge that Annie, Rob and Mike didn't seem to realise how much they'd hurt her. They'd all just assumed things would go back to how they'd been before. Daisy knew she should probably let her animosity go, but for some reason she couldn't. Annie seemed to think her apology was enough but it wasn't. Daisy's pride was still hurt and she couldn't just forgive and forget, not yet.

"All the more reason you should go, Annie. Rob's not going to be sitting in every night, is he? I'm sure he and his mates will carry on going down the pub and there are bound to be dances where they are." She glanced at Annie to see if her words were having any effect, but to her disappointment she couldn't see any sign of jealousy. She sighed and tried one more time. "Come on, it will be fun. You don't have to dance with any men, although it would obviously help with their morale if you do…" *And maybe give me some ammunition to cause trouble*, Daisy added to herself.

Annie laughed. "Oh, alright. I give in, Daisy, but I'm only coming to keep you company." She gave a loud sigh. "And because if I don't, you'll just keep on and on…"

****

Warsaw

The German officer walked up and down the ranks of the captured men. Stani and Alek stared ahead. Klemens had been killed defending the city. They had been standing in the field for ages while the Germans counted them several times and Stani would have tried to escape if he hadn't known just how hopeless it was. The Germans controlled the whole area. Any attempt to escape would result in certain death.

"If the bloody Russians hadn't invaded, we might have been able to hold out until the British and French arrived," the man on his left muttered angrily under his breath.

"That's if they're coming," Alek answered. "Other than declare war, they've done nothing."

"It takes a long time to mobilise, Alek. Look what happened to us and we didn't have to travel thousands of miles." Stani wasn't sure why he felt the need to make excuses for their supposed allies. He felt just as let down by their non-appearance as his brother.

"If the bloody French hadn't interfered, we would have been able to mobilise properly." The man beside him spat into the dirt.

"I doubt whether we could have defeated both the *Szkop* and the Russians. We didn't have enough men to cover the whole of the border." Stani answered.

"Shut up!" He'd failed to notice the German standing in front of him.

He stopped talking and stared ahead. The German was wearing an SS uniform but he didn't seem as confident as the others. Stani risked glancing at the man's face. The German looked about his age but didn't seem particularly happy. He nodded at Stani and marched back to the front.

"That was close," Alek muttered. They'd seen men shot for talking in the ranks.

Stani didn't answer. An idea had come to him and he wanted to share it with Alek, but it would have to wait until they were alone. If his plan worked, they would still be able to fight for their country's freedom, but it would be very dangerous.

****

London

"You can't say you didn't enjoy yourself, Annie. I saw you chatting with that young man." Daisy slumped down on the bed, kicked off her shoes and lay down, her arms behind her head.

"He was telling me all about his fiancée. They've only seen each other once since they got engaged and he's going overseas soon," Annie defended herself and then fell silent. Any mention of going overseas always made her nervous. She was terrified that it wouldn't be much longer before Rob and Mike were sent to France, even though everything seemed quiet over there at the moment.

Daisy shrugged. "You still enjoyed yourself. Why don't you admit it? And you cheered him up. What's wrong with that?"

Annie shook her head. There was no point trying to explain how she felt to Daisy, so she changed the subject. "I noticed you had another letter from Mike this evening? Is it getting serious between you two now then?"

"Goodness, no." Daisy looked horrified. "It's just a bit of fun and, before you ask, he knows that because I've told him, so you can stop looking at me like that."

Annie looked worried. "You might not be serious but I'm sure he is."

Daisy shrugged. "He might have been, but I've made it quite clear that I'm not interested in anything other than having a good time. It's not my fault if he feels differently."

Annie stared at her friend in astonishment and fought down the temptation to slap her. She liked Daisy but there were times her friend's selfishness astounded her.

****

Outside Lublin, Eastern Poland

"What will happen now, Wiktor?" Magda looked terrified. He shook his head. The wireless had just announced the country's surrender. He sighed. What country? The Germans and Russians had split Poland in two. His daughters and grandson were in the east and he had no means of contacting them. From what little he'd heard on the wireless, the fighting against the Germans had been heavy around Lvov, but when the Russians had arrived, the city had surrendered to them, thinking they were there to help.

His sons were missing too. He hoped they had escaped to France or England but there was no way to find out. "No news is good news," he said eventually.

Magda slumped down in the chair and put her head in her hands. "Do you really think our boys are still alive, Wiktor?"

"Yes. If they weren't, we would probably have heard something. I'm more worried about the girls to be honest." He fell silent. He'd been about to say he wouldn't trust the Russians with Polish women when he realised that would only make Magda worry more.

"Well, now we're not at war with them any more, perhaps we can go to Lvov?"

Wiktor frowned. "I don't think its going to be that easy, Magda. We'll probably have to get papers to travel…"

"Then what are we waiting for?" Magda stood up. "Let's at least go and find out whether it's possible to travel before we give up." Wiktor sighed. He admired her enthusiasm but he had a feeling it wasn't going to be that simple.

Raisa was standing outside the kitchen door listening. She'd been about to go in when she heard her mother talking about Felcia and Ala. For the first time since the war had started, she wondered if she might be the only member of the family, other than her parents, to survive. Of course she would be sad if her brothers and sisters were killed, but if she was the only one left, at least then her parents might pay her some attention.

Chapter Forty-four

London

"I can't stand another day in that bloody kitchen." Annie slammed the door and flopped down on the bed. "I've put in several requests for a transfer and nothing's happening, but if that flaming cook says anything else to me, I swear I'll stick one of his own knives in him!"

"Ouch!" Daisy laughed but she could see Annie was serious. "I've never known you so angry."

Annie shook her head. "I can do so much more to help the war effort, sticking me in a kitchen is a complete waste of my time, and theirs."

Daisy hesitated. "Well, I did hear that one of the other women had the same problem."

Annie stared at her. "And?"

"She began to serve up sub-standard food. They got so fed up with her, they transferred her."

Annie smiled.

"Of course it might not work," Daisy cautioned.

"But it's worth a try. I know exactly what I'm going to do. Thanks, Daisy."

Daisy hid a smile. As she'd hoped, Annie had taken the bait. Then she glanced at the clock. "Aaah, I'm going to be late. Are you coming with me?"

Annie shook her head. "No thanks. Like I keep telling you, I'm a married woman. I'm not in slightest bit interested in meeting other men, but you go and enjoy yourself."

Daisy shrugged. She'd given up trying to get Annie to behave indiscreetly. She'd have to think of something else. In the meantime she would go and have some fun. She checked her lipstick in the mirror and smiled. If nothing else, the war had opened up a world of opportunity as far as men were concerned. She was spoilt for choice and she intended to make the most of every moment. After all, these men might have to go and fight soon. It was her patriotic duty to help them enjoy themselves before they went.

****

Berlin

"Is he alright?" Hannah rushed into the sitting room where Franz was reading Gerhard's letter. He looked up and smiled but Hannah could see the strain in his eyes.

"Yes, he's fine. The fighting's finished now. Apparently he's working with Hans investigating Polish volunteers who've joined the Wehrmacht."

Hannah frowned. "Why is Hans taking such an interest in Gerhard? It's not as if you and he are great friends. It doesn't make sense."

Franz sighed. "I know. It's bothering me too." He wondered if he should tell her about Carstairs then realised there was no point. She would only worry and he could do enough of that for both of them.

****

Warsaw

Gerhard stared at the latest batch of files and sighed. He glanced up at the two men standing in front of him. Stanislav and Aleksander Sosnkowski. They'd volunteered a couple of weeks earlier but, given the large numbers, he'd only just got around to them.

"So why did you want to join the German army?"

The taller of the two men answered. "We think you're going to improve the lives of Poles, certainly more than the Russians will, anyway. We're also good fighters and you need people like us to make sure the Russians stay on their side of the line."

Gerhard stared up at him. His comments about the Russians echoed many being made by the Germans themselves. At the moment, the Russians were their allies, but who knew how much longer the peace between them would continue. The Germans did need the Poles and, in any case, as far as Gerhard could see, they were finished as a nation. There would be little point joining the German army to spy on them. In Gerhard's opinion, Hans Kohl was just paranoid. Unless there was something about the volunteer that really stood out, he was unlikely to turn them down. He nodded. "Go and wait in the next tent. You'll be given a chance to clean up and a new uniform. Then you'll be given your orders and sent to join your new regiment, wherever that is. Good luck, gentlemen, and welcome to the Wehrmacht."

Stani and Alek saluted smartly and thanked him, before spinning on their heels and heading towards the adjacent tent.

"Well that was easier than I expected," Stani muttered in a low voice.

Alek nodded. "And me. I thought you were mad when you suggested this." He hesitated. "I hope you're right about this, Stani."

His brother shrugged. "We'll soon see."

****

Lvov, Poland

"We can't leave." Felcia stared at Ala and Halina in despair. She'd just spent a fruitless hour trying to persuade a bored Russian official to give her exit papers.

Ala frowned. "But I thought there was a crossing point at Przemysl?"

"There is, but you still have to have the right papers."

"I don't understand? Why aren't our papers any good?"

"Because I was married to an officer in the Polish army." Felcia turned away so her sister couldn't see the distress in her eyes. "Even though he's dead, I'm still some kind of threat to them."

Halina buried her head in her hands and groaned. "We can't stay here. Since they confiscated all our bank accounts and bought all the goods in the shop, we have no means of feeding ourselves." Felcia sighed. She already had her son and younger sister to worry about. She couldn't carry her aunt too. She searched around for a solution.

"Perhaps we could find jobs?" Felcia looked from Halina to Ala. "They are crying out for labourers on the farms. Maybe we could do that? At least it would get us out of the city."

"Will they let you do that, if you're such a threat? And what about the shop?" Halina snapped.

Felcia shrugged. "You've said yourself there's no means of restocking and you've nothing left to sell. If we can get out to the countryside, maybe we can find a way to get across the occupation zones."

Halina nodded. "You're right, Felcia. We can't just sit back and let the bastards beat us. I'll contact some of my former suppliers and see if they need any workers." Felcia breathed a sigh of relief. Halina sounded more like her old self.

Felcia could see the fear in her sister's face. "Don't worry, Ala. I'll look after you, I promise."

Ala nodded. More than anything she wished she was back home with her parents. Then her heart sank. She had no idea what had happened to her parents. Felcia guessed what she was thinking and reached out to take her hand. "I'm sure Mama and Tata are fine. They are probably worried sick about us."

"And Stani and Alek?"

Felcia shook her head. "I don't know, Ala. Hopefully they escaped. We'll just have to keep praying for them." She didn't want to voice her fears that both her brothers were dead, but deep down, she knew that the likelihood of them both being safe and well was extremely small.

Chapter Forty-five

Lublin, Eastern Poland

Andreas looked around his new office in Distriktstrasse and shrugged. It would do until something better came along. There was damage from the shelling but he would get some Poles to clean it up. He was quite pleased with his promotion to Obersturmbannführer. At least now he was back on par with Hans, who had been promoted some time ago. Thinking of Hans reminded him of Karin, Claudia and Heidi. He frowned. He was bored with Claudia and she was much too friendly with Karin for his liking. He hadn't thought much about their relationship before and, to be honest, it had been useful to him for Karin and Claudia to be friends, but the last time he'd been home, he'd definitely felt excluded. Andreas stared moodily out of the window wondering what to do. Then he made a decision. The next time he went home, he would tell Claudia to leave. Karin didn't need her to help with his daughter. After all, she'd driven him mad to have a child in the first place, it wouldn't hurt her to look after the baby on her own. He would soon find another mistress and this time he wouldn't be taking her home to meet his wife.

Feeling better, he sat down and began going through the files on the large ornate desk that he'd rescued from one of the abandoned country houses he'd passed on his way to the city. He was to be responsible for intensifying agricultural production in the area. His orders were quite simple: larger farms and estates would be taken over completely by the Reich and the other smaller ones, clustered around villages, would have to provide a fixed quota of all their produce. Rationing was to be introduced in any areas that had escaped it so far and Polish POWs would be sent to work on the land, rather than to the Reich as slave labour.

Things were going well so far. Taxes had been raised, the zloty had been devalued so the Germans could buy Polish goods cheaply and there were no longer any large denomination bank notes circulating after the Germans had seized the Bank of Poland.

Andreas closed the file and stood up. It was time to go and visit some of the local farms. He could leave it to his men but he wanted to get a feel for the country and its people and he couldn't do that from behind a desk.

****

London

"Yes! My transfer has come through!" Daisy frowned at the delighted expression on her friend's face.

"How on earth did you manage that?" Then she shook her head. "You didn't?"

Annie grinned. "I'm surprised you didn't notice but you were probably too busy chatting up the men, I suppose." Annie ignored Daisy's offended expression and carried on, "I tried soggy chips and weak, luke-warm tea but that didn't seem to work, so I decided more extreme measures were called for. My coup de grâce was rice pudding with mustard in. Looks like that did work. and quite quickly too. It was only a few days ago I dished that up. I was just planning my new meal too." Annie managed to look suitably sad. Then she grinned. "Oh well, never mind. They'll never know what they've missed."

"Where are you going?"

"The driving depot at Camberley, but I'll be sleeping here some nights, so we'll still see each other." She glanced at her watch and reached for her bag. "I've got to be there in a couple of hours so I'd better get my skates on." She hastily shoved her belongings into her small suitcase, checked her appearance in the mirror, stepped towards Daisy and gave her friend a big hug. After a brief moment, Daisy returned the embrace stiffly but Annie didn't seem to notice. She pulled away.

"Look after yourself, Daisy and don't do anything I wouldn't do!"

Daisy forced a smile. "Well that gives me plenty of scope doesn't it?"

Annie laughed, then turned and hurried to the door. "I'll see you in a few days. Bye"

Daisy nodded. "Bye, Annie. Good luck." She watched Annie disappear out of the door and scowled. She'd expected Annie to get into trouble for dishing up substandard food, not get her transfer and now Annie was going to be based elsewhere, getting her revenge would be even harder. She wondered where her friend got her enthusiasm from. Although she hadn't minded working in the canteen at first, Daisy was now bored stiff serving food every day. But she had no intention of requesting any other duties. The work might be monotonous but flirting with the men who streamed through the canteen every day certainly wasn't. Her eyes gleamed while she thought about the young private she'd dated the previous evening. His muscled body had been a delight to explore and his gratitude that she was prepared to go all the way with him was almost embarrassing. Unfortunately, he'd said he was going to write to her when he went overseas. She frowned. She was seeing him again that evening. She'd have to talk him out of that. She didn't need letters from all and sundry dropping on the doormat, not when she was having so much fun. It could prove embarrassing. The last thing she needed was to have to explain various love sick letters to any new men in her life.

****

Outside Lublin, Eastern Poland

"The Germans have closed all the schools and decreed no children should be taught more than basic numbers up to five hundred and how to write their name. They shouldn't be taught how to read at all." Wiktor read the proclamation from the German poster on a board near the lane leading to the village, tore it down and screwed it up into a ball, and chucked it as far as he could into the nearby field.

"But that's ridiculous!" Magda began.

"No, it isn't. The aim is to destroy all Polish culture. They've already begun stealing our art. It'll be our economic resources next." Wiktor was furious. He was about to say more when he spotted a small dust cloud approaching the farm. He narrowed his eyes and peered into the distance. His heart sank. "Looks like the bastards are coming here." He turned to Magda and Raisa. "Go inside and stay there until I tell you to come out."

Magda and Raisa exchanged glances and then did as he asked. Wiktor watched the dust cloud growing bigger until he could clearly make out a German staff car.

****

Warsaw

Hans stared out of the window and tried to marshal his thoughts. Since the nightmare last night, he'd struggled to concentrate and he wondered why he was finding it so hard to throw off the bad dream this time. Normally it vanished with daylight and, providing he kept busy, it wouldn't recur for ages. But the dream had woken him for three nights in a row and last night he'd been unable to go back to sleep at all. Instead, he'd lain tossing and turning, restlessly waiting for dawn. He frowned. There must be a reason he couldn't shake the dream. Perhaps it was a warning of some sort?

"I've got the papers you wanted, sir."

Hans started. He hadn't heard Gerhard come into the room. "Good, leave them on the desk. If you've finished, you can take the rest of the day off."

"Thank you, sir." Gerhard saluted and marched smartly out of the room. It was unlike Kohl to give him any time off, so he wasn't about to argue. Gerhard frowned as he ran down the stairs. Kohl looked almost grey. Perhaps he was ill. Gerhard tried to feel sorry for his superior officer but failed miserably. Some of the orders coming across his desk made him feel sick but he had no alternative other than to obey. The latest ones had stated that rations for Jews should be reduced to five hundred and three calories a day. The Poles were only on six hundred and he'd heard rumours the German Central Government was trying to reduce them even more.

Gerhard reached the street door and tried to put work out of his mind. He had a few hours off. He would try to enjoy himself.

****

Outside Lublin, Eastern Poland

Wiktor watched the *Szkop* return to the large staff car with clenched fists. Somehow he'd successfully resisted the temptation to shoot the SS man and his German driver with the pistol he'd hidden in the barn. Fortunately they hadn't searched the farm buildings, just given him a long list of instructions about quotas and the penalties for not meeting the target. Wiktor had argued unsuccessfully that he couldn't guarantee the kind of grain crop or vegetables they expected because he was reliant on the weather. He'd had more luck when he'd mentioned the lack of workers to help him. The SS man had promised some Polish POWs to help. Wiktor had tried to look grateful but he had a feeling he hadn't fooled the SS man, who knew exactly what he was thinking.

Andreas walked back to the car and was about to get in when he suddenly spotted a movement from inside the house. Curious, he stopped and went back to the farmer.

"Who's inside?"

"Just my wife and daughter." Wiktor was immediately defensive.

Andreas nodded. "Call them out."

Wiktor opened his mouth to object, then realised there was little point. "Magda, Raisa, come out here."

Andreas turned towards the house and watched the door open. An older woman appeared, followed close behind by a younger one. Andreas stared. He'd only insisted they come out because he didn't like the farmer's attitude. The younger girl was surprisingly pretty with long dark hair, soulful eyes and a delightful pout. He could see anger in her eyes as well as fear, but he could also see something else and he smiled. It looked like he'd found a replacement for Claudia already.

****

Beltring, Kent

"So, how's life in Camberley?" Rob smiled into the receiver wishing she was in his arms instead of on the other end of the telephone. He knew he should be grateful that at least he could speak to her but he couldn't help feeling sorry for himself.

"It's much better than working in the canteen. I don't think I'm suited to being a cook."

"What about Daisy? Is she still there?"

"Yes. I don't think she likes the work particularly, she just enjoys flirting with the men." Annie stopped abruptly and cursed under her breath. She'd forgotten about Mike. Rob hadn't.

"Has she found someone else?"

"No, she just flirts with them." Annie crossed her fingers behind her back hoping he couldn't tell she was lying. "Is Mike still keen on her then?"

"Yes, although he laughs it off every time I ask him when he's going to ask her to marry him."

Annie hesitated. "Probably best not to encourage him too much, Rob."

"Why not?" Even down the telephone she could hear his confusion.

Annie sighed and thought quickly. She didn't want to cause trouble but she liked Mike and didn't want him being hurt. "Because Daisy's probably not in much of a hurry to settle down."

"Ahh, wants to wait until the war's over I suppose?"

"Yes, that's it exactly." Annie breathed a sigh of relief.

"All right, I won't mention marriage again. Anyway, enough of Mike and Daisy. I miss you so much, Annie. I want to make love to you desperately."

Annie felt a warm glow rush through her body. "I miss you too, darling. I think of you all the time when I'm driving."

Rob laughed. "I hope not. You don't want to have an accident."

"I won't. I'm a very good driver." Annie gave a loud sigh that echoed down the line. She knew the pips would go soon and then she would have to leave him again. "I hate this wretched war. All I want is for us to settle down together and have a normal life. It's so unfair, Rob."

"I know. I was thinking the same thing. I wish we'd never gone to Spain, we could have got married and…"

"But the war would still have come…"

"Yes I know, but at least we would have had some time before…" The pips went and Rob leant closer to the receiver as if that would give him more time. "I love you, darling. We will be together again eventually…"

His voice echoed down the silent line and he realised he was talking to fresh air.

****

Outside Lublin, Eastern Poland

"So Raisa, how old are you?" It was the first time Andreas had managed to get her on her own. He'd called back at the farmhouse a couple of times but had been told she was in the fields. This time he'd waited down the long winding lane and watched the farm through his field glasses.

The farmer had left for the fields with his wife and two of the Polish POWs and, after a few moments, he'd seen the girl go into the barn nearest the house. He ran back to his car and drove quickly towards the farm.

Raisa jumped. She'd not heard him come into the barn, her attention on the loudly clucking chickens. "I'm nin… nineteen." She was annoyed with herself for stuttering but there was something about him that she found attractive, despite the dreaded black SS uniform.

Andreas pulled the barn door closed behind him and Raisa felt her heart beginning to pound loudly against her chest. She glanced around, even though she knew there was no other way out, and then back at the German. She licked her lips and saw the expression on his face. She suddenly felt angry.

"Why have you shut the door?" Her voice was more aggressive than she'd intended.

Andreas smiled. "I'm sorry. I didn't mean to frighten you. I promise you, I've never had to force myself on a woman." Somehow her anger made her even more attractive than if she'd just let him take her. He could see she wasn't convinced, so he turned around and opened the barn door. "Look. If you want to go, you can."

Raisa shook her head. "And walk past you of course?" She was feeling more confident now and, in a small way, she was actually beginning to enjoy herself.

Andreas smiled again and stepped away from the door, his hand outstretched.

Raisa hesitated and then walked slowly towards the door. Andreas made no move until she'd stepped outside, then he followed.

"So, how about coming out to dinner with me one evening?"

Raisa pretended to consider. In reality, she knew she had little choice. He had the power to insist but it was nice to pretend the invitation was genuine.

"Just dinner? You wouldn't expect anything else?"

Andreas grinned. He was tempted to tell her not to push her luck but he was enjoying the conversation. "Just dinner, I give you my word."

Raisa nodded graciously. "That would be nice, thank you."

"I'll pick you up at six-thirty tomorrow evening, then." He could hear voices in the distance so he glanced at his watch. "I have to go now. Until tomorrow." He saluted, strode swiftly towards his car, climbed in and within moments was driving off at speed.

Raisa watched him go and wondered why she was looking forward to dining with him. He was the enemy, she should hate him, but there was something about him… She shivered suddenly and pulled her thin cardigan tighter around her.

Having given the POWs their instructions, Wiktor and Magda were returning from the field. "I'm very worried about Felcia and Ala, Wiktor. I think I'll try again to get a pass to go and see them. Maybe I'll have more luck this time. I might even be able to bring them home…" She tailed off realising he wasn't listening. "What is it?"

Wiktor pointed to the German staff car pulling away from the barn and began running towards the farm, Magda close behind.

"Are you alright?" Wiktor ran up to Raisa, panting heavily.

She nodded. "I'm fine honestly, Tata."

"What did he want?"

Raisa hesitated. "He wanted to ask me out for dinner tomorrow night."

Wiktor stared at her in horror. "You said no… Please tell me you said no?"

Raisa shook her head. "How could I? He could make me have dinner with him if he wants, so I thought it might be better if I said yes. That way he might treat me with more respect."

Wiktor grabbed her arm. "Are you completely stupid, girl? He doesn't just want dinner."

"Yes he does. He gave me his word," Raisa shouted back.

"And of course you can trust a Nazi, can't you?" Wiktor was still holding her arm and Raisa tried to pull away.

"You're hurting me."

"If you do anything to make me ashamed of you, I'll do more than hurt your arm." Wiktor was beside himself with rage.

"Wiktor, let go!" Magda had heard enough. She grabbed his arm and tried to pull him off. He shrugged her away but she continued to pull at him. "Wiktor, leave her alone. You're just making things worse."

Wiktor finally let go. "Just you behave yourself," he yelled at Raisa before striding off towards the house.

Magda stared at her daughter. "That man... he's almost old enough to be your father. Surely you can't find him attractive?"

Raisa didn't answer.

Magda sighed. She had no idea what went on in Raisa's head sometimes and maybe that was a good thing. She made one last attempt to talk some sense into her. "Be careful, Raisa. You'll never find a husband if you get a reputation. And if you start spending time with a German you'll be hated for being a collaborator."

Raisa shrugged. "I know, but I don't have much choice. If I'd said no, he might have threatened you or Tata."

Magda shook her head. Yes, the German might threaten them if she didn't cooperate, but that wasn't why her daughter was going to have dinner with him. She'd seen something in Raisa's face that had made her heart sink.

Chapter Forty-six

Driving Depot, Camberley, Surrey

Annie was really enjoying her new job. At the army's insistence she'd been ordered to take a refresher course on driving ambulances. However, the instructors were so impressed with her knowledge, they cut the course short and she was able to concentrate on the other vehicles she was learning to drive. These included staff cars, lorries and even a steam roller. Because they would often be sent to the local quarry to collect the rocks that were being used to make roads, she also learnt to drive a tipper truck.

Having come top of the class in all her courses she was soon trusted to drive vehicles down to the ports ready for embarkation. This was done at night in long convoys and was at least varied and interesting for the most part, although she found some of the mechanical requirements of the job taxing, especially as winter approached and the weather deteriorated.

Despite her enjoyment, missing Rob was like a constant ache in her heart. No matter what she did, he was always at the foremost of her thoughts. When driving along quiet roads in convoys delivering stores, she found herself talking to him in her head as if he was with her. But it was at night she missed him most. When she lay down to sleep, her mind would replay the conversations they'd had and she would initiate new ones, telling him all the things she had done in her day. Much of this she would put in letters; pages of adoration and how much she missed him, mingled with the day-to-day mundane happenings, as if by committing everything to paper he would still be sharing her life.

****

Berlin

Claudia had just helped Karin put Heidi to bed. At ten months old, she was already developing a personality of her own. She was extremely determined, had a wicked temper and would scream when she couldn't get her own way.

"She looks just like Hans when he was about seven." Karin laughed, completely missing the expression of horror on her lover's face. "I can remember quite clearly seeing him stamp his feet when he wasn't getting his own way, and he used to pout like that."

"Have you heard anything from Andreas?" Claudia changed the subject rapidly. She knew Karin had almost completely convinced herself that Heidi was her child, hence the constant references to how she reminded her of pictures of herself or Hans at that age. But one day she would realise that Heidi couldn't possibly look like her or Hans, because the girl wasn't related to her.

Karin frowned. "I had a brief note yesterday saying he definitely wouldn't be home for weeks, until Christmas at the earliest, thank goodness. Why? Hasn't he written to you at all?"

Claudia shook her head and tried to ignore the niggle of unease in her stomach. Karin stared at her. "He used to write to you all the time."

Claudia nodded. "Yes, he did." She sighed. "I'm wondering if he has become bored with me."

Karin looked horrified. She was silent for a while. "What if he tells you to go?"

Claudia shrugged. "There's not much I can do about that, is there?" She saw the concern in Karin's eyes and tried to reassure her. "Don't worry, Karin. It's probably nothing. When he comes back, I'll have to show him what he's been missing." The thought didn't excite her. She loved Karin and would be happy if it was just the two of them and Heidi, but Andreas was in control of the household. If he decided she was no longer needed, she would not have a choice.

Karin nodded. Claudia might be right. Maybe they were worrying about nothing. But if Andreas was planning to send Claudia away, she would have to stop him. For the first time in her life, she was truly happy and no-one was going to spoil it.

****

Outside Lublin, Eastern Poland

"You're absolutely sure there's no way we can travel to Lvov?" Magda stared at the German official and tried hard to hide her fury. The German was young, about the same age as Alek. She decided to try and play on his sympathy. "I haven't seen my daughters or my grandson since the war started. I don't even know if they're still alive. Can't you please see if there is some way I can travel there?"

The German sighed. He felt sorry for her but there was nothing he could do. "We don't have any control of the Russian sector unfortunately, and they aren't being very cooperative." He winced inwardly. He wasn't supposed to have said that. He'd allowed his feelings to get the better of him, probably because she reminded him of his own mother. He cleared his throat and tried to sound more officious. "If there was a way I would tell you, madam. I am sorry."

Magda gave up. "Thank you anyway." She turned to go. The German watched her. He wondered if he should have mentioned that there were rumours the Russians were rounding up Polish citizens and sending them to Russia. He shook his head. If he told her that, she would be even more worried and, as there was nothing she could do, there was no point. In any case, the rumours could be wrong.

Magda hurried home, her thoughts on her children. Wiktor had received a brief letter from Stani that morning, saying he and Alek had joined the Wehrmacht. Wiktor had been almost apoplectic with rage.

Magda was still shell shocked. She couldn't understand why her sons, who had been so patriotic, had suddenly decided to join the enemy. Wiktor had torn up the letter into small pieces and thrown it in the bin, so she'd not had a chance to see it herself. She fought back her tears. Wiktor had disowned them, so she would probably never see her sons again.

She had no idea whether Felcia and Ala were even alive and now she had Raisa to worry about as well. The SS man who'd come to the farm might have fooled her daughter, but she'd seen the expression on his face when he'd first seen Raisa. Unfortunately, if he wanted Raisa, there was probably nothing she or Wiktor could do to stop him.

****

Outside Warsaw

"Do you think they've got our letter yet?" Alek glanced around nervously, even though he knew they were on their own.

"I should think so." Stani sighed. His idea about joining the Wehrmacht to spy on them had seemed like a good idea at the time, but unless he could find a way of getting the information to England or France, they were not making any difference. Perhaps they should try to escape to the west while they still had a chance. He voiced his thoughts out loud. Alek didn't answer for a moment.

"It'll be a hell of journey trying to get to France now. The Germans are completely in control of the western border and, even if we go that way, we'll have to cross Germany. If we were going to do that, we should have gone earlier, much earlier."

"We could still try and get to Danzig and cross to Sweden?"

Alek was silent for a moment then he shrugged. "I'll do whatever you think is best, Stani. Just try not to get us killed, eh?"

Stani gave a wry smile. "I'll do my best!"

****

Lublin, Eastern Poland

Raisa sat back in her seat, sipped her wine and glanced around the very expensive restaurant. She wondered briefly who was running it now the Jewish owners had been effectively thrown out of their own business. The only other customers were groups of German soldiers or single Germans with local women. Although she had enjoyed the meal of pork roast with wine, sauerkraut and boiled potatoes followed by sernik, food she hadn't seen since the beginning of the occupation, she felt uncomfortable to see so many women collaborating with the enemy.

Andreas downed the rest of his cognac and refilled his glass. He could see Raisa struggling and he wasn't sure what he could do to make her feel better. He was a member of the occupying forces; something he couldn't change.

"I'm sorry if you're feeling uncomfortable here. That wasn't my intention. Perhaps we should have gone somewhere else."

"It would be the same wherever we went… all these Polish women with Germans." Raisa sighed as she looked around. Then she gave a tentative smile. "But I'm doing the same thing and that's what's making me feel awkward." She returned her attention to Andreas and her smile widened slightly. "I've had a very nice evening, honestly."

Andreas relaxed and smiled back. "Good, I'm glad you've enjoyed yourself. Perhaps you would do me the honour of dining with me again?"

Raisa nodded. "Yes, that would be nice."

"And now you'd like to go home?"

Raisa gave a small sigh of relief. "Yes, please. If you don't mind, of course?" The words were out before she could stop them and she cursed inwardly. What if he said he did mind, that he had other plans?

But Andreas just smiled, nodded and glanced around for the waiter. "Could I have the bill, please?"

The waiter appeared a few moments later, scowled at Raisa and handed Andreas the bill. Andreas pulled out a handful of Reichsmarks, and placed them on the table. As the waiter reached for them, Andreas placed his hand on the man's arm and leaned forward. He lowered his voice. "I do hope you weren't glaring at my guest?"

The waiter shook his head. "No, sir, of course not."

Andreas relaxed and pulled out another note which he handed to the man. "In that case, thank you for your excellent service. I'm sure we'll come again."

Ignoring the fury he could feel emanating from the man, Andreas stood up, stepped round to pull back Raisa's chair and helped her on with her coat. Then, gently taking her arm, he led her towards the door.

It was cold outside and she shivered. "Here, take my coat." Before she could object, Andreas was removing his coat and had placed it over her shoulders. After Iwan's brutal assault, Raisa had switched off her emotions, determined no man would ever hurt her again, so she was surprised to feel a warm sensation in her stomach.

Andreas opened the passenger door for her and she climbed in. He closed her door, walked round to the other side and got into the driver's seat. He started the car and eased down the small side street.

Raisa stared out of the window but she wasn't paying any attention to their surroundings. She could feel the tension between them and, although it initially reminded her of that awful day with Iwan, somehow this felt different.

Chapter Forty-seven

Beltring, Kent

With the arrival of winter, the temperature dropped rapidly and life in the Hop Houses became even more primitive. The water supply froze solid, as did the outside latrines. Finding water to shave in was extremely difficult and washing was done very quickly in cold water.

"We're still here, Rob. We could be in France." Mike was beginning to get fed up with Rob's miserable face. "At least you can call Annie regularly."

Rob nodded. "I know. I'm sorry, I don't mean to keep moaning…" He was trying to count his blessings but queuing for hours to use the one red telephone box in the village was not his idea of fun, especially when he only had three minutes to talk to her.

"More conscripts have arrived." Mike flung himself down on the straw mattress and pulled his blankets over himself. The hop house was freezing and they spent most of their time trying to keep warm.

"We must be almost full strength now." Rob pushed thoughts of Annie out of his mind and made an effort to cheer up. He and Mike had both been promoted to Lance Corporals and they had also been resupplied with brand new Norton motorcycles, Humber Snipe Radio trucks and some new 30cwt Bedford trucks.

"Marty's rendered all the 50mph governors on the new trucks useless." Mike grinned. "I got 80mph out of mine today."

Rob laughed. "You wanna watch out for the ice, especially around these winding country lanes."

"A chap's got to have some excitement, Rob, especially as we still don't have enough rifles. I sometimes think we're back in Spain."

Rob nodded, his face serious. "I was using a Lee Enfield from 1914 yesterday. You'd have thought they'd have enough weapons by now. It's not like they haven't had any warning."

"Yeah, but they weren't listening, were they?" Mike shivered and shook his head. "They should have been preparing for war while we were in Spain instead of pandering to that maniac."

"Too busy burying their heads in the sand." Rob could feel his good mood evaporating. If the country had acted sooner, they might have stopped Hitler and he could be with Annie, planning their future instead of being stuck in frozen Kent awaiting orders to go to war.

****

Warsaw

Hans glanced up at the large wall clock. He was due to meet with members of the Judenrat in a few moments. Their headquarters was on Grzybowska Street. He'd visited their offices back in September out of curiosity. Once was enough; being surrounded by Jews in their strange clothes, squalor and poverty had made him feel ill, so now they came to him for their meetings. No doubt they would be whining about their lot as usual. He couldn't understand why they bothered to complain to him. They must know he didn't care. Heydrich had demanded the Jews set up these councils to facilitate the Germans' management of the Jewish problem, not for their benefit.

Hans smiled to himself as he thought back over all the recent laws he'd brought in. When in public, all Jewish men, women and children over twelve had to wear a white armband with a blue Star of David; small shops and firms had already been confiscated and those that remained had been marked for easy identification, and there were restrictions on Jewish train travel. He'd also ordered all Jews to deposit their money in blocked bank accounts and told them they were only allowed to draw out two hundred and fifty zlotys per week. He was still pondering the latest idea of setting up a specific area for them to live in when there was a knock at the door.

Hans closed the file that was open on his desk. "Kommen!"

The door opened and two men entered. Although it was very cold outside, both men were wearing thin coats and neither was wearing gloves or a scarf. The taller man was wearing glasses, which immediately steamed up in the heat of the office. He took them off, and wiped them with an old cloth, which he hastily replaced in his pocket. They glanced around but there were no chairs, so they stood awkwardly in front of Hans' desk.

Enjoying their discomfort, Hans leant back.

"So, gentlemen. What's the problem this time?" His tone indicated quite clearly that he had no interest in whatever they'd come to talk about.

"Good morning, Herr Kohl. We've come to ask for an increase to the rations. We cannot live on such a small amount of calories and the children are being given even less."

There was silence. Hans stared up at them and then shook his head. "I'm sorry, gentlemen, I can't justify an increase in rations for people who aren't doing anything productive. If your people were working… well you might have a case. But you're not, are you?"

The men exchanged glances. "You have closed down our businesses and the Polish firms and factories cannot provide enough work in the city for everyone. If we could work, we would. Perhaps you could consider lifting some of the restrictions on the kind of work we can do." The man with the glasses tried not to sound critical, knowing that would only antagonise the SS man.

Hans tapped his fingers on the desk and sighed loudly. "You Jews. You think everything revolves around you. There is not enough food to go around so we have had to prioritise. We come first, then Poles who are active and then you. If you don't like it, you can always move across into the Soviet occupation zone. Perhaps they can give lazy people like you more food. Now, is there anything else? I am busy."

The men glanced at each other. "No, Herr Kohl. There's nothing else."

Hans watched them go, a smile on his face. Food was going to be the least of their problems if this latest plan went ahead.

****

Outside Lublin, Eastern Poland

Magda watched Raisa feeding the chickens, a dreamy expression on her face, and sighed. To her surprise, the *Szkop* had brought her daughter home at a respectable time. She'd been watching through the curtains and seen him climb out of the car, open the door for Raisa, salute smartly and say good night. He'd not even attempted to kiss her.

Of course they might not have gone for a meal. He might have taken her back to his apartment and… she shut off the thoughts. No, she was sure Raisa was telling the truth. He had taken her to a restaurant and then brought her home.

Raisa couldn't get Andreas out of her head. On the drive back to the farm, he'd told he was going home to Berlin for a few days for Christmas but, when he came back he would take her out again. He had not tried to kiss her or do anything else, much to her surprise. He had behaved like the perfect gentleman and she knew she should be pleased, but she couldn't help feeling a little disappointed at the lack of any intimacy. For a brief moment she wondered if Andreas didn't find her attractive but then she shook her head. Raisa knew men and she'd seen the expression on Andreas' face when he looked at her. He was definitely interested. She gave a wry smile. It was a new experience to be treated with respect. Perhaps it was because he was much older than her.

On her return from Bydgoszcz and in an attempt to forget about her experience with Iwan, she had wasted little time in sleeping with Vada. Unfortunately, afterwards he'd made it quite clear he hadn't wanted to see her again. Feeling even more depressed, Raisa had slept with two other men in quick succession, only for them to treat her exactly the same way. Realising the only way to keep a boyfriend was not to jump straight into bed with him, she'd decided to play things differently with Andreas.

Her only worry now was that when they did eventually sleep together, he would know she wasn't a virgin and then he might be angry he had wasted so much time. She would have to come up with a very good reason for not having slept with him and at the moment she had no idea what she could say. She was sure the only reason he hadn't pushed things was because he thought she was still a virgin, so the moment he found out she wasn't he would feel she'd taken advantage of him. Raisa shivered. Although Andreas was a Nazi he'd only ever been nice to her and she rather liked him. She didn't want to upset him but unless she came up with a convincing explanation, she was going to be in a lot of trouble.

****

Lvov, Poland

Felcia stared up at the latest propaganda poster dominating the street. A white eagle wearing the four cornered Polish soldier's cap on its head was clawing at the back of a handcuffed worker. A Bolshevik soldier was sticking a bayonet into the eagle. She shivered. She'd grown so used to the large posters of Soviet leaders that had been erected on the sides of buildings, she barely noticed them. More intrusive were the loudspeakers that had been installed in the streets broadcasting Soviet propaganda from early morning to late at night.

Like most Poles, she'd taken to stuffing cotton wool into her ears in an attempt to lessen the continual row.

There was virtually no food to be had and, if it wasn't for Halina's friends, they would have starved by now.

She stepped back as three Russian lorries drove past at speed, turning her back to protect Mariusz. But she was too slow and they showered her in the filthy water that had been lying in the gutter. Felcia did her best to comfort Mariusz while cursing them under her breath. It didn't do to say anything out loud anymore. People disappeared for no reason and she was terrified the same thing would happen to her. She carried on walking, passing several empty buildings that had once been thriving businesses. Having emptied the shops, the Soviets were busy dismantling factories and sending all the machinery back to the Soviet Union. They were like a hoard of scavenging locusts but they were also amazingly ignorant. She'd heard tales of Soviet soldiers washing in toilet bowls and wondering out loud why the water ran so quick, and Russian women going to the theatre in Polish nightgowns.

Ala and Halina had finally found some work on one of the farms on the outskirts of the town. She was still unable to work because of her connection to the Polish army, so she had resigned herself to staying at home with Mariusz and doing what housework she could. Halina had said she thought they would be able to move to the farm in the next couple of days. Felcia prayed she was right. Anything had to be better than living in Lvov.

****

Outside Warsaw

"I think we should take our chances and make a run for it." Stani had been thinking about it for ages and had finally made his decision.

Alek shrugged. "Sounds good to me. I'm not sure I can put up with living with this lot much longer."

"We'll wait until the weather gets better, probably later next spring, then make a run towards the coast and Danzig."

"As long as they don't move us elsewhere by then…"

Stani thought for a moment. "I think we'll have to take a chance on that."

Alek shrugged. "Alright. We'll keep our ears to the ground and if we hear any rumours about being transferred elsewhere, we can always think again."

Stani nodded. "The sooner we're away from here the better, but we need to plan a route properly. We've got a few months to work out the best way to do it and, in the meantime, we'll be model soldiers so no one suspects anything."

Alek gave a loud theatrical sigh. "Really? A model Wermacht soldier?"

Stani laughed. "It'll be worth it, Alek. Just think of the look on their faces when they discover we've gone."

****

Berlin

"Darling, how nice to have you home." Karin kissed Andreas dutifully on the cheek. "Look how your daughter has grown." She held Heidi up to him and Andreas stared at the smiling baby. After a brief hesitation, he held out his arms and took his daughter. She gazed up at him, with an intense expression in her eyes that reminded him of someone, but he couldn't remember who. Then she smiled again and this time he smiled back.

"Hello, Heidi. You are such a beautiful girl." He leant down and gave her a kiss before handing her back to Karin. "Is Claudia here?"

Karin nodded, her heart thudding. "She's upstairs."

"Good, I won't be long. I have something to do." He turned away and headed up the stairs, leaving Karin staring at his back, her stomach in knots. She had a horrible feeling Claudia had been right all along. Andreas was no longer interested in her lover. He had either found someone else, or he'd just grown bored. Karin fought down the rising panic. She wouldn't let him spoil her happiness. Maybe she should tell him the truth. Perhaps then he would leave her and Claudia alone. After all, he had his mistresses, surely she was entitled to the same? Karin shook her head. Of course that wouldn't work. He would be horrified and it would give him even more of an excuse to send Claudia away.

Karin scowled. Andreas was not going to send Claudia away, she wouldn't let him. She would do anything to keep her lover. If she had to she would involve Hans. Karin shivered at the thought of approaching Hans, especially as she would have to come up with a good reason to convince her brother to fight her corner. Saying Claudia was her friend probably wouldn't be enough and she couldn't tell him they were lovers. But she'd think of something. She had to. Claudia was the most important person in her life and no one, least of all Andreas, was going to interfere.

****

Romford, Essex

"I can't believe we're finally together again, even if it is only for two days over Christmas." Annie snuggled into his arms on the settee, glad her parents had tactfully gone to visit some neighbours, leaving them on their own. As soon as she'd known Rob was able to get a forty eight hour pass for Christmas, Annie had put in for the same. Fortunately things were still quiet on the continent and she'd had little difficulty, her Commanding Officer pleased to oblige one of his best drivers.

Rob pulled her closer and kissed her passionately. He slid his hands under her jumper and with Annie's help, eased it over her head. He reached behind her and undid her bra. Annie's breath shortened to small gasps, her fingers already undoing the buttons of his trousers. Rob lifted her skirt, ran his hands up her legs until he reached the top of her stockings, pulled aside her knickers and slipped his fingers inside her. Annie moaned with pleasure and Rob lifted her hips and slowly eased her panties down.

Annie opened her legs invitingly and within minutes Rob was inside her and trying hard not to climax almost immediately. He failed and after a few more seconds rolled off her in frustration.

"I'm sorry, I wanted make it last longer."

Annie smiled. "It doesn't matter. I just want to lay next to you and feel your body against mine. I've missed you so much." Her smile faded. She'd promised herself she wouldn't keep thinking about the New Year, that she would keep her mind on the present and make the most of their short time together, but she couldn't help it. Knowing they only had two days and then he would return to Kent and… She shut down the thoughts that came tumbling into her mind. Europe was quiet, it might stay that way. Rob might not have to go away at all. She might be ruining their time together, worrying about things that might never happen. *And this might be the last time you ever see him…* The words burst through the calm thoughts and tears pricked her eyes. She blinked them away, hoping Rob hadn't seen but he was watching her with concern.

"Are you alright, Annie? You're not crying, are you?"

Annie shook her head but she was too late. Rob pulled her closer. "Please don't cry, my darling."

"I'm sorry, I don't mean to…" Now she'd started Annie couldn't stop and Rob felt helpless. He hugged her tighter wishing he could say something, anything to make things better, but he couldn't, because he felt the same. They stayed like that for several minutes before Annie calmed down.

"I'm sorry. I promised myself I wouldn't do this." She pulled out a handkerchief, wiped her eyes and blew her nose. Seeing the pain on Rob's face she put the hankie back in her pocket and tried to make a joke. "I bet you're glad you made love to me before I started crying… I must look dreadful."

Rob took her hands. "You're beautiful, Annie. You always look amazing." He reached up and wiped away some mascara from her cheek. "Even with a red nose and blotchy make up." He was relieved to see her smiling. "And to prove it to you… Perhaps we should have an early night?"

Annie nodded and stood up. She didn't really want to make love again but she did want to lay beside him, to hear him breathing next to her, to feel his arms around her. For the next two days she would do her best to fight off the demons of her imagination and enjoy his company. There would be time enough to cry when he had gone back to Kent.

Rob watched her go upstairs and breathed a sigh of relief. He knew exactly how Annie felt only he didn't have the luxury of tears. He had to be strong for both of them. Spending time with his young wife was all he wanted to do and, in normal times, he would be able to do that. If only he didn't have to go back to Kent in two days, he would be in heaven. But even the short time he had with Annie was ruined by the war that was always in the back of their minds. He stood up and, while he followed her upstairs, he made a decision: for the next few hours he would try and enjoy the present and forget about the future. This might be the last time they were together before he went overseas and then who knew when, or even if, they would ever see each other again.

Made in the USA
Charleston, SC
07 January 2017